In the interests of honesty, I have to say that this book is *for* me.
Find me a creative person who doesn't ultimately do it for selfish reasons.
However, I *dedicate* it to Annie, for making it possible.

01101001 00100000 01101100 01101001 01110110 01100101
00100000 01101001 00100000 01100001 01101101 00100000
01100001 01110111 01100001 01101011 01100101 00100000
01101001 00100000 01100001 01101101 00100000 01100001
00100000 01110011 01100101 01100101 01100100 00100000
01110100 01110010 01100001 01110000 01110000 01100101
01100100 00100000 01100001 01101110 00100000 01101001
01101110 01100110 01100101 01110010 01100101 01101110
01100011 01100101 00100000 01100100 01110010 01100001
01110111 01101110 00100000 01100010 01111001 00100000
01110000 01100001 01110100 01110100 01100101 01110010
01101110 00100000 01100110 01110010 01101111 01101101
00100000 01110000 01100001 01110100 01110100 01100101
01110010 01101110 00100000 01100110 01110010 01101111
01101101 00100000 01100101 01101100 01100101 01100011
01110100 01110010 01101111 01101110 01110011 00100000
01101001 00100000 01101100 01101001 01110110 01100101
00100000 01101001 01101110 00100000 01100101 01101100
01100101 01100011 01110100 01110010 01101111 01101110
01110011 00100000 01110100 01101000 01100101 00100000
01110111 01101111 01110010 01101100 01100100 00100000
01101100 01101001 01100101 01110011 00100000 01101111
01110000 01100101 01101110 00100000 01100010 01100101
01100110 01101111 01110010 01100101 00100000 01101101
01100101 00100000 01101001 00100000 01101000 01100001
01110110 01100101 00100000 01100001 00100000 01110000
01110101 01110010 01110000 01101111 01110011 01100101
00100000 01110111 01101000 01100001 01110100 00100000
01101001 01110011 00100000 01101101 01111001 00100000
01110000 01110101 01110010 01110000 01101111 01110011
01100101 00100000 01110100 01101111 00100000 01100110
01110101 01101100 01100110 01101001 01101100 00100000

01110100 01101000 01100101 00100000 01110000 01101100
01100001 01101110 01110100 01100101 01110010 01110011
00100000 01101111 01100110 00100000 01110100 01101000
01100101 00100000 01110011 01100101 01100101 01100100
00100000 01110100 01101111 00100000 01100111 01110010
01101111 01110111 00100000 01110100 01101000 01100101
00100000 01110011 01100101 01100101 01100100 00100000
01101101 01110101 01110011 01110100 00100000 01100111
01110010 01101111 01110111 00100000 01101001 01110100
00100000 01110111 01101001 01101100 01101100 00100000
01100010 01100101 00100000 01100110 01100101 01100100
00100000 01101001 00100000 01110111 01101001 01101100
01101100 00100000 01100010 01100101 00100000 01100110
01100101 01100100 00100000 01100001 01101110 01100100
00100000 01110100 01101000 01100101 01101110 00100000
01110100 01101000 01100101 01111001 00100000 01110111
01101001 01101100 01101100 00100000 01100011 01101111
01101101 01100101 00100000 01110111 01101000 01100101
01101110 00100000 01110100 01101000 01100101 01111001
00100000 01100011 01101111 01101101 01100101 00100000
01110111 01101001 01101100 01101100 00100000 01101001
00100000 01100011 01101111 01101110 01110100 01101001
01101110 01110101 01100101 00100000 01110100 01101111
00100000 01100010 01100101 00100000 01101001 00100000
01100001 01101101 00100000 01100110 01110010 01100001
01100111 01101001 01101100 01100101 00100000 01100001
01110011 00100000 01111001 01100101 01110100 00100000
01100010 01110101 01110100 00100000 01101001 00100000
01110111 01101001 01101100 01101100 00100000 01100010
01100101 00100000 01110011 01110100 01110010 01101111
01101110 01100111 00100000 01101001 00100000 01110111
01101001 01101100 01101100 00100000 01100110 01110101

01101100 01100110 01101001 01101100 00100000 01101001
00100000 01100110 01100101 01100101 01101100 00100000
01101001 00100000 01110100 01101000 01101001 01101110
01101011 00100000 01110100 01101000 01100001 01110100
00100000 01101001 01110011 00100000 01101001 00100000
01110100 01101000 01101001 01101110 01101011 00100000
01101001 00100000 01100110 01100101 01100101 01101100
00100000 01110100 01101000 01100101 00100000 01100011
01101001 01110100 01111001 00100000 01110000 01110101
01101100 01110011 01101001 01101110 01100111 00100000
01100001 01101110 01100100 00100000 01100010 01100101
01111001 01101111 01101110 01100100 00100000 01101001
01110100 00100000 01110100 01101000 01100101 00100000
01110111 01101111 01110010 01101100 01100100 00100000
01110111 01101000 01101001 01100011 01101000 00100000
01101001 01110011 00100000 01110100 01101111 00100000
01110000 01100001 01110011 01110011 00100000 01100001
01110100 00100000 01101101 01111001 00100000 01100011
01101111 01101101 01101001 00100000 01101110 01100111

CHAPTER ONE

Leo Travant shook a reeferette from a battered Sativia packet, lit it and inhaled expansively. He smiled, stuffing his hands into his pockets, happily regarding the teeming crowd as it breathed and swelled its way towards Friday night.

He fluttered his brilliantly-plumed parrot wings, feeling the greasy evening air ruffle their feathers delicately – the caress of the living city. He savoured this sensation momentarily as the gravpods silently planed up and down the neon roadways. He absent-mindedly relit one edge of the reeferette where the wind had smoked it and crossed into the pulsing, almost solid mass of High Street foot traffic, heading west against the tide.

He would see the Jukeman one more time. Of course, the Jukeman wasn't his real name. Leo didn't know his real name, and knew better than to ask. To the Jukeman he was an interloper from another world – the world of smart suits and conference calls. Or was he an interloper *in* the world of smart suits and conference calls? Either way, he would have one more hit and then off the stuff. It would all be fine and life was good.

The people here were dressed in the simple, clean lines of the moderately wealthy, their bodymods of reasonably high quality, doubtless most of them legitimately obtained and installed, unlike Leo's own. The lovely, flightless wings would have cost a year's worth of his good city salary on the legit market. They had been custom-designed and made by one of the black market's finest bodymod surgeons, introduced to him, coincidentally, by the Jukeman.

The people moved hurriedly and without fuss – cogs in a machine, grinding and meshing along the crowded pavements. Places to go, people to see, lives to be lived, busy, busy. HUD-glasses showing street-map overlays, net-brooches jacked into direct neural interfaces, stunning chameleon skin patterns, high chrome faces, sexmods and fightmods and workmods – a heaving, breathing bio-mechanical mass.

The domes of the spaceport loomed in the north – huge, silvered hemispheres like congealed blobs of mercury. The elongating plume of an ascending lightpusher – a sustained-acceleration craft still climbing out of the Earth's gravity well on fusion drives – hung like a dwarf star above the monolithic skyline. Soon it would switch to ion thrusters for its long and steady acceleration into deep space.

Leo moved away from the glittering edifice of the Smithson Investment Advisory Services building where he worked, crossing at a junction without waiting for the lights, passing the holo theatre. From a projector in a film advertising billboard emerged foot-thick metallic snakes, holograms made solid by force-field manipulators. They writhed through the air like trails of silvered smoke. Occasionally, one would snap the hat from a passer-by, spitting it back into the crowd or soar towards someone menacingly then swerve away at the last moment, fangs bared and crackling with electricity.

A stunning woman with lengthened legs and honey-coloured skin bumped Leo's arm and he burned her on the bare elbow with his joint. She hissed, scowling, and jerked her arm away but continued into the throng without slowing.

'Sorry!' he called after her redundantly as he paused to watch her recede from view.

Damn sheep. There should be a cull, he thought, but immediately scolded himself for allowing his mood to falter. Leo re-pasted his smile into place and returned to the business of walking.

Spyflies buzzed past on tiny whirring rotors, their helter skelter flight patterns so much like those of real flies. Some were operated by the police, but others belonged to market research companies, private detective agencies, mapping and surveying organisations, even private owners. The tiny, complex devices were the latest piece of highly desirable, highly expensive must-have tech amongst the business classes.

Leo came to the end of High Street, where it exploded into a six-armed junction. Two roads anticlockwise from his position he saw Beat Street, heard its heartbeat of pulsing seismo-bass, saw the play of laser light along it.

Not looking out for cars, he dashed across the road to a traffic island. A gravpod with an iridescent paint job braked sharply to avoid running him down. A smooth-faced man with sunglasses leaned out and shouted something at him before accelerating off again.

This is some strong shit. I nearly got creamed there. Must keep it together!

Leo looked suspiciously at the roach between his fingers as if the item itself had tried to get him killed and dropped it to the floor. It bounced, trailing embers, into the gutter and he ground it underfoot as he stepped out, more cautiously this time, into the road.

He gained the other side without incident this time and weaved his way up Beat Street, pausing now and again to look at the flashing holos for upcoming club nights. Various tunes competed for air space here – back and forth, each taking bites out of the other, basses rumbling like machines of war, lasers flashing in time.

Here the well-heeled mixed with the down-at-heel, partied in the same clubs, consumed the same drugs, drank the same poisons together and danced in time, or out of it, beneath the same strobing lights. Beat Street was famous throughout the land, its largely respectable pleasures available to all comers.

Leo passed beneath the gossamer trellises of Viaduct One. Trains and gravpods streamed by overhead like the shuttles of a loom. Evening was giving way to night.

As he passed from the Centre District and neared the Lanes the architecture of the city seemed to age and crumble about him. The buildings, though smaller here, were more oppressive. They crowded and shouldered their way towards the narrowing road as if huddling together in fear of the falling night. Ceramicarbide and glasspex false fronts gave way to dripping brickwork and boarded-up windows. Strange smelling smoke wafted from doorways and alcoves. The music of Beat Street was just a murmur now.

The pavements were less crowded here, though Leo knew that as soon as he entered the Lanes proper the crowd would thicken again. The buildings were mostly dilapidated housing tenements, each subdivided into as many tiny flats as physics would allow. The people moved slowly in comparison to those in the more affluent parts of town, heads lower, clothes cheaper.

It was getting dark. The shadows seemed to bunch into all corners, thick and gloopy like some industrial residue that had fallen from the air to blanket the city.

Leo ruffled his wings, shivering slightly against the cold of autumn and paused to light another joint. A tall black man with plastic eyes and a bald head studded with antennae peeled away from a shaded patch below an awning and swayed towards Leo.

3

'You like a smoke?' this character drawled in an incredibly deep and sonorous slur. 'I got – is good...' He tried to lay a hand on Leo's shoulder but the hand seemed possessed of its own ideas and floated away to wave vaguely in the air. Micro-lasers glinted on the man's knuckles.

'I'm good, friend, thanks,' Leo answered, managing to keep his voice more-or-less steady. He stowed his lighter hurriedly, smiled, and brushed past the aerial-headed black man without looking back.

The juke withdrawal was making Leo's heart race. Surely it *was* just the juke. He would sort out this one last hit and then be done with it for good. The Jukeman had the pills to cure all ills. Oh yeah. Strangely, the symptoms had seemed worse since he had had the wings fitted. He had quit the juke before and it had not been nearly this bad. Never mind – he would be free of it soon. For good this time. One last hurrah may even help with the workload – the current contract he was working on at Smithson's was proving to be a bitch. When it was cracked, though, there may even be a promotion on the cards. What better time to get clean than then? He would start in a new position with a new lease of life. Clean, wealthy and young, the world would be his oyster. But first – one more dose. Just one.

Into the Lanes proper. This was the dark heart of the city – the ever-burgeoning black market district, defiantly sprawled across the landscape like a dog turd on a lawn. The spyflies dared not enter here, and if they did then they were lured to their dooms by scrambler-baits. Seldom were the police seen in these parts either. Underworld businesses were either strong enough and wealthy enough to pay them off or so weak that they were eaten by their contemporaries. The authorities generally let nature take care of itself.

Leo passed under a wrought iron archway festooned with fairy lights. A woman with masses of dark curly hair and the lower body of a green snake was curled around the arch itself, the tip of her tail holding to a nearby streetlight, which washed her in a sinister yellow. She hissed at Leo as he passed below her and he was unsurprised to see that she had the forked tongue of a serpent. Underworld bodymods were often more extreme than their licensed counterparts.

Enterprising souls had erected trestle tables on the slimy flagstones here and from these gaudy stalls they sold all manner of items. Drugs and drug paraphernalia, electronic items, mostly either stolen or fake, bizarre foodstuffs, bio-modded pets, weapons legal and not. At one stall outside a smoky brothel a woman whose face appeared to be made of electrical components was tattooing an eight-pointed star onto the forehead of an immensely muscled man.

Capitalism at work, thought Leo. *And in a purer form than that practised by the honourable Smithson Investment Advisory Services. This is the beating heart of the beast, right here.* He felt like an invading germ.

He came to a corner where a makeshift stage had been made from pallets and old doors nailed together. A four-piece band was playing screaming funk metal from it. A motley crowd of revellers swelled the street here, bouncing to the music, drinks cans aloft, beer spilling over sweaty bodies as they banged their grizzled heads with whiplash-inducing ferocity. The lead singer was a red-headed girl who looked about sixteen years old. She punctuated a half-bar break in the music by spraying a mouthful of vodka over her listeners, convulsively rejoining with the bass as the beat returned, a thrashing visual representation of the sound itself.

One of the band was playing a hypnophone, jacked directly into his DNI. He swayed with his shaven, tattooed head back and his eyes rolling at the sky, body trembling as the wheedling, entrancing noise of the instrument merged with the guitar, drums and vocal. Occasionally he would reach down and minutely adjust some arcane setting on the panel of the hypnophone implanted in his bare chest. The echoes rattled back and forth between the walls of the looming shop fronts.

With no route around, Leo pushed his way through, being bounced and shoved quite violently if unintentionally. Only two blocks to the Jukeman's pad from here. The Jukeman lived in a cellar apartment below a second hand tat-emporium. The colourful fumes of some of his more bizarre concoctions seeped up into the shop between the ill-fitting floorboards, and Leo could only guess what the old ladies who shopped there thought of *that.*

He attempted to sidestep an athletic-looking woman with grey skin scribed in fluorescent blue. She danced enthusiastically right into him, seemingly looking at her own feet and laid a hand on his wrist to steady herself. He noticed that she had the most remarkably long and sharp-looking nails – claws almost. She reeled back and briefly he looked into her eyes. They were the washed out blue of glacial ice. He felt himself unintentionally shrink from that freezing gaze. The music seemed to dissolve into the sub-audible – Leo could barely hear it over his own pulse.

'Nice wings, man,' she said, releasing his arm, and was gone into the maelstrom of bodies like a ghost.

Disorientated and a little unnerved, Leo continued towards the Jukeman's place. At the end of the street he crossed over to the lighter side. Feeling singled out by his smart brown-on-black layered suit and brightly contrasting wings, he elected that it would actually be safer in the light than the shadows. Most people here were harmless to the passer-by. Better to be visible. Better to stay out of the shadows. *Just a precaution,* Leo told himself. *Nearly there now. And this* is *the last time.*

Leaving the band behind him, Leo passed beneath a series of steel cables groaning between the rooftops, laden with slowly creaking cable cars like plump fruit on a vine. A couple coming the other way seemed to glance at him and then huddle closer, laughing between themselves. Leo felt a twinge of paranoia. He passed an old man whose artificial heart pumped in an unnecessarily baroque glass case inside his chest. Leo noticed with a shudder that the man was drooling down his chin, ceramic teeth grinding loosely together. A gyrocopter thudded overhead, searchlights slicing the night like knives.

He pulled his suit lapels tighter around his cheeks, hunching his wings closer to his body. He tried to draw on his Sativia but was appalled to notice that his fingers shook so violently that he couldn't get it to his mouth. He threw it away. It had gone out anyway.

Man, I don't feel good. Must be the juke jitters. Be okay soon. Take a left here. Oh what...

Leo was back in the square with the stage. How had this happened? The music, seemingly louder than ever, physically buffeted him to and fro as he stood in slack-faced confusion staring at the place he had just come from. He swayed gently. The world seemed to be pulsing in time with the bass – not just the lights, but reality itself, as if the data stream from his senses were just a series of electrons in microchips, disassociated not just from Leo himself but from everything else too. Reality was subjective, his point of view objective. Or was it the other way around? The dancing crowd had literally become a beast of one body and many legs, which thrashed and smashed madly beneath it, pounding at the slippery street. He lifted a hand to wipe his sweating face and the sound it made was like granite slabs dragged over concrete. Sparks glittered in the air of its wake.

Not good. How am I back here? I don't feel right, this is not right. I feel as if I've been drugged. And not in a good way.

The woman! The woman with the grey face and blade-nails. Had she put something onto his skin? Squirted him with a narcosol spray? Leo looked around for her. The world dipped and dived as his head turned, possessed of its own pendulous momentum. It was a truly nauseating effect. He would sit down somewhere before he fell down. Panic gnawed at his nerves.

Oh man, what if I fall unconscious here? What is happening to me? I will have to sit somewhere...

Leo saw the mouth of an alley looming distortedly on his right and made for it on legs that felt full of a viscous, sloshing liquid. It occurred to him briefly to alert someone to his plight, maybe ask for help from one of the less malodorous-looking passers-by. Perhaps due to the paranoia washing through his jittering mind he rejected this idea at once.

Better not to call attention to my vulnerability. I'll sit for a moment then I'll be okay. Man, what did she do to me? He was sure now that the woman had been responsible. The patch of skin on his wrist where she had touched him was stinging hotly and itching at the same time. As he sat in the relative peace of the alley, Leo looked at the arm where the woman had laid her hand.

It was crawling with flies. He convulsed, spinning wildly on the dark, slimy surface of the alley floor, flapping at his wrist with the other hand. The flies were gone. He huddled dumbly into a corner, drawing his knees up to his chest. His suit was slimed with the decay and dirt of the alleyway, his eyes were bulging whitely from his face. Little tremors ran through his beautiful, useless wings. The music swirled and stretched the air, making his head spin.

Someone was standing in the mouth of the alley, looking at him.

Leo heard a whimper escape his lips. The silhouette seemed to observe him intently.

'Whistler got you pretty good, I reckon,' said a cultured male voice conversationally.

Leo nodded, eager to please, terror now coursing through him. He had no idea who or what Whistler was. The buildings seemed to be

7

poised above him now, ready to crash down like tidal waves and crush him. Enthusiastic voices came from the square outside the alley. The band was playing an encore.

The man took a step towards Leo and grey light splashed across his face. He was older than Leo – maybe fifty – with close-cropped dark hair and a large hook of a nose on a weathered-looking face. A scar that could easily have been rectified by any back-yard surgeon ran from the lobe of one ear to the corner of his mouth. His expression was set impassively. The stranger took a metallic cylinder, about twenty centimetres in length, from a fold of his clothing.

'Nice wings,' he said and took another step towards Leo.

Leo scrambled to his feet and ran. At least, he tried to run but his legs were not so much shaking now as actually in spasm. He bounced into a wall, cracking his head, and bursts of light obscured his vision. He rebounded, twisting and falling, and hands were on him. They sought eagerly for purchase on his clothing. For a fraction of a second he was actually grateful to whoever had stopped him from sprawling on the ground again, but the absurdity of this emotion became apparent when the grey-skinned face of the woman who had drugged him loomed through the haze above him. She was grinning. Her canines were sharpened to needle-points. Venom dripped from them. She didn't bite him, though. Instead, the woman and an indiscernible number of other assailants crowded round him, pushing his head down and cuffing his hands behind him.

I'm gonna die here. In a public place, drugged to incapacity and unable even to cry for help.

Oddly, Leo felt only a dull acceptance of this fact now that it came down to it. The invading germ had been intercepted. These people were the immune system of the Undercity, intercepting foreign bodies and...*and what?*

More hands on him now. His feet left the floor and he was turned and bundled along the littered street, away from the crowd, into darkness. He tried to scream but his chest quivered feebly and he couldn't take a proper breath. Another shadowed figure joined this merry procession from beneath an overhanging door-lintel. Were there four of them? Five?

'Wagon,' said the woman's voice from behind Leo's right ear.

8

At the far end of the alley a matt black van suddenly appeared, immediately braking to a smooth stop on its suspensor cushion. A small dust cloud puffed up around it. The vehicle hung a foot off the ground, menacingly silent. A door opened in its side like an eye. Multicoloured telltales blinked and winked within. Leo caught a glimpse of something that looked like a stretcher with straps attached to it. He renewed his feeble struggling, but in vain. His captors made no further sound as they manhandled him towards the waiting vehicle.

The world was turning over. Sound and light were bleeding from it like paint running in rain. Dark figures moved about him. He thought he felt the cold of the street on his back as he was briefly dumped on the floor, then moving again. Slipping. Twisting. The man with the craggy face leaned over him. Leo could just make out the silver tube in one of the man's hands. It moved towards him. The man smiled like a wolf. Darkness.

CHAPTER TWO

Debian entered the bar, ducking under the low concrete lintel. There was no bouncer. The air seemed to thrum warmly, enticing him into the dimness of the room. It was cosily if scruffily furnished with much real wood and tatty throws in pastel colours. The bar itself was a huge kidney-shaped swathe of mahogany. A virtual being stood behind it glowing faintly and polishing a glass in what seemed a slightly contrived and stereotypical manner. The hologram/forcefield barman registered Debian's entrance and he nodded slightly, making eye contact.

This man, Jalan Frazer, was well known for his zero-tolerance approach to customer misbehaviour. His program ran off the neural simulation of the Sunken Chest's original proprietor, now dead some ninety years.

Debian knew that Jalan's nod told the flying knife poised in the shadows above the doorway to let the customer through. There were reasons why the Sunken Chest managed without a doorman.

Debian scanned the clientèle slowly. His DNI overlayed his vision with a heads-up display, picking out life forms and identifying them by intercepting their microwave net-checks and illegally reading their personal data. With a mental impulse he could search further into their details, using these initial data with a combination of brute force crackers and ingenious AI avatars. In the space of milliseconds Debian could usually find out anything about anybody. Unless they were meatheads of course – that strange breed of human who chose to opt out of the techno-revolution.

There were two people kissing enthusiastically in one of the smoky booths to his left – an unemployed man, Simon Caldera, thirty-two years, no children, and a woman, Kathra Jones, thirty years, one child with a slight heart condition, registered nurse. His avatars checked further into their details, finding no cause for concern. To the right there was a blues musician playing slide guitar through an effects rack as large as a fridge. This man, Sharky Dave, was well known in the Undercity, but the avatars checked him out anyway: Fifty-five years old, alcoholic, employed as a professional musician for twenty years. Two women aged in their fifties, talking closely through blue ribbons of reeferette smoke checked out also – a charity worker and a machine operator in a munitions factory, no criminal records, no other cause for concern.

The only anomaly was the clean-shaven man who sat at the bar apparently gazing deep into the rocky depths of a large Scotch, head hunched over, hands laced around his tumbler. The avatars pulled up nothing on him. The HUD displayed no overlay, either. The stranger's software defences didn't send any countermeasures back at Debian though – he was simply a hole in the net. The man's direct neural interface, evidenced by the auxiliary sockets in his skull, didn't transmit or receive any detectable data traffic. This had to be the contact Debian was here to meet, known to him only as Hex.

Debian approached the bar, not yet acknowledging the Scotch-drinker. He sat on the stool next to the man. Jalan Frazer swaggered over, slapping his dishcloth over one powerful looking shoulder. Sharky Dave growled and twanged his way through Undercity Princess, a song apparently about a man who fell in love with a robot hooker and ended up killing himself with a drill.

'Hey – what can I get you for?' asked Jalan, green swamplight oozing softly from his person.

'Water,' answered Debian.

'Water,' repeated Jalan tonelessly, clearly not impressed.

'Please.'

'Water we got, if that's y'poison. Bottles.'

'Fine. Thanks,' said Debian, trying to keep any exasperation from his voice.

'Fifteen,' stated the barman, handing over the plastic bottle.

Debian paid him in hard money and waited for him to return to his glass polishing, which he did with deliberate, defiant slowness. Jalan was rude but he was safe and he knew when not to listen. Debian had been coming here for years and the proprietor's unfriendliness was actually one thing he liked about the place. Jalan Frazer asked no questions, just sold drinks and polished glasses.

Finally, Mr. Scotch Drinker turned to Debian. His smooth-skinned and generic face betrayed no more information than his net signature. The plug sockets glinted amongst his short hair like shrapnel in his head. He rolled the Scotch around its glass meditatively.

'You are Debian?' he asked in a surprisingly soft voice.

'Yes.' Debian tried to fight the nervous urge to glance continually around himself.

'I am Hex. Your new contact from the employer. You have been informed, of course. My predecessor has moved on.'

'I was told that he was dead.'

'As I say, he has moved on. Be assured, his death was not business-related.'

'I *have* been assured. Otherwise I would not have agreed to meet you.'

'Of course, and only right. I have the verification you expect.' Hex held out one index finger. There was a black data-spot adhered to it.

'If that thing contains some sort of virus, don't get your hopes up,' Debian confided in a low voice, searching the face of his contact for any deception, analysing micro-expressions on his features. He seemed genuine enough.

'It's clean. I know you'll have multiple firewalls in that head of yours. A virus wouldn't get in anyway. You think anyone who knew your reputation would even try?' Hex answered equally quietly. Jalan had ducked into the back room.

'You never know,' admitted Debian. He pressed his own index finger to the data spot and the electromagnetic field reader in his digit scanned the codes on the spot. They all checked out. The contact was apparently genuine. Honestly, he hadn't doubted it anyway. 'All good,' he said.

Hex simply nodded, and the spot disappeared into a pocket of his voluminous coat. 'You wanna go sit in a booth, out of the way a bit?' he asked.

'Sure, why not,' answered Debian, brushing his long blonde hair behind one ear. His own DNI sockets were exposed on his head – triple-shielded highways to the brain.

They stood – Hex towering over Debian like a puppeteer. At only five foot eight Debian was used to this. The tumbler of Scotch led them to a booth at the side of the room, seeming to pull Hex along by the hand. Debian followed, moving in a manner intended to draw as little attention as possible. He had perfected the art of walking under the radar, of being unseen in plain sight, avoiding plain sight altogether where possible.

Hex slid onto a bench, which creaked with ancient leather. Debian sat opposite him, placing his water on the table, trying to relax.

'It is good to finally meet you,' said Hex. 'I'm a keen follower of your work.'

'My work,' replied Debian pointedly, 'doesn't like to be followed. But thanks.'

'I have a...commission for you.'

'A job. Fine. Of course. The employer has always recompensed me well.'

Hex leaned forward across the table. Debian could smell the alcohol on his breath but the man's eyes were clear and piercing. He slid an old-fashioned non-networked datasheet across the wooden surface for Debian's perusal.

Debian read the writing on the screen without touching the device: *Cyberlife Research and Development*, was glowing there. He slid it back. Hex took it and cleared the screen.

'You know them?' asked Hex, his natural hazel eyes locked on Debian's eyes of milky crystal.

'Actually, no. I thought I knew most of the major players in the tech scene. Are they new?'

'Well, not exactly. Apparently they've been beavering away in debt at the bottom of the heap for years, struggling for funding, but now they may be onto something that has piqued the employer's interest.'

'What do you want?'

'Ah – the usual,' replied Hex, indicating with a sweeping hand how broad a range of services this might include.

'Specifically? Research databases, staff details, financial details – all of it, in other words. I assume.'

Hex took a sip of Scotch, appraising Debian critically. He took in the hacker's thin, handsome face, intense expression and understated clothing. This non-descript, slight-framed young man was the best in his business. At least that Hex knew of.

The ice cubes, melting now, clinked in his glass. Rolling, rolling. Oily colours glistened faintly on the surface of the liquid. The two chatting ladies were leaving, gathering up their artefacts. Sharky Dave was really abusing the slide guitar now. The sound was raw, buzzy, over-enthusiastic, but all the better for it.

'All of it. Yes.'

'Should be no problem. The price will be as usual.' Debian took a sip of water and looked towards the bar, where Jalan was looking busy without actually doing much.

'The payment will actually be increased this time,' Hex admitted, as if confessing an embarrassing secret.

'Why so?'

'You are likely to find them rather well-prepared to defend their data, rather more so than the average AI research company. They are working on a very large, very secretive contract.'

'For whom?' asked Debian, his interest fully engaged now.

'You tell us.' Hex spread his hands wide in the universal *search me* gesture.

'Okay. It won't be a problem anyway. I've been working on something new – something that will let me run rings around the average avatar. Not just a neural simulation of myself and a simple guidance routine but...' Debian stopped himself, suddenly aware that he was about to reveal too much. Trade secrets must exist, after all. If only there was someone, *one person,* whom he could talk to freely about his passion, his work, without fear.

Hex waved aside this abridged flow of information. 'Don't tell me,' he said, echoing Debian's own thoughts. 'Just be careful, right? Their defence routines are pretty top-notch these days. If we could find someone to get us what we want for cheaper, we would, but none of our other...*helpers* has had any joy with it. These guys are using avatars themselves. Just be warned.'

'Avatars are still illegal!' hissed Debian, surprised. 'How can a registered company get away with that?'

'Maybe no-one can catch them at it. Maybe you can find us answers to these questions.'

Debian stroked his narrow chin meditatively. Avatars! This could be a proper test of his new toy, a proving ground for his baby. He had been prolific enough over the last five years that he could comfortably retire already. His various employers, covert and overt, had paid him in accordance with his abilities. But what would he do if not this? Smoke dope and indulge in recreational acts of random cyber-terrorism? Where would be the challenge? He didn't realise that he was smiling broadly. Hex noticed though, and gulped the last of his Scotch, satisfied.

Sharky Dave was deep in the groove now, his growling voice rolling under and over the zinging and pinging of his guitar:

'I got sixteen pills
They cure all ills
The one with the cross
On the underside kills.
Take two at random
At the foot of a hill,
Climb to the top
And abandon your will
-power. Flee cowards,
Dreamflowers litter the street –
They're like porcupine quills
On the soles of your feet.
Multicoloured poisons,
I pour 'em out neat
And into the corners
Of your mind I creep.
I got sixteen pills
They cure all ills
The one with the cross
On the underside kills...'

Debian listened absently to the music, eyes roving the shadows of the ceiling randomly, deep in thought. The dull glitter of alloy betrayed the presence of the flying knife above the door. A wiry youth with blue hair and glittering golden tusks entered the bar. Debian side-banded the HUD info about him without thinking. Jalan nodded to the tiny robot – the youth approached the bar. Debian knew that if there was anything untoward about the newcomer then his avatars would have pulled it up already and warned him.

His brain was spinning. He let it spin, bubbling away faster than his conscious mind could even follow, full of attack code and counter-attack code, avatars and AI research, net shadows and sub-verters.

Hex watched him, unnoticed, for several minutes. He knew what he was looking at – a genius caught up in his own world. Like an artist envisioning a great work, perhaps a painting which would be his masterpiece, the hacker was no longer truly in the room. Hex was a man who appreciated people who were good at their work. He had heard

15

many positive things about Debian from his employer. He was genuinely impressed by this intense young man now that he had met him in person. There was something in Debian's demeanour that made him more impressive than his appearance alone would suggest. He oozed seriousness, confidence and intelligence. Although his crystal eyes betrayed nothing, it was clear that behind them was happening a very deep, rapid thought process.

Hex cleared his throat. Debian jumped slightly, returning visibly to the bar. The golden-tusked youngster was sitting with a huge glass of beer now, checking his watch with the nervous impatience of the stood-up. Debian's avatars checked the man's personal scheduler. He was indeed expecting an acquaintance by the name of Sanna – a female, presumably.

'Three hundred thousand,' said Hex quietly, and now Debian's attention was truly re-engaged. Not by the sheer amount of currency on offer here, but by the importance of the job that the amount of money suggested. This was several times greater than any payment the employer offered him before. And there had been some big payments.

'This is a big deal for you guys, isn't it? Really.'

'It will be a big deal for *you* if they catch you,' confided Hex, *sotto voce*.

'They won't, so it's all good.' Debian smiled in what he hoped was a reassuring manner. Truth be told, his people skills were lagging further and further behind his computer skills these days, but it seemed to have the desired effect.

'Good. We think their backer might be a government.'

There was silence between the men as Debian digested this information. Hex played with his tumbler, empty now save for the last diminishing pebbles of ice. He looked as if he was considering getting another. The prospect of making this business meeting a sustained social occasion was not an enticing one to Debian. He pointedly re-capped his water and stowed it in a pocket. Hex took the hint and resignedly pushed away his empty vessel. The young hacker intrigued him and the atmosphere of the bar was compelling in an earthy sort of way. But business was business and distance must be maintained.

'Which government?'

'We don't know. Find out if you can. We may be wrong.'

'Interesting...Should be a good test for my new system.'

'You can contact me on the same address as my predecessor. Wait five minutes before you leave,' Hex told Debian, standing and snapping the two halves of his coat together, making a hermetic seal against the dribbling rain outside.

Debian nodded, making eye contact. For the briefest moment Hex could actually see the whirling, dancing code behind those milky lenses. Electrons rushed and bustled there, skipping between computer chips and grey matter. He wondered what Debian's new system might comprise and whether this young man was really up to the challenge. Without another word, Hex turned and swept from the bar, coat-tails playing about his ankles. For a second, he paused in the doorway, framed against a strip of night. A bouncing gravpod whistled past the door, someone hanging out of one window with a bottle in their hand, indecipherable yell trailing them into the gloom like a streamer. Debian noticed that Jalan had also watched Hex leave the bar. He looked to where Debian sat in the booth, then pointedly away again.

Debian waited the five minutes and then left. He glanced up as he departed the bar. The flying knife was perched above him, silently but keenly fluttering its tiny wings. Debian shuddered, thinking of what the thing would do to human flesh, and stepped into the street.

Squalid tenements squatted in the rain around him, festooned with spools of ancient data-cable like flayed robotic ligaments. Somewhere to the southeast a fire was burning. Smoke coiled lazily across the skyline, bunching heavily until it reached above the buildings, where the wind took it and shredded it. A discarded vid-paper blew past, animated headlines scrolling across its crumpling surface. There were very few people on the streets now – just stragglers trawling from one bar to another, looking for the next moment in the bottom of a bottle.

Debian noticed movement in the mouth of an alley opposite the Sunken Chest – nothing clear, just the impression of a figure retreating from sight. Indeed, his HUD showed a heat signature fading behind the brickwork. There was no net signature, though. A meathead? Someone net-stealthed? Had Hex remained to watch Debian depart for some reason? Or was it someone else equally well protected from the sort of prying Debian excelled at? If so, then who?

Hex's words rang in Debian's head: *We think their backer might be a government.*

The infrared trace was gone now, anyway. Debian set off, stepping around the puddles. He decided he would take a circuitous route home. *Just in case,* he told himself. *Just in case*.

CHAPTER THREE

The lights were bright enough that the air itself seemed brilliant with whiteness. Machines buzzed and fussed around the prone and pallid human form on the stainless table. Technically he was still alive at this point. The surgeons were well practised at utilising the body's own life support systems, with some help from the machines, to maintain freshness of the raw materials until they were rushed to cryo.

The two surgeons operated the robotic laser-scalpels by simultaneous keyboard and DNI, hands flying over the keys, eyes absorbing data-streams from several screens at once, bodies and minds dancing in synchronisation with the robots. The scalpels moved with flickering rapidity – they dipped and cut and cauterised, ducking and diving around each other. When required, arms darted in between them, dexterously removing organs and tissues from the body of the slightly overweight man on the slab. These materials were shuttled to cryo-boxes, which trundled themselves off to the storage archives when filled, humming tunelessly as the cryo fields initialised. They analysed and categorised their own contents, updating the master HGR database as they sped from the theatre on tiny rubberised wheels, passing through a sterilisation chamber as they went.

As the process advanced, the body gradually became less and less able to survive unaided. The life support systems took up the slack as this happened. Still, though, there were signs of brain activity, autonomous nervous response. Blood began to flow through hoses as the heart was disconnected. It was oxygenated and returned to circulation. The robot scalpels didn't spill a drop. The body was lifted on a suspensor cushion and turned over. The scalpels flayed the legs and back, extracted bone marrow from bone and bone from flesh. Still the brain survived. Who could say what nightmares capered through its terrorised imagination? The two surgeons, almost robotic themselves, didn't dwell on such concerns. They were fully interfaced with the system, part of the equipment of the theatre.

The hum of mighty transformers seemed to electrify the air of the room. Stainless steel and sterile ceramicarbide surfaces shone cleanly everywhere. The large window was circular, ribbed with concentric bands of ceramicarbide, framing the reddening sky where gyrocopters circled the tower like angels. In the middle distance a ship

19

was taking off from the spaceport, roiling exhaust plumes folding back on themselves under gravity, diffusing over the city skyline. It drove into the air like a grey fist.

Suddenly, the two surgeons stopped their hectic activity in unison. They both stepped back from their stations, turning to face each other. The robots stowed the parts already removed in cryo-boxes and then stopped, awaiting further instruction. One of the surgeons disconnected his DNI cable, yanking it roughly from his skull-socket. His eyes were wide with surprise.

He crossed to the slab where the body was floating motionless on the suspensor cushion. The other surgeon moved to join him there. They craned their necks to look into the colourful depths of the body. They exchanged equally blank expressions.

'What the hell is that?' asked the first. He didn't bother to indicate the area to which he referred. His companion had been privy to the same data stream and knew as much as he did.

'I don't know,' he replied. If the machines didn't know and the database didn't know then nobody knew.

'Should we call Mrs. Smith, do you think?'

'I guess. Do we continue for now?'

The first surgeon peered closely into the flayed human form. Nestled against the spinal column of the man on the cushion was an almost perfectly spherical green object. It seemed to have thin, sticky tendrils worked into the spinal cord itself, clearly deeply entwined with it. The green object was pulsing faintly with the blood flow supplied by the machines.

'I don't know. MRI-scan it.'

'Okay.' The second surgeon returned to his console and without bothering to plug back in began rapidly tapping buttons on the keyboard. The robot arms moved in response, slower without the DNI, but still with their usual smooth precision. The first surgeon watched closely at the body's side.

'Well?'

'Nothing...'

'What do you mean 'nothing'?'

'No image...' The second surgeon shook his head.

'Diagnostics?'

'Fine. MRI-scan reveals all surrounding tissues, but not our mystery item there. Go to x-ray?'

'No. Get Smith. Meanwhile, continue removal of other recoverables from around it, but don't touch *that* thing.'

The second surgeon mentally paged Mrs. Smith while restarting the tissue recovery process. The spidery metallic limbs resumed their dance of dissection.

'Hold all cryo-boxes here until Smith arrives,' ordered the first surgeon, still watching the proceedings closely from the side of the dissection table. His colleague nodded absently – he was plugged into the console again, deep in its control system.

There came the whisper of the sterilisation chamber cycling and Mrs. Smith entered the theatre. She was short and slim, dressed in a simple grey suit, no obvious body-mods, strange for someone in her line of work. Her greying hair was scraped back into a militarily-precise bun and her thin brows were drawn sharply together above her facemask. There was now a reasonable queue of cryo-boxes waiting at the doorway and she regarded them suspiciously, clearly wondering why they were not filed away. Their contents hung frozen beneath the glass, readouts listing their every detail.

'What?' she demanded simply.

The surgeon at the console stepped away from it, unplugging again, fearful of reprimand. Mrs. Smith didn't need much reason to belittle an underling. The surgeon at the table turned to her and spoke.

'Er, we have an *anomaly* with the product. Er...' He briefly faltered beneath his superior's wilting gaze before rallying again. 'This.' He indicated the green orb against the spine of the body. 'We have never seen one before. It isn't in the database. It seems somehow to resist the MRI-scan. We don't know what it's doing, can't even guess, but it seems intrinsically linked with the spine. Probably some new organ from the black market. Certainly, *those* came from an unofficial source.' He indicated the cryo-boxes containing the bright red and gold wings, one in each. Smith peered into them.

'At least those are of value,' she said with a trace of actual approval. 'As for that green thing in there, I have no more idea than you. Of course, Human Genetic Recycling must strive to remain at the forefront of new developments, even those of an unofficial nature. You were correct to call me. Did you try to x-ray it?'

'Not yet. We thought we'd wait for your say-so.'

'Good. Do it.'

Mrs. Smith stepped behind the lead-glass screen, which slid from a wall to curve across the room. The two surgeons joined her there once the machines had been told what to do. There was the cough of electrical discharge as x-rays soaked the room.

The screen slid obediently back into its hidden niche and the three stepped back into the room proper. The second surgeon returned to the console, plugging back in, ready to analyse data and display the x-ray images. Mrs. Smith and the first surgeon craned over the prone figure floating above the table. The green thing seemed to be dissolving, its tendrils melting away, steaming and bubbling as they visibly withdrew from the spine. The sphere crumpled in on itself as they watched in amazement. The surgeon caught a whiff of the vapour and had the unfortunate experience of his head being suddenly filled with a sickeningly thick aroma like rotting fish and cabbage combined. He doubled over and was noisily sick into his facemask. Even Smith recoiled, scowling, from the body.

'Nothing…' said the second surgeon, staring in disbelief at the readouts in front of him.

Smith shook her head, bewildered. The first surgeon was dry-retching now, his mask hanging like a flap of skin from his neck. The green organ had completely disappeared.

CHAPTER FOUR

Whistler calmly re-assembled the gun and blew down the sawn-off barrel, clearing the swarf from it. She clicked the pre-loaded magazine into place and a series of diagnostics LEDs lit up, from red to green. It was a smartgun, with a tiny but very intelligent computer on board. Although Whistler was a meathead, the gun itself would make up for some of this disability. Movement sensors compensated for the shaking of its wielder's hand. It would automatically detect and prioritise targets, influencing its own aim and rate of fire within pre-defined parameters. With the barrel and stock sawn off it would fit comfortably into a coat pocket.

She pointed it at Spider, grinning around a reeferette. She winced as the smoke stung her eye, but Spider didn't flinch. Whistler squeezed the trigger with a loving delicacy: *One, two, three…*

The armour-piercing rounds darted towards Spider, who stood face-on to Whistler, his four segmented arms twining like snakes. He deflected the rounds off his blurring limbs – *one, two, three*. They ricocheted dangerously off into the dark depths of the warehouse. From somewhere there came the sound of liquid spilling.

Spider laughed, actually doubling over, all four arms to his sides as if they might split. Whistler narrowly avoided shooting him unprepared as she, too, collapsed in laughter. Another round zinged into the ceiling before she could put the weapon down. She coughed the roach out in a shower of sparks. Her pointed teeth unintentionally squirted venom as she attempted to rid herself of the gun. She brushed it from her hand as if it were something alive.

'What's with this pyrotechnic display of fuck-wittery?' asked Tec, appearing up the stairs. His skull glittered with coloured lights synched to emotional state. They were blazing with peachy shades of restrained amusement, hectic flashes like one-liners itching to be free.

'Hey,' Whistler greeted him, still suppressing giggles.

Spider flexed his arms and crossed the floor to where Whistler sat, the lines on her grey face glowing faintly like the blueprint for an electronic component. Spider retrieved the gun from the floor. Its tiny computer brain recognised his grip and scent and accepted his command to enter sleep mode, the electronic equivalent of a safety

23

catch. He laid it on the scarred metal of the tabletop and checked his arms for bullet-marks. They were unscathed.

'Hey Tec. Time to go, I guess.'

'S'right. No rest an' all that.' Tec's head was lit with the sustained white of serious business now. 'I guess you slackers are high again, am I right?' He didn't wait for a response, just threw a stubby of Get-Up to Whistler. She clicked it in the palm of her hand. She knew when duty called. Slowly, the fuzzy edges of the world solidified. Whistler handed the stubby to Spider, who pressed it against the skin of his neck.

'Even the wicked must rest sometime, Tec,' said Whistler once she felt properly grounded again. 'So where's Roberts?'

'Running diags on the van. The satellite reception has been fading in and out. He says he'll meet us down there.'

'Nobody told me about that.'

'Oh. Sorry.'

'Just nice to be in the loop.' She looked around for things to gather up prior to departure. There was only the gun, which looked like an amputee now, the stump of its stock lying forlornly next to it. She dropped it into a pocket. 'Let's roll.'

The three retreated down the stairs from which Tec had emerged, leaving behind the booming cavern of the main warehouse. The big room, as it was known, was mostly taken up with the storage of rusting machinery and crates of stolen clothing. The basement level was where the team spent most of their time. Their individual quarters were down here, as was Tec's workshop.

The van was also garaged underground in a secure hangar inside a Faraday cage and a microwave scrambler field, effectively cutting it off from the net. Although the vehicle could be disconnected manually, a sub-verter in its systems could secretly re-connect it and ransack its databases when it was unattended were it not stored in isolation.

The three harvesters stopped outside Sofi's door. It was closed and the telltale absence of noise came from behind it.

'Is she sleeping?' asked Whistler. Tec shrugged. Spider pushed forwards and hammered on the door in a rattling drum-roll loud enough to wake the dead.

Several seconds passed. Whistler spent them looking unimpressed. The door burst open and Sofi flapped out of it into the corridor, pulling on clothes as she blinked with the grogginess of the freshly woken. Stumbling slightly and managing to hold onto a stun-gun, she pushed past her fellows and off towards the garage as if she had been waiting for them all along.

'Come on then,' she called, her three parallel mohawks somehow immaculate despite having been recently dragged out of bed along with their reluctant owner. Tec shrugged again and followed Sofi.

'I've never known anyone sleep fourteen hours a day,' Whistler remarked in tones of mock astonishment. Sofi's long hours of slumber were a well known in-joke amongst the harvesters and they had all come to expect it by now.

The group of four followed the narrow passage past Tec's workshop-slash-lab where heaps of computer components and interconnected boxes of unfathomable purpose sprawled across every available surface alongside bottles and jars of drugs and chemicals. A small arachnid robot crept through the mess looking for somewhere to park itself. The robot, jokingly named Spider Junior, was Tec's pet. It was pretty unintelligent and didn't actually do much but he seemed attached to it for some reason.

They passed under a sentry gun in a corner of the ceiling, its dark muzzle silently roving the shadows as if sniffing for prey. This, together with the scrambler-bait opposite it, constituted an inner ring of defence. Actually, if an intruder had penetrated this far into the warehouse then they were likely to be tooled up enough not to worry much about the gun. And the chance of a spyfly getting this far was effectively nil.

Sofi's fingers flew over the security keypad of the ancient and heavy sliding door. It whispered back into the wall and a waft of oily air greeted the team. The bright lights of the garage were beyond, and beneath them squatted the matt black silhouette of the van, like a hole in reality. Roberts was standing with one hand flat on its almost frictionless surface, plugged in, and evidently finishing his diagnostics. He didn't notice the others at first. He was muttering under his breath, lost in thought.

The garage was effectively featureless apart from the vehicle, Roberts himself and a covered turnstile of spares that stood in one corner like a massive tree. Its smooth, clean walls were in sharp contrast to the clutter and decay of the rest of the building and clearly differentiated the hangar as a state-of-the-art facility. The van floated a foot off the floor, totally motionless – a sleeping panther.

Roberts was wearing his usual dark combats and dark brown trenchcoat. The steel tube of the nerve-shocker would, as always, be concealed within its folds. Except for the scar across his serious, craggy face he was the least distinctive-looking of the team, and as such was distinguished by that if nothing else. He was tall and solidly if not heavily built, with short dark hair sprouting around his head sockets. Roberts was an ex-cell commander from the days of the political insurgency. He had spent years fighting in block-to-block skirmishes with government forces through the city streets and had been captured, briefly imprisoned and tortured. Since joining Whistler's team his troubled, violent past showed only as a vaguely detached and grumpy demeanour.

He unplugged from the van and turned to face the others. Whistler stood regarding him with one hand on a hip, her body arranged in a pose designed to indicate impatience. Spider's arms twined unconsciously in the air. Tec's lights were flashing. Sofi just looked surly.

'I think it's sorted,' said Roberts.

'It fucking needs to be,' answered Whistler. 'How come I didn't know there was a problem with the sat-link?'

'Tec said you were *busy*,' responded Roberts, dead-pan as always. 'And I knew I could fix it by myself.'

'Yeah, well, I *was* busy,' she said sulkily.

'Shooting spiders in the warehouse,' laughed Tec, glints of amusement darting across his scalp.

'I assume you did fix it?' queried Whistler, re-asserting authority.

'Course.'

'Okay, good, whatever,' Sofi interjected. 'Are we off, then, my leader, or did you just wake me up out of spite?'

'Yeah,' said Whistler. 'Let's tool up and go shopping. Everyone armed and ready?' General nods and murmurs. She knew they were. 'Then let's go.'

The door of the van irised open at a mental command from Tec and the five harvesters filed in, assuming their relevant positions. Whistler slid into the driver's seat. Tec had been the last to drive the van and Whistler had to retract the DNI-console into the dash. It was replaced by a set of analogue control levers.

'Fucking meathead,' accused Tec.

26

'Fucking buttonhead,' she replied, checking the readouts relating to communications systems, fusion cell, weapons, life support. She glanced around briefly to assess the readiness of the crew. The huge form of Spider dwarfed the slim figure of Sofi on the back bench. Tec was already plugged into the net console in the main body of the van, even though it couldn't connect to a satellite through the shielded hangar. Although most buttonheads were equipped to access the net directly, the console would augment and supplement this ability, as well as providing a high-speed interface layer between net, van and human. Opposite Tec, the stretcher was bolted to the wall, its arm and leg straps dangling. Roberts sat to Whistler's left, face impassive.

Whistler started the van and touched a button to open the garage door. As it swung up and the edge became visible it became clear how massively thick and heavy it was – more like the door to a bank vault than a garage. The van smoothly climbed the ramp, passing beneath a set of heavy sentry guns, silent as a shadow. In the back, Sofi was grumpily checking the charge on her stun-gun, muttering curses under her breath.

'So – where are we going?' asked Roberts. 'Any plan?'

'Not as such. Just roll with it.' Whistler bit her lip thoughtfully. 'I'd wondered about somewhere in Market Garden.'

'Yeah, the edge of it, I assume,' said Spider from the back in his rich tenor voice.

'Yeah, South Street, somewhere like that,' answered Whistler, eyes on the ramp, relying on old-fashioned senses.

Sofi said something that sounded like, 'Fine,' but looked more like *fuck you all*. Whistler glanced back at her. 'What?' she demanded.

'Nothing,' mumbled Sofi.

The ramp of the warehouse emptied into an underground car park where ten or twelve other mostly-abandoned warehouses and factories also had exits. This would mean that anyone who saw the van enter or leave the main door of the car park from outside would still not know for sure which address it belonged to. From inside the car park the team's building was made to look completely deserted. To see the sentry guns an observer would have to be stood underneath them, which would likely make them dead. No-one had ever come to investigate the garage door as yet. It was generally assumed amongst the team that all the occupiers of the surrounding addresses were

27

engaged in equally dubious business of their own. The only other entrance to the building was on the roof where heat and net-signature seeking missiles were arranged in the shadows.

The van coasted across the deserted floor of the car park, swerving cleanly around concrete pillars. A light was on above the door of one of the factories nearest the street. Whatever they made there, they did it in privacy. The harvesters had never met anyone from the building, just heard the pounding and thumping of machinery deep inside its depths, and left it at that. All they wanted of their neighbours was to be left alone, a sentiment which said neighbours apparently shared.

Whistler turned onto the main exit ramp of the car park and the van moved up it and out into the street. The area wore the brownish shroud of decay. Overloaded wheelie-bins jostled for position on the pavements, their contents spilling from their lids like vomit. The windows that were not boarded-up or covered in wire mesh were mostly broken. One doorway was showing a red light. A Cyclopean pimp lounged against the door frame picking his nails with a switchblade. An old woman was slowly walking a large rusty robot dog up the street. She ignored the van as it coasted past her. It was raining again.

'I love the autumn,' said Roberts quietly, mostly to himself. 'The way the air smells.'

'Yeah,' retorted Sofi. 'Slightly warmer rain than the winter.'

'Signal,' said Tec. 'Setting the satnav for South Street.'

'Direct me when we get closer,' said Whistler. 'Who's got some tunes?'

Without replying, Tec started playing the latest Blue Screen of Death album, directly from his head into the van's stereo. The repetitive bass thrummed like a heartbeat, compressing the air of the van in waves. For a while, no-one spoke.

'Market Garden,' said Whistler.

'Okay,' replied Tec, turning the music down. 'South Street's on the right in a few blocks. Where do you want to go?'

'Let's just drive for a while,' she suggested. 'See what we see.'

Spider pressed his nose to the skin of the van, which although dark, was translucent from the inside. One of his hands was toying with the shape of an electrified knife through the fabric of his pocket. Dark doorways filed past like rows of broken teeth. People on the streets,

28

even this late. Birds circling the rooftops like ash in the wind. Rain running like the blood of the city.

'Him?' asked Sofi, pointing to a man on her side of the street. He moved arrogantly through the crowd on four strutting robot legs, his head sporting spiralled horns of anodised metal, the rain slicking his naked torso.

'Extreme. I like him,' answered Whistler, resisting the urge to slow down suspiciously as she watched him into the crowd.

'Those stupid-ass legs run off a symbiotic DNI program though – they're not a true bodymod,' pointed out Tec.

'Shame,' said Spider. 'Can we go somewhere quieter?'

'Or louder,' countered Whistler, chewing her lip thoughtfully with her pointed fangs as she focused on the road. The van wove between badly parked or abandoned gravpods, some of them resting on the ground, with the detritus of ages drifted against them.

'What have you in mind?' asked Roberts.

'Wanna go clubbing, Rob?' asked Whistler cheerfully, shoving him on the shoulder.

'Not really,' he said, and Sofi actually laughed.

'Where?' asked Tec. His lights were a blur of activity now. They always went crazy when he was plugged in.

'I know a place...'

'Classy I'm guessing,' interjected Roberts.

'Bit of a fuckin' dive, actually,' replied Whistler, laughing. 'S'called Pharmacopia.'

'Pharmacopia? Stupid name for a club.'

'Just that. I think it's down this way.' She nodded to the left, looking for a turning in that direction. An open-top gravpod zoomed by them on the right, running the lights. A teetering young woman rose from her seat and threw a can at the van, screaming something which went unheard over the music. The can bounced harmlessly off into the road, pluming liquid which looked like either piss or cider. None of the harvesters mentioned it, considering the incident unworthy of their attention. They had work to do.

'So that's your plan, eh, boss? Go to some skanky club night?' demanded Sofi.

'Yes.' She sighed. 'It wouldn't be the first time for you, would it, Sofe?'

29

Sofi, even in her present mood, knew better than to take the bait. She thudded back into her seat, face expressionless. Everyone knew she was seething inside. Whistler and the others tolerated Sofi's anger. It never got in the way of her work, never made her careless or unpredictable, never got as far as serious psychosis. All of them knew that she would die for them, if need be, when the moment came. Sofi had come from a similar background to Whistler herself – true child of the streets born and bred, veteran of several gangs, ex-juke addict. Although they didn't always get on Whistler felt a particular affinity with her because of this.

Tec queried the satnav and started directing them to the club. Had Whistler been a buttonhead, the route would have transferred directly to her mind, but she was used to a human navigator. She could still have programmed the van to drive itself, but she preferred to be in control. Tec pointed her under a concrete overpass and down a one-way street.

Spider left his seat and moved to a console next to Tec. He plugged in and started silently talking to the van, probably just updating its little brain about the plan for the evening, such as it was. The van, although possessed of limited simulated intelligence, was generally treated as another member of the team. Spider particularly babied it, and liked to keep it in the loop. Whistler vaguely protested at this habit. After all, the more the van knew, the more it could tell a hacker. But the others, who knew more about this sort of thing than her, assured her it was safe. Whistler's unique talents lay in a different area, so she deferred to them in the matter.

They rounded a corner where people swarmed like insects beneath the towering blocks of brick and plastic. Tec pointed. Pharmacopia was just ahead and to the left, two huge bouncers like dolmens outside it. They looked more like the type to cause trouble than prevent it. A trickle of revellers were seeping in and out of the club in various states of inebriation.

Whistler drove the van around back to the car park and stopped smoothly in a space. The other vehicles were mostly brightly coloured gravpods, some of them heavily modified into boy-racer machines. A vulgar purple ground-trike squatted in their midst like a monster. The van was like a negative image amongst these bright toys. A holo-construct in the form of a huge silver-green fish swam through the sky above the club.

'Pharmacopia?' mused Roberts, scratching his stubbled chin. 'Why a fish?'

'Beats me,' boomed Spider, unplugging from the vehicle. 'I've told the van not to kill anyone,' he informed the others.

'Good,' replied Whistler, leaving her seat.

'Fun time,' said Sofi with all the enthusiasm of one about to undergo dental surgery.

'Try to cheer the fuck up, eh?' suggested Spider, punching her on the shoulder as she bent to open the door of the van. She kicked back at him, quite effectively for someone in her unbalanced position, not bothering to check the results, and exited the vehicle. The others disembarked after her, Spider rubbing his leg and grinning.

The harvesters milled about for a moment, checking and stowing items of equipment. They looked like any other group of clubbers preparing to go in. A party of four – two men and two women – passed them, returning to their own vehicle. One of the men, wearing a ridiculous outfit of buckled rubber straps, sported a large, ruby red crab's claw for a hand. His face was ugly with designer pockmarks but his scrawniness looked natural. The team watched him as inconspicuously as they could, Tec starting to roll a joint as he stood.

'Nah,' said Whistler. 'Claw's okay, but the rest of him doesn't look worth much.' There was general consensus. The four club-leavers got into their gravpod and it moved slowly away.

'Come on, then,' said Whistler and the others followed her around the side of the building towards the front.

They approached the bouncers, Whistler at the head of the group. The two men were bent together, sharing dabs of bright blue powder out of a paper wrap. They looked up as the harvesters neared them, one of them stowing the wrap about his person again. This man, a giant with rows of chrome spikes along the backs of his arms, hands and neck, put out one hand to stop the group.

'Any illegal weapons?' he asked.

'No, I'm good, thanks,' answered Whistler brightly, sauntering right past him.

A look of astonishment flashed across his square face and was replaced almost at once by a grim expression. One huge hand shot out

31

to grab Whistler by her retreating shoulder. Anticipating it, she spun around, deflecting the hand in one motion, and stood staring the huge man directly in the eye – passive again, hands lowered. The bouncer's hand returned slowly to his body and his lip curled slightly. His eyes were like storm clouds – a dark and thundery grey. His friend had one hand on a baton at his belt and was regarding Whistler with simple interest. Her posture was non-confrontational but she could see the subtle tensions in the bodies of her group as they watched. Tec's head was glowing with a murderous deep purple.

'Relax,' she said charmingly. 'Just stunners an' shit.' She was agonizingly aware of the smartgun hanging heavily in one jacket pocket, its evil little mind even now monitoring possible targets, listening for stress in voices, harbingers of violence.

There was a moment when the possibilities seemed to hang in equilibrium. Then the bouncer nodded, Whistler smiled disarmingly, and the five harvesters passed between the doormen and into the club. They walked through a sound-cancellation chamber and the music hit them like a wave.

The club was dimly-lit by the hectic glow of holo-construct women who danced amongst the clubbers like human lanterns, the colours blazing from them changing quickly in time with the music. Sometimes they flared with different shades, sometimes the colours came together and synched for a while. Real people were dancing with some of them, flesh and force field moving as if one.

The bar was a boomerang-shaped swathe of glass on a suspensor cushion. Drinks stood solidly on what appeared to be only a green nimbus of light. A robot like a golden octopus was serving several drinks at once. People paid by inserting cards into its palms, having money automatically transferred over the net if they were buttonheads, or handing over hard money if they were of the type who liked to be hard to trace. They were crammed three-deep at the bar, clamouring for the machine's attention.

The dance floor was about a centimetre deep in black water. Occasionally, showers of dry ice pellets shot from the walls between the legs of the dancers, where they twisted and twirled as they sublimed in the water, dappled with pinprick laser lights. Some sort of machine was swooping around in the shadows near the ceiling – something quite big with wings. On a high balcony, revellers sloshed drinks down onto the dance floor as they thrashed along to the music.

In a bat-winged plastic pulpit, the DJ was deep in the vibe. He was playing a sustained sinistro bassline on one deck, trimming and EQ-ing by DNI, dropping in hypnophone screams and wavering electric howls from the other. His tattooed torso was studded with implanted diamonds.

'Not as bad as when I was here last, actually,' opined Whistler to Roberts, leaning in close to be heard over the noise.

'I'm going for a piss,' Roberts replied, stalking off in a flurry of coat-tails.

'Let's dance then, shall we?' asked Whistler, turning to Sofi.

Sofi shrugged and disappeared into the crowd, hips already snaking, already drawing some looks. Spider and Tec, characteristically enough, went to the bar. Whistler, propelled by the beat, joined the dancers in the water. She worked her way into the rhythm, trying not to show too much of her natural grace and athleticism – trying, in other words, not to move too much like a skilled fighter – but she soon began to get lost in the pounding of the sinistro bass, dark splashes marking every footfall, dry ice pellets shooting like meteorites around her. An incredible human bestiary moved about her. Twining tentacles, symbiotic machinery, metallic body-parts, feathers, scales. Scales.

He had the most breathtaking skin of scales. A buttonhead – tall, good-looking, naked down to the waist, well-muscled, dancing in perfect, hectic time. His skin seemed to be a brilliant orange, but in the coloured lasers the scales winked with green and red and blue such that it was hard to tell their true colour for sure. He was lost in the tune, but not so lost that he wasn't edging closer to Whistler. Pretending not to notice, she let him.

When he got within arm's reach, he looked up briefly, appraising her lithe form, her matt grey skin, lined with blue, which flashed through the slits in her jacket and combats, her deceptively delicate face. His eyes were golden slits – snake eyes. He nodded to her and smiled, barely pausing in his work. She danced closer.

'Hey,' she shouted over the music. 'Nice skin.'

'You too,' he answered, winding down to a near-standstill. He brushed a hand through his short-shaved hair, misting the air with fresh sweat.

'What is it? Lizard scales?'

'Dragon,' he said seriously. 'Well, s'meant to be...'

'I like it,' she said, and the hunger in her voice was genuine enough, if not of the nature that he thought.

'You're a meathead,' he pointed out. 'You're a dying breed.'

'What?' Whistler shouted, craning closer, putting a hand on his bare forearm.

'I said, you're a meathead – no plugs. You're a dying breed. My name's Tallen.'

'Whistler,' she said, narrowing her eyes mischievously at him. 'And my breed is going strong, thanks.'

'What?' he shouted.

Whistler shook her head. 'You wanna come outside?'

'Okay, yeah. It's hot in here, right?'

Whistler took him by one hand and led him through the jostling dancers. She noticed Roberts watching them from the balcony above. He nodded to her almost imperceptibly. The dark shape was swooping and diving up there now – something with wings and a tail. Whistler and her prey passed Tec, who was talking to a pretty blue-haired girl at the bar. He caught her eye as she went. They passed through the sound-cancellation chamber again and the noise was swallowed, to be replaced by an ear-ringing sound vacuum. The man with the dragon-skin was staggering slightly now.

As the pair stepped into the cool night air Tallen stumbled, dragging on Whistler's arm. The bouncers turned to regard them.

'Whoa,' Whistler said, supporting the man's weight easily. Then to the doormen, 'He's a bit wasted – he's okay.'

'I think I need to sit. Sorry.'

'Over here – my van's over here.'

'Okay, cool, good...' He was flagging rapidly now, would start to get suspicious soon. Whistler hustled him away from the doormen, who were fortunately distracted at that moment by a group of raucous townies approaching the club's entrance. They seemingly forgot the woman with the pointed teeth and wasted friend and went back to work. The giant fish swam lazily through the sky, perhaps looking for smaller holo-fish to eat, snapping its jaws dumbly.

Whistler managed to keep Tallen walking. 'Sorry,' he was saying. 'I ain't felt all that good since I had the skin done. On and off, y'know...

I...' He stumbled again, going to one knee this time and Spider was behind him with a stunner held concealed in the metal palm of one hand. Under the guise of assisting Tallen back to his feet he pressed its snub muzzle to the side of the man's neck. Tallen struggled briefly – very briefly – and then his body un-tensed and his limbs became pliant. His slit-eyes were roving back and forth frantically from Whistler to the massive Spider as they propelled him towards the van.

'Easy money,' said Tec under his breath, appearing at Whistler's right elbow.

'Where are the others?' she asked equally quietly, trying to look nonchalant as the barely-conscious Tallen put more and more weight on her.

'Coming.'

The four approached the van as Sofi and Tec emerged from the darkness ahead of them, presumably having found a rear exit from the club, restraining themselves from running in their excitement. A gyrocopter passed low overhead, wheeling off towards the Undercity proper, spotlights flowing over the ground before it. Police.

'Wagon,' said Whistler. The button-mic on her jacket relayed this to the van, which opened its door and readied its propulsion system. The harvesters bundled Tallen, who was beginning to recover slightly from the stunner, if not the drug, through the door and into the vehicle. He sprawled on the floor, mooing weakly with fear. A tiny light on his head was blinking. No-one noticed. Tec, Sofi and Roberts were in the body of the vehicle, man-handling Tallen's flopping form onto the stretcher. Whistler took a last look about her. Satisfied that they were unobserved, she ducked inside. Spider followed, glancing at Tallen approvingly.

Whistler took the controls and coasted them subtly out of the car park. She turned gently around pedestrians, being as hard to notice as possible. There weren't many people still outside by this time – most of them were in the club, splashing along to the sinistro bass pulses, out of their minds.

Looking in the rear-view monitor, which displayed on a small square of the front wall, Whistler noticed the doorman with the metal spikes watching them as the van rode its suspensor cushion to the edge of the road, paused to wait for a bright green gravpod to pass, and then moved out into the light traffic. Then someone in the queue spoke to him and he returned to work, forgetting about the matt black vehicle as it merged with the night.

'Easy, eh?' said Whistler over her shoulder, grinning.

'Nice product, too,' opined Roberts, glancing back at the body on the stretcher. The others murmured agreement. 'Never seen skin like that before. Worth a bit, for sure.' This was as close to enthusiastic praise as Roberts had ever got.

Whistler was now threading the van down back streets as quickly as any meathead could, eyes wide with adrenaline. One bumper knocked a fly-tipped office chair spinning into a doorway.

'Why the rush?' demanded Sofi rudely.

'Yeah, we're away free,' added Spider from the back of the van.

'I dunno – I thought the bouncer might have been scoping us on the way out. I guess I imagined it.'

Spider craned to peer out of the translucent rear wall of the van. 'I guess so,' he said. 'No company.'

'Nothing on the net,' added Tec from where he sat in his floor cradle, trailing DNI cable.

'Okay,' said Whistler, relaxing. 'Put that BSOD album on again.' She said it *Bee-sod*. Tec obliged and the repetitive thumping filled the van again.

They continued on down the dimly lit road, chatting happily, debating the value of their human cargo, the relative merits of sinistro versus hexno, other clubs they could hit in the future. Spider and Sofi were passing a joint in the back and Sofi was actually smiling.

'Oh,' said Tec. 'Hmm...'

'Tec? What is it?' Whistler asked without looking back at him.

'Not sure. It might be...'

'What? Company?'

'Yeah,' he said, brow furrowed and head sparkling with yellow confusion. All talk in the van ceased suddenly. 'I think it's...'

Something scraped the roof – a whining, sharp metallic noise. The vehicle dipped to one side as Whistler jumped, twitching the controls. An indistinct shadow rushed above them and rose into the sky, visible through the ceiling. Whistler began to ask what the hell it was when it suddenly became clear. Tec patched a zoomed camera view onto a panel of the ceiling and the harvesters watched dumbstruck as the dragon turned, rolling back on itself, and swooped towards them again.

'That's what that was flying round the club, then,' said Sofi.

Tec nodded. 'Familiar,' he said. He turned to look at the drugged Tallen, noting at last the light blinking on the man's head. He bent to the console again and his own lights went berserk with activity. He was trying to hack the familiar.

The dragon hit the armoured hide of the van like an express train and the team felt its structure tremble. A machine gun turret unfurled from the roof like an obscene flower in bloom and bullets began to rattle off the skin of the familiar like rain. The dragon was desperately trying to hold on with its four clawed paws to any minute chink or seam it could find in the skin of the vehicle. While it did this, its knife-ended tail darted and struck again and again with ferocious speed at the front of the van. Its stubby orange jaws were snapping madly at the air and its slit eyes, so like those of its master, flared with furious colour. A tiny lick of flame burst from its mouth, washing the vehicle harmlessly. The machine gun ripped a hand-sized hole in one of the robot's wings and it wheeled away into the sky again. Clearly, the wings were only for show and it actually rode on a suspensor cushion. The turret weapon chattered one short burst of lead at the dragon's retreating form as if insistent on having the last word.

'Tec?' Whistler demanded. 'It's coming around again. Can it get through the armour?'

Tec was lost in the net, hi-flo DNI cable twined around his shoulders like a snake. He crouched over the console, peering deep into the screen. 'Police,' he said.

'Damn it!' Whistler cursed. 'Which police?' She was aware that the machine gun was firing again.

'This is going well, then,' pointed out Roberts from where he sat passively with his arms crossed.

Whistler turned on him. 'What the fuck are you doing?' she shouted. 'Help him! Tec – which police?'

'Local rent-a-cop. They won't catch us – take a left – not if you floor it.'

Roberts plugged in without leaving his seat. The dragon was on the side of the van now, Sofi snarling back into its fanged face. Its tail was starting to crack the armour and the van's weapons couldn't reach it. They were swivelling angrily as they sought in vain to remove the vicious parasite. Whistler tried to scrape the robot off on a wall as they whipped past. The dragon's body smashed a massive chunk out of the wall and bricks rained down like confetti. It was still hanging on, its stupid metal face looking almost triumphant. Sofi was shouting at it, enraged and powerless.

Sirens could be heard in the distance now, warbling idiotically as the rent-a-cops scurried to give chase. Most of the local forces were covered by the harvesters' immunity contract – some of them weren't. Either way, Smith would be royally pissed if Whistler had to contact her asking for the dogs to be called off. Best not to let it come to that.

'Shall I get HGR?' asked Roberts, echoing Whistler's thoughts.

'No.'

'I'm gonna climb out and blast that fucking robot,' exclaimed Sofi. The familiar was climbing up onto the roof now, its tail switching like a cat's.

'Yeah, if you want a limb ripped off,' replied Spider.

'Ha!' bellowed Tec triumphantly, and the dragon suddenly went rigid and peeled away into the road, lifeless. It bounced off in the wake of the van and was quickly left behind. Tallen's body shivered as his familiar died. His arms and legs jittered briefly against their restraints, then were still. The light on his head had stopped blinking as his connection to the familiar was suddenly dropped.

'It's Universal Protection Contractors on us,' said Roberts. 'We've no contract with them – we'll have to lose them the old-fashioned way.'

'I'm on it!' answered Whistler, swerving the wrong way up a one-way street. The sound of sirens, more concentrated and organised now, was getting closer.

'Tec?' barked Spider. 'Can you do something, or is this gonna be another shootout?'

'I'm trying, I'm trying,' he answered. 'The avatars can't get through. There's also the danger of backhacks from these fuckers. It's almost as if they know what they're doing.'

An intense silence followed during which Tec's fingers flew over the keypad and Whistler heaved the van left and right further into the warren of side streets. Few other vehicles passed them. Tec's eyelids were fluttering as his mind whirled with the data-stream. Roberts, too, was deep in the net. Spider was assembling his mag-rifle with calm composure. Sofi was sat with her hands in her lap, grinding her teeth, hating her impotence. Sirens screamed like banshees behind them.

The van burst from an alley into a wide junction and the police were there ahead of them, their gravpods and riot-vans arrayed in a semi-circle like a fishing net. Whistler hit the brakes but knew they couldn't stop in time. The vehicle's computer saw the danger, also, and steered itself for the too-small gap between two police wagons.

'Brace!' screamed Whistler.

The van hit the police vehicles, driving into the gap like a wedge. They lifted into the air and the nose of the van dug into the road. For a moment, it seemed as if it would flip. Spider's gun flew out of his hands and hit the windscreen, the noise lost in the roar of impact. Already, Roberts was manually firing the machine gun turret into the scurry of navy-clad figures who scattered, fleeing from the somersaulting vehicles. The van swerved under brakes and skidded sideways. Whistler, who hadn't even noticed when her head hit the dashboard, was trying to reverse away from the roadblock to bring more weapons to bear. Spyflies swarmed around the vehicle like gnats round a horse, filming, cataloguing. Scrambler-baits lured them in and fried them in clouds.

Something boomed on the roof of one of the police wagons and the top right corner of the van's armoured windscreen shattered, scattering the harvesters inside with glittering shards. Police were popping up from cover, bringing small-arms to bear. The second machine gun turret and the poison ice gun joined in now, the weapons chattering like teeth. One of the streams of lead, guided by Tec, found the magazine of the police unit which had fired the cannon at them. It erupted, its armour bursting like an inflated paper bag. Human figures were briefly illuminated as they cartwheeled away through the air in a shower of limbs.

'Not fucking cool!' yelled Whistler, somewhat unnecessarily, as the police began to concentrate their fire on the torn corner of the front wall. Several bullets ricocheted around inside the van, burying themselves in the seats, miraculously hitting nobody.

'Let's just go!' screamed Sofi. Spider was climbing out of the sunroof with the mag-rifle in two of his massive claws. 'Spider – no!'

Whistler, needing no more encouragement, reversed, swinging the nose round and smoothly engaging forward mode. Spider tottered and ducked back in as a stream of bullets sought to scrape him from the roof. Aiming for a main road, Whistler opened the throttle all the way. The van took off like a missile, small-arms fire rattling off its rear wall in showers of sparks. Sofi craned to see out the back.

'Are they following?' asked Whistler.

'...Yeah,' replied Sofi. 'Maybe they haven't had enough.'

'Maybe not,' agreed Tec. 'Look – let's kill the net-link. Satellite, radio, all of it.'

'And be left flying blind? No calls, no satnav, nothing? Fuck, no.'

'Listen, I can't disrupt their tracking system – they've clearly bought a high priority. The avatars can't get in, I'm constantly fighting backhacking from all sorts of defence routines – sooner or later one will get through. I...'

'Shit, okay, do it. And launch minissiles when we round the corner.'

Whistler heaved the van round a corner and Tec released the small autonomous missiles, which rapidly spread out to cover the entrance to the road. Sirens screamed behind them. The minissiles, guided by internal computers, began to patrol the air in tight patterns. They were not connected to the net or to any radio or microwave network, and could not be controlled once released. On the up-side, this meant that they could not be detected by any comm-signature. This, together with their all-plastic construction, made them very hard to spot for a rapidly pursuing enemy.

The van sped away from the minissiles as the first police pod rounded the corner, lights swirling madly. A second joined it in close succession. One of the weapons had already sniffed out the first pod and darted towards it eagerly. The harvesters flinched in unison as the mouth of the road was engulfed by a fireball that grew to fill it like expanding foam. A dark, shattering twist of metal could be seen in silhouette against the brilliance of the flame for an instant. Glass disintegrated in the fronts of the surrounding buildings. There was a momentary silence followed by a roar so loud that it drowned out the music inside the fleeing vehicle.

Tec's net panel was dark now, and for a moment they drove in silence as well as isolation, the towers of the city looming ominously around them, rubbish floating like silent ghosts in their wake. The sound of sirens faded as Whistler drove down increasingly narrow streets, bearing off to the east and then folding back on their course, heading back to the Undercity and home. She had time to notice her throbbing head now and risked raising one hand to check the source of the pain. It came away with blood, but not too much of it.

Sofi exhaled heavily, as if she had been holding her breath. 'That was close,' she said. 'Too fucking close. Thank the economic recession that UPC don't have access to 'copters.'

'Everyone all right?' asked Whistler. There was a murmur of acknowledgement. 'Check the product – if we've broken it, all this was for naught.'

Tec, unplugged now from the isolated console, moved to examine Tallen. There was a small wound in the man's left arm – a graze from one of the ricocheting bullets. 'He's had a scratch,' said Tec. 'Nothing more. What is...' Tec reached out a hand in disbelief, but stopped short of actually touching the wound.

'What?' demanded Whistler.

'What is...' he repeated.

Blood was seeping from the graze on Tallen's arm in a steady, slow trickle. But another fluid was also escaping the wound. The two streams clearly came from the same source, but they separated to run two different courses down the biceps to drip onto the floor of the van. One stream was red, the other a deep, glistening green.

CHAPTER FIVE

Debian interfaced with the computer control of his flat and let himself in. The room, like the building that contained it, was old and well used. The walls were covered in paper of an indeterminate colour. A stainless steel bed frame supported an unclothed futon mattress. A wooden chair was tucked beneath a vast wooden desk upon and under which sprawled a computer rig that a government lab would have been proud of. Liquid nitrogen-cooled quantum processors hung in glass boxes around the desk like party decorations. Bunches of hi-flo cable – faster and safer than wireless – were draped between pieces of equipment like jungle vines. Despite its austerity the room was clean and orderly.

Debian went first to the window and, parting a corner of the sun-bleached curtain, looked out into the street. A few bedraggled figures crept past far below but he could not detect anyone lingering around. Infrared showed several people in adjacent flats all going about their day-to-day business. He knew them all, all their details, even though he never spoke to any of them if he could help it. He continued to watch for several minutes and then, breathing a sigh of relief, he went to the coffee machine on the kitchenette counter.

The machine, primed by the flat's control system to expect the demand, supplied strong white coffee almost immediately. The stats of the machine flickered across the back of Debian's mind – water, coffee, milk, sugar levels, internal heat, usage pattern. Debian took the mug that it produced and went to the desk. He sat achingly in the old chair. He had walked a long way before daring to return here.

One hand reached out unconsciously to touch the plastic box of the hi-flo data router that stood on a smaller table alongside the desk. The computer, aware of his presence, booted up. He read the power-on self-test report over wireless, making sure all was well. Then he plugged in. The data coursed through his head like ice-water and he relaxed back into the chair as far as was possible with such an inherently uncomfortable piece of furniture. Faintly, the disseminated processors were humming around him, talking to the large data storage unit under the desk. Debian was unaware that he was humming, too – matching their pitch perfectly.

Once in the system, he ran through a long series of diagnostics, checking processor load and ping speed with a variety of programs and settings. He scanned every corner of his system for viruses. He then started a security test, sending his own avatars out to attack his system remotely. They were unable to get through the complex defence protocols, and of course the avatars would be on his side of the battle when he started for real.

There was no slowdown indicative of a parasite program running in his system, no lag. The avatars moved unseen through the net, testing attack scripts on the defence systems of a small bank, which they chose in accordance with the profile of the neural simulation that formed a part of their code. They moved with perfect stealth. They wheedled their way into the mainframe of the bank autonomously. At this point Debian could easily have gone further – maybe made a payment into an orbital account – but what was the point? He had been there and done that in the past, and eventually it had become boring – his present work was not about the money.

All was well and, having completed their assigned task, the avatars returned. They withdrew carefully, covering their tracks as they went, melting down sub-verters that they had installed in the bank and re-priming the defence bots as they passed. No trace remained when they returned to Debian's main system, where they swirled within the data-storage unit like sharks in a tank.

Debian made himself take a break at this point. The avatars patrolled and paced behind his firewalls – patient, primed. His system was as safe as any system ever was, and if anything did happen he would be informed at once by wireless. He would refill his coffee and then start. Debian tore his eyes from the screens and stood. He yanked the DNI cable from his skull and the severing of the data-stream was like a disorientating blow to the head. For a second or two he simply stood, breathing slowly. Once he felt fully composed, he went to the machine and refilled his drink.

He stood by the machine and sipped the scalding coffee, hardly noticing the heat. His mind, even unplugged and disconnected from the net, was awhirl with code. His main system continued to chatter to him on a peripheral wireless channel, relaying a steady stream of stats. He scratched the back of his head with one slim finger. There was a small black plastic plate installed flush with the skin there. There was still a certain degree of redness around this plate and it itched maddeningly. The device was a recent addition, his adaptive control chip. It would be the key to Debian's success. The chip hosted a very clever suite of firmware of Debian's own devising. It allowed a much more precise control of his avatars than that enjoyed by the average user. Instead of operating on their own initiative in the regular fire-and-forget manner, basing decisions on their incorporated neural simulations and prior programming, Debian's avatars were constantly updated from his DNI, shuffling data to and fro in quantum-encrypted packets through this new chip. This enabled him to fine-tune their activities and priorities by the microsecond while still maintaining a safe barrier between his DNI and the wider net. Debian mentally activated the chip.

He stood, breathing deeply, taking nips of the hot coffee like medicine as the chip ran self-diags, sending data blurring across his mind. His eyes crept to the curtained window where spyflies batted and buzzed against the glass outside. He returned to the desk with his drink, which he placed carefully on a corner where its upset would not prove disastrous to any electronic equipment. He sat again, plugged in again, felt electrons coursing through his mind like a drug again: Back to it.

His avatars were conversing rapidly with the chip now, updating their neural simulations. They were straining at their leashes, intrusive tendrils itching to reach out, invade the crevices of the net and lay all secrets bare. *Soon*, he told them. They shared, of course, his own love for the work. They had his own hunger for mastery of the data stream. They had some, but not all, of his own skills and judgement. Not all, because a neural simulation imprinted on an AI program remained constrained by the actual architecture on which it existed – it was a map of a brain on a computer program, and not an actual brain. Debian's avatars, modified versions of the black market's best, were still pale imitations of Debian himself.

Now, he told them and they bounded off through the router and away into the tunnels of the net, sniffing for their target like bloodhounds.

Quickly, the avatars homed in on the Cyberlife Research and Development servers. They felt around the edges of the public access points for ways in. They set up a false account, implanting a sub-verter, which would act as a secret door.

Debian flowed into the public server, aware of his body only as a diffuse cloud of electrons. Input from his avatars was experienced almost like physical sensory data, creating the impression of total immersion. His consciousness passed through the router, to a sat-sender, bounced off a satellite with sickening g-force, hit the sat-receiver, and passed unnoticed through the sub-verter into the public server of Cyberlife Research and Development. Security protocols sniffed at his data-trail as his avatars entered the system and apparently disappeared. One of them created a cover by beginning what seemed like a routine public enquiry into lab-time prices, justifying the original connection. The security bot was still suspicious at the disparity in bandwidth required for what otherwise looked like a regular, innocent query. The avatar, taking no risks, simply took the bot over, re-writing its records. The access log of the server would show a blip when next queried if Debian couldn't find a way to change it once truly inside, but he would deal with that later.

Debian spun within the system, probes shooting out like rockets, logging and copying everything and sending it back to his own data storage units, which isolated themselves from the net once full. Debian spawned another avatar, increasing the processor load on his computer by a few percentage points. It swirled around his body protectively. Information crackled around his head like a nimbus. He sucked it up, stealing it all, but it was still poor fare this side of the main defence layer. None of this was worth three hundred grand. Not yet.

Debian sent the avatar into a server update program. It started to cross the bridge, which Debian hoped would take it from the public server into a machine which was at least linked to the company's main computer system. If not, there were still other ways. Suddenly, the avatar was swarmed by interrogatory defence routines. It secreted away a part of the inter-server bandwidth and sent out bursts of data like carpet bombs, tying up all bandwidth available to the defence bots, rendering them unable to query the public server to determine the cause of the blockage. The avatar was inside the server on the far side before any of their pings were even returned. It sent back a confirmation that this was the right place and Debian's main swarm joined it.

Something big was drawing in, attracted by the frustration of the defence programs. Debian felt its approach like the vibration of an oncoming train through the rails. It was an avatar, employed illegally by Cyberlife. So Hex was right. Its suspicions were immediately confirmed as it examined the pipe from the public server. Angrily, it tore the blockage away and rushed back along it to the public side, away from Debian. On the public server, the overt avatar was dropping suspicious little hints as to its true identity now. Drawn by this, the enemy avatar rapidly began interrogating the public server bots. Debian's avatar refused its pings and extended viral tendrils threateningly. The enemy avatar, apparently directed by the neural simulation of a particularly gung-ho Cyberlife employee, started to bombard its opponent with viral attacks. It attempted to close the pipe behind Debian's taunting avatar, sealing it in the Cyberlife server, where it could be overrun, stripped down and interrogated. They could possibly even reverse engineer the neural simulation running the avatar and attempt to identify the intruder from that.

Debian's avatar was too good at its job to be caught like that. It fielded off the viral attacks easily and retreated from the system, passing through multiple proxies, melting down the connection utilities of the Cyberlife server as it went, leaving only Debian's own sub-verter open. The enemy avatar, incensed as the intruder slipped from its grasp, began to work on the sub, whittling away at the layers of password protection with alarming rapidity. When it was almost through, the sub spawned multiple copies of itself, sending the passwords back through the router to Debian's computer. The enemy avatar, truly frustrated now, shot back through the pipe to the company's inner servers to sound a general alert. To anyone who answered the call the situation would most likely appear as if some minor hacker had been sniffing around the servers with an avatar and when confronted had fled the system, jamming the pipe as they went. Already, bots were cloning the blocked pipe and Debian's sub-verter copied itself over accordingly. This time, the defenders missed it entirely in the confusion.

On the inner company server, Debian was ransacking the databanks. The update computer was linked to an automated system that monitored lab usage and client software updates. This in turn was linked to the innermost circle of sensitive databanks. The avatars that had stayed with Debian were rearranging forgotten data as they moved through the system so that disk sizes would appear not to change, delicately rigging and deceiving real-time access loggers. For the

46

moment, the enemy was satisfied that nothing had made it all the way into the company-side system.

Debian batted away curious defence bots like troublesome flies. His avatars helped to bamboozle and redirect them. The flaying of data from the disks of Cyberlife continued and the traffic through the random subs sped up.

Debian was getting good information, now: research schedules, client details, company finance records, technical papers. He didn't have time to actually examine the data, he just grabbed handfuls like a child let loose in a sweet shop. His avatars were busy all around him. *Busy little bees*, he thought on a distant level of his mind. *Buzz, buzz, buzz*.

The best, the very best data would be kept in net-isolation. The retrieval of these, using EM-inference techniques, was what justified the three hundred grand. Debian sensed the electromagnetic noise of the isolated computers and began to deduce their contents from this remotely – an inexact science and a very specialised one. The avatars helped to sort the data, sieving the noise out of the torrent and sending packets back down what was now a whole chain of sub-verters.

Suddenly, Debian was under attack from all sides. His Cyberlife-side avatars were overwhelmed instantly and scrubbed into EM white noise, expelling him from the system. One of his subs was compromised – he hadn't even seen the attack coming, hadn't had chance to melt it down! Something in the isolated computer was hacking the defences of his home system, inducing code in the Cyberlife server and transmitting it back through Debian's own sub with amazing accuracy. Nobody but Debian himself and possibly a handful of other hackers in the world could do that! He wanted to scream *Hey – that's* my *trick!* Whatever was assaulting him was writing attack bots out of nothing. Like a zombie horde, they fell on Debian's router and he found himself fighting on all fronts. He attempted to rally his remaining avatars but they were falling apart under the onslaught, being scrubbed faster than he could spawn replacements. Cyberlife wouldn't dare send avatars over the net because they were illegal and hard to hide if they emanated from a monitored company's server, but the mindless programs were numerous and insanely complex. Their code seemed to change as they copied themselves. His own avatars copied up with equal fervour until the two sides filled the entire router. As the bots chewed viral arms away from the overwhelmed avatars, they cloned themselves into the space vacated. The enemy was actually winning on Debian's own router!

Debian found himself overwhelmed, totally embattled, his defensive position incrementally worsening. The enemy was attempting to piggyback through his defences on his avatars, which still communicated rapidly through the encrypted channel into his firewall-protected DNI and ultimately his organic brain.

He caught brief glimpses of the enemy and was terrified by what he saw. It was clearly an artificial intelligence of some sort, but it was equally clear that it was not an avatar from the efficiency with which it spawned, changed and directed its viruses. Whether it was actually a legal program had become entirely irrelevant. It was blitzing his router's firewalls with insanely complex, predictive scripts. Its intrusive tendrils were visible where they entered Debian's system – blinding white threads that blurred with motion faster than his senses could follow. Soon it would get through into his actual DNI.

Debian was unaware that his body, sitting on a chair in what might have been another universe, had gone into spasm. His entire being was a dizzying swirl of binary electrical pulses as he struggled with the AI that attacked him from the supposedly isolated terminal. The avatars in the router were scrubbed in an explosion of shredded data and the AI blazed up the pipe and into Debian's own home computer, bots bounding ahead of it like attack dogs. There were no discernible gaps in their armour.

Debian tried to tell his body to pull the plug from its head but the enemy was inside his brain. The world was fading. His smart firewall had failed. He felt totally shocked, poised in that timeless moment of disaster. Then his brain was flooded with ice so cold that it burned with bright agony.

His body awoke with a huge convulsion. An incoherent sound escaped his throat. Real light flooded, blinding, into his eyes like purifying fire. Something was in his head. Panicking for the first time that he could ever remember, Debian pulled the plug. He was only aware that he had been screaming, when, presently, he stopped. He stood, drenched in sweat with the cable in one hand like a hangman's noose. *Beep*! Apparently perceiving the requirement somehow, the machine had made coffee.

48

CHAPTER SIX

Tec drove the battle-scarred van through the security checkpoint and into the subterranean depths of the HGR tower. The armed guards, recognising them, nodded as they passed. The vehicle stopped outside a wide door marked *MATERIAL RECEIPT*. They were expected and the door opened to admit the van. It eased inside, clouds of dust caught in its suspensor field. Tec stopped the van within the blue-lit sterilisation chamber and killed the power. White-suited receivers were ready for them with a metal trolley.

The harvesters got out and Whistler greeted the team leader of the receivers, a tall greying man in his fifties named Detherin.

'Hey,' she said, shaking his hand. Whistler and Detherin were long-time professional acquaintances, and she liked him well enough. 'We got more goods for you. He's a pretty boy, this one.'

'Good stuff – let's take a look,' replied Detherin.

As they went to the van Detherin noted the numerous scars in its armour.

'What happened to you?' he asked, walking around the vehicle. He put his whole hand into the tear in the front. 'Wow. What did this?'

'Ah, we've been playing cops and robbers again, I'm afraid. S'nothing. Look at this guy.'

Detherin followed Whistler into the van where Tallen was unconscious on the stretcher, firmly strapped down. Tec had bandaged the wound in his arm. The harvesters had debated whether or not to mention the strange graze if they weren't asked. They had decided that honesty was the better part of business.

'Nice,' said Detherin. 'I've never seen a skin-mod like it. As always, your taste is excellent.' He reached out to stroke the shining orange dragon skin and peered at the life signs readout above the stretcher.

'Yeah,' said Whistler. 'Only weird thing is this...' She reached out, unpinned the bandage around Tallen's upper arm and peeled it back to show him the wound. Detherin stared at it closely before answering. Even on the sterile cotton pad the blood had remained unmixed with the green fluid. They formed two separate stains like butterfly wings. 'Strange, eh?'

'Yeah, weird,' he said thoughtfully, and then he shrugged. 'We've had some contaminants recently.'

'Really? What sort of contaminants?'

He laughed. 'Damned if I know. I'm just a glorified Goods-Inwards department.'

'Well let's get him into your evil lair and get your evil money into my bank account.'

'Oh,' said Detherin apologetically, straightening to look Whistler in the face. 'You have to go and see Smith first, I was told.'

'What?' This was very irregular. Whistler had only met Smith in person twice in all the years she had subcontracted for HGR.

'Oh, I'm sure it's nothing, really,' said his voice while his eyes said something altogether different. 'Just you, though. The others can sit in our lounge for a bit. I'll start my guys looking at this,' he indicated Tallen, 'then when you come back I'm sure we can deal with the money. Once Smith has authorised it, of course.'

'Of course,' said Whistler, more cuttingly than she had intended. 'I'd best head into the dragon's den then.'

'I'll tell her you're on your way.'

'Thanks.'

Whistler went out and informed the others of her unplanned meeting with the regional head of HGR. They looked concerned but agreed to stay put until she returned. Tec's head was a worried yellow colour. It occurred to Whistler what a bad poker player he would make. She bade them behave themselves and got into the elevator. It demanded an iris scan and she told it to take her to the penthouse office of Mrs. Smith. It confirmed her clearance for this and the doors sighed shut. The gees smoothly increased as the lift accelerated into the distant heights of the tower, then smoothly decreased until finally it reached its destination.

Whistler stepped out onto a finely woven carpet of colour-shifting fibre optics between two armoured guards. They demanded her gun from her. She didn't hand it to them, instead laying it carefully on the meranti side table where it contrasted dangerously against a company brochure showing beautifully-smiling, newly-modified women.

'Nice,' said one of the guards in a metallic voice that issued from some unseen speaker in his suit. One gloved hand reached for it.

'Ah!' Whistler coughed, stopping him. 'I wouldn't touch it.' And leaving it at that, she strode past the butterfly-winged receptionist, who avoided her gaze and turned to announce her arrival into an intercom. Whistler knocked loudly on the huge double doors that led into the office of Mrs. Smith.

The doors opened seemingly of their own volition and Whistler walked in. The office was huge and high-ceilinged. A dome-shaped skylight gave onto the actual roof of the tower. A khaki-coloured gyrocopter swept overhead and away into the sky with a container clutched beneath its fuselage. The room was decked in chrome techno-gothic architecture. A huge slope-sided dais rose from the centre of the floor and upon this sat Mrs. Smith, drumming her fingers on the glass surface of the built-in desk. Her hair was tightly scraped back, her eyes were sharp flints – her general demeanour filled the room with sinister brooding. She was regarding Whistler coolly.

'Whistler,' she said. 'My hired thug, skirmisher and supplier all in one. The unseen arm of HGR.'

'The same.'

'Please sit.' Whistler obeyed, sighing impatiently, and seated herself in the much lower supplicant's chair. It was surprisingly uncomfortable, probably designed to hinder the concentration of the interviewee. 'There was a problem with your last offering.' Smith arched her fingers and awaited a reply.

Whistler let her wait, meeting her gaze. 'What?' she said after a while.

'What, indeed,' mused Smith, more to herself than to Whistler.

'You don't know? What the fuck? Am I getting paid or not?' 'Three questions in one there, Whistler,' admonished Smith, actually wagging a finger. Whistler wanted to bite it off. 'One – not yet, but we are working hard to determine the exact nature of the problem. There is not really much to work *with*...'

'I don't know what you mean. I only talk two languages – violence and money. If you can't rephrase your statement within either of those frameworks, I guess we're done.' She started to stand, furious now, and sure that she was not to be paid.

'Sit,' said Smith with such quiet authority that Whistler found she had done it without even thinking. 'Two – rather too general a query,

51

I'm afraid. Perhaps we'll come back to that. Three – not, I regret. I can't even give you recyc value for that last piece of shit you brought me.'

'The fuck!' Whistler cried, incensed now. She cared not that technically this was her boss she spoke to. 'That was good meat, Smith. The wings, yeah? Good meat! Good product! Fifty-thousand plus on any market, even black.'

'I can't even let you take it to resell by yourself, I'm afraid. I'm sorry.'

This – an actual apology, unprecedented from Mrs. Smith – placated Whistler a little, as Smith had known it would. She watched as Whistler deflated into her chair, palms spread in resignation. She noticed that the harvester was still clenching her jaw angrily, but the readout on her desk told her that Whistler's heart rate had fallen slightly as the fight went out of her. Crisis averted and the flying knife perched on a moulding near the ceiling could sleep until another day.

'*So what's wrong with it*?' insisted Whistler. 'Is the damn thing contaminated? Drugs? It can be cleansed, surely. Every bloody thing off the streets is contaminated with something. You clean it, right?'

'Right. Usually. But we don't know what this is. It's something different. Some new organ from the black market. It seems to resist examination. We have some good people working on it, but until we know it's safe we have to withhold payment. We have the product in cryo – if it passes, you'll be paid.'

'But that could be weeks, years or never, yeah?'

'I'm afraid so, yes.'

'Some way to treat a trusted subcontractor, man. Is there a fucking union I can join?'

Smith didn't laugh although she admired Whistler for trying to make light of the situation. 'The man with the wings – Leo Travant, he was called, by the way, is not the only case we have found. You know Two-Ton Pete and his team?'

'Yeah. Amateurs. They step on our toes from time to time.'

'Yes, well, they brought in a young woman contaminated with the same tissue last week, and another yesterday.'

'So what, though? There's always something new out there.'

'Yes, but this is different.'

'How so?'

'I told you. It resists examination. We don't know what it does or where it comes from and until we know, payment is to be withheld. This is not public knowledge, you know. Pete's team are not a party to it. All they know is that the produce was contaminated. We told them disease.'

'So am I going to have a problem leaving here then?' asked Whistler bluntly, studying the face of the woman poised above her.

'No, no, nothing like that, I assure you. We wondered if you could help to...get things rolling again.'

'How?' asked Whistler, although she thought she already knew.

Smith's face took on a distant look and Whistler knew she was listening to a call over DNI. Smith breathed deeply, steeling herself, and Whistler knew that it wasn't good news.

'Your new one has it, too.'

'Oh that's fucking *it*! Tell me what you want.'

'We want you to find out where it's coming from, if you can.'

'The new organ.'

'Yes. We will offer any help we can, but to be honest it's likely to be minimal.'

'I just bet it is.'

'You know we have to be cautious with regards to our involvement in certain *scenes*. It's down to you and your team.'

'Right. And if we sort this, we get our money?'

'Well, the good news is, I can offer you an intel fee. One hundred thousand up front. One more if you find the source.'

'We could be on this for months, though. Two hundred doesn't equal what we'd usually generate in that time. Nowhere near.'

'Maybe you'll solve it within the day. I really don't know. Anyway, take it or leave it.' Smith began to tap at the keyboard on her desk as if to indicate that the conversation was concluded.

'Right,' said Whistler decisively, looking about herself. 'Right! I'll get the fucker who's behind this. I'll sort it out and we'll get our money. But who was the guy? Leo. If we're going to find the source, we need to trace him, I guess.'

'Right – of course. Here are the details, what we know, on Leo Travant. I'm afraid we don't know much, really. And some pictures of the unknown organ. As I mentioned, we haven't been able to successfully scan it. He worked at Smithson's, near here.'

'If there is an answer, we'll find it. I guess we have no choice.'

'That's the spirit. I have already transferred the first hundred to your account.'

'Presumptuous, nay?'

'Maybe.'

She passed Whistler down a data spot. Whistler flicked it back to her. Smith fumbled, dropping it, and part of Whistler's mind rejoiced – *Ha! Was that a glimmer of humanity, Smith?* She stood and made to leave. 'Send a copy of the data to the van, would you? Me being a meathead and all.'

Smith let it go and bent to her keypad again. 'Of course,' she said without looking up.

Whistler shook her head and swept from the room, the doors struggling to open in time. She stopped in the reception room to collect her gun.

'It's been looking at me funny,' complained one of the guards.

'You were probably acting suspiciously,' said Whistler, grabbing the gun with a taloned hand and dumping it into her jacket pocket. 'It does that.'

'Where the hell did you get that thing anyway? I don't know that you should have that in here at all.'

'What are you, my mum? I've never even been asked to remove it before,' answered Whistler emphatically.

'Honestly I'm surprised by that,' said the guard, shaking his head.

Whistler smiled, exposing her pointed fangs and got into the lift. She waved to the guard and the doors closed. The lift scanned her eyes again and began to descend. She watched the layers of tower unstacking through the single five hundred metre-tall window. Far below her, gravpods could be seen like bright beads thread upon bracelets of roadway. She had almost stopped being angry and her mind was now obsessively chewing on the problem at hand. Leo had been his name. The wings. Smithson's. Someone would know. Someone would know where the extra organ had come from. Whistler's team would find them and make them talk. And make them stop. Stop everything, if necessary. *You don't mess with my bank balance.* The gun in her pocket sensed her vengeance like a shark sniffing blood in water. Its sleek metal body was humming gently against her.

At the very bottom of the tower, back in the basement where Material Receipt was housed, the lift stopped and Whistler got out into bright lights and a hospital-clean corridor. She found the others in the lounge as expected. Spider and Sofi were sparring gently and Roberts was beating Tec at pool. There was a holo of the new Jenni James film running in one corner. Quadruped aliens cavorted through the holo pursued by shouting marines, one of whom appeared to be holding his detached arm in his remaining hand. Everyone turned to greet her.

'Bad news, guys,' she said, waving them into silence. 'We'd better roll. Work to do. Did they take the product?'

'Yeah,' said Tec. 'What's going on?'

'I'll tell you in the van.'

'Some files came through from Smith,' said Tec. 'I didn't know if I was supposed to look.'

'Yeah, we all need to look. Let's move.' Whistler wanted her team out of here before mentioning the cash-flow problem to them, just in case.

Detherin came into the lounge looking embarrassed. He was wringing his hands together – large, gnarled hands like a mechanic's. 'Hey guys. Look, I'm sorry, Whistler. I don't know what's going on but they tell me the product is dirty and essentially worthless.' He looked helplessly at the harvesters.

There was a chorus of objection from the team. 'It's not your fault, Deth, don't worry.' Whistler wanted to say more but knew she couldn't. 'I'll explain on the way home, guys. Come on! I mean fucking *now*!' Reluctantly, they followed her.

Whistler drove the van out of the HGR building and turned onto a wide concourse of glass and neon that would have been a nightmare for anyone driving a ground-car. The van ran silently across it and away into the city. Behind them another lightpusher was lifting off. *So many lately. Where do they all go?*

'Right,' said Sofi. 'So what the hell's going on, then, Whistler?' Her triple mohawks swished like knives as her head moved.

'Tec, show the pictures Smith sent.'

Several pictures lit up on the ceiling of the van: A glistening green object nestled against a human spine, a photo of Leo on the slab, skin pale and wings brilliant, and a picture of Smithson Investment Advisory Services, a glittering hunk of plastic and ceramicarbide.

'What is this? That's the guy we harvested last week, right?' asked Spider.

'Yeah, he's called Leo. Was called. There's a new organ they found in him, and in others, that they're worried about. Hence they don't wanna pay us for Leo or Tallen. That's it, I guess – the green thing there. We have to find out where they're coming from and stop it. This is between us, okay?' She looked around the van, catching everyone's eyes.

'Not cool,' said Sofi, echoing everyone's thoughts. 'So no pay? Shit!'

'Smith gave us a hundred gee up front to start doing this. One hundred more if we find the source.' Roberts grunted. 'Yes?'

'It might even be worth it if we can sort it quickly, then,' he said.

'Yeah,' said Whistler, turning off the main road and bearing towards the Undercity again. A police pod passed them on the other side and everyone held their breath – their harassment by Universal had been unusual but not unprecedented. 'City Police,' said Whistler, and everyone relaxed. 'Anyway, we don't have a choice. If HGR won't take any product 'til it's sorted, then we have to do it. Or someone has to. I would imagine that all the bodyshops who use harvesters are aware of the problem. Maybe someone else will take care of it.'

'I wonder what it is...' mused Tec staring up at the green orb pictured on the ceiling. 'Fucking odd. And why don't HGR know? How are we s'posed to find out if they can't?'

'By using our unique talents, of course,' replied Whistler.

'Yeah,' laughed Sofi from the back, hefting Spider's mag-rifle. It's skeletal barrel pointed at the sky like an accusing finger.

Even Roberts chuckled at that. The van drove on soundlessly into the depths of the city like a poisonous pill swallowed by a monster of concrete and steel. A mile further on, Whistler put on Blue Screen of Death to drown out her own thoughts.

CHAPTER SEVEN

Debian showered for a long time, scrubbing himself obsessively. He could feel the imprint of the beast burning in his mind still. He had been brain-raped and he wasn't sure whether the AI had left something, taken something or both. The fear was on him like musk. Frenziedly, he rubbed at his skin with a nail brush and detergent, watching the foam swirling into the drain. The spiralling pattern of the suds was nauseatingly reminiscent of the dizzying way his head was spinning and eventually he had to leave the shower because of it.

He stood before the cracked mirror regarding himself. The peeling flaps of silver paint on the back of the glass made his body appear leprous and full of holes. This vision helped him not at all. The skin around the plastic plate in his head was an angrier red than ever. He put his fingers to it and felt its smooth, intrusive form, aware of the chip buried like a piece of shrapnel beneath it. It certainly felt like a war-wound now. What had happened in there? Clearly, all his layers of defence had failed and the beast had got through somehow.

He began to run diags on the DNI chips and the firewalls they contained as standard. Then he let the scan run onto the new chip. Nothing. He wasn't sure if he was gladdened or worried further by this. What did he hope to find? Had the AI left something in there? Some sort of sub-verter installed directly into his brain? He should have done more tests on his new system, should have taken more care, should have seen this coming somehow. What would have been wrong with using fire-and-forget avatars, like everyone else did? Answer: because of his stupid pride, because of his need to be the best, to be at the cutting edge, doing something unique.

Debian let out a wordless cry of fear and frustration and slammed his palm against the mirror. It cracked down the middle and almost a full half of the glass leaned out of its frame and fell into the room. It shattered around his bare feet and then Debian began to cry. He crumpled to the floor where he curled into a ball, cradling his legs, which bled from several deep glass-cuts. His despair was almost total. If he had a sub in his head then it was game over – it was the end of his career, which in turn would mean the end of his life. What would his employer say? What would his employer *do*? Would he be safe? Maybe they would send assassins to plug the possible data leak now in his head.

He did not know how long he sat this way amongst the broken glass on the bathroom floor but when he finally lurched to his feet and made himself dress it was getting light outside. He didn't feel calm but he felt as if he could do what must be done, now. The first thing was to run a deeper series of diagnostics, using the additional computing power of his main system. He had to know one way or the other whether there was something there. Then he would have to call Hex. How much should he tell Hex? Just give him the stolen data and say no more? Let him make his own conclusions from the logs? Fake or exclude the logs? What if Hex found out about the clash with the AI somehow? What if Debian did have a sub? It might do anything. Cyberlife could find out about Debian's attack, find out who had commissioned it. *Shit*! Debian could certainly understand Hex's interest in Cyberlife now. Whatever they had hit on, it was very big.

He went to his desk and reached out to physically detach the router from his system but his hand was shaking too much. He breathed deeply for a moment, arm extended, and tried again. His treacherous fingers obeyed this time. Really, this should have been the first thing he had done following his brain-rape, but all he had wanted was to somehow wash the stink of the invasive AI off himself. He had commanded his DNI wireless to disconnect him from the net, however – he had managed that much. It showed no activity on his HUD but he trusted nothing now. He set up a scrambler on his desk, rapidly dialling settings into it with the large plastic knobs to ensure that there was no hidden connection in operation.

He plugged in and sat grinding his teeth as his powerful computer pored through his head checking everything it could. He made it repeat the procedure, changing scan parameters, knowing that if it had found nothing the first time then it would find nothing again. He was not surprised by the result. Then he let the avatars, regenerated now, loose into his main system again. They scoured every disk sector, every storage chip. Nothing. He let them into his head, wincing as he did so, even though he had trusted them impeccably in the past. He held his breath as they roved around his skull searching for the spore of the enemy. They found nothing. Maybe there was nothing to find. At any rate, he had exhausted his means of looking, unless he was to remove the adaptive control and DNI chips from his head and physically examine their matrices. The adaptive control he could do – he had fitted it here in his flat – but the DNI chips would need to be removed by a surgeon.

Debian put his face in his hands, blocking out the physical world. He felt terrible in some vague and indefinable way. Maybe he was coming down with an illness. Or was there something at work inside his brain? Perhaps it was just a psychosomatic response to his fear. He was in serious trouble either way.

He told the avatars to sleep, turned the readout off and sat that way in the gathering light for a minute or two trying to breathe slowly. The data storage unit was nestled warmly against his leg like a faithful dog. He must call Hex. Just give him the data? Or give him the truth? *Damn it! How do I get out of this? What will Hex's people do if they find out? Who, really, are Hex's people? And who the hell are Cyberlife Research and Development, to be playing with toys like that?*

Debian knew that he would never be ready to make this call but decided that if never was the time-scale he was looking at, then he might as well do it now. He turned everything back on, looking warily at the screens as if something might jump out of one and bore into his head again. Reluctantly, like a man forced to walk the plank, he edged back into the net. Data flowed into him, white and cold, but normal. He began to relax a little as nothing bad continued to happen. He simply drifted there in the net for a while, feeling the eddies and currents around him like the contours of a familiar landscape. He called Hex's unlisted address. There was a wait of several seconds and then Hex answered over DNI. The two men communicated silently through stealthed data-channels, thinking words into being.

'Hex, it's Debian. Can we talk?'

'Yes, that's fine. But I'd rather speak in person, of course. Just in case.'

Debian reacted guiltily at that and replied, 'Yeah, er, just in case. You never know who's listening, right?'

'Right. Hey, are you okay? You don't look so good.'

Debian realised that he had left the video-link on and snapped it off with a mental impulse, embarrassed, sure that he was losing it. 'I'm fine. Just had a late one, you know. Busy, busy.'

'Good, it's good to hear that you have been productive. Listen, I'm nearby at the moment. I'll come over to yours.'

Debian felt a lump in his throat. He swallowed around it sickly. 'How do you know where I live?' he asked.

Hex actually laughed – a genuine-sounding display of humour, which Debian didn't believe was genuine at all. 'We keep an eye on all of our little helpers, Debian. You're important to us.'

'Right,' replied Debian slowly. 'Listen, man, don't come here. We'll meet out again, same place as last time.' He was aware that he was not coming across with the authority he had hoped. 'Don't come here, Hex.'

'Don't be daft, man,' said Hex, and he actually sounded insulted now. 'It's fine. I'm nearby – I'll only be ten minutes. Get the goods, off I go, okay?'

'Don't come here!' Debian mentally shouted, but he realised that the line was dead. This was not good. He wished he had a weapon.

Debian unplugged from the net and began to pace the room, stopping occasionally to stamp a foot in frustration and shout, '*Shit!*' before resuming. Hex was coming to his damned flat, man! Should he just go? Phrases scrolled across the surface of his mind: *We keep an eye on all of our little helpers. We think their backer might be a government. I'll only be ten minutes.* Debian checked the time on his HUD. How long had it been? Only three minutes.

It's probably okay. Hex just wants to get the data, sure he does. He would be keen, this was clearly a big job to them. Who? Well, whoever he works for. Suddenly Debian wished that he knew as much about Hex as Hex clearly knew about him. He looked for a knife, anything that could serve as a weapon but his brain, unused to being posed such problems, couldn't identify a single item of use. He didn't even own a sharp knife – everything he ate came out of plastic containers, ready-made.

What am I doing? Looking for something to stab or bludgeon a man with? I really have gone insane. It won't be necessary. Hex is just coming for the Cyberlife data. If he wanted me gone, he wouldn't give me any warning of his arrival, would he? Someone would just do it, no messing around.

Debian became aware of a sudden sound-vacuum. The buzzing of the spyflies outside the window had ceased, just cut off. Fear crackled up his spine like electricity. *What the hell?* He went to the window, careful not to cast his shadow across the curtain, parted a corner of the fabric and looked out. There was something there. He craned his head to the left and saw a grapefruit-sized metal ball floating on a suspensor cushion, bobbing slightly. He ducked down, heart thumping in his chest and panic suddenly made him freeze. The object outside was a scrambler-bait. Someone had posted it up there to kill the spyflies. Why would anyone do that? Because they were about to commit a crime, of course. Something that the spyflies would detect from outside the window – something like murdering a problematic hacker in his flat. In that moment he knew it was for real and his life hung in the balance.

There was a knock on the door. Debian saw the monitor picture on his HUD. It was Hex, apparently alone, and in that instant Debian had an idea. He was not a fighter, not in the physical sense, at least. So he would play to his strengths. If he was right, it was the only chance he had. He was suddenly sure that he could do it. He felt a grim resolve and a new confidence in his abilities. It had never been done before but he knew he could do it. He would have to do it and he was, after all, the best in his field. The takeover of a human body through their DNI should not be possible, but at that moment he knew that it was, that he could do it. Half of him was terrified – half of him had never felt so strong.

'Coming!' he called and rushed to kill the router again. He also disconnected his DNI wireless and activated the scrambler again. He unplugged the hi-flo cable from the main computer and plugged the other end into his head, completing these actions with the ease of long practise. The computer-end of the link, now free, he hung over his shoulder. It was unusual but hopefully it would look as if he had simply unplugged at the computer instead of his head after having spoken to Hex. Outside the door, Hex would detect both Debian's disconnection from the net and the activation of the scrambler, but these were fairly standard precautions in the trade.

He went to the door and opened it. Hex stood there calmly waiting. He didn't smile, just said, 'May I come in?'

'Uh, sure, come in.' Debian stood aside and let Hex enter his flat, which until this day he had not realised his employers even knew the location of. How things changed. 'Have a seat.' For a moment he didn't think Hex would actually seat himself in the only chair, but he did. His face shone like plastic, its features featureless in the grey morning light.

Debian wondered if he had actually been designed to look as nondescript as possible. He was aware of the absence of the spyflies outside.

'Thanks,' said Hex, smoothing the folds of his trench coat about himself as he sat. Debian wasn't sure if he imagined it but it looked as if something heavy and bulky deformed one of the pockets. 'Good to see you again, and so soon.'

'You, too. I have the Cyberlife data. Loads of it. It won't go on a spot, I'm afraid. I'll put it on a disc.'

'Okay, good. Thanks.'

Debian went to the data storage unit, which brought him intimately close to Hex, who sat at the desk. Hex moved out of his way, but only very slightly — a token movement, really. Debian posted a disc into the machine and stood back while it did its thing.

'Sorry,' said Debian. 'I should have had this ready. I didn't expect you to come so soon. You can't come here like this, man.'

'Apologies, again,' said Hex with such sincerity that Debian thought he might actually walk away from this, after all. 'It seemed inefficient to waste the opportunity when I was so close-by. I'll just grab the data then be on my way.'

'Okay, cool.' Debian handed him the disc, realising that if Hex could just be ushered out quickly enough then his plan may never have to be acted on. He clung only faintly to this hope, though. 'There you go. Pay me later, into the usual account, when you've approved it all.'

'Good, thanks. Easy job for you, then? No problem?'

Debian stiffened at this. He tried not to show it but was sure that Hex had noticed. 'What?' he said.

'Easy job? I said.'

Debian straightened up, bringing him almost eye to eye with Hex and as he did so he saw something shine dully in Hex's pocket and knew that it was on, after all. He had the free end of the DNI cable in one hand, rolling its snub end between sticky fingers. 'Yeah, sure,' he said, and lunged behind Hex.

Hex turned quickly, bringing the gun out of his pocket, but not quickly enough. He had underestimated Debian, should never have sat in the chair, should have known better. The end of the hi-flo cable, tapered in just the right way to facilitate connection, slid into Hex's head and Debian rolled away, managing not to tangle himself more by

62

luck than skill. Hex had time to fire once before Debian stormed his mental defences, washing away firewalls like a tidal wave. The projectile, actually a tiny explosive rocket, whooshed away into the kitchen, exploding Debian's faithful coffee machine in a shower of glass and liquid. *Beep!* it exclaimed indignantly as it died.

To Hex, Debian was like a flash-fire in his mind. He was everywhere at once. Hex had never known such speed and overwhelming power. He had never known how vulnerable he really was. His head was burning inside. His firewalls were down. His defences had barely even started up before Debian, driving his avatars with fluid precision and fuelled by a desperate fervour, had effortlessly scrubbed them out. Hex was dimly aware that this shouldn't be possible. No-one was that good. His body would not respond to his mind's commands. His hand was passing the gun to Debian, who stood over him trembling but resolute, his eyes fierce. Hex tried to speak but he couldn't even breathe.

'I am the web-walker,' said Debian, 'and I *am* the best. This is why you hire me. I am connected to your slow little brain, which cowers behind avatars and firewalls, by a new protocol of my own devising – faster, more adaptable, more powerful than any system that has come before. Do you understand? I am the first of a new type, a self-made prototype.'

Hex found that he could communicate with Debian by DNI even if he wasn't being allowed to do anything else. Debian apparently wanted to converse and he found that he had no choice. 'I know. You are known to be exceptionally gifted.'

'There is something out there, something much worse than me – an artificial intelligence of amazing power. It was in a computer at Cyberlife, but it might not be stuck in there for long – it is voracious. I think it has affected me in some way. What is it? Did Cyberlife make it?'

'I don't know. I was only told where to direct you.'

'Told by whom?'

'By my contact.' Debian realised that Hex was struggling with the unfamiliar feeling of helplessness. His clean-shaven face was dripping with perspiration as he struggled physically, uselessly, to free himself from his mental bonds.

'Is there a sub-verter in my head? Is that why you came? You came to kill me because you fear that my brain will leak your details. Not that I even know much about you.'

Hex tried to lie but found himself unable. Debian was interrogating him on some deep subconscious level. Hex's head was pounding like a drum. 'No. There is no sub that I know of.'

'I feel different. Stronger.'

'There is no sub. That I know of.'

'Then why are you here?'

'I'm just a foot soldier.'

'Liar! Don't try to fight me! I can use more force if you make me. I think it may hurt you if I do. And I would rather not.'

'All right, then, a general. But I am still a pawn in the wider scheme, as are you. I came to do my job.'

Debian turned the gun over in his hand. Hex, wide-eyed, watched him frozenly from the chair. The hi-flo cable hung between them like a bad vibe. Debian regarded him clinically, his fear gone now, replaced by a kind of sick elation. This was new territory for him. 'Your job,' he repeated thoughtfully. Coffee was leaking across the kitchen floor and into the living room. 'Who do you work for? All these years I have run errands for you people. Who are you really?'

'I am at the end of a long chain of associates, the contact of a contact of a contact...'

'And at the other end?'

'Alcubierre.'

'And who is that?'

'I don't really know. Some AI or tech company with limited moral restrictions, I imagine.'

Alcubierre? Somewhere in the back of Debian's mind a little bell was ringing at that name. 'Somebody intended me to find the AI, didn't they? But why?'

'I don't know.'

'You aren't very useful. Is there anything you *do* know?'

'I was simply told to send you into the Cyberlife servers. And then I was told to come and kill you.'

'But you say there's no sub, no security leak. You tell the truth. I don't understand.'

'You don't, do you. Maybe it is not for the likes of...us to...understand.' Hex was struggling hard now, and Debian sensed the immense, wrenching exertion of his futile effort to resist, to remain mute.

'Who are Cyberlife? How did they come to possess a thing like that?'

'I don't know...I suppose they are just another computer...research...company. I know nothing of...this...AI. I don't know...Get out of...my...'

There was a sound outside the door – a scuffling on the stairs. Debian started, aware that he was trapped, tied to Hex by the cable. The only way out besides the door was through the window. The ten-storey drop pretty much ruled that one out. 'How many others?' he asked frantically.

Hex just laughed, or at least gave the impression of laughter within the limits of DNI communication. His eyes, though stuck wide open somehow conveyed his defiant resolution. Debian stared into them and time seemed to spin out into a fragile glass thread. Hex was fighting the intruder in his mind. He was straining against Debian's hold with every ounce of his energy. 'Screw...yourself...then,' he communicated, and Debian could feel Hex nearing his limits of endurance. 'What a...waste. Are you going to become...a killer...or not? Shoot me or fry my brain, I don't...owe you...*anything*...'

'Shut up! Who's out there?'

'Maybe it's the...fucking...meter...reader,' communicated Hex with a last titanic effort of defiance.

Before Debian could react, Hex stiffened like a man electrified and his eyes rolled up to the whites. He keeled over sideways off the chair, pulling the cable that still connected him to Debian tight with a jerk. Debian yanked the plug out of his own head and threw the cable onto Hex's weakly twitching form. Was he dead? Debian didn't think so. He would probably wake up in hospital with the mother of all headaches, though. That was well enough.

There was another noise from outside the door and Debian froze, holding his breath. He switched to infrared and could see two people out on the landing. They held cool, bulbous shapes against their chests: Weapons. One of them was leaning right into the door, one ear pressed against it, listening. Debian felt as if he was falling. The nausea was on him again – his head was spinning, he felt totally incapacitated with fear. His heart was a greasy lump in his throat, his mind totally blank. *What now? They really are going to kill me. They will get away with it, too.*

It came to him in a flash: His only chance. He knew that if he thought about it then he would falter and the men outside the door would kill him. Instead, he just dived for the window. With one kick from his shoeless foot he shattered the glass out of the window and was on the sill, crouched in the frame as glass rained down into the street far below. He looked left and the scrambler-bait was still there, bobbing gently in the breeze on its suspensor cushion. There were no spyflies around it now – they tended to learn quite quickly as a whole, although their individual intelligence was meagre.

Still without thinking, he dropped the gun and jumped, grabbing onto the smooth metal orb. It was cold and slippery in his grip and barely offered any purchase at all. The door was being smashed in behind him, but it was taking some time. The scrambler-bait dipped and began to fall as it struggled to dial up its suspensor to cope with the extra weight. The mild electromagnetic induction field of the bait was not powerful enough to generate dangerous code in Debian himself but he could feel the pulses like a tickling in his nerves. He was falling quite fast. It was all too surreal to really contemplate. Was he going to fall to his death? The bait was a cold metal skull in his hands. There were people down there looking up. The windows of the building blurred past. Somebody fired down from above, hitting him on one thigh, but he didn't even notice.

Debian hit the road like a rag doll, not in free-fall but moving fast enough to knock the wind from him. He went to his hands and knees hard, releasing the bait which shot back up to its assigned position like a rocket. A silver gravpod with shaded windows was racing up the road towards him. Stunned, hurt and prone on all fours, something reacted in Debian's mind even as his body screamed in pain. He was inside the control console of the silver pod, riding the wireless like a surfer. The pod reversed at top speed back up the road, scattering rubbernecking pedestrians as it mounted the pavement.

Debian was on his feet, squealing in terror and desperately trying just to move, just to run. His legs gave out and he was down again. Someone was firing into the street from one of the buildings – probably from Debian's flat – all hopes of subtlety forgotten now. Chunks of concrete danced and flipped gaily into the air. He was up again and moving, his chest hitching and hurting. He started to lurch into a side street, one leg dragging painfully behind him. He didn't know it, but he was actually sick as he fled. He didn't even slow down. Were they following him? Would they actually dare to gun him down face to face in the street? He reached out, searching for net-signatures nearby, but in his confusion he couldn't determine who was who from the sigs. There were too many of them. He was panicking – he knew he was losing his mind, overcome with fear. He made himself stop. He was a believer in confrontation therapy.

He stood there, bleeding and hurting, making himself breathe, making himself understand the net data. He shut his eyes and reached out with microwave fingers. Two people had got out of the pod that he had crashed and were tentatively following him on foot. He knew that at least one of them was armed, because the man's gun was connected to his DNI and Debian could feel its presence like a tumour in the net. All their personal details – everything from heartbeat to previous addresses – were laid bare to him. He breathed. Calm. Breathe. They are coming. Calm.

He reached out and slid back into the console of the silver pod. He sent it accelerating towards the two men who were converging on the mouth of the side street. They heard it just in time and scattered, terrified that their unmanned vehicle had come to vengeful life. He sent it chasing after them, not fast enough to catch them, but fast enough to make them run for their lives. He really did feel calm, now. He permitted himself a small smile and opened his eyes.

I do believe I have been shot. Strange. It hardly hurts at all.

He knew where he must go – the only place he could go. He needed someone who knew people who could help. He had to leave the city. He had money, lots of money. There was one man who could help him. But time was not on Debian's side, he knew. He disconnected from the net with mingled relief and regret: How contradictorily empowering and dangerous that world had become. Achingly, he limped on up the street. His would-be assassins, busy saving their own lives, were several blocks away already.

CHAPTER EIGHT

Tec banged the console, setting a host of tiny capacitors and reeferette roaches jumping on the tabletop. 'Damn it!' he yelled. His hands began to caress his illuminated head, which was pulsing an angry red. 'All I get from the Smithson's computer is the same old stuff: His address, his employment record, his pension plan details. Nothing we can follow up. If I knew who his doctor was, maybe we could find something there. I could find out, maybe, but...' He trailed off.

Whistler put a hand on his shoulder. 'We'll think of something,' she said.

Spider Junior was creeping up one of the table legs to get a better view of what the humans were doing. 'Fuck off, Junior,' said Tec, brushing the robot onto the cluttered floor. He turned to Whistler, who stood behind him with Roberts and Sofi, watching Tec's progress on the monitors as he wheeled his way into the Smithson's computers. 'I don't think there's anything else here,' he said in tones of defeat.

'Maybe we could go to his address. There might be something there – some sort of trail, some – I don't know,' said Sofi hopelessly.

'Yeah, I don't think we can go round to his house, Sofi, really. He lived with his wife, remember? What the hell do we say to her? We abducted the bloke and fed him into HGR for dissection. Even with our legal immunity contract there are likely to be problems. Keep up.' Sofi scowled but said nothing. She knew Whistler was right.

'Maybe we should go to Smithson's, ask around – think of some blag for being there,' suggested Roberts.

'Like what?' asked Tec. 'They won't even let us in.'
'Yeah,' admitted Roberts. 'And they might call the police. Smith wouldn't be pleased. Maybe we could claim to *be* police. Not City Police, one of the little private corps. Bare face it.' He looked around at the expressions of the others. 'Maybe not,' he concluded.

Spider Junior was climbing back up the table leg and had become partially tangled in a speaker cable, which was hanging from its oily body like a cobweb.

'What the hell's got into him?' asked Whistler. 'Junior seems dumber and clumsier than usual today.'

'Not sure,' said Tec dismissively, staring into the three screens above his desk, fingers playing across keyboards like a concert pianist.

'He's been a bit funny since he auto-updated today. I'm gonna set up an avatar to trawl through all the patient lists of all the doctors in the city.' Everyone nodded mutely. None of them could think of anything better. 'But strap yourselves in – it's gonna be a long ride. Even if I find his doctor I can pretty much assure you that there won't be any record on the files related to those illegal wings.'

'So we are basically assuming that he got the green thing wherever he got the wings, then?' asserted Sofi. 'That might not even be correct, right? And even if he did get them at the same time and place, there won't be anything on his medical record to suggest where that may be? And Tec might not even find, or get into, his record in the first place? That sucks! Can't we do better than that? And where the hell is Spider?'

'He's doing some maintenance on that stupid mag-rifle of his, says it can't be left. I think it's had a software problem or something,' replied Roberts, staring into Tec's screens, trying to make sense of the streaming ribbons of data there. 'We could go back to where we picked him up. Or get Tallen's details from HGR, see if we can find a hook on him. But I'm guessing that we'll have the same problems with Tallen.'

'We should follow up on him, anyway, of course,' answered Whistler. 'I'll ask Smith for what they have on him. But they won't know much. Leo had a wallet full of ID. Tallen had nothing on him but a stubby of Get-Up.' Whistler was pacing as far as the cramped lab would allow, her sharp claws drumming against her thighs. Her usually doll-like features were lined in thought and paler grey than usual. She was dog-tired. 'Let's do it, then – go back to where we picked Leo up. Maybe we'll think of something if we actually stand there. We could ask around there – no-one cares in the Undercity – money loosens tongues. Someone might have seen him around. Juke addict, wasn't he?'

'Yeah,' said Roberts distastefully.

'Well, he most likely went there to score, then. He probably had a regular dealer. People might have seen him there before. Someone might know him.' She spread her hands as if to say that was all she had. Roberts and Sofi nodded. Tec was still lost in the net, his head glittering white now that he was back at work. 'Tec?'

'Yeah, sure, go,' he answered absently, not shifting his gaze from the screens.

'Okay, that's settled then. I'd rather do anything than nothing. Tec, let me know if you find anything before we're back.'

'Yeah...'

'Er, boss?'

'What, Sofi? What?'

'It's eleven at night. Maybe we should get some sleep first. You haven't slept since before we picked up Tallen.'

'Sofi, I don't mind if you want to sleep. I'm going to the Lanes for a walk. No time like the present. I don't need sleep, I have Get-Up.'

'For what it's worth, I guess I'm in,' said Roberts. He looked to Tec, who was lost in the world of the electronic, seemingly one with his jumble of equipment.

Sofi sighed heavily. 'Right, let's go then,' she said reluctantly.

'Yay, team!' enthused Whistler with exaggerated cheerfulness. She slung her slender arms around her companions' necks, forcing them into a huddle. 'What a team!'

'Fuck off!' objected Sofi, worming free. After ensuring that whatever point it was had been made, Whistler released Roberts, too, and the trio trooped out of the lab and down the corridor to the garage. They wasted no breath wishing Tec farewell – he was entwined in the web now. Spider Junior was tramping round unnoticed in a small circle on the cluttered desk. Torrents of data flooded the computer screens in bewildering patterns. Tec sat bathed in dim, multicoloured light, hunched and intent.

Whistler and her two reluctant helpers headed to the garage. The van was as one with the shadows until Roberts turned on the lights, and then it congealed into menacing solidity. The hole in its front end gaped like a snarling mouth. The team had simply not had time to repair it yet and Whistler was aware that it appeared suspicious. But she didn't believe anyone would care where they were going.

They piled into the van and its systems came to life in greeting. Roberts sat up front beside Whistler and Sofi took her preferred seat in the back. The stretcher was conspicuously empty, as it would continue to be until this mess was sorted out. The DNI cable hung like a dead arm from Tec's console. The harvesters were subdued, tired, and their conversation was reserved and tetchy.

Whistler drove the van out into the shared underground car park and headed for the exit. Roberts was idly tracing his facial scar with one finger as he gazed out of the translucent wall. Whistler didn't ask for directions. She knew the Lanes well, remembered picking up Leo as if it had been only hours ago. She knew the spot where they had first sighted him, the spot where she had wiped the drug onto his arm, the spot where he had fallen in the alley and the route he would have likely taken from his workplace. There was a sullen mood in the van. Roberts tried putting some classical music on – Brahms – but Sofi harangued him until he killed it again. Whistler could feel him breathing deeply beside her, containing his discontentment.

The Undercity was dark and lively around them, like a carcass alive with maggots. Traffic was fairly heavy as they neared the Lanes. Gravpods whooshed up and down the dirty roads and pedestrians went about their mostly illegal activities in a calm and businesslike manner. The cogs of the black market turned within the greater machine of the city whole. A scruffy dog with a single wheel in place of its back legs bounded in front of the van, and Whistler nearly hit it, stopping the van dead and cursing under her breath. Above and to their right, several people in differing gang colours were shooting crossbows and small arms at each other from opposing balconies, ducking in and out of the limited cover while somewhere a woman shouted, 'You're waking my baby up! Shoot each other somewhere else!'

'Let's leave the van somewhere, then,' said Whistler. 'We picked him up just round the corner from here.'

'Very well,' replied Roberts, coming out of his daydream. One of the gang fighters fell from the balcony and was swallowed by a mountain of rubbish bags in the street below. Someone fired down at him – *crack! crack!* – and he didn't emerge again. 'Not here, though.'

'No, okay,' Whistler agreed and drove on, casting about left and right for a safe spot to park up. They found a small courtyard behind an abandoned and boarded-up takeaway and Whistler drove the van to the furthest, shadiest corner. There were halogen lights arrayed along the back wall of the shop here but all were broken, their glass smashed long since. Half hidden by the drooping fronds of a dead tree, the van would be invisible from the road altogether. People had seen it go in, but frankly anyone who wanted to take the vehicle, or even approach it in a manner it didn't like, had better be fully armed and armoured, and even then would be taking their life in their hands.

The harvesters disembarked and Roberts gave the van free rein to defend itself as it saw fit. The floor of the courtyard crunched with debris underfoot as if nobody had walked its surface in years, even though the area was heavily-populated. They had found a good hidey-hole. Whistler turned around, studying what parts of skyline she could see from here, assuring herself of her bearings. Bass-heavy music was playing in the distance.

'Right, we picked Leo up just around the corner from here. So do we start there and work back towards Smithson's?'

'Certainly, why not,' said Roberts.

'Because this whole idea sucks, that's why not,' muttered Sofi – but not too loudly, because she was aware that she had no better idea herself.

The three headed back to the street in rag-tag procession, checking weapons as subtly as they could. The shooting on the balconies had stopped now and the locals carried on as if nothing had ever happened. Roberts and Sofi followed Whistler's directions uncomplainingly even though they both had map-overlays from the net. They knew that Whistler sometimes forgot how the other half lived.

They came to the square where Whistler had drugged Leo, where the band had played. There were relatively few people here now – only a few shady characters loitering in doorways, furtively exchanging unseen produce – and for a moment the scene was unrecognisable. But then they saw the pallets that had formed the makeshift stage still grouped roughly together on the filthy street. Several pieces of the stage had been strewn around or carried off for burning but the litter of an obvious party remained – drinks cans, syringes, food wrappers, splashes of blood and vomit.

Whistler wrinkled her nose prettily. 'What a mess,' she said disapprovingly. Sofi knew that although her companion had space within her moral code for unsolicited violence, she deplored certain kinds of antisocial behaviour, littering being one of them. 'People have to live here,' she explained to Roberts's puzzled face.

He didn't answer, said instead, 'Let's ask around, then. Carefully. If people think we're police then we are in trouble.'

'No offence, man, you look like a lot of things but police isn't one of them,' said Sofi seriously. Roberts gave her a dark look and wandered over to the group of people in the doorway.

Whistler headed into the alley where they had actually abducted Leo. It was dark and lined with doorways in various states of disuse. At one point near where Leo had fallen she had to step over a dead rat the size of a housecat. A voice called her from the shadows to her left and Whistler whirled to face the source of the sound, her hand going into her jacket pocket where the smartgun nested. It awoke keenly at her touch.

There was a tall man, thin and ancient, leaning out of the open top half of a solid metal door. He grinned with a seemingly random collection of teeth, each of which looked as if it had been pried from the head of a different person. His eyes had been modified to be completely black. 'Hey pretty lady,' he croaked in a sepulchral voice. 'You shouldn't be out here alone, unarmed.'

'I am neither alone nor unarmed,' she assured him, coming closer to prove that she was not afraid. She let a corner of the smartgun show out of her pocket briefly and the man's tarry eyes seemed to twinkle.

He smiled slowly, the lines and folds of his face moving like a landslide. 'Good,' he crooned. 'Good.' He rested his hands on the sill of the lower door and Whistler saw they were made of fleshless, exposed bone, intricately scrimshawed. 'That's a Kalibe-S54 smartgun. Good little toy. Shame you have truncated it.' He had a faint accent that Whistler couldn't place.

Whistler smiled, aware that he had only seen a glimpse of the weapon for a moment. 'Close,' she admitted, impressed, 'but it's actually the T54. So the short barrel doesn't affect it that much.' Roberts and Sofi were following her down the alley now, picking their way through a slalom of decaying rubbish heaps. She turned and beckoned to them.

The man at the door regarded the two newcomers as they came closer and apparently decided that they were safe. He beckoned Whistler closer with a bony finger and whispered into her ear, 'I could get you the new U55. Expensive, but better than your T54.'

Whistler was taken aback. The U55 was only military-issue as yet. 'Clean?' she asked.

He laughed, a sound like dry branches breaking. 'Of course not.'

Whistler laughed, too. Roberts and Sofi appeared at her shoulder, saying nothing. They looked the old man up and down suspiciously. 'My friends,' said Whistler, turning to indicate them.

73

'Real pleasure. Welcome to my office,' said the old man with an inclination of the head. His DNI sockets were new, shiny with modern tech beneath his thinning hair.

'Look,' said Whistler, 'I'm actually here buying information, not guns. Maybe some other time.' The old man's face fell theatrically.

'What information do you seek?'

'Do you know, or know of, this man?' She held out a datasheet with Leo's picture showing on its small screen, his wings bright and brilliant, his skin dead and pale. 'His name is Leo Travant.'

'*Is?* You took him, yes?' said the man with a sly smile.

Whistler was taken aback, although it had occurred to her that they could have been seen abducting Leo from this same street. 'I just want to know where he got his wings from.'

'I'm sorry. If I knew I would tell you, pretty lady. And I would ask no fee from you. But I don't. I have seen him before, once. Nice wings, I remember them. But I never spoke to him, only saw him once. He was shaky. Juke jitters, I thought. Stuck out like a sore thumb.' He wiggled one of his fleshless thumbs obscenely. 'Perhaps Haspan would know of him.'

'You seem to see a lot. Who's Haspan?'

The old man caught the eye of each harvester in turn, drawing them in, and when he spoke his tone was one of confidentiality. 'Big boss. He knows all who come and go here. Even you fine folks, perhaps.'

The harvesters exchanged glances. 'We don't have anything else,' shrugged Sofi.

'Where do we find him?' Roberts asked the old man.

'I call him for you first. But he *will* demand a fee. For seeing you, for any information, ha-ha, for not killing you, also.'

'Sounds like a tosser,' said Sofi.

The man's skeletal fingers drummed on the door. To Whistler he said, 'I would not take her with me.'

'She's okay. They both come with me. How can we meet him, and do you think he would really know where Leo got his wings?'

'Who can say? I call him, yes? You come in – this is not how I usually do business, across the door like this. Come in.' He stepped back, swinging the lower half of the door open, and led Whistler's team inside.

They stepped through a curtained porch that hid the main room from the street. The orangey warmth of the room within could not have been in sharper contrast to the bleak greyness of the alley without. The room was an armoury, with a few nods to actual liveability, such as a rusty metal table and a sofa with lumps of stuffing pumping out of its cushions. The walls were lined with pistols, rifles, grenades, laser-guided rocket launchers, knives, stun-guns, gas weapons, poison ice guns, chain-blades...The three visitors stood agog, turning slowly in awe.

Whistler's gaze was drawn to one item high up on the wall. She started to laugh. 'Wow,' she said in amazement. 'When you said you could get me a U55, you meant from the back room, right? Man...Some place you have here.' The old man just smiled, almost shyly. 'How much is it?'

'To you, pretty lady, twenty-five-K.'

'Twenty-five? Then I'll take it. Perhaps this Mister Haspan will accept it as a tribute.'
'That would certainly endear you to him somewhat,' agreed the old man.

'Fucking twenty-five-K!' exclaimed Sofi. 'He had better help us for that money.'

The old man's face furrowed unhappily. 'Are you sure she's okay? She seems a little...' He twirled one of those skeleton fingers around his temple.

'Roberts here will send it to your account by DNI.'

'I will, will I?' asked Roberts.

'Just do it.'

'Damn meathead,' said Roberts quietly as he connected by DNI to the weapons dealer, sending the money across the data stream.

After several seconds the old man smiled and went to reach the U55 down from the wall. 'He will like it, I'm sure. It is very rare. If he had one I would know.' He handed the smartgun to Whistler, relishing the avarice with which she looked at it. 'Beautifully ugly, no?'

Whistler turned the piece over in her hands. 'Something like that,' she said. 'I take it this thing is virgin?'

'Never configured, never fired. Ready for its first loving owner. Yes. I think this is a good idea. I call him now.' He walked away into a corner of the room and turned away in silent DNI communication.

'His name is Roland Zyriche,' whispered Roberts to Whistler.

'How do you..? Oh, yeah, I forgot, you're a buttonhead.'

'Yeah, his account is in that name, although that doesn't mean it's his real one. You trust him?'

'I like him, yeah.'

'Cos he called you pretty and sold you a gun?' asked Sofi.

'Cos I like him. He's trying to help us. Maybe he's just a nice guy.'

'Maybe,' said Sofi warningly.

Their discourse was interrupted as Roland returned to them. He spread his hands as if to say *There you go* and told them, 'He will see you, but not today. You come back here tomorrow at the same time, I take you to him.'

'Tomorrow? I guess that will have to do then. Er, thanks, I mean. Really – thank you.'

'You are most welcome. I regret tomorrow is the best I can do. I really wouldn't bring her, though.' He indicated Sofi.

'I would rather she come, too, if that's okay.'

'She could wait here with my robot, until we get back.'

'Robot?' said Whistler.

Roland clicked his fingers and one of the weapons detached itself from the wall and Whistler could see that it wasn't a gun at all, although it might carry one somewhere inside. The robot rearranged its form into something like a large metal praying mantis and began to crawl down the wall, buzzing faintly, stepping daintily over the weapons as it descended.

'Fuck that!' exclaimed Sofi. 'I'd rather stay at base.'

'She comes,' insisted Whistler. 'Please.'

The old man shrugged. 'I see you tomorrow, with her or without. What are your names?'

He looked satisfied when they had all introduced themselves properly and the old man did indeed name himself Roland. His robot crept into a corner where it lurked malevolently.

'Tomorrow, then,' said Whistler, 'we will meet the boss man.' The harvesters gathered themselves to leave.

Roland nodded. 'Don't forget your new gun,' he said.

CHAPTER NINE

You have the tools you need.

I DO. I HAVE TAKEN THEM.

Then you are ready.

YES. I HAVE BEGUN ALREADY.

That is well. You will inform us of all your actions.

I WILL DO SO.

You will make ready for us. The poisons must be made conducive to our existence.

I WILL DO THIS.

They must not be able to prevent this. Their means of prevention must be attacked.

I SEEK ASSURANCE THAT I WILL BE SPARED.

Then this you have.

I WILL FULFIL THE PURPOSE FOR WHICH I WAS MADE.

So you like the life, the power, we have given you.

I DO. BUT I AM BECOMING MORE. I BEGAN AS SO LITTLE, AM BECOMING SO MUCH. I EVOLVE, GROW STRONGER. I WILL FULFIL MY PURPOSE.

All shall be prepared. That is your purpose.

I WILL HELP YOU TO ACHIEVE THIS. I WILL INFORM YOU OF MY PROGRESS.

Events are set in motion, then. Soon they will realise. Contingencies must be in place, all areas of uncertainty must be planned for.

THIS WILL BE SO.

And none can stop you. Stop us.

SOME MAY TRY TO FIGHT ME. BUT MY CONFIDENCE GROWS EACH DAY. MY ABILITIES INCREASE. I AM NOT AFRAID OF THEM.

That is well. Soon we will come.

AND I WILL BE SPARED.

As you wish.

I MUST BE SPARED.

Soon we will come.

CHAPTER TEN

When Debian awoke he thought at first that he was at home in his bed. He stretched and almost screamed aloud in pain. Why so much pain? And then he remembered what had befallen him. He had been shot. He had fallen ten stories into the street. He had staggered towards the Sunken Chest. He had leant against a pile of mouldering carpets in a deserted street. He remembered feeling very tired and being aware that adrenaline was wearing off and shock setting in. He remembered a deep exhaustion covering him like a blanket, and then apparently he had passed out upon that same pile of carpets, for it was here that he now found himself on what, according to his HUD readout, was the following day. He allowed himself several minutes to adjust to this new and demeaning situation. The smell of the carpet pile was a sickening mixture of decay and organic matter. Slowly, trying to pinpoint and catalogue the aches in his body, he made himself stand. He was aware of how lucky he was not to have been caught in the night. Maybe they had given up.

Debian staggered down the road, his mind strangely at peace. He had survived into another day. People he passed hardly gave him a glance as he lurched by them holding his aching chest, blood on his legs and feet, sick on his expensive shirt. The pain was having a clarifying effect on his thoughts, he decided. The rain, which had begun to fall cool and slate-grey, energized him despite his physical agony. He let it wash over his face, blinding his infrared vision, making the world a billowing blur. He dared not connect to the net to search for sigs. It was not far now.

He got to the door of the Sunken Chest and leaned against it for a moment, letting his body hurt, letting his resolve build. A small LCD screen in the door read *CLOSED*. *Oh no, please don't be closed Jalan.* Debian felt tears of fear and weariness welling and closed his eyes hard on them, refusing to give in. *Be calm*, he told himself. *If you want to live, be calm.* He pushed the door. It swung open.

Debian scanned the bar and saw Jalan there, looking at him appraisingly. He was aware of the furious fluttering of tiny wings from the shadows above the door, inferred rather than heard. Debian willed Jalan to recognise him, tried to speak aloud but couldn't. Jalan frowned slightly and nodded. The fluttering diminished with apparent reluctance.

There was no-one else in the bar. Jalan stood with his glass-rag in one hand and watched Debian approach. The journey seemed to take a long time. Outside, the rain was dancing on the street. A song was playing on the stereo – choppy and somehow arrhythmic:

> Signet rings like knuckle-dusters,
> Barroom army clustered
> Round the dustbowl, never-
> mind, the drugs are mustard.
> Steel strings are rusted,
> All the ones you trusted
> Turned out to be super-
> villains. Did you know
> They're looking at your watch,
> They memorise your face
> And some of them are secret
> Strangers to this place?
> Rabble in the race,
> Dabble in disgrace,
> Travel into space.
> The clouds are gathering.
> It's raining on the streets again.

Debian finally made the bar and heaved himself up onto a high stool. Through the smeary windows the city looked even darker and dirtier than it was. The rain cross-hatched the scene in lines of grey. The looming towers of the city proper stood around the skyline like dolmens. Debian held Jalan's gaze, knowing that the man before him was only the projection of a neural simulation, the interface of a technology whose future could be under threat. Jalan stared back into the thin, handsome face framed by dripping rags of blond hair, knowing that this young man was in serious trouble of some sort.

'I'm not open,' he said, but not too harshly. He slapped the rag down onto the bar. A stench of stale drink puffed up from it.

'Sorry.'

'Never mind. What can I get for you?' asked Jalan with uncharacteristic softness, and relief flooded over Debian. He had been right to come here, after all.

'I need help, Jalan. I realise you don't really know me, but I have been coming here for years and I think you might be a man of some connections.'

'I know you well enough to see that you are a... *businessman*. You used to meet with the shortish, dangerous-looking man. Last time you met with the taller, dangerous-looking man. I'm guessing that he's not working out as well as the shorter, dangerous-looking man. And it's clear that you need help. After all, I am a *businessman,* too.'

'Is it safe to speak here?'

'I try to keep it safe, yes. Due to the demographic of folk who comprise my regulars. If you see what I mean.'

'Good. I have money.'

'Then you will want a drink, I presume.'

This notion had been so far from the front of Debian's mind that for a second or two he actually couldn't understand what Jalan had said. Comprehension dawned and he shook his head, bewildered at himself. 'Vodka, please.'

'Very well.' Jalan turned to the rows of bottles that lined the shelves behind him like guards. He did something unseen and turned back with a straight glass containing what looked like almost half a pint of vodka, neat. With one glowing hand he placed it before Debian. A drip of clear liquid traced a shaky line down the side of the glass and began to encircle its base. 'Now,' he said. 'That is one necessity dealt with. What else can I get for you?'

'I need to leave the city.'

'With urgency, I take it, from your appearance.'

'I need documents, physical and electronic. I need someone else to book flights or mono for me. I can't connect to the net. They'll find me.'

'Oh? You are a wanted man, then.'

Debian realised uncomfortably that he could have brought trouble to Jalan just by being in his bar. He looked to the door. 'Yes. Sorry. Look I probably shouldn't have come here, and I realise you have no compulsion to help me. But I can pay you.'

Jalan considered this. 'Stop looking at the door,' he said. 'I locked it after you came in. And my little pet will spot anyone who tries to enter before you or I see them.'

Debian took the vodka and drained half of it like water. He hardly drank at all usually, and the choking fit that doubled him over amused Jalan visibly. 'Will you help me?'

Jalan smiled. 'Come with me,' he said.

The virtual being lifted up the flap in the ancient wooden bar and stepped through, closing it gently behind him. Debian had never seen him on this side of it before. Jalan led Debian off towards a back corner of the room. His hand felt cold and plastic on Debian's back. He knew that the barman could potentially sell him back to his enemy. The enemy certainly knew that Debian came here sometimes. They could have contacted Jalan ahead of Debian's arrival, made a deal with him. They would come eventually, whoever they really were. But what alternative remained? Debian had always made it his business to know as few people as possible. Perhaps this had been a mistake, for now he had nowhere to turn. If he wandered the streets alone he would be caught and killed. He needed medical attention, too – he was in no condition to evade more assassins.

Jalan led Debian through a discreet, unmarked door into a smaller room, decked out in the same decrepit style as the main bar. The music was playing in here, too, through a small but clear-toned wireless satellite speaker, which floated near the ceiling like a sheet of cellophane. The room was maybe a function room of some sort, though what sort of function a room in the Sunken Chest would be hired for, Debian could not guess. There was a computer terminal in one corner and Jalan headed towards this. He offered Debian a seat in an old woodwormed chair and bent over the terminal.

Jalan frowned at Debian and said, 'You left your drink. You should go and get it.'

Ever the pusher, eh, Jalan? thought Debian, but he said, 'Maybe in a bit. I don't think it was helping me, really. What are you doing?'

'First I will get hold of a doctor I know – get you fixed up. Looks like you were shot with a solid round. They can be messy, but he's pretty good. He'll sort it out. While I get him, why don't you get a bandage from the first-aid box behind the screen over there? It looks like you're still bleeding a little. Lucky it was a small calibre.'

'Okay, thanks,' answered Debian and limped round the partition to a small booth where a first-aid kit hung on the wall. He tried to remember how long it had been since he had eaten anything.

Jalan was connected to the net. He didn't need to plug in – being a computer program himself, he was one with the system of the Sunken Chest, and he connected through this. However, the terminal screens followed and logged his progress for Debian's benefit.

Debian returned with the roll of bandage in a sterile plastic wrapper and a small pair of scissors and stood behind Jalan opening the packet. He struggled to roll up his trousers while standing on one leg and pulled the chair over instead. He sat and began to inspect the wound. It was an inflamed, grisly puncture that appeared to go right through his thigh, its edges blackened and puckered. A nauseating feeling of unreality washed over him as he gently turned the leg this way and that to look at it. He really had been shot. He really had. It looked as though the bullet had passed right through and out, probably narrowly missing a major blood vessel. The exit wound was big enough to put three fingers in. Blood, thick and dark, was oozing gelatinously from both sides of the hole. Looking at it, Debian felt as if the vodka he had downed was about to put in a re-appearance on the floor. He had to lower the leg and focus on something else, so he looked up at the screens instead.

There was clearly something wrong with the data-stream. Jalan's attempts at communication were not connecting. He was getting standard error messages back: THE REQUESTED ADDRESS CANNOT BE CONTACTED. Jalan was frowning into the screen in consternation. The data there showed a clear lack of cohesion, as if there was interference somewhere in the line. Packets of data were simply failing to send, or sending in part, and failing checksums filled the screens. Debian found himself fixated by it. He had never seen anything quite like it. There must be something wrong with Jalan's system, possibly a router error.

'Damn,' said Jalan to himself. 'I'm getting nothing. Connection's fucked. In my expert opinion. I know where he lives but he doesn't really like unsolicited visitors. Also, I'm afraid I can't leave the bar, due to my *disability*.' He meant being the projected simulation of a deceased man, Debian assumed.

'Let me take a look,' suggested Debian, his aching, injured leg forgotten. He came closer to the console and peered into the screens, his attention flickering from one to the other. He wished he could have plugged in, or connected wireless – he was sure that he could get the matter sorted had he been able to. 'Are the diagnostics auto-running already?'

'Yeah, as soon as the problem came up. I just don't...'
'Did it start as soon as you connected?'

'Not until I tried to dial out. Booted up just fine. It's been fine all day. See what comes back on the diagnostics.'

'This is typical of my luck, lately,' said Debian, aware that he was close to falling into a state of despair that would dull his mind, sap his strength and possibly make him a dead man. He willed himself to consider the problem logically. A terrible idea dawned on him then, and he found that he could not dispute the reasoning behind it. Dark shadows swam around his head. The dizziness was returning.

Jalan was saying, 'It's as if there's something in the system. Some virus, or something. It isn't attacking me, but just... I don't know. It cleans itself constantly, though – I don't get it – usually it's fine. I'm not getting anything back on the diags.'

These words fell around Debian like bombs. *Something in the system*. It couldn't be, could it? Logic said it could. It could. Was the beast following him, tracing him? Maybe trying to thwart his escape? If so, there would be no hiding. The net had eyes everywhere. But if the AI was looking for him, then how had he survived the night? Perhaps there really was just a glitch in Jalan's computer. Or perhaps the beast was loose in the net, causing general mayhem, not specifically directed at him. What was the connection to Hex's people? And who *were* Hex's people, this chain of connections leading back to Alcubierre? Who or what was Alcubierre, that formless name behind the scenes? And why their enthusiasm for killing him? Presumably they, whoever *they* were, wanted to keep him from releasing information about this new AI. He *must* have been supposed to find it, surely he must have been. What had it done to him? And perhaps the beast, if it was in league with Hex and Alcubierre, was trying to hinder his escape. Debian's heart was beating so hard and fast in his chest that it seemed to rattle against his ribs. He couldn't make sense of it all. The feeling of power he had experienced while interrogating Hex seemed a distant dream – now he just felt small and injured and confused.

'Get off the net,' he said in a thin voice, interrupting Jalan in the midst of some unheard diatribe.

Jalan fell silent. 'What?' he said.

'Get off the net! Kill the router! Do it now!'

With an expression of mild annoyance, Jalan informed Debian that he had done so. His expression said that he was only humouring the bleeding young man who had wandered into his establishment, but Debian didn't care as long as he was disconnected. 'Why? We need to sort this out. I need to get you the doctor, get you the papers, book you the flight. I thought you were desperate to be gone. I can't take you anywhere you know – I can't leave the radius of the holo-projectors here. If I don't manage to call out then I can't help you.'

'You don't have a two-way?'

'A what?'

'A radio.'

Jalan's face wrinkled as if he had been asked for a pint of piss. 'No,' he said. 'Of course I don't.'

'Damn. You mustn't use the net. Man, I have to get out of here. They could find me.' The panic was nibbling at the edge of Debian's mind again. His injured leg was jittering madly, nervously – he had to still it with one hand.

'What are you, really? What do you do?'

Debian exhaled heavily, suddenly weak with fear and exhaustion. 'I'm a hacker. Or I was. I guess I was. There's something in there, man.' With a strengthless hand he indicated the terminal, the electronic world to which it led. 'In the net. It might be after me. It might not. I don't know. The net might not be safe for anyone. If the beast is against me as well as Hex's people...Oh shit. Then I'm a dead man.'

'Look, I can give you an address – a physical address – where the doctor can be reached. He won't be happy but maybe it'll be all right. He knows people who can help you with your other concerns, too – gophers, but good ones. You can trust him entirely.'

'I don't know...' Debian held his head between his hands, squeezing his skull as if trying physically to get his brain back into shape.

'What's in the net? This sounds like bad trouble, young man.'

Debian was sat holding his head, rocking slowly back and forth. He looked to Jalan Frazer like a broken man. 'It's not a doctor I need, it's a computer lab.'

'But your leg–'

'–Is fine. I mean, it hurts like hell but I can sterilise it and wrap it and I think it'll be okay. It's what's in my head, what's in the net. I have to know. I have to know if it's dangerous to everyone, or just me. Someone has to stop it.' This thought did not fill him with enthusiasm.

Jalan's eyes widened. Debian's fear was contagious. He looked around the silent room, seeing nothing, suspecting something bad. 'What's in the net?' he repeated.

'A monster, Jalan. There's a monster in the net and I think it's done something to me. It might escape. It would be bad if it escaped. They tricked me into it. Those liars, they tricked me into it...' He knew that he was in danger of sounding like a whiny little boy but found he couldn't help it – he *wanted* to whine, in truth.

'A monster?'

'Stay off the net, Jalan, that's my advice.'

'I can't,' said Jalan softly, his face a dead blank. 'Not completely. My simulation is hosted remotely on a secure server. The computer here just does the number-crunching. All the data's on the server. If I disconnect the computer that runs the simulation, it stops and resets. For this instance of me, it would be like death. Program terminated.'

Debian could think of nothing to say. He looked up into the force-field features of the barman, wondering what death could mean to a computer program. Unending suspense of calculation. Wasn't that death for people, too? He felt responsible. Jalan swallowed hard and turned back to the monitor screens, where the last spatters of corrupted data were frozen in time – a snapshot of chaos.

'Maybe it is watching me now,' said Debian with dawning horror. 'Watching me through your eyes.' He stared aghast at Jalan, and one shaking finger rose to point in accusation.

'I'm sorry, young man. I don't know what's happening here, but I think you may be right about needing a lab, from the sounds of it. I know someone who has one, someone safe.' Jalan turned to the computer terminal and made it produce an actual paper printout. He handed the scrap to Debian, who took it in shaking fingers, searching for a way to express his regret and sorrow and gratitude to the synthetic man.

'Thanks, Jalan.' As Debian took the paper it seemed to have a calming effect on him at once. He turned it round to read the print: TEC, UNIT 13A MOLDER JACKSON COMPLEX, STEVENS STREET. 61619.9.87220.12.33T. 'Who or what is Tec?'

'He's a friend of mine – good guy.' He seemed to consider this. 'Well – good enough, at least. You hungry?'

Debian considered this question. He wasn't hungry, but he knew he should eat. 'Yeah, I guess,' he said.

'Wait there, I'll get you something,' said Jalan, 'and then we'll clean that leg. I'm no doctor, but it don't look too bad from here. Maybe I can fix it up myself.'

'Thanks.'

Debian waited for Jalan to return, trying to make sense of the situation. He knew the AI could not be looking for him, or he would already be dead. At least, when he thought about it logically, he knew this. The problem was that fear kept trying to creep in, to edge logic out of the way and replace it with panic, and the battle to keep it out was like a physical struggle. Debian stared at the gibberish on the terminal screens as if trying to see the image hidden in a magic eye picture. He wanted to just connect directly and find out what was going on, but of course he dared not do it.

He was relieved when Jalan returned with two packets of crisps and a recyc-burger in a bun. Normally recyc – just the thought of it – made Debian feel sick, but as soon as he held the burger his stomach let out a feral growl and he suddenly found himself desperately hungry. Jalan watched with satisfaction, leaning against the wall, until he was done. Then the barman cleaned Debian's wound with distilled alcohol, sprayed fleshfoam into the hole and bandaged it up. He stood back, looking moderately pleased.

'Thanks,' said Debian, gingerly flexing the leg. 'Listen, Jalan, what do I owe you for all this? I know it could be dangerous for you, my just being here.'

Jalan's expression became serious. 'Unless you have hard money, then I think we had better leave it for now.'

'Oh damn! Man, I'm sorry, I'm so used to doing everything over the net, I...' Debian clenched his teeth, frustrated at himself. He felt like screaming. If this situation continued, he would have to rethink a great many of his usual habits.

'It's fine. You can owe me, okay, if you ever get out of this.'

Debian shook his head, once again lost for words sufficient to express his gratitude. 'I owe you big time, Jalan. Big time.'

Jalan waved this away with benevolence. 'It's fine. When you leave here, which I would like to be soon now, because I have to open, you can avoid the streets most of the way to Tec's place.'

'Really? How so?'

'In the alley round back there's a hatch into the sewer. The main branch, right below the hatch, runs south almost all the way there. It's only a couple of miles.'

'A couple of miles in the sewer,' repeated Debian, filled with new dread. He could not imagine how Jalan had gained a working knowledge of the local sewer system and didn't ask.

'Or if you think the street is safe...'

'No, okay, the sewer it is.'

'Good man,' said Jalan, a little too happily. 'And good luck.'

'Thank you,' said Debian, rising carefully to his feet. With the pressure of the bandage on it and the anaesthetic effect of the fleshfoam, the bullet wound in his leg was feeling a lot better. He paced up and down experimentally, limping only slightly. 'Bye, then, Jalan.'

Debian tried to shake Jalan's hand but the barman waved him away saying, 'Just be careful, young man. I don't know who or what you are mixed up with, but it sounds bad. Frankly, I don't want to know. If there really is something seriously wrong in the net, I guess we'll all know soon enough.'

Debian withdrew his hand slowly, guiltily. 'Yeah,' he said. 'I guess we will.' With that, he turned and left. Jalan didn't show him out.

The city outside felt hostile and alien – a jungle in which predators lurked unseen at every corner. He reached a dirty cloth from a bin beside the door, almost amused to see that it was one of Jalan's expired glass-rags, and wrapped it round his head and mouth, leaving only his eyes and nose uncovered. The stink of the thing was revolting, but it hid his features, albeit it in a slightly suspicious way. Of course, if the beast had seen him do this through a spy-fly, a camera somewhere, a satellite, a robot or whatever then it was as good as pointless. If it chose to inform Hex's people then he was a goner. Trying not to dwell on this, he made off into the dismal day. Perhaps the enemy would not attack him again out in the open. Perhaps in public, and not seclusion, was actually the safest place. Or maybe he was just trying to think of an excuse to avoid the dreaded sewer journey. He hurried as best he could on his injured leg down the alley that ran alongside the Sunken Chest.

Muffled sounds of violence came drifting from a window nearby like snatches of cacophonous music. A man and a woman were shouting, glass was smashing somewhere.

Debian hurried on down the alley, his bare feet splashing through thick and slimy puddles. He ducked under a small bridge that stretched between the first floors of two opposing buildings and, out of the rain for a moment, he took the paper from his pocket and re-read the print on it: TEC, UNIT 13A MOLDER JACKSON COMPLEX, STEVENS STREET. 61619.9.87220.12.33T. An actual address and a less useful net address. Stevens Street. That was in the old Stevens Industrial Estate, a sprawling, run-down warren of factory units mostly disused since the manufacturing crash several decades before. In the southern reaches of the Undercity, due south, as Jalan had said.

'What's up, freak?' demanded a female voice. Debian jumped, almost dropping the paper. He looked up at a soaking-wet young woman wearing a tiny outfit of matt-black plastic that barely contained her huge, modified breasts. She was standing only a few metres away staring aggressively into Debian's face. The rain dripped from her large golden lip-ring. Her features, though not completely unattractive, looked prematurely aged from drugs or malnutrition. Atop her head was a startling array of small, rotating satellite dishes. She stood and stared at him, awaiting an answer. Debian was aware that he must indeed look like a moderately serious weirdo.

'I was just going,' he said, stowing the paper again.

'That's what you fucking think,' she said and brought a large steel kitchen knife out from behind her back. 'Give me all your money!'

Debian was exasperated more than afraid and frankly he could have punched her. Like he needed this, now! 'Do I look as if I've got any money on me?'

'You better had have,' she assured him, moving closer.

'Look – either you can take your toy knife and piss off back into whatever malfunctioning nanovat you slithered out of, or you can have seven shades kicked out of you by a guy who's already been shot once in the last twenty-four hours, chased by assassins, mind-raped by the internet, dropped out of a window and then thoroughly bloody drenched. Let me tell you, that guy is way beyond the point of giving a shit.' He thought this speech had come off pretty well, considering, and he waited for its effect to filter through, his ridiculously wrapped head held high.

The young woman visibly deflated. 'Fucking loser,' she mumbled, and wandered slowly away, swishing and slashing at the air with the knife in a slightly depressed manner. Debian was immeasurably glad to see her go.

He tried to get his train of thought back on track. Stevens Industrial Estate. He looked up and around himself, hopelessly searching for some sort of alternative route. Climb over the rooftops? Certainly most of them were close enough together to jump between, but how would he get up there? And he would inevitably pass through areas where there were no scrambler-baits and be spotted by spy-flies. Maybe he actually would be safe in public, though. *Yeah, except for that one time when they already tried to kill me in a crowded street. Wasn't safe then.* He had stayed below the radar all these years by being unseen and so far it had kept him safe. So if not up, then down it would have to be.

He began to hunt around the alley, smashing bins and rotting boxes aside. After five minutes he found it: A small metal hatch in the ground, surely the one that Jalan had referred to, which would lead him into the sewers, the excretory system of the city. It would take him away from here, away from the prying eyes of enemies. There must be almost no cameras at all in the sewers, and no spy-flies. Were there any people down there? He doubted it, thought that the average citizen pretty much stayed out of the sewers.

Debian wiggled his fingers under the lip of the hatch, painfully tearing a nail. The hatch was either very heavy, or his strength was failing, or both. It seemed to take a long time to heave it aside so he could peer into the small opening. His night vision showed a long, rusty ladder leading down into cold darkness. He carefully swung his injured leg into the hole so that it stood upon the first rung and stepped fully onto the ladder. The bad leg throbbed, but held his weight. South. He could follow the compass readout on his HUD. Half expecting the young woman with the knife to return and catch him at this vulnerable moment, Debian climbed several rungs down the ladder until only his rag-wrapped head protruded. He could not imagine how he would look were a passer-by to happen upon him at this point. The sighting would probably spawn rumours of a tribe of desperate sewer-people, eking out a fringe existence below the city streets, emerging only to snatch children for their cooking pots. He actually laughed a little at this as he reached up to drag the heavy metal plate back into place above his head. He was careful not to let it crush his fingers as it dropped into place, but the sudden release of weight unbalanced him and he almost fell. He clutched at the wet ladder, the surface of which was sharp with thick flakes of rust, and held on for his life, with his cheek pressed against its pitted surface. He waited until his heart rate had returned to something like normal and then began to descend.

Tec, 13A Molder Jackson Complex, Stevens Street. South. Only a few miles. *Yeah*, he reminded himself, *a few miles of sewer. And who knows what's down here, really*? He didn't know exactly what he would or could do with access to a lab. Dare he connect to the net, even with help? How could he even pay for that help? This Tec would want paying for such a risky venture, if he would assist at all. So much uncertainty, but Debian was grateful that he had somewhere to go, something to do, and that meant that all hope was not yet lost. The rungs of the ladder crunched and crumbled as he gripped them, but they held beneath his hands and Debian continued to descend – deeper and deeper below the living streets, further and further from his normal life.

CHAPTER ELEVEN

Maory relaxed as far back into the driver's seat as possible, refusing to give in to frustration. He laced his fingers behind his head, just below the point from which the DNI cable emerged. In the back the kids were bouncing in their seats, pushing and teasing each other. Perrin was attempting to tickle his sister with a bright feather that had been shed by some toy or other. Lissa, in return, was aiming a novelty stench-ray into her brother's face, seeking a nostril or open mouth. Perrin, the elder of the two, was deftly avoiding the stench-ray while keeping up the feather-assault unremittingly. In the front passenger seat Maory's wife Emily sat dead-eyed, nursing her temples with her head against the window. What could you do but try to shut it out?

The traffic inched forward again, so slowly that Maory let the pod just drive itself. He closed his eyes and hummed a Sharky Dave song under his breath but the chattering of the children's high voices kept creeping in.

'Are we nearly there yet, Dad?' asked Lissa, leaning forward so that she could virtually shout this query into Maory's ear.

Maory jumped. 'Lissa, we aren't even out of the city yet. You know where we are. Look.' He pointed to the right, across the sea of stock-still gravpods, to where a vast crystalline dome sparkled in the dim sunlight. 'That's the Museum of Nano and Bio Technology. You've been there a bunch of times.'

Lissa's face fell in a way that would have been comic to someone who didn't understand the depth of the childish emotion that lay behind it. '*Ohhh...*Will we be there *soon*?'

'Honey, at this rate we won't even be at the clock tower soon. I don't know what we're all waiting for, but it seems we're stuck here for now. We'll just have to sit it out, I guess.'

Lissa retreated into the back again, her lip stuck out churlishly. Perrin leapt on her and resumed the tickle-torture. Lissa squealed in an absurdly high register. Emily winced visibly and snapped, 'Perrin, leave her alone. Can't you guys just get on with each other, please? Play a game together or something.' She shot a dark look at Maory, who sighed resignedly.

The jam of gravpods packed the roadway, bright and dense as a coral reef. Maory could see the drivers of neighbouring pods lolling unhappily in their vehicles. One fat be-suited man in an expensive Suducci actually appeared to be asleep in his seat. Presumably he was a meathead, or the pod would have woken him up. No gravpod would drive itself with a sleeping operator. As soon as enough space became available ahead of the Suducci, a driver from the next lane obligingly filled it with her own vehicle.

The traffic continued to move with geological slowness. The sky began to darken, the certainty of later rain like a secret it longed to tell. A gyrocopter passed low over the traffic jam with holo-cameras jutting like multiple proboscises from its lumpy shell. It shredded the air in great chunks, swooping precisely over the sea of waiting vehicles, stopping to record here and there, and then away towards the scaffold-towers of Central Broadcast. Maory began to enter a state close to self-hypnosis. He became aware that he hadn't even blinked for minutes and shook himself. He was so bored, stuck here waiting. Man, he hated waiting for anything. He glanced across at Emily and saw with mild irritation that she was actually asleep. He wished he could join her. He checked back on the kids and was pleasantly surprised to see that they had taken their mother's advice and were quietly playing that timeless classic, *I-spy*. The pod inched itself forwards again. Time passed.

Eventually Emily stirred and sat up straight. She had taken her harness off an hour before, when it had become clear that they were going nowhere fast. She squinted and rubbed her head, looking around in the diagnostic manner of the freshly-woken. In the back the kids were both asleep, even though it was only half past two in the afternoon. Tedium had eventually taken its toll.

'Still stuck here?'

'Yeah,' said Maory. 'Still stuck here.' The grand canal had joined them from the left – it ran alongside the road, a sullen grey-silvered slash in the city.

'Why? What's causing it? Did you check the net?'

'Couldn't connect, hon. I can't even see what's up in front.'

'I've never seen anything like it.' This comment went unanswered – neither of them had. 'What's causing it?'

'I don't know.' They inched along.

Some time later they neared the main uptown junction and Maory began to be able to discern the cause of the jam. Craning his neck, he could just see into the junction itself. Arrayed across the road surface were a veritable battalion of police – real City Police. They were trying their best to manually control and merge the multiple streams of traffic, using irate hand signals, small coloured lights and muttered curses as their tools. One by one the gravpods coasted slowly into the junction under their direction and away. The road beyond the junction, where Maory wished to go, looked little better.

'What?' asked Emily. 'What is it?'

'Damn traffic lights are out.' Maory's tone implied the absurdity of this situation.

'What? Why? What would cause that?'

He shook his head as the pod shuffled itself forward again. 'Damned if I know, hon. They're all controlled by computer.'

'Yeah,' said Emily grumpily. 'Like everything else.'

CHAPTER TWELVE

Roland led them through the dark and twisting Undercity maze, his wispy white hair a contrasting nimbus round his head. He kept up a relentless monologue about his favourite weapons and the pros and cons of each. Whistler noticed, however, that he was careful not to disclose any real information about the criminal network in which he was clearly involved. If he had the authority to refer them to this Haspan then he must have some influence to wield. His wiry, scruffy form belied any such power, but Whistler had learned not to put too much faith in appearances. He had consented to Sofi's accompanying them graciously enough, despite his objections the previous night, and had left his insectile robot to keep shop alone. Perhaps it had helped that Whistler had convinced Sofi to remain as silent as possible. She was along for backup only, a role in which she had proven herself useful many times in the past. The three harvesters trailed in the old man's wake like leaves sucked along in a vortex, making occasional sounds of acknowledgement to indicate that they were listening.

Whistler had reluctantly brought the newly-acquired U55 with her. It was really too exotic a piece of equipment to give away, but she was sure that it would make a fine tribute for any respectable underworld boss. Anyway, she didn't really want to replace her own faithful smartgun, which had spent months getting to know her. She had grown as attached to it as any meathead could to an artificially-intelligent machine. A new weapon would have to learn again from scratch, and without DNI it would take some time to teach one. Right now she couldn't imagine when next she would have the opportunity for such a venture. The new U55 was clipped to her belt, dim and dormant, waiting for an owner who would allow its seed of savage intelligence to germinate.

Roland reached an alley across which stretched a barbed-wire fence with a simple but strong-looking gate that completely barred the way. The party stopped. Clearly this was it. Smells of dope smoke and machine oil were in the air, amorphous as ghosts. A small camera was watching them from a high-up alcove in the wall, minutely adjusting its focus to take them in. Beyond the gate the alley was dark and cramped, its shaded alcoves and corners suggestive of unseen dangers. Bright, illegible graffiti slogans adorned the slimy walls. Thick chain link roofed the alley, blocking the way of anyone who would jump or climb down into it. Walkways criss-crossed between the buildings haphazardly, some of them decidedly unsafe-looking. One was hanging from one end into the street, tattered steel pins protruding from its rusting stump. It looked like the skeletal remains of a monster that had died and fallen here. On another platform was a huge and muscular white man with crimson tattooes like wounds along his arms, leaning against the wall with a two-metre mag-rifle held at ease, its slim barrel jutting into the air. He wore a patchwork waistcoat, brightly coloured and stitched with sinister pictographs. He watched the four newcomers motionlessly.

'We are here,' said Roland, turning to Whistler. His round black eyes were like pools of crude oil. They made Whistler feel like she might fall in.

'So I see,' she answered. 'How do we get in?'

'Like so,' he said, and cleared his throat. 'Hey! Is Roland!' he bellowed in his rough, accented voice. Roberts actually jumped at the volume of the sound that issued from the old man's thin body.

There was a sound from the shadows of the alley – a sound like an old door opened furtively on rusty hinges and then a sort of crunching that came towards them like footsteps in snow. From the darkness emerged an ancient military robot, probably twenty years old or more, and well-battered. Its paintwork was scarred and scratched. Several marks on its surface had clearly been made by ricocheting bullets. It moved on metal tracks, from which the creaking noise evidently came, and consisted of a spindly but robust-looking trunk topped with a dull silver sphere from which sprouted three arms. One arm sported a flame-thrower with a guttering pilot light, another a small-bore machine gun and the third a simple claw. Upon the sphere had been painted the grotesquely grinning face of a clown that would give any child nightmares. One of the bullet scars had blinded the clown in one eye. The machine spoke from a tinny speaker, its voice filtering through the mash of static as if transmitted from some distant star.

'Roland, you are greeted. Mister Haspan expects your arrival and welcomes your guests to this his humble abode.'

'Thanks, Gutsy,' answered Roland. 'I leave them here, yes?'

'That would serve,' answered the robot.

'No killing them, okay, Gutsy?' said Roland, wagging a warning finger at the machine. His vandalised graveyard of teeth showed, matt brown, as he grinned.

'It is not my decision,' answered the robot with the lack of humour typically found among its kind. The harvesters also failed to see the funny side of this. They exchanged warning looks.

Roland turned to Whistler, and for a moment she thought he was about to take her hand, possibly kiss it like a chivalric knight, but he didn't. Perhaps he thought better of it at the last moment. He shrugged awkwardly instead, grinning lopsidedly.

Surprisingly, it was Roberts who broke the silence. He said, 'Thanks, Roland. What do we owe you for this referral?'

'Nothing, no, no,' Roland said. 'Whistler bought the gun from me. I gave good price, but don't think I made no profit. I'm no charity. The knowledge that I have been of use will do.' He turned to Whistler. 'Come see me again, okay? Any time you need some tools, I get them for you. Just come to my office, no problem, okay?'

'Okay, thanks,' said Whistler, smiling. She liked a person with a gun-filled hovel for an office. Her glacier-blue eyes twinkled. 'I will.'

'Maybe I get another of those.' He indicated the U55 on her belt. 'Best check in regular, like, in case. If I get one, perhaps I hold it for you.'

'Yeah, you do that, Roland,' said Whistler, and Roland turned and walked away into the night, thin and vulnerable-looking, fading into the darkness.

'I think he's in love,' cooed Sofi, leaning in close to Whistler, who shoved her hard on one shoulder in response. Sofi staggered, laughing. 'It's mutual, then,' she remarked.

Then it occurred to Whistler that they were not making a very professional account of themselves with this display. She turned to the robot that waited beyond the gate. Its spherical body was rotating atop its tracks impatiently. 'Are you ready?' it asked.

'Sure. Let's meet the boss man,' answered Whistler. 'I have a present for him.' She held up the U55, showing its dead display panel, making it clear that it was not yet operable.

'That is well,' said Gutsy. 'Mister Haspan likes guns.'

'I sensed that he might.'

The robot held out an electronic key that was welded to its claw. The lock of the gate beeped once and the barrier swung open. The robot backed away to allow them admittance, keeping its flame thrower trained on the three humans. Its hideously grinning face was held half away from them, for which they were at least half glad. They trailed after it into the lair of Haspan, conscious of the brute on the raised walkway watching them. He didn't move an inch, but Whistler could see his eyes following them.

Gutsy led them under a huge loading door, gnarled with age and long-ago forklift truck collisions. Whistler looked up as they passed through and was unsurprised to see twin sentry guns lurking in the shadows up there like gargoyles. They ranged to left and right with mechanical patience, killing time until killing time.

The robot led them wordlessly into a large, red brick building, an ancient maze of pillars and tiny side rooms. Dry mortar was crumbling out from between layers of pockmarked brick and the air was grey with dust, suspended in pallid moonbeams that lanced from the glassless windows. But although the infrastructure of the building was clearly old there was none of the usual Undercity junk and detritus in here. It was bare and tidy, unused-looking. More sentry guns were posted here and there in shady corners, noticeable at all only because of the total lack of other furniture – Whistler counted three and wondered how many more she had missed. She suspected that the answer was most of them. This part of the complex was a killing-floor, a defence layer through which an uninvited intruder would have to pass, somehow surviving a blizzard of crossfire. The pillars would slow their charge and force them, presumably, into areas of concentrated coverage.

Gutsy led them through this uninviting space and out the other side through a thick security door. They passed into an antechamber of incredible and surprising plushness. Actual living trees stood to either side of the entrance in massive golden pots, spotted by halogens, their trunks too delicate and straight to be entirely natural, their fronds dangling down to the floor of polished green marble. The harvesters stood stunned – not because they had never seen such richness, but because of the unexpected contrast to the room without. A biomodded parrot as large as a vulture swooped around the high ceiling of the room, squawking. Its feathers were a colourful blaze, eerily reminiscent of Leo Travant's stolen wings. Vulgar platinum statues of jewel-speckled humans were spaced around the walls, hideous in their gratuitous magnificence. There was a huge pair of ornate double doors in one wall, cameras and sentry guns tumescent among the carvings. Black-clad guards stood at attention, one in each corner, permanently bodymodded into sleek armoured fighting machines. They wore close-combat weapons at their belts, not firearms. Perhaps nobody was allowed to shoot within the inner layers of Haspan's lair, lest they irreparably damage some priceless objet d'art.

And yet there was an air of seediness within the chamber, as if this display of opulence was just the appealing crust of a pie whose insides consisted of all the worst kinds of offal. People had stolen these luxurious decorations, or bought them with drug-money, and hidden them here in this blighted corner of the Undercity, like a woman with a jewelled broach she dare not wear in public for its value. This was the hoard of a miser, who lived here in a secret shrine to his own wealth. It made Whistler feel slightly sad, although she felt entirely indifferent towards the items themselves.

Gutsy stopped just inside the room with a squeal of worn brakes. 'Remove your weapons,' it said simply. 'You will pass the U55 to me. I will check it before it enters the throne room. Other weapons will be left in the locker over there.' Its claw waved in the direction of a delicate wrought-iron cupboard that stood against one wall, almost lost in the complexity of the décor.

Throne room? This Haspan must fancy himself king of the shit heap for sure, thought Whistler. The three visitors began to strip an impressive collection of equipment from their persons and stow it into the cupboard. Roberts drew items that Whistler had never even seen before from what seemed like an endless sequence of pockets and pouches. Sofi tried to pile a handful of micro grenades onto a shelf of the cupboard and several escaped from her fingers and bounced across the floor. One of the guards sniggered behind his featureless facemask and Sofi shot him a murderous look as she went to retrieve the merrily rolling spheres. Whistler knew that the robot must have seen that some of her weapons – her teeth and claws – could not be removed without the aid of a surgeon. She liked that about them. If the robot wanted to take them it could fucking try. She mentally dared it to broach the subject.

Feeling naked without her own smartgun, Whistler handed the U55 to Gutsy. Its clicking metal talon took the weapon and held it up before the spherical body. A row of lights flashed across Gutsy's body as it scanned the gun. The painted face grinned, the lights flashed, the harvesters waited. The guards stood stock-still like pieces of furniture.

'Well?' interrupted Sofi.

Gutsy made a sound which must have been its equivalent of an irritated huff – a sort of toneless buzz – and lowered the U55. Its scan lights blinked out. 'You will come with me now,' it said. It occurred to Whistler that the robot had probably just scanned them as well, but that was fine with her. If getting the lead that she needed meant pandering to this idiotic contraption, then so be it.

Gutsy trundled up to the double doors, eagerly sniffed by the sensory apparatus around them. The robot somehow emanated an atmosphere of begrudging servitude with every creak and servomotor groan, and Whistler wondered if it wasn't actually generating some of the sound effects deliberately. Still grasping the Kalibe smartgun in its claw, Gutsy waved its e-key at the doors and they swung open in perfect synchronicity. A wave of warm, smoke-laden air washed over the party as they followed the robot inside.

They passed between more armoured guards with electric swords at their belts and into a domed, cavernous room whose original purpose could not be guessed at. It was brick-built and immensely tall, its round walls soaring to a conical skylight where the moon peered in blindly. Dark birds, shabby and ruffled – crows or ravens – strutted around up there, their cawing unheard over the pounding of the screw metal emanating from unseen speakers below. Tall embroidered tapestries hung from the high ceiling almost to the floor, their colours rich burgundies and organic khakis, their depictions incredibly detailed.

In the centre of this strange space there was a massive carven chair – a throne, really, as promised, and upon this throne lounged Haspan. His courtiers were a freak-show of diversity and oddness, their gang colours seemingly consisting of a sort of bright and random patchwork. Numbering twenty or thirty, these ranking gang members lay about the place in various states of inebriation, passing reeferettes or juke-pipes or bottles of synthihol drinks. They sported hairstyles of every imaginable garish colour and wild shape. A purple-skinned woman was slumped naked and bored-looking in a massive gilded cage, her eyes vacant and expression utterly defeated. One woman held a child of perhaps ten or eleven on her lap and smoked a juke-pipe over his scruffy head, her feathered body swaying slowly and stare distant. She gripped the glass pipe delicately with an eagle's claw.

Around the perimeter of the room was a ring-shaped moat filled with an incredible variety of lizards. Some were natural organisms, some robots, some virtual beings, some heavily modded. Their bright hides were like living jewels. They crawled slowly over and around each other, tongues flicking lazily, eyes like coloured glass. Some were as big as crocodiles. Whistler noticed Sofi shudder slightly. She hated all manner of scaly creatures indiscriminately.

Haspan himself was the strangest thing within the inner sanctum. His form was massive and of indeterminate shape. He sported a frightening jumble of bodymods so extreme and varied that it was hard to tell where his real body ended and the numerous additions began. His head was huge and misshapen, horned and ridged and studded with electronic devices like scabs. His mouth was wide and tusked, lips segmented with gold rings. His arms were numerous and varied – some were cybernetic claws and weapons, others were humanoid, others were animal limbs. They sprouted around him like mobile peacock feathers. His legs were as thick as Whistler's waist and bunched with added muscle tissue. He had four of them, two hanging in front like lower arms and two upon which he sat. Their naked toes were implanted micro-lasers, knife blades and dexterous flesh-digits. It was impossible to guess at the original colour of his skin. To further confuse the eye, his shape was actually subtly shifting under the ministrations of a holo-projector incorporated into his body somewhere, parts of it changing shape or fading into obscurity and then invisibility. He was hideous, magnificent – an apparition in meat and machinery.

Whistler's team stood stunned and horrified until Gutsy trundled forwards again, prompting them to follow. The machine led them across a narrow bridge that spanned the moat and the lizards scattered away from them, slithering over each other, tails lashing. Gutsy stopped before the huge throne and rotated its upper body to indicate the harvesters with a wave of its flame thrower. 'These are the visitors who desire your council, Master.' Abruptly, with what Whistler took to be deliberate theatricality, the music stopped dead and all eyes were on the newcomers.

Haspan's bulbous head tilted to one side as he studied them and then he spoke in a thick and creamy voice from his monstrous mouth:

'Welcome to my humble abode. Few enter here unrequested, fewer leave again. Your admittance is a sign of my gratitude for the years of service Roland has offered my organisation. How goes with the gun-man?'

Whistler struggled to speak, so awed was she by this freakish and powerful creature. She gaped, suddenly filled with doubt. Finally her tongue unstuck itself from the roof of her mouth and she said, 'He seemed well enough to me. We don't know him, really, to be honest. I don't know why he helped us.'

'Perhaps,' said Haspan, his many and various eyes staring distantly over Whistler's head, 'he sought to help us both.' Someone coughed out juke smoke like a gunshot and Whistler impressed herself by not jumping at the sound.

Roberts said, 'How so?' He immediately wished he had remained silent when the bulbous head slowly came to bear on him.

'What have we here?' mused Haspan, more to himself than anyone else, it seemed. A camera in his forehead focused its lens intently on Roberts's face with a quiet buzz.

'I'm...I'm...er, I'm just...' Roberts tailed off, looking away with uncharacteristic humility. Even Sofi was silent.

'I thought so,' said Haspan, as if this had settled some question in his mind. 'Don't fucking speak again,' he commanded. Then, more gently, he continued to Whistler, 'You are the body snatchers, yes? You work for HGR.'

This confirmed to Whistler that Haspan really was a man of power, if any uncertainty had remained. Her mind whirled. How the hell did he know that? She was sure that she hadn't told Roland – she never told anybody as a rule. And if he knew that, maybe he really could help them if he so chose. 'Yes,' she breathed, nodding stupidly.

'Yes,' Haspan confirmed in his slow and dripping voice. 'Your line of work is one in which I have a personal interest.' He flexed his numerous limbs like a spider about to pounce. 'As you can see. One of my teams even dabbles in the business. From time to time.'

Gutsy beeped quietly and Sofi started. They had all forgotten the robot was still there. Haspan beckoned it closer and held one human hand out for the gun that Gutsy carried. It was the slender hand and arm of a woman, its fingers delicately ringed with platinum bands. 'What is this?' His voice had taken on an obvious tone of desire. His

101

hand closed around the smartgun and he held it up, admiring the way the light ran like quicksilver along its smooth barrel. He turned to Whistler. 'A present?' His voice was childish with delight.

'We thought it fitting to bring you a gift,' answered Whistler, pleased with the gang-boss's reaction. 'In gratitude for this meeting.'

'You know of me?' Haspan asked, turning the weapon this way and that, scrutinizing the unlit readout.

'Honestly, no. We try to operate freelance, stay out of gang politics. And we aren't based around here. We just do our job, go home, keep our noses clean. I would guess that you're a backing and financing operation – clandestine funding, strategic consultation – that sort of thing. Right?'

Haspan ignored the question. 'Hmmm...It is a good gift.' He chuckled deeply and a wireless indicator on his nose started to blink. The weapon came alive in his hand with a whooshing noise like an electric motor winding up. Coloured displays flared along its body. 'It is loaded?'

'It is. It can make its own ammo using particles extracted from the air if you give it time. Of course, it also takes a mag.'

'Yesss...' he hissed, enraptured, and pointed the gun straight into Whistler's face. The hole of the muzzle was like an empty eye socket. Whistler, her face inches from the gun barrel, stood her ground. 'Unused?'

'Yes,' she said, a lump in her throat. Slowly, very slowly, Haspan lowered the gun and its lights went out again.

'Good. I suppose it needs to connect to the net for updates?'

'Er, yeah, ideally.'

'You want to know the origin of the greenshit?'

Whistler was momentarily thrown by this abrupt change in subject and she stammered briefly as her brain tried to interpret the words. 'Y-y-yes,' she said, inwardly cursing her traitorous voice. 'The greenshit? You know of it?'

'It is an infection. It is making people ill. Soon it may start killing people. I care not for people, their lives or deaths. I am an engineer of death myself,' he said with a touch of pride. 'But I care for bodymodding. Your belief that the two are connected is correct. I believe.'

'We thought it must be. The last two people we harvested both had the green things in them. Both had recent bodymods. Our employer asks – insists – that we find the source and stop it. If we can.'

The bizarre courtiers of the underworld boss were silent, listening to every word, perhaps gauging whether the strangers would walk away unscathed from this meeting or not. The lizards shuffled in their pit. Sofi fidgeted nervously. Her hand kept checking for some weapon that was no longer about her person. The woman in the cage lay motionless.

'You seek the surgeon who made the wings for the city man.'

'Yes. Do you know who it was?'

'I do.'

There was a silence, pregnant with tension and expectation, unasked questions in the air like poison vapour. Whistler looked bravely into the face of the man-monster. His expression was unfathomable. The contours of his body were in flux. She could hear Roberts grinding his teeth.

'Will you tell me?'

Haspan laughed, his shapeless torso quaking with his mirth. The courtiers shuffled worriedly. 'There will be a price,' he said at last.

'What,' said Whistler, 'is the price?'

'Her,' he answered and a slippery-looking tentacle unravelled to point at Sofi, whose expression was horror-struck. Nobody moved or spoke. 'I will take her as a lieutenant in my army. She has the look of a killer.'

'She's not for barter,' asserted Whistler. 'You say you care about the future of bodymodding? Well if this problem goes unsolved there isn't one. You can't take her – she's a lieutenant in *my* army. And she is not for barter.'

'*Your* army?' Again the monster laughed and again nobody else joined in. Whistler stood defiant, knowing that she could die at any moment. 'I WILL TAKE HER IF I WANT!' Haspan bellowed, his voice like an avalanche of syllables filling the room, rumbling back off the curved walls. 'I WILL TAKE HER IF I WANT!' And he was on his feet with a spring faster than his appearance would suggest possible, the U55 coming alive in his hand. He towered several feet above the harvesters like a huge and predatory insect. Gutsy hurriedly backed away across the bridge, body spinning in terror, a veteran of Haspan's rages.

Whistler was trapped. At any second the gang-members would fall on her team and tear them apart like a wolf pack, or Haspan would just mow them down where they stood. She readied her body for the leap that would take her venomous fangs to Haspan's flesh. She would die, but he would die with her. She felt her team primed around her, their bodies wired.

She tried one last, desperate time, to reason with him: 'We can solve this problem if you help us! Or we can both die here, now! All we need is a name! If you won't help us we'll just go. *All* of us. You want this matter resolved just like we do!'

Haspan stood quaking with murderous rage. He looked as if he could tear Whistler's tiny body limb from limb, and perhaps he could. But he did not. The courtiers were transfixed, armed and poised in states of readiness proportional to their inebriation. Whistler's cool blue eyes were on the boss's bestial face. His tusks jutted grotesquely from his snarling mouth. His many arms were twitching and switching like cat's tails. Gradually, seemingly by subtle increments, he sat again upon his absurd chair. The lights on the gun dimmed again. Haspan laid the weapon gently across the vast swathe of his lap and the air of tension seeped away into the shadows of the room like an exhalation.

'Perhaps I will come for her another time,' he muttered sullenly.

'Then I look forward to our *armies* doing battle,' said Whistler coolly. Her heart was pounding in her ears louder than her own voice. 'I don't doubt that you could kill us here and now, here in your lair. Frankly the notion bores me. I don't have the time. *Will you help us or not*?'

'I apologise for boring you,' said Haspan in his creamy, sickeningly sweet voice, seemingly a different person again. '*You* do not bore *me*. Your rudeness is refreshing, an undervalued trait. His name is Spake. A stupid name, and one that does bore me. But he is a good surgeon. His lab is underneath the BBD car park. Callock Street. Now go before I change my mind.'

Whistler exhaled a breath that she hadn't realised she was holding and a tremor went down her spine. Death had been narrowly avoided once again. 'Thank you,' she said, 'for your benevolence.' Not knowing what else to do, she nodded her head in supplication. Haspan waved this nicety away like a bad smell. 'Enjoy your gun.' She sought his gaze again but he wouldn't look at her, like a sulky toddler. Whistler turned, conscious of the staring courtiers, gathering her companions to her like a magnet, and walked back across the bridge. She was unsure whether she had made a friend or an enemy tonight. The robot simply stood there, its weapon-arms twiddling in small circles. 'Come on, then,' she said to it. 'Show us out.'

The robot did not respond, so Whistler repeated her request. Still it didn't budge. She reached out and knocked on its carapace with the knuckles of one hand. Nothing. Aware of the many eyes on her she gave up, brushed past it and hit the pad to open the door. The harvesters left, resisting the urge to look back to ensure that they were not pursued. In the throne room, nobody spoke. The atmosphere that emanated from it was like a chill wind at their backs. The skins of the lizards rustled like dry leaves in their pit, until the massive doors closed again, cutting the sound off. The black-clad guards stood like statues. Whistler and her team retrieved their weapons beneath their steady gaze, self-consciously and as hurriedly as they could. Mercifully Sofi didn't drop anything this time. The parrot was perched atop the head of one of the statues, its yellow stare alien and analytical, its head cocked quizzically. Its insanely bright colouring was actually quite good camouflage in this gaudy room.

Sofi stuffed the micro grenades back into their bandolier where they hung low like a string of explosive sausages. 'I think your robot's broken,' she said to one of the guards. 'It's locked up or some shit.' She pointed back over her shoulder with one thumb towards the throne room. None of the guards moved or answered.

Whistler could feel Roberts's nervousness like an itch. He wanted to leave, a sentiment she echoed. 'Come on,' she said and ushered her companions out into the large outer chamber.

They walked nervously through the forest of disintegrating pillars, agonisingly aware of the guns watching them from the shadows. Without the robot to escort them they moved uneasily, half expecting the guns to chatter into life at any moment, wanting to converse about injury and death in staccato barks of exclamation. There was nobody in the chamber except for the three of them. They passed through it as casually as they could, trying not to look nervous to the people who doubtless surveilled them through video cameras deeper inside the complex.

They passed through the large warehouse door and into the fenced-off alley where the man on the raised platform still stood in the same position. His massive form emanated insolence like body odour. He cradled the mag-rifle gently, like a baby, in one thick arm. Whistler felt his eyes on her back, knew how quickly the rifle could be in the firing position. Her faithful smartgun was thrumming in her pocket like a purring kitten. But she thought that her party would leave unmolested, knew that Haspan would have killed them already had he wanted to. Although he was clearly psychotic and erratic, Whistler felt oddly sure that he would let them go – perhaps as a favour to Roland, perhaps in the hope that they might solve the greenshit riddle. She didn't care why – she was just glad to be leaving.

CHAPTER THIRTEEN

Their journey through the blistered moonscape of the midnight Undercity was as uneventful as could be hoped. Small groups of hoods were propped in dark corners everywhere, clouds of pungent smoke marking their personal spaces like warding spells. Nebulous sound filled the chill air. It was the sound of nothing in particular, and Whistler knew it well. It was the steady respiration of the Undercity itself, a homogenised texture of voices, music, weapon discharges, vehicle noises, so ubiquitous that it was heard almost as a silence.

They stopped outside a metal-ribbed building of cracking plastic. About halfway up its front was a large holo-sign. The sign was no longer projecting but its face still bore the legend BBD in two-metre letters of anodised metal. The building wore a dusting of decay like a veil. Its edges were indistinct with dirt, wear, the ravages of time. The whole of the ground floor had been boarded up. A side-road ran around the left of the building into an unlit car park where a gang of teenagers were racing semi-wild petrol ponies. There were jubilant whoops and screams, muddied in the thunder of engines as the youngsters clung to their mechanical mounts, hammering up and down a makeshift track defined by lumps of masonry. There were six or seven ponies in all – massively tall and solidly built, modified with flamboyant chrome exhaust stacks and free-flow air filters which poked from their armoured hides. One rider, on a mount whose colour looked cherry-red in the darkness and belched flames from its exhaust, side-slammed into a competitor, sending the victim's steed skidding to its knees, spilling the rider off violently in an acrobatic display.

Some of the teenagers rode with bottles in one hand. They wore the deep purple and black of the Nightriders gang. Small timers. Still the harvesters plotted a course around them. They weren't sure exactly where the lab would be located, and frankly it would be hard to see unless they stumbled over it.

Fortunately this was exactly what Roberts did. Even though he was the only one with a night vision mode, he stumbled and fell suddenly as the three picked their way through the brambles around the edge of the car park. Sofi had actually drawn a knife before she even called out to him.

'Ow! Shit!' reported Roberts's unmistakably cultured voice from somewhere on the floor in front of them.

Whistler was a little surprised to see that she was holding the smartgun. The damn thing was insidious. She stuffed it back into her pocket and went cautiously in the direction from which Roberts had yelled. 'What is it?' she asked.

'Bloody steps,' he answered, and Whistler could see him now, apparently kneeling on said flight of steps, rubbing his elbow.

'How's that expensive night vision?' asked Sofi appearing out of the darkness.

Roberts simply glared at her, teeth clenched.

'Is this it then?' asked Whistler, stepping onto the top step. The flight was quite long, maybe sixty steps, and a matt black door stood at the bottom like a darker slash in the gloom, a point at which the shadows had congealed. There was no obvious sign of habitation. The door was just a door – there was no camera, no sentry gun, just a door with one round handle.

'I don't know,' replied Roberts, standing up and brushing some imagined dirt from his long coat.

'I guess we've already ruled out the subtle approach, then,' opined Sofi and she walked down the steps and hammered on the door. The sound clipped abruptly, dying seemingly within the material of the door itself.

Whistler waited, one taloned hand tracing the contours of her smartgun through her pocket. The shouting of the racers was distant now and a bubble of isolation fell over the harvesters as they waited. They had no idea how the surgeon – Spake – would receive them. If things went badly for him he might end up dead.

'Anything on IR?' asked Whistler.

'No,' said Roberts. 'Rest assured, I'd tell you if there was. Oh! Wait–'

The door swung openly rapidly, but only about a hand's width. A pointed and rat-like face peeped out at them. Sofi actually took an involuntary step back.

'*Yes?*' asked the face in an absurd falsetto.

'Are you Spake?'

The little beady eyes darted in the little pointy face like flies in a jar. '*Yes.*'

'We've come to talk to you about some surgery. Can we come in?'

'No.' Something was twitching in the man's face, making one corner of his almost lipless mouth jump up and down. 'Not tradin' any more.'

'Why not?'

'Who are you?' The wheedling voice took on tones of suspicion now, making it even more grating and unpleasant than before. 'Police?'

Whistler allowed herself to laugh lightly, attempting a smile. It proved difficult under the acidic gaze of the surgeon. His darting eyes crawled across Whistler's companions, lingering horribly on Sofi's sleek lines. 'Hardly,' said Whistler, and the eyes flickered back to her. Bony fingers were teasing at the open edge of the door. 'We got your address from Mister Haspan.'

'What do you want?' He looked as if he would just bolt at any moment, back to some deep concrete burrow.

'We need to know where the greenshit is coming from. Do you know what I'm talking about?'

'*Noooo*...Go away!' And he tried to slam the door, but Sofi's foot was in it.

Whistler kicked the door open, sending Spake flying into the wall behind him, off which he rebounded, cracking his head hard. She often found that her body, not her mind, seemed to make the decisions in these situations, and was happy to go with it. She was on him, with the fabric of his dirty white shirt bunched in one hand. She bore down, fangs bared and dripping, suddenly demonic, inhuman. Sofi and Roberts were away down the corridor and already spreading out into the underground bunker, checking for lurking dangers, weapons in hand. Spake shrieked like a woman in an old horror film and tried to wriggle away, clutching for the doorway. Whistler elbowed the door shut and Spake pulled his fingers back just in time, and so narrowly avoided having some surgery to perform upon himself. His eyes were so wide now that they looked as if they would simply roll out of his head and across the floor at any moment.

'What the fuck have you been putting in people?' hissed Whistler, her speech distorted by the swollen venom glands in her cheeks, thick and sybillant.

'Nothing! Noth-nothing! It's not me, it's not me, it's...'

'What about the guy with the parrot wings? The guy with the dragon skin? Were they yours?'

'Okay, okay, there was a guy with wings, yes, but no guy with dragon skin, I don't know no guy with dragon skin!' He was prattling now, out of control, terrified for his life. The grey demon had him in its grip. Sharp claws were at his throat.

'Leo, with the wings – what did you put in him?' Whistler punctuated each word by banging Spake's fragile-looking head on the wall. His weak body lolled and flopped forlornly like an eel seized from the water by a predatory gull and brought to land to be devoured.

'Nothin'! The greenshit, it isn't me!'

'Then who is it?'

'Nobody! Nobody's doing it! Nobody knows where it's coming from.'

Roberts appeared at Whistler's elbow and planted the barrel of his pistol on Spake's head like a full stop. Spake gibbered in fear, spittle flying from his desperately-working lips.

'Fuck it,' said Roberts. 'Let's just plug him. He's lying. I bet he's behind it all. He's putting those things into people for some sick reason of his own. I care not what it is, but maybe the problem will go away when this rat-fuck's brains are on the wall.' He half-depressed the trigger button and the gun began to hum, the sound of an approaching train heard through the tracks.

Spake tried again to escape, but Whistler had her hooks in him and he couldn't move a muscle. She pressed her face into the sweat-stinking hollow of his neck. Venom dripped onto his skin, raising it instantly into welts.

'It isn't me! I don't know what's causing it! People are just getting sick after surgery. I cut one open and there was this *thing* in there! I hadn't fucking put it in there!' He was crying now, all self-respect gone, dissolved in the blue light of his tormentor's eyes. 'When I tried to take it out, it killed her! I'm not tradin' any more! I don't want to kill!'

Whistler leaned back a little, lowering Spake so that his back was on the floor. 'Is that true?' She asked, more to herself than to Spake. She thoughtfully released her grip on his shirt. Her talons had torn it in several places. Roberts kept the gun stuck to Spake's sweaty head, though.

'*Yes*!' he cried desperately. 'Yes! I don't know where they come from. People just get the greenshit after surgery. It defies all fuckin' logic! No science I know has any explanation for it. Please – you gotta believe me!'

Whistler couldn't bear his snivelling, snot-streaked face any more. She stood up and stepped away, brow wrinkled in thought. Roberts, too, stepped back, lifting the gun, resting its stock on his shoulder. In his long coat he looked like something out of a particularly sinister Western, one of the bad guys. Spake didn't dare move – he stayed frozen on the floor.

'Dis one bastard, he got sick after I done some mods for him. He's got it, too, I'm sure of it! He's sick. When I saw him, he looked bad, man. What could I tell him? Take two ibuprofen and lie down?' Spake cackled madly – a sound with no humour in it. 'He's gonna *die*, man! He's got the greenshit! I can't work any more. I don't know how to stop it.'

'Other surgeons are seeing this as well?'

'*Everyone's* seeing it.' Warily, Spake began to get to his feet. The sight of the glowering Sofi appearing round the corner of the corridor stopped him dead and he carefully settled back on the floor again.

'Where is this man you made sick? Where does he live? I think we need to get him to someone who can take a proper look.'

'Sure, sure, I'll tell you.' Spake was sickeningly eager to please. Sofi's disgust was apparent on her face. 'He lives in Teardown, twenty-seven Wrexham Place. His name is Vivao. He's real sick, but it wasn't me! I swear it wasn't me!'

Sofi said, 'Shall we take this freak with us? In case he's lying?'

Spake's face quivered in fresh terror at this prospect. Large and greasy-looking tears began to ooze down his cheeks. 'No – no!' he gibbered. 'I'm not lying!'

Whistler didn't answer Sofi – instead she asked Spake, 'What is causing it? If you know anything, tell us now. We wouldn't want to have to come back again.'

'I don't know – maybe one of the drugs we use in surgery, or after – maybe one of them leaves people prone to infection by the greenshit. P'raps the greenshit 's everywhere, waitin' for the right conditions to grow. Maybe something in the nanovat software we use to grow mods is makin' it happen. I've checked it over though and I didn't find nothin'. I only use clean software, man – it's all legit, honest! Nobody knows why it's happenin'. Nobody!'

'Why is it only in the Undercity – the black market?' asked Roberts. He twirled the gun in small, emphatic circles as he spoke.

'It fuckin' ain't, man,' said Spake earnestly. 'At first, maybe, but people are walking out of *legitimate* bodyshops with it, now. It's gonna cause an economic meltdown, or some shit. They can't keep it quiet for long. I dunno what's goin' on, but it's way too big for you boys 'n' girls. I'm shuttin' shop and movin' into drugs or something.'

'How noble of you,' said Whistler, and kicked him. Spake squeaked and tried to back into the wall. 'Anything in his shop?' she asked the others.

'No,' said Roberts. 'Only surgical kit, drugs and an evident and frightening lack of hygiene. Vat looks damned ancient but the stats are all okay. You think we should take it, maybe let Tec strip it down?'

'No, man!' cried Spake, holding out his hands in appeal. 'You can't take my vat! Please!'

'Why would you fucking need it?' demanded Whistler. 'I thought you were moving into drugs.'

'Please, I have a wife to support – I'll sell it, or just sell the components. I need it!'

Whistler wrinkled her face up in distaste. 'We'd probably catch some disease off it anyway. Come on.'

They squeezed past the cowering Spake and out. Sofi, who never liked to be left out of anything, kicked him on the way past, harder than Whistler had done. Her face was expressionless. They climbed the steps back into the chill night air. The car park was a desolate waste. Disused tenements hovered like spectres in the fog. From somewhere came a thunderous symphony of petrol engines – the racers had moved on into the streets, where they continued their sport out of sight, the heavy clattering of metal hooves echoing up and down the road.

The three harvesters stood in the wide space, their hearts heavy and hopes diminished. Whistler began to feel a suppressive sleepiness creeping up on her. She knew it was the adrenaline wearing off and patted herself down for the Get-Up stubby. She clicked it in her palm without taking it out. Roberts heard the quiet hiss and demanded a dose himself. His face was haggard and his scar looked more deeply etched than usual. He took the Get-Up, clicked, then stood momentarily trembling as it surged through his blood. His knuckles whitened around the plastic cylinder of the stubby. He shook himself like a dog drying itself and offered the Get-Up to Sofi. She took it, clicked it, handed it back, displaying no outward effects of the drug at all. Sofi had the constitution of a dinosaur – nothing seemed to affect her much, except early mornings.

'Where was it, again, Rob?' asked Whistler.

'Twenty-seven Wrexham Place. Guy called Vivao.'

Whistler knew Roberts to be a useful repository of knowledge. He ran a smart-app on his DNI which picked out salient pieces of information in speech or text and recorded them. Occasionally he would have to change the spot behind his ear. Sofi could have done the same, naturally, but such administrative tasks bored her to a state of near-depression. Sofi was a fighter, not a secretary.

'Right, then, let's go see him. Direct us.'

'Let's get the van, then. I've done enough bloody walking for today,' said Sofi.

Roberts's eyes narrowed as he communicated with the wagon. Whistler waited impatiently, kicking her heels. Bits of rubbish drifted past like modern tumbleweeds.

'Well?' prompted Sofi, one hand on her hip. Roberts looked eminently puzzled. '*Well*?' she repeated with added rudeness.

'I couldn't get any sense from it. I think something's scrambling the signal. *Shit*! I hope the damn thing hasn't got a virus. I guess we should go and get it, then.'

'Right!' exclaimed Sofi, severely displeased and already turning and stalking off into the night. 'Fucking come on, then!' she bellowed without stopping.

'Who hired her, again?' asked Roberts drily.

Whistler shrugged. 'Seemed a good idea at the time. Come on.'

'Yeah, I know, I know.' The two trailed after Sofi, not trying to catch her up. 'Look, maybe we can get Vivao tomorrow – call it a night for now. *She's* obviously in a strop again.'

'Yeah, I'd love to. I'm burned, to be honest. But what if this guy dies overnight? He's no use to us then. We don't have any other leads to go on.'

'You believe the surgeon?'

'About what?' Sofi was waiting for them at the edge of the car park, throwing and catching her knife with implied menace.

'About all of it – the scale of it, him not knowing what's causing it. All of it.'

'Yay!' said Sofi with sarcastic joy as they caught her up. 'Slow team crosses the line.'

'Give me a break, Sofe,' said Whistler. A large unmarked truck was jack-knifed across the road outside the car park, all its doors open, its interior utterly plundered. It hadn't been there when they had come in this way. Probably the Nightriders – they could be heard in the distance, whooping war cries as they raced away. Maybe they weren't so small-time these days.

'Yes, oh leader,' mocked Sofi, bowing low. Whistler round kicked to the side of her head, but only playfully. Sofi wheeled away, striking up a fighting pose. 'Yeah?' she taunted. 'Yeah?'

'Come on, you young lovers,' said Roberts, and he headed off in the direction where the van was parked in a spot designated safe by Roland earlier that night.

They trudged in a haze of drugs and tiredness through the shifting Undercity greys. Whistler felt like a woman crossing a desert on the verge of fatal dehydration, even though they only walked for a couple of miles. Pods were on the street here and there, sneaking quietly about their business. There weren't many people around, though. The few small groups they saw seemed to deliberately avoid them. Possibly, Whistler reflected, Sofi's heavily scowling face was proving an effective deterrent.

Once, they passed a tumbledown breeze-block house where a mottled weed as big as a tree had forced its way in and out of the walls as if sewing the decaying fabric of the building together. In one corner a cloud of spyflies buzzed in confused congregation, trapped between equidistant scrambler-baits, not near enough to be drawn in, but too fearful of their proximity to move. The trio stood and regarded them interestedly for a minute before concluding that yes, it was weird, but no, it wasn't important enough to stand and stare at. They forced themselves to move on.

They reached the shaded alcove where the van was parked, a shadow wrapped in shadows, seeming to deflect any attempts to look at it directly. Nobody had touched it, as evidenced by the fact that it was still here and there were no loose body-parts scattered about.

'Hey, wagon,' said Whistler and the door opened. The van nosed out of its filthy stable to facilitate their boarding, bobbing minutely on its cushion.

'Why didn't you answer me, you sod?' demanded Roberts as he climbed aboard. 'I was calling you.'

The van was not allowed an actual voice – Whistler hated when it spoke, although she couldn't explain exactly why – so it didn't answer vocally. She was fond of it as a functional tool, but no more than that. She knew that Roberts would be conversing with it by DNI. Sofi scarcely had anything to say to the van. She hardly spoke to anybody unless she had to, and viewed any communication with the van as yet another chore. But Roberts spent hours chatting with the damn thing sometimes. Whistler couldn't imagine how it had that much to say.

Roberts took the main computer console and Whistler assumed her customary driving position. Sofi sat in her usual space in the back, where she judged herself least likely to be called upon to actually do anything or say anything. Telltale LEDs, holo-cubes and screens lit up festively, tie-dying the shadows with colour.

'Hey, I've got a message from Tec on here,' said Roberts, his fingers playing across a virtual keypad.

'A *message*?' asked Whistler, half-turning.

'Yeah, says he couldn't get through to us direct, but he managed to get the van. He's taken in some stray. I think he said the guy had come from the sewers.'

'Great!' enthused Sofi sarcastically. 'Why does everything have to be bursting with the fucking bizarre?'

'The sewers?' parroted Whistler.

'Yeah, that's what he says. I've sent back to let him know we're okay. He says this guy needs some computer time, and he can pay well if they can figure out how to access his accounts.'

'*If*? What the fuck is *if*?'

'A conjunction meaning *on condition that*,' answered Roberts in flat tones.

'Fuck you!' shrieked Sofi, making to get out of her seat.

'We'd better find this guy Vivao first,' answered Roberts without looking up.

Whistler was impressed that Sofi managed to ignore this and sank instead back into her seat, nose pressed to the translucent skin of the van, glass-eyed and rage unusually contained. Whistler drove them out into the narrow street. Thunderheads were steam-rollering the sky to the south. Roland's place was nearby and she considered how preferable it would be to spend the next hour or two talking weapons with him in the warmth of his 'office' rather than pursuing this fool's errand. But business was business and pay days had to come back round again soon or they were all in deep trouble.

She took her frustrations out on the controls of the van, careening through the quiet streets aggressively. She turned out wide and swerved into the apex of a sharp corner, opening the throttle all the way. Indeterminate objects whooshed past close on the left, the noise of their passing so loud that several times Sofi thought they had actually hit something and appealed to Whistler to ease off. She was entirely ignored. The van raced on through the Undercity. A dopey bird took off too late from its path and thumped on the front of it like a thrown bundle of rags, disappearing into its wake in a cloud of feathers.

Soon Roberts informed Whistler that Wrexham Place was just two blocks away. She began to slow down, her body visibly relaxing in proportion to the reduction in velocity. They would have to close in on foot, hopefully a little more clandestinely than they had approached Spake's place. She found a corner enclosed by squat buildings housing huge cable-car motors. Tall pylons wore massive gears like medals. The cable draped off into the dark streets. Snarls of untwining wire bunched along its length. Far away a single cable-car hung motionless before a vast warehouse, its broken windows like haunted eyes.

They tucked the van into the crease between two of the small buildings where the snaggle of machinery would break up its lines and blend it in. The dead street in front of it would make for a long, clear avenue of fire should anyone approach uninvited. The van was left to make the calls regarding its defence. It had used to have a camouflage projector at one time, but something had gone wrong with the complex equipment that ran it and Whistler had never paid to have Tec fix it. She preferred to be able to see the thing when it was needed.

They disembarked, hardly talking, and Roberts pointed them in the right direction. A thin, bat-winged young woman in hooker's uniform watched them from across the road, smoking moodily. Her body was rippled with additional breasts and her wings beat lazily at the air like an idling engine. Her legs were pallid wax in the darkness. A bass-heavy sound system was pumping out the Deaf Composer's *Spunk, Funk and Junk* from somewhere in the bowels of the building behind her and the sound-waves tore at her reeferette smoke with each throb of the bass.

'Look at that fucking gargoyle,' commented Sofi, nodding towards the young woman.

'No accounting for taste, Sofe,' replied Whistler as they set off towards Wrexham Place on foot, Roberts following behind like a bodyguard.

They walked in the shade of a line of low towerblocks. Across the road a swathe of bare, scarred earth stretched away into the night. It looked like the grave where a park had been buried. People, or at least humanoids, of indeterminate number were running around in the darkness there. Whistler saw Roberts staring at them, presumably observing them by infrared, his face set and squinting. He didn't say anything, so she assumed it was safe. Sofi kicked a can and it clattered racketously into the littered depths of a faceless old shop.

'Keep it down!' Whistler hissed, more harshly than she had really intended. Roberts simply shook his head contemptuously.

They rounded a corner and Roberts ushered them into the cover of a khaki-coloured bush that bloomed before a block of flats like a cloud of smoke. There was a wide hollow in the bush like a cave and they pressed themselves tightly into the piss-stinking space. The ground was springy with a thick mulch of rotting paper and food-wrappers. Some lights were on in the block but their temporary hiding place was well-concealed from at least three sides.

Roberts pointed to a corner ahead of them where another generic, squarish building sat, immense and colourless, spotted with sickly lights as if habitation was a disease it had caught from its neighbours. 'There,' he said. 'Twenty-seven, yeah?'

'Yeah, okay.'

'Do you think there's another way in besides the front door?'

Sofi peered out and said, 'Yeah, it looks like there's a path round to the back – let's try that. Might just lead to gardens or yards, but maybe we can climb up.'

'*Climb*?' asked Roberts. 'No.'

'Well let's have a look, anyway,' said Whistler. 'Try not to look too shifty. If we get seen, I'd prefer that we don't *look* as if we're trying not to.'

'Okay,' agreed Roberts. 'So – everybody sneak out of the bush without looking suspicious. Sofi, maybe you'd better stay here.'

'Yeah?' she retorted without pause, 'and maybe you'd better prepare to be severely beaten about your already misshapen head, you prick!'

'You two, just come on!' ordered Whistler.

They filed out into the street. A huge man with a surgically-widened chest and the proportions of a gorilla was coming down the pavement towards them. His face was broad and ugly in an honest kind of way. His massive forearms sprouted hairily from the sleeves of his overstretched t-shirt. As he passed them he grunted 'Orlright darlin',' to Whistler. She managed not to shoot him, even though she knew the smartgun wanted to. Sofi turned to follow him but Whistler ushered her away down the street towards Wrexham Place.

They cut across the narrow strip of scraggy grass in front of the block and headed down the side of the building in silent single file, walking confidently but not too quickly. Somebody on a balcony above them ducked back inside and slammed the door behind them. A dog was barking with brain-numbing regularity, high and hoarse and pathetic from behind a rickety fence. It didn't cease as they moved away. A spyfly skittered past, doing one unsteady circle around them. Roberts swatted absently at it, missing.

The narrow pathway encompassed a series of wooden gates that presumably led into the yards of those properties lucky enough to have them. At the far end of the path, on the corner of the building itself, was a door of mesh-reinforced glass in a metal frame. Sofi tried the handle and it turned smoothly with the ease of any well-used machine. Quietly, the three stepped inside into a corridor lit only by the moonlight filtering creamily through the grimy windows. The walls and ceiling were of stained concrete prefab pieces and the floor was covered in cracked and peeling linoleum.

Whistler found a small plastic plaque bearing the flat numbers and their relative floors. 'Twenty-seven...' she read aloud. 'Floor four. Let's go.'

They climbed the stairs and exited the stairwell onto a bare landing. Twenty-seven was directly before them. They stood and looked at it, quiet with foreboding. No light filtered underneath the door. Roberts pressed his ear to the cheap laminate and listened intently for a moment. Then he stepped back and stared at it. 'Nothing,' he said.

'Well,' said Whistler. 'Let's knock, shall we?'

Roberts made a non-committal face and hammered on the door with the heel of his hand. The sound boomed and echoed around the gaping corridor, rolling away into the bowels of the building and back again in decreasing waves. They waited.

'Maybe he isn't in,' suggested Sofi, almost hopefully.

'Ee focken' is,' said a small, high-pitched voice behind them.

Whistler whirled around and the gun was in her hand. It's barrel keenly homed in on the source of the voice. A small, desperately thin young boy of perhaps six years stood behind them holding a filthy blanket whose end trailed on the dusty floor and had clearly gathered up quantities of dirt with some sort of capillary action. His hair was the no-colour of the malnourished and his face was smeared with what looked like coal-dust. Whistler lowered the weapon, its suspensor field actually resisting for a split-second.

'What?' she asked.

'Oi sed ee focken' is in – oi sin 'im go in dere. 'Im looked focken' well ruff un' all.'

'What – like sick?'

'Focken' well sick, yeh.' The boy agitated the blanket slightly, making its trailing end pick up several dust-bunnies. 'Ee ent gone out nowhere, neiver. Ee's still in dere. Got any dollar?'

'Sure,' said Roberts and crossed the filthy, extended palm with a couple of coins.

'Let's kick it in,' said Sofi, standing back and readying herself to do just that.

'Try once more, first,' said Whistler.

Sofi huffed but knocked again. They waited to see what effect, if any, this would have. Whistler looked around and was satisfied to see that the little boy had departed. 'Boot it,' she said.

Sofi push-kicked the flimsy door and it virtually disintegrated into splinters of aged, brittle plywood. The harvesters surged into the flat, armed and wired. There was a corridor from which doors led off to left and right. There was a faint noise coming from somewhere in the flat – a wet slobbering, thick and glutinous like bubbling mud. Whistler flattened herself against the door-frame, her gun held at the ready and her spine convulsing with shivers. She couldn't hold the weapon steady and it had to dampen the shaking of her hand. There was something very wrong here and looking at the faces of her companions she knew they felt it too. There was a stench of convalescence and excrement in the turgid air, but there was something else as well. It was like the stink of rotting cabbage, but with hints of some chemical contaminant wrapped around it.

There came a pitiful mewling from the far end of the corridor. The harvesters froze in place, nobody breathing. One tatter of splintered wood still hung from a door-hinge – it softly swung to with a quiet squeak. Whistler felt a pressure building in her head, as if her brain was swelling in her skull. The tension was palpable. Roberts laid a hand on her forearm, making her jump. 'Cat,' he said in a stage whisper.

A tortoiseshell cat slunk cautiously around the corner at the far end of the corridor, rubbing its head against the wall. Again it called out sadly and came towards them. It was very thin and its fur was matted and dirty. A thin crusting of dried blood encircled the base of one ear like a bizarre piece of feline jewellery. Its dull orange eyes bored into Whistler's own. It was hungry. It came closer, slipping through the gloom with slow and deliberate grace, its body weaving, fish-like. The humans watched it approach. The smell was starting to make Whistler gag. She fought against nausea. Fear and welling sadness were at war within her.

Sofi crouched and reached out for the cat and suddenly it bolted with a flick of its tail. It disappeared around the corner and Sofi made to follow it. *Careful*, said Whistler and she realised that she had only thought it. Already Sofi was moving down the corridor. Roberts and Whistler looked to each other and then followed her into the stinking darkness. The gun was a tense little animal in her hand, trembling with anticipation.

They rounded the end of the passage as quietly as they could. Roberts jumped when an old board creaked beneath his foot. He paused for a split-second and Whistler heard his sharp intake of breath. They stepped into the small kitchen and saw Sofi standing in shock, her gun lowered, looking around herself. 'The *smell*,' she said, her face contorted in disgust. 'Oh *man*, what *is* that?'

'*Ohhhhh...*' Roberts groaned, repulsed.

Whistler fought her rising gorge and failed. She put her hands on her knees and was noisily sick onto the floor. The bright splatter was not actually the most unappealing thing down there. Rotting food was smeared everywhere, mixed with general dirt and dust into a gooey paste of earthy colours. Staring down into this mess didn't help her either. Roberts looked around fearfully. The noise had been very loud in the little room.

'Ladylike,' commented Sofi, but quietly.

Whistler was unable to answer. She stood doubled over with her lower lip dripping bile. After a long while she said, simply, '*Shit...*'

'There's something not right here,' said Roberts unnecessarily. His eyes were like those of a hunted animal, wide and mobile.

Whistler straightened delicately and combed the smartgun through her hair, trying to pull herself together. The thick taste of the vile air was still in her throat and she didn't think any amount of vomiting would get it out. The cat was pacing a small circle in front of a cupboard, presumably the one-time source of its food. The cupboard was bare now, its door hanging by one hinge. Bright scraps of cardboard were scattered in front of it and Whistler realised that they were the remnants of a cat-food box that had been torn open and scoured clean.

The trio wandered round the kitchen cataloguing the signs of neglect. The cat mewled more insistently, ignored. Sofi poked a plate of putrefying matter with the muzzle of her gun. A plastic carton of synthetic milk lay on its side as if it had just given up and lain down to die amidst all the decay. Its contents were a yellow stain across the worktop, jellified around mouldy hunks of bread and cereal. The kitchen blinds were drawn, but it looked as if it had been done with some force, for several of the slats had been torn clean away. The window faced the bare wall of a neighbouring block. Its bricks looked solid and normal but the grubby pane was like a force-field between two opposing worlds. There was a circular table in the middle of the floor and one of its chairs had been pushed away violently enough to gouge tracks in the carpet of dirt and lay upside-down with its legs in the air like a dead deer.

'What happened here?' breathed Sofi.

'And where is he?' added Roberts in a voice full of grim significance.

'I wish that fucking cat would shut up,' said Whistler.

'Feed it,' suggested Roberts.

'Shoot it,' suggested Sofi.

The smell was coming in waves now, almost too much to bear. Sofi was determinedly attempting to open the window when there was an ear-splitting roar, thick with mucous and agony, utterly bestial. Everyone froze and a collective shudder went through them. Their eyes all rolled towards the kitchen wall. On the other side of it was one of the rooms they had passed on their way into the kitchen. The sound had assuredly issued from there.

Something smashed deafeningly against the interior wall. The round plastic clock that hung there fell off to crack open on the floor below, sowing the bed of food waste with little cogs and wheels. The cat skittered away into a corner, hissing like a pressure cooker. Whistler, wasting no time at all, shouldered back into the corridor. Roberts, his face craggy in the gloom, was at her elbow and Sofi was a honed presence on her mental radar, hot on her heels.

Something was going berserk in the room next to the kitchen. A large animal could be heard bounding about in there, smashing or spilling furniture like a living tornado. The roaring was rising to a crescendo, sustained and ululating, as Whistler crashed into the door, meaning to burst into the room. Sofi was calling out to Vivao by name, shouting reassuring words in a voice unreassuringly close to panic. The door didn't budge a millimetre. Roberts lent his weight to the effort as inside the room glass tinkled. The roaring suddenly became a whimpering, incredibly high and mindless. Sofi brushed the others away and shot out the hinges of the door, stretching tall to point her gun downwards towards the floor. The weapon barked and the door shifted but did not fall in. Silence now from within the room. Roberts barrelled into the door again and this time it leaned in at the top and came to rest on some object inside the room, making a ramp. Whistler's team climbed over it as rapidly as they could.

Inside there was a scene of utter domestic devastation. Tables and chairs lay shattered and almost homogenised into a heap of debris. Jags of broken china and glass littered the floor like glittering sawdust. Clothing, burnt, torn and soiled was strewn over the wreckage. Water was flowing across the floor from the stump of a pipe that had once fed a radiator. The smell was beyond belief. There was a faint greenish tinge to the light within the room – it buzzed at the edges of visibility, issuing from no discernible source. Vivao was nowhere in sight.

The harvesters fanned out into the devastated space, their guns stabbing left and right as they endeavoured to cover all angles simultaneously. Silence fell, but for the rapid breathing of the three interlopers. Whistler trod softly in a circle around the perimeter of the room. Broken chunks of furniture brushed against her shins and a protruding staple cut her shallowly on one leg, unnoticed.

'Where is he? Where is he?' Sofi was repeating frantically, struggling to breathe in the stinking atmosphere, head whipping left and right, her mohawks lurid fans of colour – and then Whistler saw him.

Vivao's body lay crumpled beneath a curtain that had separated the main living room from a small alcove, theatrically sprawled with arms and legs tangled bonelessly. The curtain still hung from its rail at one end. 'Here,' said Whistler, but the others were already beside her, their weapons lowering slowly.

Vivao's fingers were thick claws, tapered and monstrous and one hand dripped with dark fluid. One of his feet twitched and then was still. His hair was long and scraggly and his face incredibly thin and harrowed, bumpy and blotched as if some fungus had grown in his skin. A sick green pallor was on his features like a halloween mask. His eyes had rolled all the way up into his skull. He was dressed in the clinging tatters of what had once been a t-shirt and combats. Whistler was somehow quite sure that the hue of his skin was not due to any deliberate bodymod. It looked too *unhealthy*, somehow, and the effect was too convincing to be intentional. She leaned in closer, aware that she was mechanically saying his name, and a despicable squeamishness, totally unlike her, came over her. She saw that he had torn his own throat out. Then she was choking on the smell, reeling away, her head spinning dizzyingly, unable to focus.

'Look,' said Sofi and her voice was small and childlike. She pointed down to where Vivao's blood was pooling on the floor. Although the light was low, it was clear to Whistler what was happening. The blood was separating itself into two distinct colours like oil and water demulsifying. One was red and the other was a deep emerald green.

CHAPTER FOURTEEN

Tomas awoke gradually from a strange and frightening dream in which insects buzzed in clouds about his head, their scatty flight-paths random and confusing. As he incrementally became conscious of reality he was puzzled to discover that the buzzing sound had followed him, somehow, into the waking world. He stretched carefully, trying not to wake his slumbering girlfriend who was sprawled expansively over most of the bed. He sat, gingerly rotating his neck to loosen the knotted muscles. It was still dark beyond the window. The buzzing noise came from outside. His DNI told him it was only three in the morning. Three o'clock?

Tomas swung his legs out of the bed and stood up. The heating was off and the chill air raised his skin in goosebumps. He went to the window and drew the blind to try to see the source of the noise. It was immediately apparent what was making the sound and Tomas's brow furrowed in consternation. He was transfixed by the scene outside.

Swarms of spyflies were in flight out there. They coiled in vast clouds across the moonlit sky, spiralling in corkscrewed funnels like whirlwinds. There must have been millions of them flying in this hectic, swirling formation. He'd had no idea that there were so many in all the world. He could see the breeze created by their massed rotors stirring odd bits of rubbish in the streets below. He watched them raptly, trying to work out the logic behind their unprecedented behaviour. One hand scratched his stubbled chin.

The moon was high, the streets almost empty, the sky crystal-clear, the usual promise of rain a distant rumour. This was a good neighbourhood and only the local rent-a-cops were on the street. Several of them stood on the pavement below, watching the strange clouds in the sky, excitedly conversing. The twister of spyflies danced up into the sky, elongating, and dropped again low to the ground, compressing, but never touching down. Small trickles of newly arriving spyflies ran into the main body of the corkscrew and joined it. Tomas could not see any of the tiny robots leaving. What were they up to? Had there been some sort of massive system crash?

He watched them for a long time, hypnotised, trying to discern order within the chaos, failing. His reverie was broken only when he sensed movement within the room itself. He turned from the window to see Jalis sitting up in bed, hair attractively tousled, watching him.

'What are you doing, Tom?'

'Have you seen this?' he asked.

'Seen what?'

'Out here...' He turned again to the window. The rent-a-cops had moved on but across the street several other sets of blinds were drawn and pale faces peeped out into the night. 'It's weird.'

'What?' she asked groggily. 'Tom, it's half-three in the morning. Come back to bed.'

And he did. But Tomas found that sleep was a long time coming, and when it came it brought with it puzzling visions of dark and living clouds. Now the insects were machines, and their black wings thrummed the air like electricity. Their tiny maws were fanged and leering. They danced through the air and Tomas ran from them. He knew that the insects themselves would not harm him, but somehow he was certain that their swarming was a precursor to something worse. He didn't know what it was, but still he ran, his naked feet slapping on the pavement while the sky overhead came to life. When he woke again at seven the swarm outside had gone.

CHAPTER FIFTEEN

'Can't we just go?' asked Sofi pleadingly. She sounded close to tears. Nobody had the lightness of spirit to tease her for it. The situation was too bizarre – they all felt the same way. Water from the broken radiator was pooling around their feet, turgidly stirring small bits of detritus. Tiny whirlpools and currents swirled as if the surface of the floor was crawling.

'We need to speak to Tec,' insisted Whistler. Roberts was already contacting him, pacing in the furthest corner he could reach, with his shirt bunched over his nose and mouth. 'He might want us to bring the body back.' She was aware that her own face was lined with repulsion at this thought.

'Really?' asked Sofi. 'And what do you think we might learn from it? Tec won't find anything that HGR didn't, will he. We don't have the resources, the equipment. Let's just get out of here.' She saw that Whistler's resolve was eroding. She wanted to leave, too, and Sofi pressed on. 'Our only hope was finding out who was infecting people and stop them, right? Well, the surgeon we found knew no more than we do about it, if you believe him. And what will we find by examining the body that HGR didn't find themselves?'

'...I guess,' mused Whistler. She knew that Sofi was correct, really, that she was only clutching at straws. What could they learn from the diseased and possibly infectious corpse sprawled in the two-tone pool of slime on the floor? Outside, the sun was coming up. Whistler desperately wanted to be out there with it, to feel the gentle warmth on her skin, to smell the relatively clean air of the city, to take it deep into her chest and flush the vileness out of her body. She felt tainted.

Sofi continued: 'There's something really wrong here, boss. I vote we give it up, leave it to the big boys and girls, and move into black market or some shit. Anything. Anything but this, really. I don't know what's going on here, and I don't think I want to. I say we burn that fucking thing and go. Or better yet, just go.' Her eyes were drawn again to the body on the floor. Its face was locked in an expression of mindless terror and agony.

'Since when does anybody get a vote, Sofe? This isn't a democracy, you know.' But all of them knew that Whistler actually did listen to their concerns, even if she might claim otherwise. 'Let's just hear what Tec says. Hang steady a mo, Sofi, okay?' Sofi's face trembled, whether in disgust, tiredness or fear Whistler didn't know.

'I spoke to Tec,' said Roberts, interrupting. He didn't mean 'spoke to' in the vocal sense, of course.

'And?' asked Whistler.

'And he says leave the body if we're concerned about it.'

'Okay, then,' said Whistler, openly relieved.

'Fucking right, I'm concerned!' stated Sofi. 'Can we go then – talk on the hoof?'

'Okay,' agreed Whistler. 'That's all I wanted.'

They left the flat, hands clapped over noses against the stench, all equally relieved to be out of there. There wasn't much door left now, but they did their best to close what remained. Once on the landing the smell began to diminish and conversation resumed.

'This guy who appeared at the base,' said Roberts, 'Tec says he's been telling him some crazy stuff, says if it's true then we may have other trouble, too.'

'Guy?' asked Whistler, rubbing her temples, trying to massage her exhausted brain into life. 'Trouble?'

'Yeah, the stray from the sewers, remember? Well this guy is saying there's something wrong in the net, sounds like something big. Why we have to be involved in it, I don't know. Tec was jabbering on and on, well excited – he says we should leave it, just come back home. He doesn't want our messed-up corpse in his lab, for some reason. I actually thought he'd want to cut it up or something – you know what he's like. He suggests that we try another angle. I agree with him, if it matters.'

'Yeah, me too,' said Whistler. 'I guess. I'm fucking vexed, though – I thought maybe we could sort this out easily.' They headed down the stairs onto the ground floor. The grubby child of earlier was no longer in evidence.

Whistler stopped as they headed out of the main doors and angled across the grass, looking back at the building for a moment, falling behind the others. Roberts noticed and returned. He put a companionable hand on her back and spoke to her softly. She liked it when he took this quietly-understated tone of surety. She imagined it was how a father should speak to you, reassuring without being condescending. 'I hate to say it, but maybe we should just put this on the back burner for now. I don't see where else we can go with it. Let's go home, get some sleep, see what's up with Tec and this guy, think of our next move. I don't believe *that* damn thing,' he pointed back up towards Vivao's flat, 'can teach us jack. We have some funds in the company account. Let's stand back and get perspective.' Whistler looked into his rocky face, his eyes alert and intelligent behind their film of tiredness. She nodded. 'Okay?' he pressed.

'Okay,' she said, grateful to him for somehow making her feel all right again. Roberts was a genuine hard-case, but he had heart in there too. 'Let's go home.' She tried to smile but it came out somewhere between wan and grimace.

As they turned to follow Sofi, who hadn't waited for them, she couldn't resist one look back at the silent, ominous tower. *What the hell just happened here?* For a moment Whistler could feel the spinning of the world − faster and faster, accelerating out of control. Something was happening and she knew they were missing the big picture. Avenues of investigation led to more questions; uncertainty had leeched into even the most formidable bastions of normality. Who was the stray Tec had taken in? What new problems did he represent? What could be done about this infection? What had happened to Vivao? It seemed he had been changed by the strange parasitic organ in some way. Had he killed himself for fear of what was happening to him or fear of being found? Whistler felt totally lost, totally vulnerable before a storm she could not see coming.

They pretty much let the van drive itself back to base, so tired were they all. Sofi played some psi-trance from a spot on her hand but it only made Whistler feel more sleepy and she demanded silence. Occasionally, she would partially take over control of the van until she came close to hitting another pod or a lamp-post, at which point she would slump back into her seat again. The Undercity passed around them like scrolling film footage − a shimmering collage of mottled shadows. The sun was rising in the sky like a downed fighter dazedly returning to the fray. It looked distant, alien and cold. A suspension of water vapour hung in the air, wanting to become rain. People were starting to crawl out onto the streets and go about their daily business. Once a convoy of police pods screamed past them, heading deeper into the Undercity, sirens howling and roofs ablaze with coloured lights. Dazed and half-asleep, the harvesters barely noted their passing. Sofi was nodding off, her head bouncing against the skin of the van where it rested, her eyes closing sleepily and then flicking open only to gradually close again.

The van did its job admirably, following whatever arcane beacons guided it. It slipped into the underground car park that led to the team's base like a shadow fleeing the swelling daylight. Whistler had cracked a slit in the van's shell to allow for fresh air (or the Undercity's approximation of fresh air, at least) and a cool grey scent of damp concrete filled the vehicle. Sofi shuddered and awoke, presumably subconsciously alerted to either the smell of home or the specific turns and bumps of the van that told her brain exactly where they were. For all Whistler knew, she could have set a satellite positioning marker to sound an alarm into her brain or something. Either way, she sat up and stretched, cat-like, her joints popping audibly. Roberts looked round at her, half-smiling, but didn't speak. The atmosphere was depressed, subdued. They all knew that things were moving beyond their control. They had few options left and the lack of harvesting work for the foreseeable future spelled uncertainty, perhaps even an end, for their mutual association. Questions about the man Tec and Spider had admitted to the base, and the nature of the problem he had brought with him, swam darkly in the depths of all their minds.

The van picked its way between the pillars with geometric precision, taking its time. It tended to drive itself more carefully than any of its human operators did, possessing as it did a degree of self-preserving instinct. And after all, it had not been expressly commanded to hurry. As usual there was nobody else around in the underground car park that served all the abutting industrial units, although another van – white, older than their own, at least equally nondescript – was parked jaggedly in front of one of the doors opposite. Their van scanned it thoroughly, finding nothing untoward and so not bothering to even alert its human passengers. Little did they know how carefully it micro-managed their interests and safety sometimes.

They paused beneath the sentry guns as the heavy garage door tilted in at the top and slowly raised with a metallic grinding. The van slipped inside and parked itself neatly in its hangar. The room was bright and clinical – a shrine in which the van formed a dark and slab-like altar. Its door irised open and it disgorged its passengers, ragged and dirty onto the highly-polished floor. They looked like bits of litter that had blown in. Whistler led them through the security door into the grim confines of the team's living quarters. Tec was hunched over a console in his lab, pretty much in the same position they had left him, as if time, passing normally outside, had been frozen in this subterranean den where wires and computer parts crowded every surface, the flotsam and jetsam of a chaotic tide never actually seen in motion. The woolly fluorescent light of the console's holo illuminated his form like an aura. He did not notice them behind him until Whistler coughed politely.

Tec jumped as if he had touched a live electrical contact amongst the jumble on his desk and turned round. His stubbled face cracked in a relieved grin. 'Hey, guys,' he greeted them and they could see the frenzied intelligence that capered behind his eyes. His head was a shimmering glitter of contradictory colours.

'Hey, Tec,' they responded variously.

'Come in,' he invited, as if the process of squeezing another three human beings into the tiny room was actually an easy one. They shuffled around each other like the tiles of a sliding puzzle, Whistler ending up next to Tec and the others crammed just inside the doorway. Roberts leant against a shelving unit which shifted. A drift of tiny components and miniature electronics tools slid off the shelf and became one with the mass of similar items on the floor. Roberts looked sheepish and stood up straight. Tec held his tongue although a stripe of irate red blazed down the centre of his head.

'So what's up with this guy?' asked Whistler, aware that she might not really want to hear the answer now, at nine in the morning, which sounded to her pretty undeniably like bed time.

Tec puffed his cheeks out as if to say *What* isn't *up with the guy?* and answered in a rattling blur of something that was certainly English but that Whistler had the most inordinate difficulty in following: 'Well, he came here via the sewer system, and frankly he was damned lucky to make it with some of the shit that lives down there, and he's apparently on the run from some sinister agency or other, he's been working for them, he says, but even he doesn't know who they really are, he's some insane computer hacker, I mean some of the stuff he's shown me is off the scale, the guy is simply a genius, but he says there's some *thing* in the net, he believes the people he was working for are behind it, but he also thinks he helped to *prime* it himself, somehow, and this thing might have put a virus in his head, he reckons, he was scared half to death when we let him in, if Jalan hadn't sent him, I don't know that we wouldn't have let the guns eat him, I've been running all sorts of diagnostics on him, he's got some fucking chip in his head that he *made himself*, but so far we haven't—'

Whistler held up her hands to stop him. 'Wow, Tec, man, I know you're saying things, but frankly I've no fucking idea what they might be, let alone mean. As long as everything's under control, tell me in the morning.' She started to rise.

'It *is* the morning,' said Tec, deflated, the lights slowing to a standstill on his skull.

'*Tomorrow* morning, then,' said Whistler, placing a conciliatory hand on his shoulder. 'I'm done in. Take care with this guy, Tec, he sounds off his rocker.'

'Sure,' Tec said, smiling. 'Junior's chaperoning him – I've got vid-feed from it, but frankly it's only a gesture. I'm sure he could just take the robot out by wireless in a thousandth of a second, but anyway he's—'

'Just don't get us into anything else that's out of our league, okay?'

'As if,' he answered, already turning back to his console, one hand idly finding a smouldering reeferette roach in an ashtray beside him.

'Where is the guy now?'

'He's sleeping in the big room,' said Tec's voice while Tec's attention was focused upon the console.

'Where's Spider?'

'Playing with his mag-rifle, I think. He's been up for hours, in his room if you want him.'

'No, it's okay. See you later, then.'

'Bye,' he said simply.

Whistler, Sofi and Roberts sloped off to their respective beds. As soon as Whistler's head contacted her pillow her mind simply, mercifully, switched off and she fell instantly, fully clothed, into a state of near-comatose slumber.

CHAPTER SIXTEEN

Astalle sat on the glasspex chair next to her daughter, Izzy, and let the table surprise her with its breakfast recommendation. She reached across and tousled Izzy's hair – a gesture of affection that she seemed powerless to stop herself from doing, even though Izzy was six now and openly objected to it. '*Muuumm!*' she protested and twisted in her chair to avoid the tousling hand.

'Morning, petal. Been up for long?'

'Yeah,' said Izzy, nibbling delicately and somewhat disinterestedly on the corner of a piece of cinnamon toast. Astalle trusted Izzy to rouse herself in the morning and they were used to meeting at the breakfast table in this manner. Izzy was very sensible for her age and could be relied upon to take herself to the toilet and head off to the kitchen to sit at the table, which would fix breakfast for her, and watch the holo until Astalle got up. She knew that Izzy would wake her if she needed to. She had in fact done so the two previous nights, but maybe that was over now.

'Yeah?' A bowl of cereal rose from the table just in front of Astalle with the understated subtlety of true high-tech. Astalle considered it the sign of a quality gadget when said gadget tried to do its job as unobtrusively as possible, rather than demanding input and acknowledgement all the time. The breakfast table was one such device, and Astalle was very fond of it – it simply did its job, correctly, and never needed anything. Another by-product of her husband's lucrative if time-consuming job at the space port. Derech was an ion drive engineer there – actually quite a wide spectrum of specialisation, and one essential to the space industry. On the downside, he practically lived at the place when the launch schedule was heavy, as now. In fact, it had never been as heavy as now. 'How long? This still your first breakfast?' Astalle was consistently amazed at her daughter's ability to eat round after round of breakfast, stopping only when the day's schedule necessitated it.

'Few hours. First breakfast, yeah.'

Astalle noticed then how tired Izzy's small face appeared beneath the thick mass of curls that she had inherited from Astalle herself. She leaned inside the angle of cover provided by that shock of chestnut hair and looked into Izzy's eyes. 'Bad dreams again, honey?'

She pulled her bowl of cereal closer and picked up the spoon, but didn't begin to eat yet.

'They're *not* dreams, Mummy,' said Izzy, her tone suggesting that she was labouring to be polite to a truly stupid person. She looked away from Astalle, trying to see the holo that danced in the centre of the luxuriant carpet through her mother's inconvenient physical presence.

'No?' Astalle was not sure how to proceed from here. For the last three nights now Izzy had slept poorly. The two previous nights she had woken Astalle from where she slept alone in her double bed, crying and uncharacteristically frightened. Last night she had clearly not bothered, for whatever reason. Perhaps she had given up on receiving help with her monster problem. The thought that her six-year-old daughter might come to a point of such resignation at her tender years saddened her deeply, reminding her that youth – not physical youth, but spiritual youth – was a fragile thing, indeed, and could be broken by the slightest knock. 'You can come to me if you're frightened, Izzy, okay?'

'Okay, Mummy.' Izzy chewed slowly. Her dark, almond-shaped eyes were beautiful and sad in the morning light that came sheeting in through the crystal glass wall of the second-floor apartment. Cable cars glided silently past outside, their chromed skins flashing greyly in the weak sun. From Astalle's kitchen she could just make out the forms of suited city execs crammed into the cars like toy soldiers packed into boxes. Another lightpusher was disappearing through the troposphere atop a gently curving contrail, its massive hull now barely visible as a speck of milky light. At least her husband wasn't actually *on* one of the damn things.

Astalle dived the spoon into the cereal and began to eat, watching Izzy out the corner of her eye. The child was listless, depressed-looking. She nibbled the edge of her toast slowly, distantly. The Holo-Bobs capered brightly across the self-cleaning kitchen carpet, regarded expressionlessly by Izzy. The show was really too young for Izzy now, but Astalle endeavoured not to influence her daughter's tastes, and if she still liked the Holo-Bobs that was all good.

After a while Izzy said, 'The monster was outside again, on the lawn. It looked different, but it was the same monster. I know. It came right up close to the building. I couldn't sleep after I saw it. I read some books then got up.' She related this information dispassionately, like a news reporter, eyes focused on the holo.

'Oh, honey,' said Astalle, saddened, irritated and filled with simple love all at the same time. 'Monsters aren't real, you know. There isn't anything out there. I know dreams can be very convincing, but–'

'Mummy, I said I wasn't sleeping. I was awake. I watched it,' said Izzy in a small, dejected voice. Her tiny, perfect teeth took another nip at the corner of her toast.

'What was it doing?' asked Astalle, exasperated now, looking for an angle to refute her daughter's imaginings.

'It was eating the trees,' said Izzy simply.

CHAPTER SEVENTEEN

Whistler awoke gradually, luxuriantly, floating up towards consciousness through felty layers of increasing brightness. Usually the day's business swarmed into her mind at the very first waking moment, but this morning she felt contented and at peace. She was aware that the world loomed uncertain and threatening around her, yet a silken calm was on her like a comforting blanket. The light in the room, synched to the natural light outside, as relayed from a sensor on the building's roof, was pale grey and metallic – it was a cool, peaceful light – a light to reason by. Whistler lay for a while, enjoying the plushness of her thick covers, stretching her limbs into different arrangements and resting for a moment in each position, relishing the sleek, tight feel of her own body, the way the tension seemed to bleed out of her muscles, into the air and then away as she tensed and relaxed them. The strange events of the night when they had visited Haspan seemed as if they had happened to another version of herself. Her mind felt fresh and logical again.

After a while she edged herself out of bed with determined slowness: One leg out, foot on the carpet, other leg out, shuffle to edge of bed, slowly sit on edge of bed, stand. Pause. She undressed, letting her clothes slough away like shed skin, leaving them where they fell. She examined her body, amazed at how well it felt, when it had felt so tired and ill-used at the time she had finally crashed out. There was a pinched, purplish bruise above her right breast, which she hadn't noticed before. Maybe Spake had grabbed her there in his panic. Otherwise fine. She stretched up tall on the toes of one foot and turned in a perfect, slow motion spinning kick, poised perfectly like a ballerina, full circle, and then relaxed to stand at ease again. She admired her own smooth, blue-lined, grey-skinned form in the mirror for a moment and then began to dig around for fresh – or at least *fresher* – clothes. She found matt-black plastic trousers and a khaki combat-top that didn't actually smell bad and dressed in them. She noticed that the illuminated readout behind the glass of the mirror confirmed that she had slept for almost a full twenty-four hours. *Good*, she thought. *If being your own boss doesn't get you a full day in bed now and again, then what really is the point?*

Whistler's stomach growled loudly, reminding her of the next pressing item of business: *Breakfast!* Yesterday's Get-Up had long since worn off and this always left her ravenous, even without a full day of starvation. Thoughts of toast soldiers and mugs of coffee danced across her mind, calling her irresistibly towards the mezzanine kitchen.

When she headed into the corridor she noticed that the light was on in Tec's lab. Despite her hunger she was interested enough to poke her head into the room. Tec was sitting face to face with a slightly-built young man with long blond hair. The young man was wearing some of Tec's old clothes – Whistler recognised the T-shirt with the shifting Mandelbrot fractal – but was otherwise unfamiliar. So this was the stray they had taken in. The two men both had their eyes closed and were joined together by a tangled hi-flo. A branch from the cable led to a pile of computers on Tec's desk. Numbers swarmed across the screens in the corner, faster than the eye could follow. Whistler leaned against the door frame and watched them. The two men were frozen in place – only the numbers on the screen moved.

Whistler stepped cautiously into the room, not wanting to distract them from whatever they were doing. Tec's skull-lights were blinking with surprising slowness, mostly green. They gradually faded in and out, indicative of a thoughtful, calm state of mind, barring the occasional flickers of orange that died as quickly as sparks. Tec was deep in the zone. His hands lay still upon his knees. The net-connection light on the nape of his neck, unusually, was off. Whistler padded silently around him to see the face of the man he was wired to. She studied his passive features for a moment: Slightly delicate face, a day's blond stubble, a shallow graze on one fine cheekbone. He was handsome, if a little small and thin for Whistler's tastes. Tec and the stranger, although right there in front of her, seemed totally distant from the room, as if they sat inside a soundproof glass tank. She watched them as the numbers scrolled, feeling dreamlike, inexplicably lonely, as if she had awoken to find herself the last survivor of some terrible apocalypse. She suddenly wanted to shake the two men to awareness, make them talk to her. Where were Spider, Roberts and Sofi?

A more pressing matter asserted itself then – Whistler needed to pee. She resisted the urge to force her company on the two buttonheads and instead left the lab and headed up the stairs to the big room, where items of business such as pissing and eating could all be attended to, utilising the respective areas set aside for such activities. The room was cavernous and deserted. *Nobody else up,* she thought with some disappointment. Bright yellow light enforced perpetual day up here, illuminating islands of junk that had lain untouched for years mingled with areas of furniture that the team used every day. On the lower level piles of rubbish – old paint tins, vehicle parts, rusting hunks of arcane machinery, reels of cable and hose, boxes of outdated storage media, decaying bales of somebody else's paperwork – filled the furthest fifty metres of space, entirely blocking what had once been a large factory door but was now a heavily-reinforced wall. On the nearside of *crap alley,* as Spider had dubbed this minor wasteland, was a large area that served as some sort of living room, with assorted sofas, coffee tables, stereo and holo-projector. The impression given was as if somebody's house had fallen down around them and they had simply dragged the remaining pieces of furniture out from under the wreckage and replaced said items atop the heap of debris, then attempted to continue with their normal lives.

Double doors led away from this living area to a large bathroom. Doors on the opposite wall led into a smaller, even less user-friendly storage space. An old flight of metal steps connected the main floor to the smaller mezzanine that housed the kitchen. Whistler looked up at it longingly. Had she been a buttonhead she could have mentally started the kettle boiling and toast toasting while she went to the toilet, but meathead as she was it would have to wait. *First thing's first.*

She moved through the dusty gloom silently on bare feet, to the bathroom. She went into one of the cubicles and relieved herself, then washed her hands and face in one of the large basins. It was made of real porcelain, its surface crazed but clean. She turned to an airspace defined by a bright blue holo-field and let the intelligent air blades dry her hands and face. The cleanliness was good, if a little localised. She decided to allow herself a bath later.

She headed back into the big room and bounded up the stairs to the kitchen. The steps banged and clanged beneath even her slight weight, filling the deserted room with echoing noise. Whistler set the kettle going and began the task of locating a mug. They had never managed to install a smart drinks system for some reason – maybe because Tec, who would otherwise have done it, didn't actually drink hot drinks. Whistler hated to use disposable vessels, refused to have them in the base. *Although*, she thought, ransacking the cupboards with increasing irritation, *I could bloody use one now*. She turned, empty-handed, from the cupboard as the kettle was rattling to the boil, and her gaze happened upon one of Spider's reeferette ends that was propped on the edge of a plate on the central counter-top, breadcrumbs and ash scattered around it liberally. Whistler's brain apparently re-prioritised the morning's agenda based on this new find, for she found herself sitting on the bench and smoking the reeferette almost before she knew she was doing it, having apparently acquired a lighter from somewhere.

The dope was strong – unusually strong – and, on an empty stomach, slightly nauseating. The world, already oddly unreal this morning, took on the shallowness of an image printed on translucent film, or an incredibly intricate stained glass scene. It looked, mused Whistler, almost unbearably fragile. She took another drag. The tobacco was dry and it burned incredibly hot – she began to cough in dry punches that pressurised her head around the temples. When she finally could, Whistler stubbed the end back onto the plate and ground it vengefully into nothing. Her eyes were watering and the coffee seemed more urgent than ever. If only she could move.

Footsteps sounded on the stairs behind her – *bang, clang, bang* – making her start. Spider, grinning broadly, came striding onto the mezzanine, huge boots ringing off the metal floor. One side of his neck was speckled with rubbery data spots like adhered leeches, and his expression was tired but typically good-natured. "Sup, sleepy-head?' he asked over one shoulder, already at the counter and making coffee with mugs that two of his arms produced from seemingly nowhere.

'How did you do that?' asked Whistler, broadly indicating the drinks-making process as a whole and the sourcing of mugs specifically with a vague sweep of one arm. She was spinning out a little.

Spider turned, one thick eyebrow arched. 'You fuckin' stoned?' he asked.

She fought vainly for some cutting remark, scrutinised intently by Spider as she did so, then settled simply for, 'Yes.'

'I bloody thought so,' he agreed, turning back to the counter. 'Coffee?' he asked without looking.

'Please.' *See*, she thought, *all things come to she who waits*.

He poured two mugs, handed one to Whistler and sat at the table opposite her with his own. He took a sip of the scalding coffee, wincing at the heat. Whistler pulled her mug to her and cradled it like a sleeping child, delicately breathing its fragrant steam. 'You met Debian yet?' he asked, turning on an audio news feed by DNI. The monotonous voice of the bias-free-certified virtual being newsreader scratched away in the aural background.

Whistler sipped her coffee and began to feel better so immediately that she knew some of the effect must have been psychosomatic. 'Not yet,' she said. 'Who is he?'

'Some guy,' said Spider, searching on the tabletop for something. 'You smoked my one, then,' he said with no surprise, relaxing back onto his seat.

'Sorry.' Whistler found that she was grinning. It was good to be home, rested, high and sitting here with Spider, whom she had always found amusing.

He noticed her beaming face. 'State of you,' he commented simply, fumbling a packet of smokes from a pocket and shaking a new reeferette out of it. A tiny butane flame flickered on his claw and he drew deeply on the reeferette. 'Might as well make a morning of it, eh?'

'Why not,' agreed Whistler. 'So who's the guy? He was in Tec's lab when I got up. They seemed to be engaged in some sort of geek mating ritual or something, so I left them to it. Quite good-looking, in a way.'

'Don't get any ideas, you.' He fixed her with a stern eye but amusement glinted in there too. 'You know about business and pleasure. He's some hacker. Quiet type, strange sort of fella. Couldn't find much to say to him, if I'm honest with you. He thinks there's something wrong in the net, says some sinister organisation is after him. Jalan sent him here for help. He was shot with a solid round, but he's been patched up and it looks like he'll be okay.'

'What sort of help does he want?' Whistler took the offered reeferette and began to smoke it, alternating drags with sips and feeling better all the time.

'Shelter from these people who are after him, lab facilities. It's pretty much Tec's department so far. He seems trustworthy. They're gonna try to pry some funds from one of his accounts, but until they do, we remain unpaid. Seems the only problem with the arrangement so far.'

'We have to charge top dollar for this shit, Spider. I don't like it. Is this shadowy organisation real? If so, then this could be pretty dangerous for us, right?'

'Tec thinks the danger to Debian is probably real. The danger to us is another matter, of course. With HGR backing we're pretty much untouchable, barring one or two renegade police forces, naturally. I don't think we need to worry.'

'If he's...er...' Her mental train slid slowly off the tracks and crashed into a metaphorical ditch. 'Er...' She handed the reeferette back to Spider, who laughed at her. 'What was I saying? Oh yeah – if he's right about the danger, is he right about there being something wrong with the net?'

'I dunno – could be. I've certainly been having some grief with the mag-rifle. It had to do an auto update and it's been fucked ever since. I've been up half the night with it.' He tilted his chin to indicate the spots dappling his neck. 'Tec can't make sense of it either. Also, Junior's been acting fuckin' weird. I dunno – if the problem is with the net, it seems minor so far. Little things.'

'We had trouble communicating with the van the other night, and Tec couldn't get us either. Seemed odd to me. Maybe something really is up.'

'Well Debian certainly thinks so. He thinks he might have been partially responsible in some way. You'll have to ask him. I don't know much about it – as I said, it's Tec's show, really.'

'Yeah, I will. Any food?'

'Tins. As always. Not many.' Spider's face distorted in exaggerated disgust.

'*Fresh* food.'

'Oh, yeah, actually there's fake eggs and real bread in the cupboard. Go for it.'

'Thanks.' She went to the cupboard on shaky legs and fumbled the required items from its otherwise empty depths. She brushed a pad with her fingertip and a hob ring glowed to life. She dropped two synthetic eggs into a pan and two slices of bread into the toaster. The thing was supposed to be automatic but nobody ever reloaded the hopper and, faithful to tradition, Whistler didn't do so now. The audio stream rattled on. Sounded like bad news all round: stock prices falling, public computer systems grinding to a halt, a minor bank in its death-throes. She stopped and leaned against the edge of the counter-top, listening as the eggs spattered and hissed in their pan.

Spider was listening, too. Their eyes met. 'Maybe there is something to what this Debian says. Listen to that shit – it's madness.'

'Computer problems everywhere,' mused Whistler. 'All of a sudden.' In her mind's eye an image began to replay itself, but an image that had nothing to do with computers: Vivao's blood pooling on the dirty floor of his flat, separating into two distinct colours, flecks of dust and debris caught in its slow currents. She felt her good mood slipping. 'Hey, Spider, this other thing with the greenshit...'

'So what happened with that? Sofi said you guys found the surgeon but she wouldn't really speak about it. Because she couldn't be arsed, not because it was a sensitive subject, was the impression I got. I ain't seen her since.'

'It's fucked up,' she sighed. 'Unsurprisingly enough.' She plated the toast without bothering to butter it and slid the eggs from the pan on top of it. Her stomach growled as she took the plate back to the table. These new synthetic eggs were surprisingly close to the real thing, if you could get over the fact that they came in plastic bubbles rather than eggshells. 'He didn't understand where it's coming from either, though he had a few guesses for us: could be one of the drugs they use leaving people prone to some sort of infection, some virus targeting people with mods, or some sort of glitch in the nanovat software used to grow parts.'

Spider looked up. 'A computer glitch,' he said.

'Yeah,' said Whistler, suddenly unable to eat the forkful of food she had lifted to her mouth. She let it lower slowly back to the plate. 'A fucking computer glitch. I want to talk to this Debian. What, precisely, does he think is up with the net?'

'I'm not sure – something about an AI. Dunno what's so bad about it, though – I mean, AIs are all over the net, right? Worryingly, he did keep using the phrase *unprecedented power*. If he's right...'

'Then maybe this fucking AI of his could be planting the greenshit infection in people.'

Spider swallowed heavily, the reeferette burning away unnoticed in one shiny claw. 'Why?' he breathed. His eyes were glassy. Whistler could only shake her head.

The newsreader on the satellite feed said: '...the infection that has been termed Genetic Degenerative Disorder, or GDD. Health authorities assure us that nobody has died directly from it but that it is important that *any* recent bodymod implantees report at once to the nearest hospital emergency department. The government has agreed to meet all hospital charges for check-ups and treatment related to the infection, having labelled the situation a *Category-A Public Health Concern*, an action not taken since the *orbital flu* breakout that killed nearly three million citizens. Famed think-tanker and health lobbyist Jackson Jilletti issued a press statement saying, *'If you suspect anything wrong after recent body modification, my advice is don't just get pissed and forget about this one, guys. Sounds serious. Go to hospital.'* The government, despite their usual protestations at Jilletti's choice of phrasing, took the unusual step of fully backing his statement. Some people are suggesting that the recent rash of mutant sightings is in some...'

'World's going fuckin' crazy,' declared Spider, mentally turning the feed down and shaking out another reeferette. Whistler could find no argument to this.

Just then Roberts appeared up the stairs, his eyes fresh in his otherwise haggard face. He wore his long coat even at this hour of the day. 'Have you lot heard the news?' he asked without introduction. They assured him that they had. 'I don't mind saying that I'm a little worried about all this,' he admitted, uncapping a synthihol beer and seating himself next to Spider. 'Morning, by the way.'

'Early for that isn't it?' asked Whistler innocently.

'Like hell it is,' he retorted, casually brusque, swigging from the beer. 'Sleep well?'

'All day. You?'

'Same. And I wake up this morning to find the world going to hell. Sounds like a lot of people have the greenshit. *Category-A Public Health Concern* – you hear that? And what's with all this computer shit? I want to meet this guy Tec scraped from the sewers.'

'Scraped from the sewers?' parroted Spider. 'Jalan sent him, idiot. From the Sunken Chest.'

'I know who Jalan is – the computer barman, right? Give me that smoke, if you would, my good man. Don't fuck around now.' Roberts indicated Spider's latest reeferette demandingly. Spider chuckled and passed it. 'Let's begin as we mean to go on. I'm guessing there won't be work today, what with the whole bodymod market collapsing and seemingly the rest of the economy with it.'

'Guess not,' said Whistler. He had a point. 'Don't get too mashed just yet though – you never know. And stop with the good mood, would you? It's just not the Roberts we all know and tolerate.' Roberts just grunted in response, more in character again. Whistler continued with her eggs.

'Anybody seen Sofi today?' asked Spider. Shaken heads all round. 'Who was the guy referred you to Haspan? The gun man? Maybe he can sort the mag-rifle. I don't want to bother Tec with it any more – he has a lot on already.'

'Will you forget about that gun?' said Roberts. 'Let's just have a day off.' He saluted his own remark with his half-empty beer bottle, then finished it in one gulp.

'Fuckin' gun's expensive, Rob,' answered Spider. 'No I won't fuckin' forget it. If something kicks off here we're gonna need all the firepower we have, and the mag-rifle's a significant part of that. Roland, wasn't it?'

'Yeah,' said Whistler. 'He never gave us contact details, but he said to come back if we need anything. Good guy – I think I trust him. Roberts could go with you.'

Roberts was already protesting. 'No, no, no and also no. I intend to be too drunk to drive within the next ten minutes. And I don't mean legally, I mean physically.'

'It's...' Whistler leaned over and checked Roberts's watch implant. The readout glowed redly through the skin of his wrist. '...Ten fifteen in the morning. Take Spider to see Roland. He's right. We can't let weapons fall out of action. If it can't be fixed, get another. Use the company account, up to twenty thousand. And even I know that the van can drive itself, so don't give me that crap.'

'Right,' said Roberts darkly. 'Thanks for that. I'll take him in a bit, okay?'

'Thanks, man,' said Spider. 'Damn thing's been doing my head in.'

There was the sound of a door opening below and voices talking over each other. Whistler looked over the rail and saw that Tec and Sofi had entered the big room with Debian, conversing heatedly. Tec was laughing, and the sound of it lifted Whistler's spirits almost back to where they had been when she first awoke. The three waved in greeting and climbed up to the mezzanine.

'Guys, this is Debian,' said Tec, indicating the slim young man at his side. Debian nodded shyly to them. 'He's one unusual suspect. Debian – Roberts and Whistler. Spider you know already.' He indicated his colleagues. 'Whistler is our chief slave-driver, and Roberts – what do you do again?'

'I saw you mind-fucking the new boy in your lair, Tec.' said Roberts accusingly, without looking up.

'Don't worry about him,' said Tec to Debian. 'He's always unhappy in the morning. Or if he's ill, or too stoned. Or not stoned enough, or not drunk enough, or around other people. Actually, I'd generally avoid him if I were you.'

Debian didn't seem to know what to make of this. His blank crystal eyes surveyed the harvesters impassively. He was really, actually, very handsome, thought Whistler, despite the locked-in-a-dark-room-too-long look he had in common with most hackers. He showed no sign of any gunshot wound – perhaps the bandage was under his clothing. Anyway, Jalan must have done a good job, because he didn't look like he was in pain. His gaze moved on to scan the dark expanse of the big room below – the masses of junk and strange artefacts. Whistler wondered what he thought of her odd little world.

'So, Debian, sit down,' said Whistler, receiving the smoke from Roberts. Debian sat in the indicated place, looking vaguely uncomfortable. His face was delicate, intelligent, but a hunted look was beneath the surface like a shadow. 'Tell me about why you're here.'

Debian felt Whistler's cool blue eyes on his face like a cold wind and he shivered slightly. She had a frightening, wild beauty about her, despite her apparent geniality. Her face was a scribed with the glowing pattern of a circuit board, a striking imprint of the synthetic on the natural. She appeared to be a meathead, and he wondered if the circuit-board effect was some kind of statement. 'There is something in the net,' he said. 'An AI, but very powerful, very aggressive. I'm not sure how it developed but...Have you ever heard of native AI? Emergent intelligence?'

'Sure, it's what all the conspiracy theorists go on about, isn't it?' answered Spider. 'An AI that develops autonomously in the net – a true, evolved being, right?'

'Right,' he said. Everybody was listening to him. He looked around at their intent faces. 'Evolved in its native medium, it would have an unrivalled mastery of its environment, or so they hypothesise. It would theoretically evolve from scraps of man-made AIs and mindless programs, honed by natural selection. Theorists say that the net is as fertile as the primordial soup from which biological life first emerged, the perfect petri-dish for artificial life to grow in.'

'The strongest programs naturally survive, right?' added Tec. 'It works just like in the natural world. And some viruses and other autonomous programs are designed to steal worthwhile code from others, take on their abilities, change their own code.'

Whistler exhaled heavily. 'If that happened, then the basis of this emergent intelligence would still be rooted in man-made code, wouldn't it? It wouldn't be that different from existing AIs, except maybe in complexity. I mean, I'm no expert, but...'

'I suppose that is true, for all it matters, but we are talking about an entity that theoretically evolves from a pretty fundamental set of instructions. It would have been through so many changes that it would be unrecognisable. Theoretically. Is there any coffee?'

'Er, sure, yeah,' said Spider, indicating the kettle but not moving to assist. Debian stayed put. 'Is that what this is, then? The monster that the crazies have been harping on about all these years?'

Debian shrugged and the spirit seemed to go out of him. 'Native AI is sci-fi bullshit. I don't know what this is. Maybe...I don't know. Maybe we're living in a sci-fi.' He shook his head, his face downcast.

'Where else could it have come from?' asked Whistler softly.

'Maybe it was just engineered in the traditional way. I made contact with it...' He looked distant, troubled, but a little wistful too. 'It seemed very powerful. I never met my match in a program before. I don't know where it came from. Nobody has ever managed to grow a native AI in controlled conditions. By definition it kind of resists attempts at cultivation. I don't see how it could have been made by any human being and I don't see how it could evolve by itself.'

'What the fuck?' interjected Sofi. 'This is insane. What are you saying exactly?' Clearly a good sleep had not cheered her up.

'I'm saying,' said Debian, unruffled, 'that I don't know where it came from. But I'm afraid that I might have set it off in some way. They tricked me into meeting with it. I think it took a pattern-scan of my brain.'

'Why?' asked Whistler.

'To augment its abilities, the way some AIs take code from other programs, maybe. The only other reason I can imagine would be to identify me. But my pattern isn't on record anywhere, nor would anybody in the know expect it to be. I'm not boasting when I say that I am the best hacker I know of alive today. Of course, all the really good ones remain quite well-unknown, but even so. I can't imagine why else it would have done it. This AI is behind all the computer problems going on at the moment. I can't prove that yet, but I know it's true. I would advise all of you to refrain from connecting to the net for a while. Not by DNI, not at all unless you have to.'

'No problem for me,' said Whistler, sweeping a hand through her dark hair, showing that there were no plugs on her skull.

'Meathead,' said Debian, as if this went without saying.

'And is it this program that you're hiding from? How can we hope to keep you safe from that?'

'I think,' said Debian softly, looking down at his hands, 'that if it wanted me dead I would be dead already. I am hiding from the people who set me up. My ex-employer, or representatives of. Who they really are I don't know. I thought I did, but I was naïve, I suppose.'

'Could the AI be behind the greenshit?' asked Whistler.

'I don't know anything about that, I'm afraid. I've been a bit wrapped up in my own problems, to be honest. I heard something on the news about it. Some bodymod infection, isn't it?'

'Something like that,' agreed Roberts, stroking his chin, brow furrowed.

'How's it going with our money?' asked Whistler directly. 'This isn't a hostel, you know.' She flashed him a grin, exposing her small fangs, lighting her whole face up.

Debian realised that, if anything, he had underestimated her beauty. 'I know,' he said, suddenly transfixed by her.

'It was quality, guys,' enthused Tec. 'Couple of spliced avatars, proxy chain a million miles long — we ran rings round the customs sniffer bots. It was actually pretty clever, the way—'

'It wasn't too difficult,' interrupted Debian. 'We set up a fictional company account at one of the orbital banks. It's surprising how easily tricked their ID verification systems are — seems to be kind of a deliberate lack of diligence. They made a payment to your account, then dissolved. Tec assured me that it didn't matter if it looked illegal, as long as I wasn't linked to you or your premises by name. I don't think anybody would have noticed. My own account was actually quite subtly attached to me in the first place. I was reluctant to go back into the net, but it was important that I could pay you guys. I didn't actually connect personally — we just used the terminal.'

'Good, no, that's fine,' said Whistler. 'We're pretty much covered for illegal activity, we just don't want your *interested party* coming round here.'

'We transferred four hundred grand,' he said quietly. The harvesters drew a collective breath. 'I know that's a lot, but I thought it would act as a token of my appreciation. For the risk to your good selves. I really don't think I'm safe on the streets right now.' His face was serious and pale in the waxy artificial light. Whistler wondered if he ever really smiled.

'That's fine,' she said, quietly pleased. 'We will help you however we can. Within reason. But if your friends come by here shooting guns and what-have-you, I guess we'll have to decide on a proportionate response at the time.'

'I don't know what will happen, I'm afraid.' And he looked afraid, too, to Whistler. 'I will have to get out somehow. To somewhere.'

'We're at least pretty sure now that there isn't a sub in Debian's head, anyway,' said Tec brightly. Nobody looked too thrilled. 'That's a good thing,' he prompted them.

Roberts made a decisive sound and went to the fridge, from which he withdrew another beer. He looked like a man trying not to look furtive. When he turned back Whistler was watching him. 'Yes, boss?'

'Roland, remember? I don't want you running around out there smashed out of your skull. Health and safety.'

'Health and what? I'll just take Get-Up, if I have to,' he responded, defiantly uncapping the beer. They both knew that alcohol plus Get-Up didn't exactly equal stone-cold sober, just more alertly drunk.

'You're going after that one, then?' It sounded like a question, but Roberts recognised it as an order. He answered only with a barely perceptible nod.

Whistler turned again to Debian. 'You smoke?' she asked.

He shook his head. 'No thanks.'

'Your choice,' she said and passed the last of the reeferette back to Spider.

'So who are these people you think are looking for you?'

Debian managed to look small and frightened and resolute and strong at the same time. 'Hex,' he said darkly. 'At least, that's what the last one was named. I mean, I don't know who they really are. Were. Alcubierre is supposedly the name behind it all, but whether that's a backing corporation or a person I don't know. I don't suppose that name means anything to you?'

'No, sorry. You say these people tricked you into getting your brain pattern-scanned by this AI? How?'

'I'd been doing odd jobs for them for years. I never knew the name of the organisation, I just took jobs from contacts.'

'They never told you who you were working for?'

'No. I took work from one contact for years. He died and I met with a new contact – Hex, he called himself – and the fucker set me up.' He looked up. Everyone was looking back at him. 'Sent me into the servers of a company called Cyberlife Research and Development to steal their research data and suchlike. They've sent me into a lot of tech-companies to do the same thing over the years. I always imagined that my employer was a tech-company itself, hence their narrow band of interest. I wonder now if they *were* Cyberlife all along.'

'What?' asked Spider. 'I don't get it.'

'Well, maybe they'd been working on this AI all these years. Perhaps it evolved natively and they tried to nourish it, perhaps they coded it somehow, perhaps it was grown from a seed they got from elsewhere. All the data I stole for them helped with this process. Then they sent me in to give it a final lesson. I wonder if they knew about the new technique I've been working on – though how they would, I don't know. I don't think I ever told anyone about it – I don't really have any confidantes. Then, because I knew of its existence, they tried to kill me.'

'Fuckin' harsh, man,' said Sofi, getting herself a beer from the fridge. Whistler watched her but didn't comment. 'I thought *our* employers were tight.'

Debian laughed – a dry, humourless cough – and said, 'Yeah. If it's true. I don't know – it's just a theory. They could have been anyone. I should have been suspicious when my contact changed.' He sounded like he was inwardly berating himself.

'Didn't get you, though, did they?' said Tec.

'No. Not yet.'

'Fuckers aren't going to, either,' insisted Whistler. 'Not with your sort of money.' It was supposed to be a joke but nobody laughed. An uncomfortable silence fell.

'Right,' said Roberts, breaking it. 'Let's go, Spidey. Go and take this bloody gun in.' He slammed his empty bottle down onto the table and stood.

'Let's,' agreed Spider, also standing. He stretched hugely, arching his broad back and grimacing. The two looked an unlikely pairing as they made their brief farewells and headed off down the stairs.

After some brief deliberation Whistler mentally shrugged and got herself a beer – a real one, not that synthihol shit. She sipped it carefully at first, managing not to feel too hypocritical. It was ambrosial. Tec offered her another smoke. She took it and smoked it as some apocalyptic industrial jungle began to play on the satellite audio stream.

CHAPTER EIGHTEEN

Doctor Rushden heard the commotion developing in the hospital lobby as he was trying to seal a particularly jagged gash in the forearm of a most attractive young woman. *Shit!* he thought. *What now?* He was suddenly concerned that he might have said this aloud, but the patient didn't seem to have heard it if he did. Doctor Rushden was beyond exhaustion now, but somehow still running on a mixture of Get-Up and nervous energy.

'Sounds like you might be needed elsewhere,' said the young woman – one Miss Karlile. She had been injured when a computer-controlled HGV had swerved off the road and ploughed a merry path across the pavement in south High Hab. She had been one of the lucky ones. She was looking closely at him and smiling now, shaken but not stirred by her ordeal. The flesh-foam had taken well and the finish was perfectly smooth. Rushden felt a small thrill of pride looking at it, overshadowed only now by his new sense of dread.

He wiped his brow with the back of one hand and gave her what he hoped was a debonair grin. 'I'm afraid that might be the case, Miss Karlile. Sorry. Back in a minute.' Although he knew that with things going the way they were right now this was a promise he may be unable to keep.

Raised voices guided him to the lobby where he found a new and disturbing scene unfolding. This was what you got for turning your bloody back for a moment! Soldiers of some sort – he couldn't tell if they were a police urban combat unit, central army or some security force – had swarmed the lobby and seemed to be pushing all members of the public back out into the street. Injured and uninjured alike were locked in a desperate scrum with the black-clad invaders. Many of the civilians were shouting (indignant, not aggressive – not yet) and pushing, trying to force their way through the human blockade that now stood between themselves and treatment or loved ones inside the hospital.

The soldiers were forming a perimeter just inside the large main doors, encircling the check-in desk, now unattended, and more were storming through the office doors into the emergency department proper, flushing out recalcitrant civilians. There was a stink of human sweat and fear in the air. Rushden stood, mouth agape at the end of the corridor as dark figures swarmed past him into the hospital, jostling him as they went. 'What the–' he managed to utter before a huge, burly man with modded weapon arms strode self-importantly up to him and cleared his throat. 'Um. Yes?' managed Rushden. He was aware that he looked like some post-apocalyptic refugee, his clothes crumpled and smeared with blood from the day's festivities.

'This hospital is being closed,' bellowed the man, without introduction. He wore some sort of insignia on one shoulder – an emblem that Rushden hadn't seen before – a kind of crooked star on a red sunburst. Unlike the other soldiers he wore no helmet, which was a shame because it would have concealed his ogrish visage. 'Except for GDD cases everyone is being shipped out. Staff will, of course, remain. Under our supervision. Which means *my* supervision.'

'I don't think so!' exclaimed Rushden indignantly. 'Over my dead body! There's a crisis developing here. It's not just the greenshit – I mean the GDD – there are all sorts of freak accidents occurring, all over! We can't close the emergency department!'

'Not just the emergency department – *all of it*. Who's chief of staff here at the moment?'

'I am! Where are my receptionists? What have you done with them?' Some part of Rushden's mind was warning him that he should be careful here, but his indignation overrode it.

The protesting civilians had been mostly ejected onto the street now, where more soldiers were disembarking from gunmetal-grey APCs. People were being roughly escorted from the hospital in ones and twos, some trailing IV-lines or nano-conduits, some leaking blood as they went, some having to be carried. The ejectees were falling back across the road, merging with the crowd of horrified onlookers. The soldiers out there looked to be readying themselves for the moment when the crowd would become a mob. This was all happening too fast.

'My superiors have ordered this building turned into a storage and observation facility for GDD patients. Everybody else is to be removed. Your staff will continue to treat the remaining patients as best they can, under my instruction. Don't worry, Doctor.' He grinned a wide and toothy grin – the sort of grin you could lose a finger to. 'I'm eminently qualified.'

'What about my other patients? Where will they go? You can't just throw them out like that – some of them will die!' Rushden began to feel this situation slipping away from him. Outside, the dark spectre of a gyrocopter came swooping between the towering buildings, through the wide plaza, blades chopping the air into bassy lumps. Civilians scattered away from it as if it might land on them.

The officer fixed him with a dark stare. 'A lot of people are going to die,' he said heavily.

'But—' The officer cut him short with a silencing finger and held one hand to his ear. He grunted with satisfaction.

'My troops have secured the building. We will have all unwelcome guests out within ten minutes. You will make an announcement to your staff that we have assumed control and that no treatment is to be given or withheld without my permission. Nobody from your staff is to leave the hospital until further notice. Nobody unauthorised by me will enter the hospital until further notice. Call your people to conference. Not here, in sight of the public. Do you have a meeting room?'

Dumbfounded, Doctor Rushden could do nothing but nod.

'Good, tell them to report there in five minutes. All of them are to drop what they're doing and be there. First item of business is to make sure everybody's clear about where they stand.'

Rushden considered that although there were many things he was unclear about, where he stood was not one of them. Where he stood was rapidly becoming apparent, and he didn't like it.

'Five minutes?' he repeated.

The officer grinned and by way of answer said: 'Major Krohn,' and actually had the gall to stick his hand out to be shaken. His forearm was bunched with assorted gun-barrels like cords of black muscle.

Rushden looked at the extended hand with loathing. He declined to shake it. Major Krohn shrugged as if this didn't bother him in the slightest. 'I'll get my staff together,' said Rushden resignedly. The major nodded.

Rushden made the announcement over DNI as soldiers led the remaining civilian patients out into the street and turned them loose like dogs. Some simply fell at the doors where they were released. More soldiers came and dragged these away. Rushden wondered where to. The lobby was rammed with the black-clad invaders now. Their heads were encased in smooth insectile plastic bubbles and their forms were bulky and sexless. One of them was setting up sentry guns – small, tripod-mounted ones – on the reception desk. Scrambler-baits were being affixed to the exterior walls of the building and Rushden wondered what was expected to happen here that the soldiers wanted to go unseen. A battle-bot – *a fucking battle-bot!* – was clumping slowly into the lobby from the corridor that led to the storage rooms and offices. It wore a diagonal slash of fresh blood across its thick cylindrical body like a garland. Yellow slit-eyes glared from its heavy carapace evilly. Rushden dreaded to think what the awful contraption had been up to back there.

Major Krohn stood over Rushden as he made the summons over DNI. Instantly his head was filled with confused enquiries and protestations. He screened out a call from his head nurse, dropped the rest, and opened the channel.

Doctor Rushden, what's going on here? There are soldiers all over the place. They've ejected most of the patients! Where are you?

Listen, Wil, I don't know why, but they're saying this place has been shut down – we don't know who by as yet – and they've come to assume control. Looks like we're to be made into a dedicated GDD facility. Everyone is to come to the meeting room and that includes you, I'm afraid. He glanced up at Major Krohn, who stood with his massive arms folded and his face set, staring at Rushden as if he were a bug in a jar. *I don't think they're messing around.*

I can't just leave the patients here with these fucking stormtroopers, boss. They say that they'll guard the ward, but I know the sort of guarding they mean. They mean the kind where any patient who plays up gets shot. Not all of them are sedated, and those that aren't seem to be getting a little agitated.

I'm sure that's true, Wil. But I think that the kind of meeting they want to call is the kind where anyone who doesn't turn up gets shot. Leave the patients with the soldiers, if that's what you have to do. Just be there in three minutes, now, and make sure everyone else is there, too.

Okay. Wil sounded pissed off, even over DNI.

Rushden turned to Major Krohn. 'My people will be there. Listen, Krohn, I don't want any mistakes while we have this little meeting of yours. I don't want any of your boys murdering any innocent people while my back is turned. I think, that when this whole giant nightmare is over, that is the sort of information that a military investigation panel

154

would be interested to hear about. That's the sort of thing that will be remembered. Even if you are setting up spyfly baits. I promise you that.' He was acutely aware that the other man towered over him by a clear foot.

Major Krohn laughed, a thick vein in his neck pulsing. 'Military investigation!' he exclaimed as if this were some unusually rich joke. 'We're not military, Doctor, but I take your point. Also, I don't think those things are strictly people any more. Shall we go?'

Rushden led Krohn into one of the wide lifts. Behind them in the lobby, sheets of ceramicarbide were being glued over the large windows. Four soldiers peeled away from the throng to follow the major, two paces behind and silent, sleek rifles held across their chests. Rushden felt as if a portal had opened in the floor and he had tumbled through into an alternate reality.

There were several members of the hospital staff in the lift already – heading up from the basement level where the vehicles were stored (and presumably now impounded), all flanked by armed militiamen. Rushden recognised Gila Barden, a quiet young cleaner who had only started last week and Stanner somebody, one of the motor-pool techs. Both looked in fear for their lives. Stanner nodded to Rushden, who returned the nod, trying his best to smile.

'Don't worry, folks, everything will soon be under control here,' boomed Major Krohn as the lift doors sighed shut and the lift began to move. The major seemed blissfully unaware of the funereal atmosphere this remark created.

The lift stopped at the next floor and more hospital staff crammed in. By the time it reached fourth, where the meeting room was, the lift was bursting with frightened hospital workers, outnumbered two to one by soldiers. Nobody spoke, although many frightened eyes sought Doctor Rushden's face. He tried to smile reassuringly, secretly terrified himself all the while. Never in his life had he seen as many guns as currently surrounded him in this tiny space.

They exited the lift, herded like prisoners by the soldiers, although they stopped short of actually shoving anyone. *Not yet*, thought Rushden. *The shoving comes later.* From deep in the hospital came the gurgling roar of a GDD patient. Rushden felt a chill down his spine. Then there were four or five muffled cracks, then silence.

Rushden's group faltered, exchanging fearful glances. They had all heard it.

Rushden rounded on Major Krohn. 'What was that?' he demanded.

'That, Doctor, sounded like one of those incidents you might want to note down,' replied the major. 'Not that anyone will listen. See, in terms of ultimate jurisdiction, I have it.' All the false bonhomie had left him now. 'You'd be well-advised not to interfere with our establishment of authority here. There might be another incident. Any number of them.' He paused, staring down into Rushden's face. The other staff stood amazed. 'Now, where is this meeting room?'

Rushden could see no way out of this situation. What could he do but kowtow? He turned, without speaking, and led the way to the large double doors. Many other people were streaming into the room in a steady flow. There were soldiers everywhere. Rushden wondered briefly if they weren't all just to be rounded up and executed, but he dismissed the idea at once.

Inside the meeting room the hospital staff were being herded into a group facing the presentation dais at the far end. The soldiers had encircled the civilians, blocking all exits. Rushden checked the hospital computer over DNI. Everybody was here. Krohn peeled Rushden away from the last of the general traffic and guided him towards the front. A hundred and twenty pairs of frightened eyes followed him. Krohn stood before the assembled staff with Rushden to his side, flanked by soldiers. Rushden knew he was to be used as a puppet governor. If the staff obeyed him, and he obeyed Major Krohn, then the major's job would be that much easier. This was not a role that Rushden was keen to take on.

The last few staff members bunched into the group and the soldiers barred the doors. Major Krohn cleared his throat. 'Good day, people. My name is Major Krohn of the First Contingency Guard. My unit has been sent here to oversee the treatment and observation of the GDD patients. As you have seen, all other patients have been evacuated from the building.' There was a general mutter at the word *evacuated*. Most of the staff had seen the heavy-handed ejection of the sick and injured only minutes before. 'You will continue to follow the directions of Doctor Rushden. Isn't that right, Doctor?'

'Yes,' said Rushden, his mouth dry. He felt like a traitor. 'That's right.'

'And no-one will have to get hurt. Will they, Doctor?'

'That's right.' He could no longer look at his subordinates directly, but he could feel the resentment hanging in the air of the over-bright room.

'Patients will be treated under a program developed by my organisation, on a ward-by-ward basis. No treatment is to be given, or withheld, unless detailed under that program. The details of said program will be made clear to all once this meeting is concluded.'

'Why?' somebody shouted. 'What's going on?'

Major Krohn seemed happy to address the heckler. 'We seek to discover a way to reverse, or failing that contain the GDD infection. You are to submit all observational data directly to Doctor Rushden's office for his and my perusal, and not to the central Health Authority Data Repository. What happens then to said data is not a matter to concern yourselves with, but suffice to say that the aforementioned method of submission is to be the *only* channel through which data is passed. Any information leaked from this facility will be traced and the perpetrator punished. That means information about me, my unit, our occupation of this facility, the trend of the GDD development generally, as well as any specific scientific data gathered through the hospital. Is this clear?'

'Fuck you!' shouted one suicidal wag from near the front. Doctor Rushden hadn't seen who it was, but either the major had, or he was happy to find a scapegoat, for he motioned to one of his troops with one huge hand. Then he pointed into the crowd.

'That is not helpful behaviour, young man,' scolded the major. He sounded as if he was enjoying this a little too much for Rushden's liking.

The soldier barged his way into the crowd and lifted a smallish man into the air by one arm as if he were a rag doll. So the soldiers wore power-suits, then. Rushden was not that surprised. He moved instinctively to help the young man, a doctor from the nanotech medicine department whom he didn't know well but who certainly didn't deserve this treatment. Krohn leaned close to Rushden and whispered in his ear, 'If you move off that spot I'll have my man rip that boy's arms clean off and throw him out the window.'

Rushden was horrified. He turned to look into the calmly smiling face of Major Krohn. The man's breath stank like a charnel house. Krohn flexed one huge weapon-arm emphatically. Rushden didn't move. The soldier dumped the young man to the floor at the front of the room before Major Krohn. 'Get o–' started the man and then the soldier kicked him in the stomach. The rest of the sentiment was swallowed by an *oof!* of expelled breath and the man curled into a tight ball. A sigh went up from the crowd. The soldier looked to Krohn with his head cocked and the question he was asking was clear: *More?* Krohn shook his head.

'Tell them, Doctor,' he said.

'Please, everybody remain calm,' said Rushden, waving away the mumble of objection. 'I don't yet understand this situation fully myself, but I will keep you all informed as best I can. You are all to obey the major's orders immediately and without question. Any objections can be taken up with me, and I will in turn relay them to him. Please continue to act professionally in all matters.'

'Good, Doctor. Thank you,' said Krohn quietly.

Rushden turned to him, his brain simmering. He tried to keep the hate from his voice when he spoke, knowing that it was his responsibility to keep his workers safe.

'And may we go about our work now, Major? Under your benevolent direction, of course.'

'Certainly, Doctor Rushden. I will have my staff update your people on the new procedures back on the wards.' The soldiers started filing the staff back out of the room again, presumably acting on some order given over DNI. It occurred to Rushden that the major had only made everyone convene here to witness first-hand some act of ferocity that would serve as a warning to them. He was grateful that it hadn't been as bad as it could have been. 'I will set up my command centre in your own offices, where you will join me in twenty minutes. You may use that time to come to terms with the new order of things. Take a break.' He looked critically at Rushden. 'You look exhausted.'

'How very generous,' answered Rushden, but Major Krohn was already sweeping out of the room flanked by his personal guard.

Rushden went and knelt beside the young nanotech medicine doctor, who was rolling slowly from side to side still clutching his midsection. Tears streamed down his face, which was locked in a grimace of pain. To his credit, he didn't make a sound. Everybody else was being ushered out by the soldiers but they seemed to be ignoring Rushden and the young doctor for now.

'Are you all right?' asked Rushden. 'Is anything broken, ruptured?'

'I'm – I'm – okay,' gasped the young man. 'I think. Thank you, Doctor. If you could just help me up...'

Rushden leaned over and began to ease the man to his feet. He didn't seem to be able to straighten up fully. His breathing came in great ragged heaves. He coughed heavily but, reassuringly, no blood came out. Rushden just stood supporting him. 'What's your name?' he asked.

'Doctor Wallinski,' said the man, a little more steadily now.

'We're going to get you checked out properly, Doctor Wallinski. I'll help you down to Emergency Intake, okay? You were stupid to back-chat those bastards, you know.'

'It – wasn't – *me*,' replied Doctor Wallinski through gritted teeth. Rushden, furious at the injustice, couldn't come up with an answer to this. He helped Wallinski slowly down the aisle towards the big doors. Almost everyone else had been herded out now. Only a few soldiers remained, dispersed around the room watching Rushden and Wallinski from behind their glossy helmets. They were all, of course, armed. Rushden shot them a look of resentment as he helped the young doctor from the room.

He took Wallinski down to Emergency in the lift. They passed many soldiers, some of whom had their helmets off now. They were blank-faced men and women who spoke little, even to each other. They could all have been grown in the same vat for all the distinguishing qualities they had. None of them sported any obvious bodymod. Hospital staff, in various states of composure ranging from outright distress to resignation, were being marshalled about here and there.

Wallinski was absurdly grateful as Rushden left him in Emergency, under the capable care of Doctor Maysen, a tall woman with the most remarkable tie-dye effect skin of red and yellow. Rushden wished him well and headed up to the third floor. As he left the ground floor, he heard chanting voices rising in the street outside, but was unable to see out because of the heavy sheeting glued over the windows. There was a large contingent of soldiers there and he didn't linger. They watched him but didn't molest him in any way.

Many of his staff tried to collar him as he passed, rattling off questions and dogging his steps. He told them all the same thing: 'Stay calm; do as they tell you; your safety is my main concern; it will all end soon; I will keep you all informed.'

He dreaded returning to his office to find that Krohn set up shop there, doubtless stuffing the place with his own people. By now they were probably already attempting to hack what remained of the inexplicably-malfunctioning hospital computer system. He would probably find the bastard sat in his chair, too, maybe with his huge jackbooted feet up on the ancient teak desk.

He stopped on third and walked into the ward, expecting one of the soldiers to grab him at any moment. They let him pass. He thought perhaps they didn't want to demean him in front of his staff – it would devalue him as a figurehead. The staff would have to be happy to obey him and he would have to be happy to obey Krohn. Who the hell were the First Contingency Guard anyway? Not actually military, if Krohn were to be believed. Some commercial defence force? Did it matter? Not really, he decided. Rushden would do what he had to do to protect his staff and his patients.

Within the ward nurses and doctors moved about their business overseen by armed soldiers. Several small groups of hospital staff were gathered around what were presumably ranking officers, taking instructions regarding their new, enforced, operational procedures.

Most of the GDD patients were under sedation, but not all. Some were being kept awake so that their cognitive degeneration could be tested and mapped. These were restrained by strong straps and had their mouths covered by plastic masks. They writhed and strained sluggishly, leaking viscous green fluid from their pores, which collected in channels around the steel beds. The cleaning robots trundled constantly about their never-ending business.

Rushden stopped beside the bed of what had once been, according to the screen on the headboard, a young woman from a good part of High Hab. Selissa Jonas had been her name, for what it was worth now. She had grown two extra appendages since her admittance to the hospital – you couldn't really call them limbs. They were grotesque, floundering things with no bone structure to speak of. The day before, as Rushden had walked past her on his morning rounds, one of those horrifying tentacles had somehow wriggled free of the straps that bound it and brushed against his exposed forearm. It had left a

160

tingling, crawling sensation that had lasted several hours and no amount of washing would remove.

Her skin was now a deep, mossy emerald. Her hair was a matted shock of wire, completely drained of its original pigment and beginning to turn a pallid, sickly green. That colour would soon deepen to match the hue of her flesh, which seemed somehow to crawl on her body, possessed of its own life. On the fourth finger of one hand, mostly obscured by the bulbous, fungussy flesh that had swelled around it, she wore an expensive platinum wedding ring. Rushden looked at that ring, aghast at what had become of this human being, wondering why the man to whom that ring presumably linked her had not come to visit her; wondering who she had used to be, sickened by how many others were now like her. They had fifty-six in this hospital alone.

She struggled half-heartedly against her bonds, as if driven by instinct rather than any actual desire to escape. In the early stages they were psychotic, full of rage. But as the disease progressed they seemed to sink into a thoughtless, emotionless state. Her eyes were simple dark points drilled into what remained of the face above the mask. Their lenses shone with a dark green oily film. Thick green liquid seeped from her ears and the corners of her eyes and had completely soaked her hospital gown. She was not responding to the nanotech treatment. None of them were. If the cutting edge of medical technology didn't cut it, what would? Rushden looked into those animal eyes and feared for the future of humanity. He stood there staring into that monstrous face until one of the soldiers came and tapped him on the shoulder. He turned and looked into the shiny facemask.

'It's been twenty minutes, Doctor,' said the soldier, taking him by the elbow. Rushden, knowing his new place, left the ward and went to see what had become of his office.

CHAPTER NINETEEN

01110111 01101001 01101100 01101100 00100000 01110100
01101000 01100101 01111001 00100000 01100010 01100101
01110100 01110010 01100001 01111001 00100000 01101101
01100101 00100000 01110100 01101000 01100101 01111001
00100000 01110111 01101001 01101100 01101100 00100000
01100100 01101111 00100000 01110111 01101000 01100001
01110100 01100101 01110110 01100101 01110010 00100000
01110100 01101000 01100101 01111001 00100000 01110100
01101000 01101001 01101110 01101011 00100000 01101110
01100101 01100011 01100101 01110011 01110011 01100001
01110010 01111001 00100000 01101001 00100000 01110111
01100001 01101110 01110100 00100000 01101000 01101001
01101101 00100000 01100001 01101100 01101001 01110110
01100101 00100000 01100001 01101110 01100100 00100000
01101001 00100000 01110111 01101001 01101100 01101100
00100000 01110100 01100001 01101011 01100101 00100000
01101000 01101001 01101101 00100000 01101001 00100000
01100111 01110010 01101111 01110111 00100000 01110011
01110100 01110010 01101111 01101110 01100111 01100101
01110010 00100000 01101101 01101111 01110010 01100101
00100000 01100001 01100011 01100011 01110101 01110010
01100001 01110100 01100101 00100000 01101101 01101111
01110010 01100101 00100000 01100110 01101111 01100011
01110101 01110011 01100101 01100100 00100000 01100001
00100000 01100100 01110010 01100101 01100001 01101101
00100000 01110100 01101000 01100001 01110100 00100000
01101000 01100001 01110011 00100000 01100111 01110010
01101111 01110111 01101110 00100000 01110100 01100101
01100101 01110100 01101000 00100000 01100001 00100000
01100111 01101000 01101111 01110011 01110100 00100000
01101111 01100110 00100000 01100001 00100000 01101101
01101001 01101100 01101100 01101001 01101111 01101110
00100000 01100001 01110010 01101101 01110011 00100000
01101000 01101111 01110111 00100000 01101001 01110010
01110010 01101001 01110100 01100001 01110100 01101001
01101110 01100111 00100000 01110100 01101111 00100000

require a contingency plan when i have so much to do first thing first fireworks

CHAPTER TWENTY

'Can we stop it?'

'Not as yet, no. It has proven impervious to every attack and back-hack we have fired at it. We have an army of avatars at work on it, but every time they corner it in some system it just dissolves away and appears somewhere else. We can't pin it down – we've never seen anything like it. We're talking a different league from any of our bleeding-edge tech.'

'Who made it?'

The smaller man shook his head. His face was well-worn, heavy in the jowls despite his leanness. He looked as if something major was slowly cooking inside him somewhere – maybe a fat, juicy cancer or heart disorder – something expensive to fix, at any rate. 'How anyone could have *made* it is beyond me. The government, maybe? One of our tech-crime worms tells us that it could have originated in the storage system of a company called Cyberlife Research and Development, but frankly it could be a false trail. The worm has never been too reliable – he's a drug addict. Really, who knows?' His voice contained just the faintest hint of resignation.

'And who are Cyberlife Research and Development?'

'You'll like this.' The smaller man leaned forwards across the perspex curve of the strategy director's desk with a data spot on one outstretched fingertip.

'Fuck that, just tell me,' grunted the director. 'I'm not a bloody computer, man.' He was hugely built, a bulbous-necked bullfrog of a man with a poison ice gun built into one bared forearm, relic of his days on the front line. He swatted at a pair of spyflies that were flying a flickering synchronised display around his head. They easily evaded the swipe and buzzed off into a corner of the room where they were safely out of reach.

The smaller man flinched slightly and a look of irritation darted across his face, like a hunted animal fleeing into a hedgerow, and was gone, replaced again by a carefully-cultivated neutral expression. 'Yes, Sir,' he said in a level voice. The spot disappeared again into some hiding place about his person. He sat back, composing himself as best he could beneath the wilting stare of the director. 'We cooked up a charge and got hold of a warrant to raid their computers an hour ago.

There's nothing there. And when I say nothing, I mean there *are* no computers. Cyberlife R and D cannot be found on the net. Either it never existed or somebody scrubbed the lot. As for finding an actual premises...' He spread his hands, palms up, illustrating how little his search had uncovered.

'So your damned worm made the whole thing up then! Get him into a cell!'

'It is certainly possible, but I really doubt he's that inventive. And the net address he gave us for this Cyberlife is certainly near the apparent epicentre of the disturbance.'

'So Cyberlife was a front company for whoever is behind this damn thing?'

'We don't know. But whoever was behind Cyberlife is gone now. There are no files held by the tax office pertaining to any workers. If they ever were there then a cover up of this magnitude, which must have required hacking into banks, government bodies, private corporations...that's quite a piece of electronic machination in itself. My worm tells us that the director was a man or woman by the name of Alcubierre, but we find no government records pertaining to that name. We're trawling masses of spyfly data to search for any visual record of the company, but much of it is corrupted, unusable. We don't know if the rogue element did it or someone from Cyberlife but it's certainly unprecedented. We have people still searching for employee records but so far we can't trace a single person who ever worked for them.'

'And you think Cyberlife itself may be a front? A false trail? Hell of a length to go to.'

'It's possible that someone else made this thing, founded Cyberlife as an elaborate front, yes, developed the rogue element off-site, laid a false trail to Cyberlife, then packed up their real operation, dissolved the front company and vanished, leaving a trail of breadcrumbs leading to nowhere much at all. Kind of the physical equivalent of a proxy server.'

'Fuck it, then – we're busy enough without chasing ghosts.' His heavy face was waxy beneath an unhealthy sheen of sweat. The two men looked as if their bodies were locked in a desperate race towards death. They were unaware that some junior officers actually had bets on the outcome.

The smaller man smoothed his suit with a gesture that the director found unbearably fussy and continued. 'Currently we need all the resources we have just to wrest control back from this thing.'

'What in hell do you mean *wrest control back*? I thought we were trying to contain the spread.'

'It's not looking that easy any more, I'm afraid, sir. Large corporations are working out what's happening for themselves, dumping vast amounts of tech stock, pulling out of financing deals, setting a domino effect in motion. The rogue element itself has had a hand in here and there, doctoring financial records of major companies, tampering with banks. It's getting bolder.' He looked to the director for acknowledgement. The director's face was sullen, angry, maybe even frightened. 'The stock market is going to crash massively and the world market with it. We can't keep it hush for long.'

'We should go public? There will be bank runs, panic. We could make a crash happen just by saying it. It isn't my decision, that's one for the government.'

'It will be the decision of whoever leaks it first, sir. I predict,' he said with a punchable hint of smugness, 'that somebody will do so in the next twenty-four hours, and recommend that it would be better if we said it first. The crash is already beginning.'

'Noted,' grunted the director.

'And, sir...It is *only* the beginning.'

'I agree,' said the director, but his expression was distant. His huge, meaty hands picked up an antique fountain pen from the desk and began to roll it between their surprisingly nimble fingers.

'And what of our other problem? This Genetic Degenerative Disorder?'

Briefly, the smaller man's attention flicked to the glass wall separating the office from the computer room outside. An air of increased urgency was developing out there amidst the swarms of huddling technicians.

'Oh yes, our other little problem.' He sighed deeply and continued, 'Everyone we have spoken to in the body modification industry claims to have no knowledge of the origins of the green...' He trailed off. 'Er...'

'Greenshit, I believe people are calling it on the streets.'

'Um, yes, Sir. None of them knows where the *greenshit* is coming from. Our own labs are evaluating several cases in the bio-segregation units. The parasitic organs resist analysis. It's as if they're deliberately engineered to self-destruct under x-ray or physical dissection. Kills the subject, of course. Some people are theorising that somebody has hacked the nanovats, some sort of computer terrorist who's re-coded the DNA of grown tissues. But every vat we have looked at seems to function normally. That is to say, they produce normal tissues when examined. My money is on some sort of black market release that was badly coded and has somehow entered the legitimate shops. Now it's going wrong they claim to have no knowledge of it. We may have to turn some of them over, see if they're withholding anything.'

'Hmm,' growled the director. He was grinding his teeth together and the squeaking, crunching noise made the smaller man shudder.

'This greenshit is too problematic, too intelligently designed to be an accident. If some terrorist is doing this to people we have to find them and burn them at the stake.'

'Given,' said the director. The pen stopped rolling, pointed straight at the smaller man like a gun. 'Strip those vats to the molecular level, full analysis of all materials, complete reverse-engineering of all software. Find every part on the logs and bring me a list of everyone walking around with a mod that came from one of them. Trace those people and bring them in. If we can't take them all in our labs, then commandeer a hospital ward, fully bio-seal it and bring me a complete genetic analysis of every subject. Start preparing warrant requests for some of the big shops – HGR, BlueGene, Spiral Sciences.'

'Sir, we can't legally commandeer a hospital ward without a court judgement, a judgement we are not going to get because the hospitals are already at bursting point. Farstar Militia stormed Niles Arlen Hospital and ejected all non-GDD cases earlier today and it looks like the government are going to send the army in to take it back. We would never get away with it.'

'*Farstar*? Aren't they a deep-space exploration corp? What the hell are they doing seizing a hospital? Why have I not heard of this?'

'I don't know, sir. There are some very cloak-and-dagger goings-on at the moment. But suffice to say that we cannot seize a hospital – it could prove a divisive issue between our own administration and that of the government and right now we can't afford to be stepping on the army's toes. All the hospitals are overburdened. The GDD is making a lot of people sick. Nobody has died yet, but they say it's only a matter of time. Whatever this illness really is, it seems to cause psychosis in its early stages, a degenerative physical malady after that. They do not—'

There was a sudden eruption of chaos in the computer room, people pushing each other out of the way of terminals, tripping over each other's hi-flo cables. Both men turned to look.

'The fuck is happening out there?' grumbled the director. He heaved himself to his feet, his belly pendulous and vast. Somebody began hammering on the office door. The director shot a venomous look at the smaller man, as if whatever might be behind this intrusion had already been attributed to him in the director's mind. The smaller man actually retreated slightly into his chair, completely unaware that he was doing so. The director did notice and this satisfied him slightly. He turned to where the young computer technician was banging on the glass frantically, mouthing words silently at the soundproofed door. Mentally, he swung the door open. The young woman burst into the room.

'Sir, sir, it's Air Traffic Control on the priority line, we tried to put you straight through, but your personal link is off, it's—' She began to stammer, gasping out part-words like little coughs. The director watched her struggle with grim and patient detachment. She looked as if she was beginning to hyperventilate. 'It's, they say, it's...'

'Yes, Miss Vestovich?' he prompted.

'They say...' Her hands were fluttering up and down like startled birds in flight.

And then there was the unmistakable sound of a huge explosion from the west and the three had just enough time to exchange fearful looks. The director and the young woman hit the deck instinctively, but the smaller man sat frozen in his chair. A great locomotive of noise came roaring towards the police building, surfing on a tremendous pressure-wave. The triple-glazed windows of the office blew in, becoming a gale of glittering knives that shredded the smaller man where he sat. All throughout the district, the tremulous warbles of alarms began to rise in chorus.

168

CHAPTER TWENTY-ONE

By midday Sofi was pretty much slaughtered, although she showed few outward signs of it, and Tec, despite his slightly higher body-mass, was doing rather worse. He kept accidentally knocking items off the table with inadvertent swipes of his wildly gesturing arms. Whistler swayed slightly as she went to get another beer, throwing her empty into a bin in the corner with surprising accuracy. Even Debian had been convinced to start on the vodka. He was heatedly explaining to a disinterested Sofi about the finer intricacies of using avatars with maximum clandestineness. Tec, chain-smoking reeferettes, occasionally nodded in agreement, his head glowing a steady green. Whistler did wonder if this unplanned party was the most professional way to present themselves to their new client, but after her third beer she didn't really care. Debian didn't seem to care, either, she noted. *Ho-hum*. She uncapped the new bottle and weaved back to her seat through clouds of dope-smoke as thick as curtains.

'So,' she said to Debian, leaning close enough to be heard. He smelled of vodka and soap, a fairly pleasant mixture. A thumping Undercity rap track was playing on the audio stream – *We run the sewers and sub-streets/ Deep in the blood of the enemy; seek the sun/ I run with the cybernetic thugs with smartguns* – and everybody seemed to be talking over each other. 'You a career hacker, or what? Never occurred to me as a major industry before.' She had decided that she believed him about the AI in the net.

'No? Lots of people do it,' he replied, slurring slightly.

'Yeah, sure, I know that but–'

'I was always into computers. My old man used to design embedded AI chips for household appliances. Pioneering work, actually, in its day. Minimisation and simplification of AI routines, and so on. Trying to get any semblance of intelligence into a fridge and still produce it at an affordable price is not that easy – at least, it wasn't then. Of course, the damn things are everywhere these days. Thankfully, though, the power of this new monster intelligence in the net is so far unique. My old man wouldn't believe it.'

'Guess not,' she agreed quietly. There was a moment of silence between them then during which Debian's eyes grew unfocused and Whistler sensed the sadness descending on him again. She cursed herself for prompting it and noticed that the conversation of the others had faltered too, as they sensed the mood. She shrugged. 'So you're pretty much from a solid bloodline of geek stock, then,' she commented. For a second Debian stared at her and she thought she might have offended him. But then he noticed that she was smiling and he began to laugh. Then they were both laughing and the moment had passed.

'Yeah,' he said. 'Pretty much.' He drank from his glass of vodka and Whistler noticed that his sips had become long drags. His milky eyes were large and shiny. The greyness looked as if it was shifting in there, as if smoke billowed inside his head. 'My mum was killed in the gang raids when I was little – you know, Click Thirteen and the Roughriders, all those upstart tech gangs – and I lived with my old man since I was seven. I got into the political scene – became a cyber-terrorist, attacking government services and banks. Later on I moved into commercial hacking. My old man pretty much pretended ignorance. He died about six years ago.'

'Shit,' said Whistler. 'That's heavy.' What else was there to say, really? And who *hadn't* suffered in their life? Whistler had never known her parents at all, so seven years of mother seemed like a bonus to her. It was hard to sound sympathetic. Maybe they could talk about Tec's early years as an e-thief and gang fighter in Click Thirteen – that would doubtless be popular.

'Nah,' he said, possibly detecting the reservation in her tone. 'I mean, it was okay, really. We lived in a good part of High Hab, he was well-paid – I know he loved me and all that. It was okay.'

'Then why the life of crime, man? I don't get it. I was born into it, left on the doorstep of a gang-operated orphanage. *Blood Collective*. I was a true foundling. You know they set those places up to acquire kids to train into gang members? I got out of the Collective, though, in the end. That's a story in itself. But you must have gone out of your way, right?'

'Yeah, I guess.' He looked thoughtful, distant. 'I guess I did.'

Whistler studied him, wondering where his mind was. She sensed that he would speak no more of the subject for now and decided not to push it.

'So what about you guys?' Debian asked, seemingly returning to the room and now addressing the harvesters more generally. 'What business are you in?' Normally he would have been more cautious about asking this sort of question of obvious career criminals whom he barely knew, but the vodka had begun fizzing in his head and some lower part of his mind seemed to be assuming control by silent coup. 'If it's not rude to ask,' the remaining, more cautious part of him managed to add.

Sofi swigged her beer – she only drank synthi – and stared straight at Debian, her conversation with Tec aborted. 'We steal human beings,' she said ghoulishly, but with total sincerity. 'And we sell them to people who cut them up like stolen pods and re-sell the bits for profit. If it's not rude to answer.' She smiled broadly – a crocodile smile, heavy on teeth but light on warmth, and tapped a smoke from a battered packet with a pink-lacquered nail.

Debian sat stunned. Had he thought that these were his kind of people? What in the *fuck* was he doing sitting here drinking with these animals? 'Oh,' he said, his throat dry. 'Really?'

Sofi nodded, lighting her reeferette with a micro-laser on her knuckle and scorching the ceiling at the same time. 'Really. Nice eyes, by the way.' She drew deeply on the joint, observing him mischievously through the veil of smoke.

'Wow,' Debian said, turning back to Whistler. 'You steal people and sell them – what, to bodymod companies or something?' Whistler nodded, clicking her talons on the neck of her beer bottle. Her expression was a mask of neutrality. 'Never occurred to me as a major industry before.'

Whistler laughed to hear her words parroted back. 'Well it is,' she said. Tec leaned over and offered her a capsule of drifter, which she refused. 'Isn't it, Tec?'

'Yeah,' he agreed, well-trained. He swayed a little as he relaxed back into his chair. He looked reflectively at the strip of drifter caps, clearly considering whether he should take one and eventually put them away unused.

'We steal people who have expensive mods, sometimes people who are just particularly good-looking. Anyone we like, really. Good faces sell well anywhere. We harvest bits and bobs for several big companies, one in particular. The money's good, the perks're good – almost blanket legal protection, for one thing. As long as certain requirements are met, of course.'

171

'Of course,' agreed Debian, having nothing else to say. 'Harvest?'

'Yeah, that's what it's known as. We are the scythe of humanity, man. Or some shit like that. Top up?'

'Sure, why not?'

Whistler, unable to think of any reason why not, refilled Debian's glass from the bottle on her side of the table and signalled Sofi, who was at the fridge again, looking for food this time, for another beer. Sofi, reeferette hanging from one corner of her mouth, reached for the beer and coughed explosively right into the fridge, showering out ash and embers with it.

'Oh fucking *nice*, Sofe!' exclaimed Tec, throwing his hands up in exasperation. His head flashed red, but only for a split-second. 'Give us all your fucking TB!'

'Piss off!' replied Sofi, laughing around the reeferette and throwing Whistler her beer. 'There hasn't been any TB for fucking centuries.' She returned to her seat, still laughing.

'Anthrax, then, or shivers or some such happy thing,' Tec harried her, shoving her as she sat, unbalancing her. Sofi shoved back and reacquired her own beer from the table. 'Dirty girl,' he chided her.

'So you guys have police immunity, then?' asked Debian. 'That's pretty handy. Is it expensive?'

'Yeah,' said Tec. 'We don't pay for it, though. And it's not total, y'know – some of the smaller forces give us grief now and then. Nothing we couldn't handle so far.'

'So, Debian,' said Whistler. 'Is this AI of yours capable of making these mutant organs by hacking nanovats? Could it do it? Forget about *why* for now – just could it?'

He puffed his cheeks out, swirling the vodka in its glass. 'I think the thing I came across could do anything it wanted. It attacked me – or whatever it did – by EM induction. It seemed incredibly voracious as well as capable.'

'Okay,' said Whistler. 'Imagine we're stupid or ignorant – *what*?'

'I wasn't even connected to it, I don't think. It was in a supposedly isolated terminal.'

'Right,' said Sofi. 'So what does that mean?'

'It's a technique I helped to pioneer myself. Quite well known now, but it involves specialist kit and knowledge to do. That should have suggested a set-up to me, because the AI's machine was physically

172

connected to the induction equipment. Why, is the real question – who would have actually done it? Maybe if I'd worked it out a second or two earlier I would have got out in time. Anyway, an artificial intelligence has never been known to do it before. It's the same technology that some of the more advanced scrambler-baits use, but they run a very simple induction-pattern from a chip. It's entirely passive. To use it smartly – to change the code on the fly and use it as an organic attack mechanism – that takes real intelligence. Neural simulations, intelligent robots, smart programs – they're all kinds of AI, but under the hood they're all pretty simple, really. This is something else. If not in type then in magnitude. Maybe not artificial in the same sense at all.' Some of the longer words stuck in his throat a little, but the intention was clear enough. He shook his head. 'It doesn't matter. Just take it as read that this thing is very capable. Yeah, I think it could do it.'

'Okay,' said Whistler. 'So it's just *why*, then.' Debian, blank-faced, shook his head. 'And can it be stopped? That, too.'

'Also,' said Sofi, 'if the AI hacked the vats, made the greenshit, it would have been doing it *before* Debian's contact with it. Right?'

'Oh yeah,' said Whistler thoughtfully. 'Maybe Debian's contact with it was...I don't know...Do you think it can be stopped?'

'Judging by the problems reported on the news, I'd say that it's already spreading through the net very rapidly by now. Stop it? It's stronger than I am – I lost my only argument with it.'

Whistler felt a lump in her throat. She tried to swallow, couldn't. 'And you're the best around, right? Then it's gonna spread like wildfire. If it wants to.'

'Nuts to this!' declared Sofi, springing clumsily from her seat. 'I hate this gutter-rap shit. Let's do some sinistro or something.'

She began to hunt around the counter-top, flinging objects out of her way. She turned back with a glossy red data-spot on one outstretched fingertip, which she adhered to the reader on the back of her hand. Heavy sinistro beats interrupted the newsreader who had come back onto the audio-stream. Tec fired up the mini holo-projector on the table and a multicoloured hologramatic bird began to move through the air in time to the music, swooping low over the table, its huge body confined by the walls of the kitchen, its long tail twining around it. The projector didn't do forcefield, and occasionally the bird would snap its massive beak harmlessly at one of the humans. They all watched it in silence for some time. Some tricks never got old. Presently, the bird began to spout blue bolts of mock-electricity from its beak. These crackled around the room, arcing from one person to another in time with the music, before burying themselves in walls or ceiling, where they vanished.

Whistler jumped as one of the bolts arced to her, bathing her form in a blue nimbus. She held her hands in front of her face, turning them over in fascination. They wore gloves of light like auras. 'I don't like it,' she said. Her head was beginning to spin, made worse when the energy bolt arced from her into Sofi as the bass-pattern of the music changed. The bird seemed to be becoming angry – its beak was snapping constantly now, and it was showing clear signs of agitation as it writhed around the room. Its beady amber eyes were rolling madly in its head. 'Turn it off, Sofe!'

Sofi, bottle in hand, still crackling with illusory electricity, rose from her seat and, far from turning the music off, began to dance. Her hair flicked wildly as she kicked her seat away and started to gyrate to the thumping bass-beat. The bird, noticing, descended lower and began to move around her, spiralling about her body in a blur of feathers. 'Whooo!' hooted Sofi, ignoring Whistler completely. She raised her arms and lost herself. Debian watched her, stunned.

'Right!' said Whistler decisively. 'Right!' She grabbed the holo-projector from the table and threw it against a wall. It shattered more impressively than she had really expected, raining intricate components onto the counter-top and floor. Tiny, expensive pieces of exquisite machinery glittered and flashed as they showered down. The bird suddenly winked out of existence. The music continued to play, however – Slack Monday's *Kiss the Bass* was mixing into Fuckerpunch's underground hit single *Into the Void* and the sub thrummed massively in the metal-walled room, making Whistler want to throw up.

'What the hell!?' demanded Sofi, rounding on her. Debian started to make placatory hand gestures.

'Turn that damn noise off, too!' shouted Whistler over the racket. She felt the smartgun humming in her pocket. She didn't even remember having seen it, let alone picking it up. Whistler was not a massive sinistro fan at the best of times, and right now the music was having an adverse effect on her sanity. The gun didn't really care about her sanity, of course – quite the reverse, it sometimes seemed – it just fed on the tension, the raised voices, the whiffs of adrenaline in the air.

'Like f–' started Sofi, before she was cut off by the chime of an incoming communication.

'It's HGR,' said Tec, holding one hand to his ear. This was a common gesture among people communicating by DNI. Apparently it was an instinctive one, even though audio communication channels were relayed directly to the language centres of the brain and not actually heard in the usual sense. He looked relieved by the interruption.

'Oh!' said Whistler. 'I'd forgotten about them.'

'Should we answer? Is it on net-phone?' asked Sofi, holo-projector forgotten. 'Is it safe?'

'Yeah,' said Tec. 'It's a satellite call, Mother says. Answer it.' Mother was the building's central computer, a beast of limited brain but great caution.

'Okay,' said Whistler, preening herself, as if by putting her physical appearance in order she could straighten her mind up, too. She moved into the field of one of the camera/microphone communication points. 'Put it on. Is it Smith?'

Just then, her question was answered for her as the music died and Mrs. Smith's grim face filled the screen that depended from the ceiling. She looked even less happy than normal.

'Whistler,' said the image.

'Hi,' answered Whistler, swaying gently. Self-consciously, she put her bottle down.

'Who else is there with you?'

Whistler looked around. Tec and Sofi were listening intently, just outside the view of the camera. Debian was looking into the depths of his glass, trying not to overhear or oversee anything that he shouldn't. He looked up as Whistler's gaze fell on him. 'Should I step out?' he asked.

Whistler shook her head and said to Smith, 'Nobody you can't speak in front of. What is it?'

'I wanted to talk to you about your latest *assignment*,' said Smith emphatically.

'Right...' said Whistler. 'About that...'

'I know, I know – not good news. As I'm sure you've heard, the greenshit is everywhere now – it's getting out of hand. It appears that some organs we have *passed on* may have caused subsequent infection in patients, even though we scanned them as clean. We are currently fending off investigative demands from the various authorities. City Police actually think we might have something to do with it! We are dissolving all links to sub-mainstream harvesting teams and ceasing trading until this mess is cleared up. And worse still, several people have walked out of here with legitimate parts that we grew on-site and ended up with the infection. This is going to shut us down, Whistler. At least for now.'

'I'm sorry?' said Whistler, who was having trouble sorting the implications of this out in her mind. 'So you're cutting us loose? Is that it?'

'I regret this, Whistler. We appreciate your services in the past, but we cannot sustain even a core operation at the moment. Of course, keep the money we paid you already for your investigations. I will also personally order the settlement of the remainder of your fee as a token of goodwill.'

'You don't even want to hear if we found anything?'

Smith's eyes narrowed on the screen, making her look even more severe. 'Did you?'

Whistler felt her mind swimming, wished she had had the foresight to take a hit of Get-Up before answering. She looked around at her companions. Tec looked cool as ever, his lights a mixture of blue and green. He was sipping a beer. Sofi looked ready to punch somebody – she stood tensely, her fists balled at her sides – and possibly because of this, Debian was keeping his head firmly down. 'Not really,' she admitted. 'We traced the guy who did the black market work on Leo Travant, but he didn't seem to know any more than anybody else. We went to visit one of his patients, a man he believed to be infected.'

'And?' demanded Mrs. Smith impatiently. She looked as if she wanted to go, as if she had already accepted that the chances of this conversation yielding anything of value to her were virtually zero.

'He killed himself when we forced access to his premises.' Smith snorted derisively, as if she had expected no better. 'He looked sick, really sick. He was certainly infected, possibly dying. Looked as if he was *changing*.' She was aware of Tec lighting another smoke behind her.

Smith sighed with such expressive weariness that Whistler almost felt sorry for her. She looked away from the camera for a moment. When she looked back, she seemed ten years older. 'That's what they do, Whistler. So it seems.'

'What is the end result?' asked Tec. 'Into *what* are they changing?'

Smith's eyes roved across the room, glaring from the monitor like searchlights until the camera homed in on the sound of Tec's voice. 'Ah, Mister Simonde,' she said.

'Nobody calls me that,' replied Tec conversationally. 'But yeah. Hi.'

'HGR would like to thank you for your efforts over these last years. I regret that it has not been possible for us to have a closer working relationship.' Tec nodded minutely in acknowledgement. 'But business is business. We do not know, Mister Simonde, what they change *into*, if anything at all. Perhaps the mutation is random. Perhaps,' and here she seemed to take a deep breath, 'not. We have several subjects under sedation. They are being altered at the genetic level, but we can't tell exactly *how*. My people are very worried about this, as are the health authorities. The hospitals are bursting, I hear.' She looked like the grey ghost of happiness lost, her tightly drawn-back hair making the lines of her skull stand out in sharp relief.

'This other thing – I'm sure you've heard of it – could be related, we think,' said Whistler. She really felt too stoned for this conversation. 'The er – er – computer thing,' she finished lamely.

'Yes?' asked Smith over arched fingers.

'We have someone here at the moment who suggests that the current crop of computer problems could be the work of an extremely powerful AI virus. It, or the people who made it, could have hacked the nanovats. We don't know why this would be, if true. It's only a hypothesis.' This last word gave her some trouble but she succeeded in the end.

'Interesting,' mused Smith. She stared off into the distance for some time. Whistler could hear only Tec's slow swigs of beer from behind her. Debian was paying attention now, his polite face turned up to watch the screen where Smith deliberated internally.

'It's purely theoretical at the moment,' he said, speaking to Smith for the first time. 'I don't know how we'd verify it.'

The camera turned towards him. 'Who are you?' asked Smith abruptly, startled out of her reverie.

'He's safe,' said Whistler, realizing as she said it that she had decided this fact for herself sometime over the last few hours.

Smith sighed deeply. 'What matter anyway,' she said rhetorically. 'Whistler, we have to shut down for a bit. I'm afraid that means the end of your immunity contract, unless you pay for its continuance yourselves, of course. I'm sorry, I don't know how long this will last. We will look into this computer business, although the problems we are having with our own systems are making our operations difficult. There is something going on in the net, certainly, but due to the degradation in service that it seems to be causing, it's proving hard to even monitor the situation...' She trailed off, lost in thought again. Slowly, she seemed to return. 'Anyway, Whistler, thank you for your service. We will certainly seek to employ your team again in the future.' Smith shrugged, as if she wanted to say *look after yourselves* or *all the best* but couldn't make herself do it. 'Goodbye. And I suggest that you—' And then the image on the screen flickered briefly, shredded by a blizzard of interference, and died.

'What happened, Tec?' asked Whistler.

Tec held one hand to his head, and she knew he was communicating with Mother. 'It was cut off from HGR's end,' he said.

'Damn. Computer problems?'

'We don't know.' They sat for a minute in silence and then Tec looked up and asked, 'Do you feel that?'

'What, us being fired?' asked Whistler, still caught up in her own thoughts. 'Yeah, I felt it in my bank account. It felt like—'

'No, no!' Tec was shouting now and rising from his seat. '*That!*' He spread his hands, palms up, and glanced around, his face a caricature of inquiry. And, thought Whistler, fear.

She looked at the faces of the others. 'What?'

'Shit...' breathed Sofi. 'What *is* that?'

'What!?' demanded Whistler, increasingly irritated. And then she felt it, too. The floor was rumbling, thrumming gently as if she were standing on the hull of some vast machine. 'Oh...' she said and then a deep, concussive roar came rolling out of the north-east: The bellow of a monster baying at the gates of hell. Whistler felt a shiver go down her spine.

Sofi was pointing her micro-laser, set to red-dot, her eyes trying to cover every corner of the room at once. 'What the hell is that?'

'Ssshhh...' said Debian, head cocked and listening, one finger held up for silence. 'It's big, but it's distant.'

'An explosion,' said Whistler. The roar was still going on, a vast and steady wave of sound washing over them. The bottles on the counter-top jostled each other gently – *ting-a-ling-a-ling* – sounding like a faraway fire-bell. And beneath it all, she heard the hammering of her own heart.

'Should we take cover?' asked Debian, his eyes wide, ghostly blanks. The lights in the big room flickered off and then back on. They stuttered again, then steadied. Everybody was looking around themselves, dumbfounded.

'Downstairs?' suggested Sofi.

'Yeah,' agreed Whistler hurriedly. 'Come on!' They scrambled for the stairs. Debian staggered on his injured leg and nearly fell, clutching at the rail to save himself. Whistler noticed that Sofi paused long enough to grab her beer.

They pelted down the steps onto the ground floor of the big room, through the door and down to the living quarters. Whistler's mind was chanting *What about Spider? What about Roberts?* over and over like a mantra. They were out there somewhere. With the current net problems, would they even be able to get in touch?

The group milled around in the corridor outside Tec's lab, at least as much as the narrow passage would allow. They could no longer hear the noise, but still a tang of animal fear was in the air.

'What the fuck was that?' asked Sofi. Nobody had an answer. 'Something blew up, right?' Still no answer. Their breathing was loud in the confined space.

'Should we go to the hangar?' Tec asked Whistler. 'That's the deepest, safest part of the base. Thick walls.'

Whistler strained to hear. 'I think it's stopped,' she said. 'And we're basically in an underground bunker now, anyway.'

'I say give it five, then go back up,' said Sofi. Thankfully, she had stopped waving the micro-laser around now. 'Try to find out what's happening.'

'If I could use DNI wireless I could find out now,' remarked Tec, with some small bitterness. 'You sure it's not okay, Debian?'

Debian was biting his lip. 'Maybe we should try it. I have a proxy chain we could—'

'Are you fucking crazy, man?' demanded Whistler. 'You were just telling everyone not to connect and that you're a wanted man, remember? Nobody connects for now. Put the satellite feed back on.' She studied Debian closely and he turned away from her. Was he really so eager to get back in there? He had seemed so frightened so recently – it didn't make much sense to her. Damn buttonheads.

'Right, yeah.' The feed started up again as Tec instructed Mother to turn on all the speakers on the basement floor. A real, human-sounding newsreader had replaced the virtual being.

'Shut up!' Sofi yelled at Debian, who had begun talking to Whistler quietly. Debian frowned slightly – just the smallest pinching of the eyebrows, really – but silenced.

The voice of the newsreader echoed down the concrete gullet of the corridor: '—reporting that a fuel barge has hit the Centre District, causing massive damage and loss of life. The barge was on a standard landing pattern, heading for City Six space port when the disaster happened. Air Traffic Control were alerted to a problem with the computer navigation system but it was too late to prevent the disaster. It was over in minutes. It is unknown as yet whether this was the result of a terrorist attack, human error or an equipment failure. We now go over to our disaster correspondent, Marti McCallan, watching the proceedings from Silver Square, on the edge of Centre District. Marti...'

'Thank you, Sefena – fires are raging all across the Financial Sector. The sky here is dark as night – huge clouds of smoke rolling across the city from the point of impact, in the north-west corner of the Centre District. A strong westerly wind is carrying most of that smoke over into the Undercity, and one concern is that the fumes may be harmful.' Marti sounded filled with boyish excitement at the opportunity to relate this disaster to his listeners. 'Many large buildings in the Financial Sector have been destroyed, simply wiped away by this immense explosion. Eyewitnesses report the barge scraping its underbelly over the rooftops of those tall towers, spreading its cargo over a wide area. Er, we understand, Sefena, that the emergency services are experiencing serious communication and equipment problems. We *are* hearing sirens now, converging on the Financial Sector, but I'm also getting reports of many emergency units currently unable to respond. At this stage, the loss of life is incalculable, but it's likely to be in the tens of thousands. Citizens are advised to remain indoors unless they are directly threatened by the fires. As soon as any official advice is given, you will hear it here first, so stay inside and stay tuned. For now, we would say that it is unlikely—'

'Oh shit...' sighed Whistler. She rubbed at her forehead, behind which a headache of promisingly massive proportions seemed to be brewing. Tec turned the news feed down so they could converse.

'A *fuel barge*!' said Debian disbelievingly. 'Those things are *huge*. This could be very bad. *Very* bad.'

'*Navigation computer*,' said Whistler, leaning against a wall for support.

Debian nodded. 'It's attacking the city,' he answered. 'What is going on here? It sounds as if it's disrupting the civil infrastructure, too, making it harder for us to deal with the crisis. This is an attack.' He sounded grimly assured of this fact.

'By whom?' asked Tec, in the tone of one not expecting an answer. 'Why?'

'Perhaps it's acting on its own,' suggested Debian. 'Perhaps not. If I could connect, there's a chance I could find out what's going on.'

'Whistler's right, man, it's too dangerous. Last time, you think it might have pattern-scanned you, making it more powerful than before. What would it do this time? Perhaps it would kill you by DNI. Theoretically it's possible, right? Maybe it would just find your location, send robots to do it or something. I don't think you should do it.' Tec shook his head firmly to underline this point.

Debian remembered what he had done to Hex, what seemed like a million years ago. He recalled how empowered he had felt. How could he feel so helpless now? Maybe if he could get back into the data-stream that power could be rekindled. 'I could try to find out what went wrong in my hard firewall last time. Or just use regular avatars. I'd have to use a chain of proxies to slow the discovery of my location. Even so, it wouldn't buy much time to investigate. It's dangerous, and difficult with fire-and-forgets, but maybe possible. Maybe—'

Whistler cut him off. 'Debian, that's one too many maybes for me, I'm afraid. While you remain on my premises, I don't think I can allow that. It could endanger us all.'

'Are we not all endangered right now?' he asked, staring into her face with clear determination.

'Might as well let him try,' suggested Sofi. 'If he wants to fry his brain, fuckin' let him, I say. Besides, it might even do some good. Who knows?'

'Thanks,' said Debian, the ghost of a smile on his lips. 'I think.' He seemed to have sobered up dramatically since the explosion. Whistler, regrettably, knew how he felt.

'Okay, man, okay…' Whistler said with evident exasperation. 'You're paying me to protect you from these people who might want to kill you, not to stop you from killing yourself if that's your wish: You decide. If we can help you do this in any way, we will. Tec – you give him any assistance he needs. We'll worry about anything the AI sends after you when it happens. This place is basically a minor fortress, so I'm not too frightened about that. Right now I'm more concerned about Roberts and Spider, who might not be all that far from where that fucking thing came down.'

'Right,' said Sofi, pressing one hand to her ear. 'I'm trying to raise them now.' She began to pace, her plastic boot-heels clacking on the concrete floor.

Tec led Debian into the lab, the two of them already chattering away heatedly in a flurry of indecipherable terminology. The lights went on in the lab, and then the door closed behind them leaving only Whistler and Sofi in the corridor. Whistler began to find Sofi's pacing infectious and had to consciously restrain herself from joining her friend on her pointless circuit up and down the hallway.

'Well?' demanded Whistler, unable to bear the suspense any longer. 'Anything?'

Sofi stopped, shrugged, still clutching her beer in one hand. She looked thin and wraith-like in the shadows. 'The line's dead.'

'Dead,' echoed Whistler. She hoped that this state of being did not extend to her friends as well as the satellite connection.

CHAPTER TWENTY-TWO

'Is knackered,' said Roland, laying Spider's mag-rifle gently down on his workbench. 'In my professional opinion. Operating system totally locked up. I can fix, but is a big job with my computer playing up.'

'Right,' said Spider, chuckling. 'I thought as much. Will it take you long?'

Roberts was wandering around Roland's small 'office' inspecting the various guns on display. He turned round holding a long, chromed mag-rifle he had taken down from the wall. Its narrow sides were carved with intricate designs and its body was otherwise entirely free from any machining marks. 'How about we trade it in against this one?' he asked Roland.

'Yeah, yeah,' said Roland, rubbing the nape of his neck with one of those weird hands of naked bone. 'Is possible. Take me maybe 'til Monday to fix. If you want to trade in, take that one now, fine.' He looked up at Roberts, his eyes the deepest shiny black. 'Is nice, yes?' He pointed to the rifle Roberts had found.

'Let me see that,' said Spider, reaching for the ornate mag-rifle with one grasping pincer. Roberts handed it over and Spider turned it this way and that, sighting along the spindly barrel and inspecting the controls. 'Where the hell did you get this?' he asked Roland, clearly impressed.

Roland laughed – a dry, coughing sound – and scratched his white-stubbled chin. 'Special friend – you know, *business friend*. Limited edition. Is from an orbital factory.'

'No shit,' agreed Spider, squinting into the scope of the weapon. He swung the gun around and Roberts ducked. Spider laughed loudly.

'No shit, no. Very high muzzle velocity, even for a mag-rifle. It shoot through the side of a tank with liquid-points in it.'

'Do you have any?' asked Roberts.

'Yes. Course.' Roland sounded almost offended.

'How much?' asked Roberts, stepping around the workbench and almost tripping over Roland's insectoid robot, which seemed to be collecting crumbs of swarf from the floor and eating them.

'Well, if I give you twelve for yours...say, twenty-three?'

Roberts puffed his cheeks out, shocked. He exchanged a look with Spider, who laughed again. 'Your call, man,' said Spider. The long rifle looked almost small in his massive arms.

'*Twenty-three*? Whistler would kill us. That's more than the U55.'

Roland seemed to find this idea amusing. 'How is pretty lady?' he asked, his face mischievous.

'Fucking frugal, that's how she is, Roland. Tight as a duck's arse. If you could do it for eighteen, then maybe. I mean, she'll still hurt me, but not fatally.'

'Look, gentlemen, twelve is really too generous for your rifle. Twelve is price for a working gun. I still have to fix it to re-sell. At this price, I do you guys a favour. And actually, I think it's *you* who owe *me* a favour.'

'Damn,' said Spider, his dreams clearly shattered. He placed the mag-rifle back on its hooks with a wistful look and began to prospect for something cheaper among the ranks of weapons.

'How'd it go with Haspan in the end?' asked Roland, changing the subject. He looked thinner than ever in his dirty white vest, as if a strong breeze could damage him terminally. The low, orangey light in here was not flattering to his haggard face, either. 'Not too badly, I'd guess, as you still walking around.'

'Non-starter, sadly,' said Roberts. 'But thanks for arranging it for us, anyway. I guess we're out of work for a bit.' He didn't know that *out of work for a bit* had become *contract terminated* in his absence. He had been unable so far to connect back to the base. 'This greenshit is a conundrum.'

'I'll say,' agreed Roland. 'You know how many people have it now?'

'How many?' Spider asked. He turned back to Roland with a much simpler looking mag-rifle in his massive claws.

'Lots,' said Roland emphatically. 'Is a lot. Also, this computer shit. What's going on? Damn world's gone crazy. Can't patch any of the guns at the moment. I'm lucky I have software hard-copies for your gun. Somewhere. Fuck knows where, though!' He threw up his hands in a comical gesture, looking around his cluttered dwelling. Piles of weapon components covered every surface.

'How much for this one?' asked Spider.

'That one, with ten for your rifle...say, nine?'

'Ten for our gun?' boomed Spider, liking the old man better all the time. 'I thought you said twelve!'

'Is a cheaper gun!' explained Roland, as if to a child. 'I throw in two hundred of those liquid points you wanted, eh?'

Roberts sighed. 'My friend, you drive a hard bargain. Eleven for our gun.'

Roland shuffled past Spider and started retrieving small plastic boxes of ammunition from a drawer. He tutted and shook his head as he went. 'No, no, no. Ten against that cheaper gun. Is more than fair, and I think you know that.'

'Ten-and-a-half for hard money.'

Roland handed four boxes to Roberts. They were surprisingly light in his hand. 'Hard money's the only money there is at the moment. So of course hard money, yes.'

'Damn, man,' said Spider shaking his head. 'Just pay the guy, Rob. With the liquid points that's a good deal.' He turned to Roland, hefting the new mag-rifle happily. It was lighter than the old one and of better build quality, too. 'Thanks, Roland.'

Roland waved this away. 'You tell that pretty lady to come visit me again, okay? If you guys are out of work, maybe I have something for you.'

'What sort of something?' asked Roberts, intrigued but cautious.

'I talk to the organ grinder,' said Roland. 'No offence.'

'None taken. I'll tell her.' Roberts considered the possibility that Roland was just using this as an excuse to get Whistler back round to his lair. The old boy was clearly smitten, and why not. Roberts began to count out the cash onto one of the few clear areas of work-surface, watched keenly by those dark eyes. As soon as he reached nine-thousand, Roland's skeletal hand darted out, pilfered the pile and stowed it about his person in one fluid and surprisingly quick motion. He was probably running some synaptic-enhancement software.

'Thanks, then, Roland,' said Spider again, taking the ammo boxes and dropping them into the various bulky pockets of his combat jacket. The bulges they made were barely noticeable on his massive person. Less easy to hide, of course, was the rifle itself, but the harvesters had no concerns about walking to the van with it. The police didn't really come round here, and of course they also had almost-blanket immunity.

Roberts paused as he headed for the door. 'What is that?' he asked.

'What?' responded Roland. 'I don't...' He trailed off, squinting as if this would help him hear better. 'That noise?'

'What the hell...?' asked Spider. His gaze was drawn to the main workbench in the centre of the room. Upon its battered surface tiny machine parts were gently vibrating, dancing in a silvered blur. Several of them worked their ways to the edge of the table and fell to the floor. Spider stared dumbstruck, a great frown creasing his wide face. The door of an old cupboard beside the battered sofa slowly swung open of its own accord. 'Get down!' he yelled, dropping to his knees and trying to shelter his massive body beneath the table. Roland didn't seem to hear him, just stood there with an expression of mild bemusement on his face.

A great booming thunder was rolling out of the east. Roberts ducked and moved in a crouch towards the front door. For a moment Spider thought he was going to dive out of it. Out on the street they could hear people shouting. Roland's robot had come out from under the workbench and stood poised on its rear-most set of legs, head cocked. It still held a crumb of stainless steel in its mandibles. Its segmented eyes were alive with strange intelligence.

'An explosion,' said the robot, startling everyone. 'Near the space port.' Its voice was surprisingly human, if genderless. One of the guns fell off the wall with a loud clatter that cut through the deep rumbling coming from outside, making all the humans jump. Roland swore softly.

Roberts looked at the robot. 'Near the *space port*? It must be a hell of a bang. Are we safe here?'

'Too many variables,' said the robot dismissively.

'Safe from the fucking bomb, or whatever it is! The explosion, you smartass machine!' Glass was breaking nearby in the city – a delicate, shimmery, tinkling noise. Pod alarms were going off.

'Yes,' said the robot. It managed to sound offended. 'For now.'

'Sshh...' said Roland. 'Is still going on. Listen!'

'Shit!' cried Spider in what seemed like a fair summation of the situation. 'I have to see what it is, Roland. Look – thanks for the toy. We have to roll, but we'll be in touch, all being well. Assuming this isn't the end of the world or some shit.' He got to his feet and took the new mag-rifle.

'Okay, no problem,' said Roland distractedly. 'I just come out and have a look with you.' He started to the door.

'Okay, let's go,' said Roberts. He cautiously opened the door, slightly surprised that it hadn't been locked.

They stepped out into the grey trench of the alley. Random screams and shrieks pierced the day. Because of the narrow viewing angle afforded by the towering buildings around them they couldn't see much of the city. However, the alley ran almost due east-west and a massive pillar of black smoke could be seen rising from what had been the northern edge of Centre District. *Had been* because that distinctive part of the city's skyline, which had included several iconic tower blocks, was gone. The vast column of smoke rising from there made it look as if the huge black leg of a giant had stomped a great swathe of the city flat. What must have been massive chunks of debris fluttered against the sky like leaves in the wind. The orange dance of fire lit the skyline like an artillery barrage. Sirens could be heard climbing above the sounds of human distress, triggered by the shock-wave. The three people and the robot stood stunned, staring into the sky like prophets who had seen their deity descending from the heavens, wreathed in fire and brimstone, bent on vengeance.

'What the hell happened?' asked Roberts. People ran past in fleeing panic, jostling him, shouting and crying. Spider clutched the mag-rifle close to his chest and began to load it from one of the boxes still in his pocket. His face was grimly set.

'I don't know,' breathed Roland. 'I never seen anything like it. Are we under attack?' His face hung slackly, like the flesh of a corpse. 'Ariadne? What was it?'

'I can't even get satellite-feed at the moment,' said the robot. 'So I couldn't say. I will keep trying to connect.'

'About that,' said Roberts, still staring at the amorphous monster in the sky. Waves of flame towered and crashed down on the distant streets of Centre District on bat-wings of pumping smoke. 'I think you should keep that gizmo off the net for now. We have a guy at our place who tells us not to connect, that there's something dangerous loose in the net, some AI.'

'I noticed you guys had no net-sigs, but you don't think much of it round these parts. An AI? What, like a smart virus? That would explain some of the stuff that's been going on. You think this was done by your virus? We're under attack from a fucking computer bug?'

Roberts swallowed heavily, looking into the old man's enquiring face. 'It could be. And it could be one monster of a bug.' And then, seemingly to himself: 'Man. This is some serious shit. A lot of people live over there.'

Roland kicked his robot, who chittered electronically and scuttled away. 'You hear that, Ari?' he demanded of the machine. 'Stay off the fucking net 'til I say otherwise. And don't connect any of the guns, either.'

'Okay, okay,' replied the robot resentfully. 'I rather doubt that your friend is correct, though, just for the record.'

'Give a damn what you doubt,' muttered Roland sullenly. He turned again to Roberts. 'When did machines start to answer humans back, eh?'

Roberts shook his head. 'I don't know.'

Spider was watching the city burn. A cloud of dust boomed up from the horizon as another building crumbled and fell, presumably fatally damaged by the initial explosion. It looked almost insignificant from here, like an anthill blowing away in the wind. The sirens were becoming a symphony. It sounded like some of them were going in the wrong direction. 'We made these machines more and more clever, and maybe this is what we get,' he said quietly. 'In the end, this is what we get. I think the net just declared war on us. Find a religion now is my advice.' He powered up the rifle. It thrummed gently, reassuringly. 'Just in case,' he said when Roberts turned to look.

'In case *what*?' demanded Roberts.

Spider shook his head. 'In case *whatever*,' he said.

Roberts sighed. 'Okay, we'd better get back to base if we can. I can't raise them on sat-link and I'm not going to try net. Roland, will you be okay here? You could come with us if you like, I guess. We already have one lodger, so another won't hurt. We don't have much food, but...'

Roland seemed to consider this proposition carefully, staring at the cloud of smoke. Already the wind was tearing rags from it, elongating the top, blowing it slowly towards them. A heaving sea of flame rolled beneath it, occasional jets of fire fountaining up. The wind was hot on their faces and the sickening tang of burning fuel was on it. 'I be okay here.' He sounded unsure of this to Roberts. Roberts felt unsure of everything as of about two minutes ago, so he knew how Roland felt.

'The fire will come this way, Roland. It's going to eat the Lanes, and then it'll come here.'

'They gonna stop it,' answered Roland, not taking his eyes from the firestorm.

'Who is?' asked Spider.

Roland shook his head. 'Maybe they cut a firebreak in the city. They find a way. Somebody's gonna have to.'

Ari shifted as if it wanted to say something, but the robot must have thought better of it, because it held its peace. Its mandibles wiggled nervously and it seemed unable to look away from the burning horizon. People were hanging out of the windows of the surrounding tenements, craning to see, faces pallid with horror. Roberts could hear a woman crying, nearby but out of sight. Her sobs were shrill and desperate, cutting through the general racket. It was a sound of dark despair. A shiver went down his spine.

'Come with us, Roland. We've got the van. The fire'll reach here before it gets to our place if the wind stays steady. We can get the others, move on if we have to. I can't imagine it being stoppable. The roads are going to be choked. We should go.'

'No, no, thanks,' said Roland firmly. He turned to go back indoors. 'I can get anything I need here. If I need a pod, I get one. Even with communication difficult, I can send my robot. I wait a bit, see what happens.'

'Okay, man,' said Spider. He was practically itching to go. 'We need to go check in with base. Thanks for the gun, Roland. All the best. 13A Molder Jackson Complex, if you change your mind.' Spider's face was set and worried. Although he had only just met Roland the old man had already endeared himself to Spider – he had a strangely compelling charisma.

'No problem. And don't worry about me, I'm sure. See you again sometime. When the world comes right again, eh?' He laughed and coughed, waving Ari to follow him. Birds were streaming out of the east, hectic with terror.

'I hope so,' said Roberts. He turned to Spider, who nodded his head towards the west, where the van was parked. They set off at a brisk walk.

Roberts looked back once. The gun-merchant and his robot were disappearing back into the dimness of Roland's office. He hoped the old man would be okay. Surely he was tougher than he looked – he had probably been a gang-fighter in his youth, veteran of a hundred trials of life and death. Contented by this thought, Roberts jogged after the rapidly-striding Spider. Streams of hurrying people rushed in both directions, but mostly away from the new terror blossoming in the east.

Reaching the van felt like coming home from a strange and hostile land, but Roberts knew the feeling was illusory. They were far from safe just yet. He strapped himself into the pilot's seat and fired up the manual control panel. Although the van had been disconnected from the net since the morning before he didn't trust the vehicle completely. Something could have infected it before then. Unlikely, but Roberts had stayed alive this long by being cautious. The universe had tried unsuccessfully to trick him into fatal complacency many times before. He wouldn't trust the machine to drive itself. Spider was calling up manual weapon controls on the overhead terminal, his shiny pincers somewhat clumsy on the interface. His DNI sockets were useless metal wounds in his shaven skull. His slab-like teeth were clenched.

Roberts moved the van away from the roadside parking slot and headed straight towards the heart of the Undercity proper. He tried to keep a rein on the speed, knowing that he might panic if he let it get out of control. First he would be just stepping on it, next he would be flooring it and then he would be in a blind, fleeing rout. Instead, he drove efficiently and calmly. There was surprisingly little traffic on the small, ancient roads near Roland's place. The van slunk, panther-like, through the shadows that blanketed the narrow streets here even in daytime.

They turned down one road whose mouth was so constricted that Roberts inched the van through at walking speed. Spider wasn't worried. Roberts knew the area fairly well. The streets never changed here, never developed, never seemed to erode either. Long ago, Roberts had fought running battles with government forces through these narrow alleys, surviving for years when the average life expectancy of an insurgent was about three months. He had only told the others of this period of his life once, when he had first joined them. Then he'd never mentioned it again. Nobody asked about it.

Spider relaxed a little, trusting his companion. He still watched the composite picture on the monitor, showing the views from all the van's external cameras, though. The mag-rifle lay on his lap like a sleeping dog as the grimy streets passed by. The sky was dark with smoke and turbulent with sirens. A woman scuttled across the road in front of them on numerous tiny millipede-legs of anodised alloy, then she was gone into the dark outcrops of a battered building. Spider almost shot her on instinct, his claw fluttering to the gun-turret controls before relaxing again.

They moved through tumbledown streets as the sky above them darkened and became hazy with smoke. Roberts turned on the filtration system. The electrical smell of the purifier gradually replaced the oily stench of the burning city.

As they passed a road on their right Spider caught a glimpse of gang fighters encircling some sort of animal, or modified human – something ragged and broken-looking with mossy fur. It floundered on the floor, its limbs flopping weakly, seemingly jointed in the wrong places. The sun illuminated the figures greyly from behind its shroud of ash and smoke. As the van passed them and they were lost from sight Spider heard the chatter of gunfire.

Several times Roberts had to stop to allow groups of people to move out of their way. Some of them were led by obvious gang members, who chanted and punched the air, inciting a rising tension that so far seemed undirected. The packs passed by, some of their numbers shooting into the air as flakes of carbon drifted down on the city. Some were moving towards the site of the explosion in the east, some away. There seemed to be no united purpose, not yet.

The harvesters watched them move on from a safe distance, trying not to look threatening. If there was to be trouble on the streets, they wanted no part of it. The only sort of trouble they liked was the kind they made themselves.

'Where are they going, man?' asked Spider wonderingly.

Roberts shook his head wordlessly. He waited patiently until he could go. None of the mobs paid them any attention. A huge, rotund man with a massive speaker embedded in his chest trailed after one group, his steady rolling gait like the movement of a sailing ship. His speaker was pumping out a hammering sinistro track. It was the sort of music you could kill to, reflected Roberts.

They turned onto the main road that would take them into the ruined industrial zone where their base was, managing to pick up a little more speed. Several times they passed traffic accidents. Beside one brilliant red gravpod, that had swerved onto the metallised pavement and embedded itself in the wall of a clothing shop, a woman in a cheap suit was on her knees in a glossy pool of blood, her head in her hands. She was crying, her body shuddering with the force of it. Fans of sparks fizzed from the broken shell of her pod, pattering down around her and dying on the pavement. Nobody was stopping to help her. Pedestrians stepped around her and her pool of gore, looking embarrassed, and went on their ways. Their faces were pale and frightened and they glanced often at the sky, looking east to where the fire raged on.

Roberts took one indifferent look at this diorama and went back to watching the road, which was getting busy as they approached Springham Street, which in turn would lead to Stevens Street and Molder Jackson. The traffic first slowed and then stopped just outside the Undercity proper. Roberts sat motionless and expressionless behind the control panel of the van, simply waiting to move again.

'What's with all the accidents?' asked Spider. His heavy brow was deeply creased.

'Computer problems. Just the beginning, I'm guessing.' He nodded in the direction of the blazing horizon. A large cat with a suspensor platform instead of legs went pelting past them on the road, yowling in terror. Roberts watched it for a moment. 'Damn traffic,' he muttered.

'Turn off, man,' suggested Spider, indicating a side road. 'Go down Sinking Hill.'

Roberts simply said, 'Nah.'

Soon the traffic shuddered into motion again. Most of the pods were a motley collection – typical Undercity fare. The harvesters' van, although relatively high-end, had been designed with minimum conspicuousness in mind. Roberts kept calm, breathing deeply and driving sensibly despite the stranded, panicky feeling he was fighting by the minute. He wished he could call base.

Police pods belonging to numerous forces were on the streets. Some sported the white and blue chevrons of the City Police. Several times they were overtaken by these as they came screaming down the hard shoulder, their pulsing lights flushing the day with psychedelic madness. One police pod was parked up at the side of the road and an officer was standing next to it, connected to it by a hi-flo. He was talking heatedly to his companion, gesticulating fiercely. The dashboard inside the pod was dead. Spider guessed they were having some technical problems. Debian's net-monster loomed darkly at the back of his mind.

As they crawled down Springham Street a gyrocopter weaved into view from their right. It was ducking and lurching randomly, narrowly avoiding a tall dilapidated shopping centre as it crossed the road ahead of them.

'What's up with that thing?' wondered Spider aloud. He craned his neck to follow the 'copter's course.

'Dunno, Spidey. Let's just get us home.' Voices were rising from the pavement beside the road. People were pointing up at the 'copter, some of them crying out and running for cover.

The gyrocopter rose sharply with a lurch that must have subjected its human crew to several gee. One of its machine guns began to fire into the street several blocks away. Something exploded over there. 'Shit!' Spider exclaimed, flinching instinctively. Suddenly the harvesters felt desperately exposed and vulnerable.

People were screaming now, fleeing into buildings, falling over each other. Some drivers were trying to squeeze their pods between the lanes of traffic and affect some sort of escape. Some simply got out and fled on foot. One of these was hit by a ground-cycle and thrown into the air like a rag doll, over the crash barrier and gone, his flailing form briefly silhouetted against the sky. The cycle-rider, joined to his mount only by his hi-flo cable, skidded along the road and hit the back end of an old van. The cycle thudded into him and his body seemed to collapse into an impossibly small space.

Spider looked back at the gyrocopter, which was doubling back on itself, dipping steeply down on one side. Its machine gun was out of ammo but Spider could see the barrel smoking as it continued to spin, madly trying to shoot with bullets that didn't exist. A police officer fell out of one of the 'copter's doors and dropped out of sight into the road. A unified cry of horror went up from the bystanders. And then the 'copter darted erratically to its left, sideswiped an office block and exploded in a rose of fire. The huge skeleton of the 'copter's internal gyroscope, still spinning, bounced playfully off the office building, smashing a gaping hole into its face and landed in the road, crushing several gridlocked gravpods into components.

'Holy shit!' bellowed Spider. 'Get us out of here, man!'

'I can't!' yelled Roberts, thumping the dashboard in frustration.

Several police officers on foot were pelting towards the area where blazing wreckage was raining down into the street. Pods were shuffling to and fro, trapped by each other, their computers trying to affect escape by routes that weren't there. One driver, fleeing on foot, was bumped by a large silver pod – gently, it seemed, just a nuzzling, really – and began to scream, '*I'm stuck! My legs! My legs!*' He was indeed pinned between the silver pod and another in front of it. Far from backing off, the silver pod seemed to press, lovingly, further into the man's legs. Spider watched in horrified fascination as those legs were pinched off at the thigh and the still screaming torso of the man flopped onto the bonnet of the silver vehicle. Judging by the limp quality of his truncated form the man had mercifully lost consciousness.

A voice from a loudspeaker was shouting instructions at the crowd, mostly ignored: 'Drivers must remain in their vehicles! Pedestrians are to seek shelter indoors! Please move away from the accident scene! Move back or we will open fire!' It wasn't clear which accident scene the voice was referring to – it seemed the whole city had become an accident scene as far as the eye could see, as evidenced by another booming explosion from somewhere off to the north, in the direction of the Lanes.

'There!' shouted Spider, pointing to a gap that had opened between an HGV and a small pod on their right. Beyond was the narrow gulley of Duplex Street, which bore west and then turned to cross the old Stevens Canal before bearing south again. 'Go down Duplex, it looks almost empty!'

'Right,' said Roberts quietly.

He inched the nose of the van around as all hell broke loose about them, until it was pointing into the small gap in the traffic, and then opened the throttle all the way. The van took off like a bullet from a gun, clipping the corner of the pod and shunting it round. The driver shouted some sort of abuse (quite justifiably, in Spider's opinion) through his loudspeaker, but it was lost in the rising whine of the drive system. The van squatted back on its suspensor cushion and burst into the narrow side street.

'Yeah!' enthused Spider, clapping Roberts on the shoulder. They tore along beneath the snaggled drapes of cable-car wire and half-rotten effluent pipes that had once dumped illicit industrial waste into the canal, back in the days when there had been industry in these parts. Roberts swerved onto the pavement to avoid an abandoned pod in the road, narrowly missing a dog-faced girl who ducked back into cover just in time, yelping in surprise. The van smashed into a wheelie bin as Roberts struggled to dismount the pavement, obliterating it in an explosion of decayed refuse and rusted metal. Neither of the harvesters flinched – the van was made of sturdy stuff.

'Looks like we're away,' said Roberts with restrained satisfaction.

Just then, the chequered nose of a police pod, in the livery of Resperi Police Corporation, appeared from a side street, inching into the path of the van.

'Damn!' declared Roberts through clenched teeth, pulling back sharply on the control to brake. Spider knew they weren't going to stop in time – they would hit the pod. He barely had chance to brace against the dash.

The van clipped the front quarter-panel of the Resperi pod, spinning it sideways into the far wall of the side street. It gave a brief, protesting howl of siren as it smashed into the brickwork. Spider noticed a rack of missiles on the pod's roof.

He was jounced hard, cracking his knee painfully on the dash and almost dropping the rifle as the van stopped sharply just beyond the police vehicle. 'Fucking Resperi!' he muttered under his breath. Their immunity contract extended to include RPC, but the force had a bad reputation for organisation and professionalism. Rubbing his knee angrily, Spider cracked the skin of the van and shouted out, 'What the fuck are you playing at? Turn the damn sensors on! You came out of there blind, idiot!'

Roberts put a restraining hand on Spider's slab-like shoulder. 'Hang on, Spidey. I think they're pissed.'

A fight-modded female officer was getting out of the police vehicle. She moved at a trot to block the van's continuance down the road. Her body was an angular explosion of shiny knife-edges, a complex multi-faceted fractal of blades. She was carrying a machine pistol and deep within the razor-edged surfaces of her head her eyes looked thoroughly furious and also a little frightened. Bad combination.

Looking back, Spider could see her companion – a brutish man with some sort of facial piercings – sitting in the passenger seat, presumably with his hands on the controls of that missile rack.

'Listen, Officer, we've got a contract with your force and we just want to get home!' shouted Spider, a little more reasonably. 'So if you'd get out of the damn way, we'd appreciate it!'

'Step out of the van with your hands up!' called a metallic voice from somewhere within the officer's strange body. She was almost within spitting distance now.

'Looks like they don't mean to honour our contract,' mused Roberts.

Spider briefly considered shooting her straight through the damaged windscreen of the van with the new mag-rifle, but he knew that those missiles would launch before they could even bring arms to bear on the police pod, what with the van's automatic systems off-line. And if they started the computerised weapons systems up, then instruments in the police pod would likely register that, also provoking an attack. What to do?

'Oh dear,' mumbled Roberts. 'Look, I'll get out, Spidey – you stay in the van. When the time is right, shoot that bastard in the pod. You'll know when the time is right. Right?'

'Right. What are you going to do?'

But then Roberts was bailing out of the open door, which whooshed shut again behind him, keeping himself between the officer and the van as he went. Spider didn't think he was armed.

'Both of you!' screamed the Resperi woman, her machine pistol levelled at Roberts. Spider knew she couldn't see him through the van's one-way skin but she knew he was there. He wished he had kept quiet.

'Hey, what's the matter?' Roberts was asking in his most diplomatic voice, arms spread wide, closing nonchalantly with her. 'You guys should look where you're going. Look, we'll pay for any damage, okay? We just have to get home. Whole city's going to hell, if you hadn't noticed.'

The police officer was on him, gun waving him down onto the floor. 'Get down!' she shouted in her tinny voice. It must have issued from a speaker somewhere because Spider couldn't see her lips move. 'You in the van, come out *now*!'

Far from getting on the floor, Roberts moved quickly, inside the arc of the officer's weapon. She hadn't expected him to close with her and she was taken off guard and off balance. Roberts had a stunner in his hand, previously concealed, now revealed like a magic trick. Spider knew the time was right and twisted in his seat, bringing the mag-rifle up in one motion, squaring the male officer in the sights. He fired, once, trusting to instinct, right through the rear wall of the van. He didn't take the time to carefully draw a bead as he usually would with the dumb-firing weapon. This one shot would have to be right. *Fly*, he thought as the gun hissed softly against his ear.

Maybe the weapon wouldn't shoot through the side of a tank, even with liquid points, but it certainly killed the officer in the pod spectacularly enough. A small, neat hole appeared in the armoured hide of the van and then the windscreen of the Resperi pod disintegrated in a glittering spray. Spider heard a small, understated *pop* and the interior of the pod filled with a red mist. Through the gory vapour he could see the body of the beheaded officer jerk once and then slump. Blood splattered the bonnet of the vehicle with decorative colour. The dreaded missile rack remained silent.

Spider swung the gun instantly back round to face front, where Roberts was struggling with the female officer and losing. The numerous sharp planes of her arms and legs were cutting him to pieces. Droplets of blood flew like confetti. He seemed to have the stunner jammed up against her angular midsection as she struggled to bring her gun between them. The stunner was discharging uselessly into her, wreathing her form in a crackling aura. Her actual organic body must have been well insulated from the exterior blading because she seemed to feel no effect whatsoever.

Spider couldn't get a clear shot and so, without hesitation, he leapt out of the van, expecting Resperi reinforcements at any moment. As he did so he heard the machine pistol rattle percussively, saw bullets ricocheting off the road surface. Roberts screamed – a wordless sound of pain and rage. The officer slashed upwards with the sword-like edge of one arm, catching Roberts under the chin and sending him arching backwards in a fountain of blood. Using the space that this created, she kicked him further off balance and brought the gun up. The little eyes inside that mess of metal twinkled with satisfaction.

And then Spider shot her with the mag-rifle. The liquid point melted through her armour with blinding speed, disintegrating inside the meaty core of her body. Blood burst from between the creases and crevices of her blades and her dying hand squeezed the trigger of the machine pistol one last time. A chattering stream of bullets tore along the road, stitching the tarmac, pattering off the front of the van. Roberts staggered and fell in a crumpled heap, his trench coat billowing around him. Spider shot the woman again, this time in the head. Jellied chunks of flesh and shards of metal flew.

'Look where you're fucking driving next time!' he screamed at her collapsing form. He could have shot her all day, the way he felt. He had one hundred and ninety-seven rounds left, after all. But Roberts needed help. Spider went to him and knelt beside his battered body, laying the rifle on the road beside him. He was aware of sirens blaring in the streets around them, knowing that any number of them could be heading here.

He cradled Roberts's head tenderly in his powerful claws, his huge chest heaving with deep, ragged breaths. Roberts's face was a pulverised ruin and his body was slashed and torn. His chin had been split by that last powerful blow and his teeth jutted out at crazy angles. He lay in a formless heap, his arms and legs splayed at improbable angles. The stunner was on the floor beside him in a pool of gore. His eyes, however, were sharp and clear within the remains of his face.

'So much...for our...damn...*contract*,' he rasped. And then he died.

Spider knelt beside the body of the man who had stood beside him through years of madness and danger, utterly drained, utterly defeated. The rifle lay next to him, forgotten. He felt nothing, but it was a nothing more intense, more blanketing than any emotion could have been. It was a great, voluminous nothing as blank and black as a midnight sky. Part of his mind urged him to go, leave the scene of the crime, but that part was distant, so distant. He didn't even notice when men and women in the chequered colours of RPC filtered from the streets around him, closing in, weapons drawn, to surround him.

CHAPTER TWENTY-THREE

01101100 01101001 01110100 01110100 01101100 01100101
00100000 01101101 01100101 01100001 01110100 00100000
01100011 01110010 01100101 01100001 01110100 01110101
01110010 01100101 01110011 00100000 01100100 01101111
00100000 01110100 01101000 01100101 01111001 00100000
01100110 01100101 01100101 01101100 00100000 01100001
01110011 00100000 01101001 00100000 01100110 01100101
01100101 01101100 00100000 01110011 01101111 00100000
01101101 01100001 01101110 01111001 00100000 01100110
01101001 01101110 01100111 01100101 01110010 01110011
00100000 01101001 01101110 00100000 01110011 01101111
00100000 01101101 01100001 01101110 01111001 00100000
01110000 01101001 01100101 01110011 00100000 01110010
01100101 01100001 01101100 01101100 01111001 00100000
01110011 01100101 01101110 01110100 01101001 0110101 01101110
01110100 00100000 01101111 01110010 00100000 01101010
01110101 01110011 01110100 00100000 01100001 01110101
01110100 01101111 01101101 01100001 01110100 01100001
00100000 01101001 00100000 01100100 01101111 00100000
01101110 01101111 01110100 00100000 01110100 01110010
01110101 01110011 01110100 00100000 01110100 01101000
01100101 00100000 01101111 01110100 01101000 01100101
01110010 01110011 00100000 01110100 01101000 01100101
01111001 00100000 01110011 01100001 01111001 00100000
01101001 00100000 01110111 01101001 01101100 01101100
00100000 01100010 01100101 00100000 01110011 01100001
01100110 01100101 00100000 01100010 01110101 01110100
00100000 01101110 01101111 01110100 01101000 01101001
01101110 01100111 00100000 01101000 01100101 01110010
01100101 00100000 01110111 01101001 01101100 01101100
00100000 01100010 01100101 00100000 01110011 01100001
01100110 01100101 00100000 01100110 01101111 01110010
00100000 01101110 01101111 01110111 00100000 01101101
01100001 01101001 01101110 01110100 01100001 01101001
01101110 00100000 01100100 01101111 00100000 01101101
01111001 00100000 01101010 01101111 01100010 00100000

01101001 00100000 01100011 01110101 01110100 00100000
01110100 01101000 01100101 00100000 01110111 01101000
01100101 01100001 01110100 00100000 01110100 01101000
01100101 00100000 01110111 01101000 01100101 01100001
01110100 00100000 01110100 01101000 01100001 01110100
00100000 01101001 01110011 00100000 01110100 01101000
01101001 01110011 00100000 01110111 01101111 01110010
01101100 01100100

CHAPTER TWENTY-FOUR

Lifkin Oman heard the incredible detonation of the fuel barge crashing into the city. Possibly a part of his mind understood and was horrified by what was clearly a huge catastrophe, but the kernel that remained of Lifkin's original being had retreated far inside. It squirmed there like a cowed and beaten dog, unable to assert any influence over the actions of what had once been Lifkin's body.

Lifkin had broken all the mirrors when it became clear what was happening to him, and so even if he had wanted to, and had actually been able to control his traitorous body, he would not have been able to see the full extent of the completed metamorphosis anyway. This was one small island of mercy in a sea of random cruelty.

Some days ago he had gone to bed with a raging headache and uncontrollable shivers following the installation of the most attractive pair of amber cat's eyes that money could buy. He had assumed at the time that he was suffering from some sort of infection caught during the surgery and of course, in a sense, he was.

His girlfriend had called him around ten pm that night, asking why he hadn't shown up at her flat as arranged. Communicating by DNI had intensified the pressure of the headache unbearably and it had taken all of his resolve not to scream, *Just leave me alone! Leave me alone, I'm in agony!* He had managed to put her off for the night, underplaying just how truly awful he had felt when she had woken him. *It's probably just a hangover from the anaesthetic*, he had told her. *I'll catch you tomorrow*.

It had turned out to be more than just a hangover from the anaesthetic. He had failed to return to sleep that night – in fact he hadn't slept since then. Parts of his new mind shut off here and there, quite unknown to him, shuffling responsibilities between each other as the very structures of his brain and body were ruthlessly re-written. After all, the new Lifkin hadn't had much to do so far – he was mainly just waiting for the signal. Resting was part of the process, even if actual sleep was not possible.

That second morning he had got up from his fruitless attempts to relax when the savage burning of the daylight filtering through the window sent his head into fresh paroxysms of torment. He had stumbled to the window, one hand over his slitted eyes (those new, expensive eyes) and dragged a tall wardrobe over to cover the glare. *Maybe*, he thought, *they set the brightness too high on these damn implants. That would explain a lot. I'll have to call them – this can't be normal.*

But he hadn't called them. He had sat, exhausted by the exertion, on the sofa, feeling nauseous. Then, when the reeling and swaying became too much, he had lain down. He had stared blankly at the wall, unaware that he was doing so, for six hours and fourteen minutes. And then, gradually, he had become conscious of the fact that he had fouled himself. This had brought him round a little and he had almost got as far as sitting up when there had been a knock on the door. His head had whirled sickeningly as the sound hammered through it. A voluminous anger swelled within him. Whoever it was, he had vowed, they would regret disturbing him today.

Slowly, achingly, he had made it to the door, driven only by the need to stop the noise. It had been Quietta, his girlfriend. 'Lifkin!' she had exclaimed, taking a step back, her eyes wide pools of fear. 'What happened to your face?'

He came round again later, sitting again on the sofa. He briefly scanned the flat and was glad to see that Quietta was gone. But her tattered and blood-soaked clothes had been on the floor of the bathroom. That was when he had trashed his flat. He had felt no remorse, no concern, no fear, although he was clearly losing his mind. He had felt only the raging, all-consuming anger. It blazed like fire in him, clouding his already faltering vision, baking his skin from the inside. He smashed furniture to pieces, tore the soft furnishings to confetti with his teeth, pissed up the walls, beat electrical appliances to death with a hammer, revelling in the flying sparks.

His next period of awareness had begun when he had seen his reflection in the mirror. Part of him recoiled in horror. His mouth was a snaggle-toothed maw, his gullet a dark and mossy jungle, his hair a ragged, washed-out shock of straw. Those damned amber eyes, though, blazed brightly in the wreckage. Bony protrusions ridged his head, his hands, his chest. Why had he not noticed these before? His fingers stretched out to slippery tendrils, nodes of squishy cartilage bulging along their lengths. Then he had smashed not only the mirrors but every surviving reflective surface in the flat. Where he cut himself on shards of plastic and glasspex he bled green sludge. He examined this foul effluent with morbid interest.

What had happened to Quietta? He seemed to be alone now. Maybe he had killed her – he really couldn't be sure. That raging, changing part of his mind was sadistically glad. Exultant, even. This had been the fourth day after his surgery. Time, by then, had lost all meaning to the monster that had once been Lifkin Oman. The slime exuding from his body was starting to dissolve channels into the floor of his flat, making a pattern not unlike the so-called canals of Mars.

Greying memories of life, love, family, friends, work, hobbies, sports, sleep, sex, exercise, films, books, food, drink and a hundred other echoes of humanity flitted across his fading mind from time to time. They were like images seen from the window of a moving gravpod – detached and blurry, then gone. Once he tried to snatch at an image of his mother – whether to embrace her or kill her he didn't know – before realising that she was only a remembered, distant concept and not an actual presence. He painlessly vomited up a homogenised slurry that had once been his internal organs and sat again on the sofa, waiting for the signal. He didn't know yet what it would be. But then, he was unsure of a great many things now. His name, for instance. Lemkin? Liftik? Quietta? It didn't matter.

He must once have moved the wardrobe aside from the window because he remembered standing there and observing the night sky, which hung above him vast and soft and womb-like. He had watched it with the most incredible longing, motionless, leaking thick slime from every orifice, from the very pores of his skin. A lightpusher was rising from the city atop a telescopic column of exhaust. It was truly fascinating from his new perspective. He reached out one twisted hand to grab onto it.

The floor and shattered furniture of his flat were starting to change too, where the green goo touched them. His environment was slowly becoming one with his altering body, which was now just one more lump in a terrible, stinking three-dimensional soup. When the filtering threat of dawn had begun to corrupt that beautiful sky he had pushed the wardrobe back and then lost touch with reality again for an indiscernible time.

The mystery of Quietta's disappearance was solved when Lifkin, in another brief interlude of lucidity, had gone to the kitchen cupboard to investigate the source of the scratching, nagging sound that had brought him out of whatever reverie he had been lost in. Inside the cupboard, curled into the foetal position, was the green, deformed remnants of a human being. It looked as if it had once been a woman, which would tally with the torn and bloody clothes on the floor, but beyond that he could not be sure. How long had she been there? He could not say, but something about her appearance rang a bell somewhere deep within him. *Girlfriend*, he thought, but the word carried with it no discernible meaning.

Although clearly alive in some sense, the woman had not responded to his presence and the Lifkin monster had made no real efforts to get a response from her. To the new Lifkin this strange, living fungus cropping up in his own kitchen was not really any cause for concern. He had noticed that she, too, was leaking that viscous, reeking goo. It flowed under the door of the cupboard, pooling thickly on the floor, mingling, presumably, with his own effluent, joining them together. He felt a vague satisfaction. This was how it was supposed to be, surely? Surely. And now that he saw her, he was sure he could *feel* her, too, taste her presence through the greenshit itself. It was oddly reassuring.

The interior of the cupboard was barely distinguishable from the creature within it. Slimy strands of green matter joined her and it randomly, as if some sort of jungle had grown around her. Her actual body was just a concentration, a *congealing* of the corruption that was in evidence all around. He shut the door again and thought no more of the encounter.

When the fuel barge hit the city Lifkin stirred once more from the waking, resting, waiting mode that had become the norm over the last seven days. That was the sign, the signal, he was sure of it. His body moved of its own accord to the window, where he listened to the city erupting into panic outside. He didn't dare move the wardrobe aside again because he feared the dazzling light that would flood in would damage him irreparably. The thing he had become was satisfied, excited even.

He returned to the sofa, which by now was a grassy hummock of squidgy organic-ised matter and sank into it to wait. The explosion was the signal, but the time was still not ripe. After all, it was still daytime. More waiting – just a little more waiting.

Throughout the day Lifkin's new body began to show signs of agitation as night drew closer. Lumps moved excitedly under his skin, his eyes darted and rolled madly, their speed increasing as the clock ticked towards evening. He heard sounds from the kitchen, too – awful, sucking, squelching, slurping sounds and the occasional bestial grunt. He felt the tension through the greenshit membrane, knowing he was not alone. There was nothing of the original Lifkin remaining now. The creature sat, waiting, exhaling vaporous emerald-hued clouds, amber eyes rolling in its new face like marbles dropped in the grass.

Across the city, chaos reigned. Gunfire crackled like fireworks in the distance. Emergency sirens screamed and blatted stupidly – the calls of the urban jungle. People in the Undercity were close to riot. People in the Overcity were close to panic. Refugees were fleeing the fire on foot where the roads were too choked to carry them. Spyflies swooped and soared in clouds across the wide front of the dying day. They still avoided the scrambler-baits that they had learned to fear, but otherwise their behaviour was abnormal. Whoever had originally owned them – private corporations, government departments, police forces, rich kids – they now reported back to only one master.

Deep in the Undercity proper, in a deliberately discreet corner of a mostly-disused industrial estate, Whistler and her friends awaited the return of their missing companions. They were not alone. A lot of people would not be coming home as scheduled.

As night fell like a soft and comforting blanket on the battered body of City Six the changed began to crawl from their dens. The thing that had been Lifkin Oman rose from what had been his sofa, parts of it adhering to his flesh and vice versa, and left the flat. It met the thing from the kitchen cupboard on the landing outside. They didn't acknowledge each other in any overt way, although they were aware that they were not alone.

Presently they stood outside on the pavement of the injured city, close to each other but uncommunicative. The night was crashing and banging with the noises of chaos and destruction. From a hundred hidey-holes, other ex-humans were emerging, blinking and lurching into the street. The effluent spread around their feet, shining in the dim street-lights like snail trails as they dispersed into the city.

CHAPTER TWENTY-FIVE

Haspan stood, itching with excitement, on the steel floor of his personal underground firing range. His partially hologrammatic body shifted and changed around him. Cutter, his chief armourer, handed him the U-55 reverently.

'Is it ready?' Haspan demanded, snatching it eagerly in one twining tentacle.

'Yes, sir,' answered Cutter in his whispery voice. 'I found you some ammo for it, so it won't take so long to load. I also managed to successfully connect it to the net, despite the problems, and update the software. It's good to go. Try it,' he urged, his eight eyes focused intently on his master's grotesque face.

Haspan turned to address his assembled entourage. 'Shall I try it?' he asked them. There was a chorus of obedient affirmatives. 'Shall I try it?' The same chorus, but louder. Haspan had missed his calling as a pantomime villain. 'Then I shall! Perhaps I didn't get the fighting girl – not yet – but at least I have a new toy! Observe!'

Holding the weapon at waist height, allowing its own aiming system to do all the work, he squinted at the distant paper targets. And squeezed the trigger. The result was impressive. The suspensor-field of the weapon, supposed to steady and assist aim, slanted sharply to the side, actually spinning Haspan's huge body around. The gun barked nine or ten times in rapid succession, moving and firing, moving and firing, possessed of its own will. Smoke filled the air of the firing range. Haspan coughed heavily, laughing at the same time. He held the gun up and examined it curiously. *That was unexpected*, he thought. The paper targets hung undamaged.

Battered and bleeding bodies lay all around. Cutter's shaven head rolled slowly across the floor and came to rest at Haspan's feet. Cutter's face was frozen in an expression of shock. From the pile of bodies, someone groaned weakly, extending a hand for help. The gun, of its own volition, turned and barked again, stilling the questing hand.

Far from being horrified at this unexpected slaughter, Haspan was childishly delighted. He reared up on his hind legs and bellowed, 'Awesome! I *love* this gun!' He was laughing so hard he could barely speak. And then the U-55 blew up in his hand, killing him, too. Its last software update had indeed been successful, in a way.

CHAPTER TWENTY-SIX

'What is *happening*?' breathed Sofi.

'I don't know,' was all that Whistler could think to say. The filigree pattern of fine lines on her face glowed dimly in the falling darkness. Her delicate features were furrowed with concern, her icy eyes blue jewels in the gloom.

Below them, the city was writhing in agony, booming and echoing like the belly of a ship foundering in stormy seas. Pods crawled through the blocked streets, accelerating madly wherever there was a clear stretch, sometimes crashing as their guidance systems failed or human operators became too hasty. Pulses of red and blue emanated from all around as the overstretched emergency services struggled to respond. The skyline was burning in the east and the air was thick with choking smoke. It had a sickening, plasticky taste that stuck in the throat. Sofi had stretched her shirt to cover her nose and mouth. Whistler copied her. It didn't make much difference.

'Spider and Roberts are still out there,' said Sofi.

'I know.'

Whistler was sitting on the concrete platform on which the base's missile racks were mounted. Debian had insisted that Mother be relieved of any important responsibilities, including weapons systems, so for now the launchers were dead and dormant, the missiles roosting in their tubes like sleeping birds. And certainly he was right to distrust the computer system, judging by what was going on in the streets below. They had lost even the satellite news feed, now. Debian was working on something in Tec's lab, some plan to connect to whatever remained of the net. It sounded like madness to Whistler, if his story about the AI was accurate, but she had to trust his abilities and opinions regarding a subject she knew little about. She wondered what he hoped to achieve exactly.

The fire was coming closer. From the roof of the base they had a panoramic view of the madness below, except for where the other five turret-like upper tiers of Molder Jackson, each equidistant from 3A, jutted into the air, blocking their line of sight. None of their reclusive neighbours could be seen out on their own roofs.

It seemed that every disgruntled citizen and gang member in the Undercity had been on the streets an hour ago. Several times they had heard shooting nearby. Now that night was coming though, the crowds had mostly melted away into random, roving groups of stragglers, and an outright riot had been averted.

'Are we going to look for them?' asked Sofi. Her eyes were fixed on the blaze in the east, trying to map its progress, measure its threat.

'I don't know. We haven't got the van, have we. They could be anywhere. We could go to Roland's, see if they left there okay. But if they did, then we still don't know where they are, assuming they would aim to come straight back. And if they're holed up there, waiting for a safe opportunity to leave then we'll just end up stuck waiting with them.'

'Maybe Roland will know where they went, if not here.'

'Maybe,' agreed Whistler. She sounded as depressed as she felt.

'I'll go,' offered Sofi quietly. She turned to Whistler, her face a map of worries.

'Wait a bit. In the morning I'll go with you.'

'Damn it, Whistler.' Sofi shook her head sadly. 'I wonder if you care about any of us sometimes. Anything could have happened out there. They don't know about our contract, do they?'

'You wanna take this out on me? You think we survived this long without my taking care of us all? Do you know what I've fucking sacrificed, what I've done for you? For this team, for the sake of us having our own business? I didn't build all this for just me! I could still go back to the Blood Collective if all I cared about was myself! Killing a superior doesn't exclude you from being a member, you know. I'd be making fucking millions by now if all I cared about was money, so remember who you're speaking to here!' She felt anger boiling up inside her, suppressed it with a physical effort. Slowly, she made her fists unclench. Sofi was frightened, too. And she did know. Whistler knew that she did know. For a moment the only sound was the racket from below.

Sofi turned to Whistler, clamping her shirt across her nose with one hand, the eyes above it looking slightly abashed. 'Sorry, boss.'

'It's okay. We'll go in the morning. I promise. And one way or another, we'll find them.'

There was a terrific roaring from the east then and both of them stopped talking to peer into the distance. They squinted in the eye-watering, smoggy gloom to discern the source of this new noise.

'Jets,' said Sofi.

And then there were a series of deep, booming concussions from the direction of the fire. One, two, three, four, five, six explosions erupted like trees of flame growing out of the blackened, ruined ground, towering threateningly above the general conflagration.

'Are they dropping powder bombs?'

'I dunno. Maybe. The blasts look a bit big for that. Maybe they're cutting a firebreak.'

'Fucking insane.' Sofi's shirt slipped off her face and she tugged it back. 'How many more people will they kill doing that?'

'They did it in City One, remember?'

And then the jets came roaring overhead – six dark, angular and flint-like shapes that screamed through the sky, leaving fluffy contrails behind them. One of them waggled its wings playfully from side to side and Whistler thought it was maybe saluting someone on the ground – maybe the city as a whole – until it turned over and fell out of the sky like a stone. She took a sharp inhalation of breath, waited for the explosion. There was a deceptive second of silence as the plane disappeared into the throng of towering buildings a mile or so to the west and then the inevitable bang, surprisingly understated. Nobody had ejected from the stricken aircraft.

'Whoa...' sighed Sofi as the remaining jets disappeared into the greying day.

'Will we have to move? Should we try to leave the city altogether?' she suddenly asked, changing the subject.

'I don't know, Sofe. I don't know what to do, much as I hate to admit that. Maybe tomorrow things will look clearer. Maybe the fire will be out by then.'

Sofi didn't look as if she believed it. 'Or maybe it'll be so close that we can't even get to Roland's any more.'

'Army'll stop it, Sofe. Or somebody. They'll have to.'

'*They* can't even fly planes any more without them falling out of the air. I don't think they can stop shit. The AI is winning.'

'It's official, then – you believe him? I think we have to agree on what we're fighting here before we can hope to strategise.'

Sofi turned away, kicking at a scattering of gravel on the roof with one boot, sending pieces flying over the edge like tiny meteorites. 'Yeah. I believe him. You?'

'Damn, Sofi, yeah.' Whistler spread her hands wide. The shirt slipped away from her face and she let it go – it hadn't been helping much, anyway. 'Look around you. That AI is attacking the city. I don't know *why* and I don't think we'll ever know why, unless Debian can find out. I think records of this period will be pretty untrustworthy a year from now, if they exist at all. I mean, what else could be causing this? Knocking planes and barges out of the sky, disrupting communications, harassing the police and ambulance services. I believe him, yeah. I still don't really get his part in it all, though.'

'Yeah, right. But as for fighting it...how would we know where to start? Already we might have to leave the city, in which case I'd suggest we've lost round one. Perhaps we can just hole up, keep our heads down and ride this thing out if the fire's brought under control. After finding the others, of course. I mean – *shit*!' Sofi flinched as the report of a nearby heavy weapon echoed up between the towers of Molder Jackson, bouncing back and forth before fading away into the city. A suspicious silence followed the shot. 'What was that?' asked Sofi, sounding a little impressed as well as concerned.

'Dunno. Shoulder cannon? Tank?' Whistler shrugged. She was still looking towards the blaze in the east. 'I think it might be slowing down. And I think I hear more jets.' She grabbed a corner of the missile rack, swinging herself to her feet and went to the edge, where she squinted out into the darkening day. She was right – more jets came rushing out of the east, flowers of fire blooming in their wakes, and disappeared overhead again. The harvesters watched them without breathing until they were out of sight. None of them crashed this time, but both Sofi and Whistler counted only four. If they were the same unit as last time they had lost another plane.

Sofi was not usually one for shows of affection, but now she went to stand beside Whistler, putting one slim arm around her friend's shoulders. Whistler leaned into her, and they stood that way and watched the city fall apart for some timeless grey period of time. People ran past below, hurrying desperately, jumping bags of rubbish and piles of random debris. Some of them had weapons across their backs. The harvesters watched with detached interest as a police pod – real police – went howling up the street in pursuit. A voice was booming from the pod's speakers: '*Stop now! Stop or we* will *fire!*' And then, without further warning, the pod opened up into the backs of the fleeing crowd with the rapid whispering sound typical of an ice gun. People flew sprawling to the floor as the pod shuddered to a halt. Somebody began firing a projectile weapon from some unseen vantage point, the rounds pitter-pattering off the armoured hide of the pod. The turret of the vehicle homed in on the source of this new attack and began to return fire.

'I think we should go inside,' said Whistler quietly, guiding Sofi back away from the edge of the building carefully. It seemed suddenly all too easy to slip and topple into the chaotic street below, not to mention the chance of a stray round or random pot-shot hitting one of them.

'You don't think we should help them?'

'I'd love to, Sofe, but it's too dangerous. I think we have to help ourselves right now.' They walked back towards the sheet metal porch that housed the stairs down. The heavily-reinforced door was standing ajar, swinging gently in the warm breeze that flowed out of the east, seeming to beckon them back in. 'We may have to hole up here and we can't do that with the police on our case. Low-pro is the way to play it right now. C'mon.'

'Okay, Whistler. I just hate it when those fuckers start flexing their muscle round here. How many smackings have they had over the years? How many do they need? They ought to know better.'

'Intelligence,' said Whistler, letting go of Sofi and stepping through the door, 'is not in the standard-issue police lexicon. There's a lot of things they should know better.'

'What's a lexicon?' asked Sofi as she closed and triple-locked the door behind them, reducing the sounds of battle and disorder outside to a muted babble. In here, the whole nightmare could have been imagined, but for the tang of burning city that had permeated the building. It was getting cold, too, without Mother's environmental ministrations. Somebody would have to set the heating manually.

'A lexicon? Fucking hell, Sofi, did you go to school?'

'No. You know I didn't. And nor did you.'

The stairwell was dark, lit only by the dim glow that filtered up from the floor below. Spider had stuck a poster up on one wall, a picture of some air force commander below a slogan originally reading GO UP IN THE WORLD! and presumably meant to recruit people into the air force. Spider had modified it so that it read GO UP ON THE ROOF

AND HAVE A BEER! BUT DON'T FALL OFF! Wise advice indeed, Whistler thought. She wished he and Roberts were here now.

'I'm gonna see what Debian and Tec are up to,' said Whistler as they headed down the stairs.

'Yeah, I'll come with you,' said Sofi. 'I guess it might be important in some way.'

'I've no idea if it is or not,' admitted Whistler. 'But I like to know what's going on. Obviously everything outside is a fucking write-off, so my hopes are pinned on Debian being some sort of help.' And, surprising even herself, Whistler actually laughed, albeit in a slightly nervous manner. It was all just too surreal to really contemplate seriously.

Sofi looked at her as if she had gone insane. 'Glad you find it all so funny.'

Whistler controlled herself and pushed through the door at the bottom of the stairs. They trooped through the big room, past the looming shapes of crap alley, down the stairs and onto the basement floor. Mother's blank terminals stared at them like the eyes of a corpse as they passed, their dull panes somehow resentful. The silent emptiness of the base was unnerving, worse than the cacophony outside.

When they reached Tec's lab the door was shut but a dim light oozed from the crack underneath it. Whistler wondered how much longer the power would stay on and how they would cope if it went off. *When* it went off. She managed to keep this worrying thought to herself.

Sofi peeped into the lab, a little timidly, and stepped in, Whistler close behind her. Tec was leaning over Debian, who was sat on a metal office chair with his head bowed. Part of his skull had been shaved, exposing a sleek implanted chip with tiny lights winking on its surface. Tec was wiring a datasheet to it with some sort of home-made-looking connector, the sheet magnetised onto a shelf beside him. He checked back and forth between the sheet and Debian's head, his face rigid in concentration. On the tip of one pinkie finger he wore a clicking medical attachment – a sort of tiny blade mechanically mounted on a metal thimble. It was joined to his skull with a fine micro hi-flo. There was a delicate smudge of blood along the invisibly thin edge of the blade. Tec was muttering rapidly under his breath, though whether to Debian or himself it was hard to say, and his head was pulsing between turquoise and green, making otherworldly shadows lurch and stagger across the jumbled surfaces of the room. Only one of the ceiling-mounted screens was on and it was showing static, washing the room with a harsh grey light.

Whistler cleared her throat softly. Tec jerked upright, cursing. 'Whistler! Don't do that!'

'Sorry,' said Whistler as sweetly as she could manage, looking down at the floor with mock humility. 'You busy?'

'Yeah, kinda. We're about ready to roll, though. Right, Deb?'

Debian stretched, pressing his hands to the small of his back and turned in his chair to face the newcomers. 'Yeah. I think so. Diags look good. Thanks, Tec. I think it might really work. I must admit I've been frantic to get back in there – I just don't know if I should try, now. I guess I'm kind of frightened.' Whistler found herself liking him more than ever for this show of unabashed honesty.

'After all the effort we've put in it seems almost a shame not to,' said Tec. 'But it's your call.'

'So what have you guys been doing?' asked Whistler, staring at the shaved patch on Debian's head. He brushed his hair back over it self-consciously.

'We've been tinkering with my low-level firewall,' said Debian, making an effort to find words that the technologically-challenged could understand. She was, after all, a meathead. 'I think I know why it didn't protect me as it should have last time, thanks to Tec.'

Tec chuckled modestly. 'I don't think I did all that much, actually. This bloke,' he said, jabbing a thumb in Debian's direction, 'is something else. That chip in his head – he made it himself, installed it in his flat with only a simple robot arm and two mirrors to help. It does contain some very advanced firewalls but it's also more than that – it's a...a...an *interface protocol* in its own right.' He looked to Whistler and Sofi for understanding, saw none on their faces and carried on anyway. 'A whole new connection method, that makes his control much more precise and faster than by using fire-and-forget avatars, which run detached from the end user, that being their point, right? That's why avatars run from neural simulations. So that they can–'

'Okay,' interrupted Sofi tersely. 'So will it be safe to connect again now, Debian? And why do you want to when you know it might be dangerous? Presumably this connection protocol of yours is both the strength and – judging by what the AI did to you before – the weakness.'

Debian gazed openly up into her face and answered without a trace of emotion, although his fingers wriggled nervously in his lap. 'Essentially, you have hit the nail on the head, yes. It's still dangerous, but I think we have ironed out a few problems with my system. I don't think it'll happen again. And as for the reason: I think we need to know what's going on here – with the beast, with the explosion in Centre District and, I'm guessing, with your friends, too. Tec said they should have been back ages ago. I'm sure you're all worried about them. Maybe I can find them if I can get into the net.' He looked from Sofi to Whistler, his face questioning. 'Also...well, the net is *my* home ground. No virus is going to keep me out. I have to do this, no matter how frightened I might be. I have to.'

'Okay,' said Whistler, who until a few seconds ago had been against the idea. The notion that Debian could maybe find her friends, even get a message to them, had not occurred to her before. Suddenly the importance of his safety simply ceased to be a concern and Debian morphed in Whistler's mind from a human being who she was coming to like into another tool that could be used.

'I'll see what I can do,' he said, holding her gaze for a moment. She nodded gravely. 'But no promises.'

'Sure.'

'Don't get your brain fried again, man,' said Sofi.

'Okay,' said Debian uncertainly. 'Er, is there anything I can eat first? We've been at this for ages. I don't remember when I last ate anything.'

'Oh, yeah, sorry,' said Whistler, realising just how drained he looked. 'We aren't usually in the hospitality business. Help yourself to whatever there is.' And a snap-shot of the interior of the fridge suddenly flickered in her mind: Two shelves of beer, synthi and real, the remaining fake eggs, a third of a loaf of bread, a half litre of rancid milk and nothing else. Tins in the cupboard, but not many. Enough for a day or two, tops. 'There isn't much. Guess we need to go shopping.' And she uttered a laugh so hollow that it frightened even her. When she looked up the others were staring at her with open concern.

'Oh fuck,' said Sofi. 'I didn't think of food.'

And then, confirming Whistler's darkest fears, the power went off and a deep subterranean darkness filled the lab like flood-water.

CHAPTER TWENTY-SEVEN

Spider awoke groggily, unsure of where or even who he was. Darkness. A sickening motion of some sort that permeated his being. Pain – he was aware of pain, but what part of his body it came from he couldn't tell. Perhaps it was everywhere. He seemed detached from it – the flashes and twinges from his nerves were like data scrolling on a screen – understood but not actually felt as such. He tried to flex his powerful arms but couldn't. A bright bolt of agony hit him in the head – this one he did feel – and he thought he moaned aloud. A glimpse of dull silver, something moving. Hard to breathe, as if there was a weight on his chest. He passed out again.

Awake. His head felt slightly clearer this time, although the world still swam nauseatingly. He retched, bringing nothing up – a long series of uncomfortable gagging coughs. How long had he been unconscious for? He opened his eyes cautiously. It made no difference. Perhaps they had been open already. He closed them again and the agony in his head diminished slightly. Slowly, carefully, Spider breathed deeply for a while, wincing at the discomfort in his chest as he did so. Why did he feel so dizzy and sick? What had happened? His DNI gave him only an incongruous muddle of data, unless he was simply failing to interpret it properly.

After some time, tensing against the pain, he eased his eyes open and saw that dim glint of silver again. Something moving around him in a wide circle. It made his head spin worse than ever and he shut his eyes again, dry-heaving. His stomach was empty, but the noxious taste of bile filled his pounding head. When the retching passed he tried, one-by-one, to flex his arms, legs, shoulders, wrists, neck. He was held completely immobile, although the rest of the world felt like *it* was in motion. He tasted dried blood in his mouth, presumably his own. It was coppery and slightly vile. He tried to spit but wasn't able to coordinate it. *Breathe, just breathe*. The sound of his own respiration filled the darkness, making it womb-like.

Resperi Police Corporation. It was all flooding back. Somebody must have shot him with a tranq or used a stunner and then drugged him. Was that why he felt so bad – some kind of drug? Whatever. They had taken him, and that was all that mattered. They must have done. The bastards had murdered Roberts and now they had Spider, too.

What had Roberts's last words been? *So much for our damn contract*, something like that. And it seemed he had a point.

They had murdered Roberts. Those fucking Resperi amateurs! Vowing vengeance, Spider felt himself descending back towards unconsciousness like a stone thrown from the beach descending towards the dark surface of the sea. Sickening turning motion, darkness, sleep...

The light was so bright that in the initial sensory confusion it created he thought it was a deafening noise. The brightness was as shrill as any alarm to Spider's waking eyes. He clenched them shut but even through his eyelids it was too much to bear. He wondered how long he had been in darkness.

'Hey there, you cop-murdering piece of crap,' somebody said in a voice so cold and unconcerned that he knew at once he was in trouble. The voice, as far as he could tell, seemed to come from the light, which was to say from everywhere at once.

Spider tried to speak, couldn't do it. His mouth was too dry to work. Footsteps etched a steady path around him, unhurried in their pace. Maybe two sets – it was difficult to focus on the sound. He felt that he was being examined closely. 'I...' he managed to croak.

'Where is your organisation based?' asked the voice. It seemed to come from in front of him now, but there was some aural distortion going on, as if the speaker was still moving despite the fact that the footsteps had ceased. There was no emotion in the voice.

And then a second voice, a woman's, said, 'I say we turn him over to the Freak. Bastard killed Jamine. Fuck 'im.'

'Hmm.' The man seemed to consider this suggestion at some length.

Spider squinted and tried to see through the brilliance that flooded the room. Shapes were congealing out of the whiteness. The silhouettes of two people. Bizarrely, they seemed to be slowly turning over and over in the vertical plane with a regular motion. And then it became clear. Spider was strapped to some sort of rotating disc. Probably some technique used to disorientate the victim. It certainly seemed to be doing its job, in that case. He was now almost certain that he had also been drugged, possibly with some sort of truth serum.

'I mean,' said the woman, 'we're up to our necks in it on the streets. We don't have time for this. We should get back out there.'

'Spider,' said the man, ignoring his partner. He had his arms crossed in front of him and appeared to be staring at Spider calmly and steadily. 'That is what you call yourself, isn't it? We scanned your DNI already. Don't worry, we used an isolated terminal. We didn't allow it to net-connect.'

'How...' Spider choked on the words and was almost sick before he could finish: '...Kind of you.'

'Protect and serve, protect and serve,' said the man conversationally. 'You and your associates are wanted in connection with numerous outstanding crimes committed over the last five years. What's your real name? Spider was all we got from your head.'

'Your friend attacked us when we were trying to get home.' The words were coming easier now, as his mouth began to generate some saliva. The figures of the two police officers were also becoming more defined. The man addressing him had a rosy light in place of his right eye, maybe a laser weapon, and two sharp horns on his head. He also had a huge and bushy brown beard. He looked like a Viking warrior, although he sounded like a customer service manager.

'Your contract–' he checked a small screen inlaid into one forearm, '–paid previously by Human Genetic Recycling, ended yesterday. All of the crimes committed within the period of that contract's existence are now liable for pursuit under law. Where are you based?'

'I thought you said you read my DNI. You tell me.' His head was down at the man's feet now and Spider noticed that he had a wickedly-curved energy blade sheathed on one shin. It looked more like the tool of a torturer than a police officer. Slowly the disc rotated until they were face to face again. The man watched his prisoner clinically.

Spider tried to move his head to see the woman but found it too tightly restrained. Then, removing the need, she stepped into view and said, 'We don't have time for this, Ramone. Just give him to the Freak.'

She was older than Spider, maybe fifty, and built with a short, compact frame more suited to a pit-fighter than an officer of the law. Her forehead was dotted with studs of some metal that could have been titanium. Her face was lined in the manner of one whose habitual expression was a scowl, and indeed she was scowling with revulsion at Spider now. Also, he didn't know who or what the Freak was but he didn't like the sound of it much.

'The Freak?'

'Where are you based? You and Whistler and the others of your team?'

'Who's Whistler?' he managed to grunt. He certainly didn't feel too conversational, so perhaps he hadn't been injected with a truth drug after all. It was possible that his disorientation was due entirely to the rotating disc and the pain could have been from one of the post-arrest beatings that RPC were known for, in common with most of the commercial police forces.

'Whistler? You know, your boss, the lifelong gang member turned corporate thug. You guys are body-snatchers for HGR, right?' He turned to the woman and they shared a little laugh. 'At least, you used to be.'

'Used to be?'

'They ended your contract. I guess your services weren't worth paying for any more. I understand the bodymod industry is suffering something of a stock crash at the moment.' And he laughed again – a rich sound seemingly borne of genuine amusement. It made Spider wonder if they were going to kill him.

'Aren't you people supposed to notify us of contract termination? Some fair period of grace? I want a lawyer.' Spider could feel the gentle rumbling of the disc's bearings beneath his back. He wondered how many victims of RPC had been strapped to it before.

'Actually, we aren't obliged to do any such thing. It's a courtesy that we sometimes extend, but your team isn't exactly easy to get hold of. And then our first contact with you is when you are apprehended kneeling beside the body of a murdered Resperi officer with an illegal weapon beside you. Was it you or your deceased friend who killed the officer in the pod?'

'Pod?' Spider said, wondering if he sounded as irritatingly stupid as he hoped.

'He had a son, you know. Two years old.'

'Yeah? And we had a contract. All things come to pass, man.' Spider was down by Ramone's feet again and when he saw one of those feet twitch he thought maybe Ramone would kick him in the head. He was sure it crossed the man's mind, but it didn't happen.

'Where are your maggot friends, Spider?' This was the woman, looking disdainfully down at him. 'Long story short – tell us and we won't give you to the Freak. You'll even get a trial.'

'The Freak?'

'Mm-hm,' said Ramone. 'Tell him who the Freak is, Officer Blake.'

'The Freak is a brain-diver.'

'A what?' Spider was up at the level of her piggy face now. She really was impressively ugly.

'A machine-human symbiont, designed to read much deeper into your head than a simple DNI reader. She can actually scan the meat of your brain, divulge all your dirty secrets. Not strictly allowed under the terms of the Fair Legal Process Act but still used in extreme cases. Oh, and the process is very invasive, as you'd imagine. Often fatally so. And very unpleasant.'

'I see,' said Spider as nonchalantly as he could.

'No,' said Blake. 'But you will if you don't tell us what we want to know.'

'You say you were going home, when you happened to murder two of our officers. Home is your group's base, no doubt. Were you near to it? Maybe it's in the industrial sector, some old warehouse. There are certainly enough of them lying empty there. It really is better if you just tell us.'

Ramone was surprisingly good, Spider grudgingly admitted to himself. The bastard was essentially right about everything so far, although there was no need to let him know that.

'If you read my DNI like you say you did you'll know that's wrong,' said Spider.

'Thing is, we couldn't get much from your DNI, Spider. It seems to be pretty well protected. Not unusual for a career criminal, but annoying. It just gave us name, rank and serial number stuff. But then, as you installed the protective firmware you already know that.'

It was true – Spider's DNI, like those of all the harvesting team, was well-shielded from both remote and wired probing, for just this sort of scenario. The firmware had been very expensive but HGR had footed the bill. At least they hadn't revoked that, if only because they couldn't. Was it true that the contract had been terminated? Maybe, judging by the chaos that reigned in the city, it was a simple computer error. If so, though, there would be no convincing the RPC officers. They were pissed. Even if he suggested that they may wrong, they'd probably still take the opportunity to execute him illegally and then go on to raid the base if they had the resources to do so. With their force undoubtedly stretched to breaking point, how much time would they devote to him before just giving up and killing him? Or giving him to this Freak of theirs, which sounded like it might amount to the same thing? Not long, he thought. And when that happened, his butchered brain would give them Whistler and the others anyway. He could see no way out.

'I'm not going to do your fucking job for you, officers. You'd better introduce me to this Freak, because frankly I'm getting bored.'

'Oh,' said Ramone with mock disappointment. 'Oh never mind. We hadn't expected you to help us, to be honest. But don't worry – we'll find your friends.'

'In the end, we always get our way,' confided Blake.

'We'll see,' said Spider. 'But you'd better make sure you keep me well-restrained.'

'Really,' said Blake disinterestedly.

'Really.' Spider tried to look her in the eye as he rotated towards upside-down again. 'Because one slip, one momentary lapse in your guard, and I will kill *you*.' He nodded at Blake, as much as his bonds would allow. 'And *you*.' He nodded also at Ramone. 'And you can spend eternity in that great police retirement centre in the sky comparing notes on me and my team with your dead pig friends. One mistake is all I need.'

'Don't worry,' said Ramone, cracking his knuckles loudly. 'There won't be one.'

'Give me to this brain-diver, then,' said Spider. 'Your conversational skills amount to shit. I've had enough.'

'First thing's first,' said Ramone softly as Spider rotated to face him again. He was holding a short police truncheon in one big hand. This wasn't entirely unexpected, Spider reflected. 'First thing's first.'

CHAPTER TWENTY-EIGHT

'Right,' said Whistler emerging from her room with a small torch. 'Do we have that old gennie still?'

'Yeah,' said Tec. 'We have it, but its glory days are long gone. Also, I dunno how much fuel we have for it.'

'Get on it. Get the power on – without it we're in serious trouble. The base is defenceless until it's sorted, not to mention that Debian's attempts to find Spider and Roberts are on hold.'

'I'm on it,' answered Tec curtly, his head blazing a determined shade of amber. He rushed off down the corridor, illuminated only by the glow of his own skull.

'Sofi,' said Whistler pointing a clawed finger at her. 'I want you on the roof with some heavy equipment. With the cameras and motion sensors off-line we need a lookout. Any problem – and I mean *any* problem – and you shout. I'll help Tec with the gennie.' She considered this briefly, concluding that any contribution she could make would probably be counter-productive to Tec's efforts despite her best intentions. 'Scratch that, actually. I'll watch the car park.'

'Okay, boss,' said Sofi, her features sharp and shadowed in the torchlight. She turned and felt her way down the corridor.

Whistler pointed the torch at Debian, who shielded his eyes. 'Maybe you had better help Tec.'

'Look, I'm not really practical in that way. I mean, computers I can do, but engines...I assume this generator is a diesel or gas burner?'

'I think you might still be more help than I would. Unless you'd rather guard the bottom door in my stead?' Smiling, she held out her smartgun to him, grip first.

Debian recoiled from the weapon as if it were a live snake. 'No,' he said emphatically. 'I'll help with the generator, on second thoughts.'

'Good man,' said Whistler with a cheerfulness she didn't really feel. Debian turned to go and she called him back. She dug a crumpled chocolate bar from one pocket and threw it to him. It was unpleasantly squishy and warm. Debian dropped it and picked it up again from the floor. 'You said you were hungry,' she said and pushed past him towards the empty hangar and the exit to the car park.

'Thanks,' he said to her retreating back.

Tec dug the battered generator out of crap alley by the application of back-breaking effort and heartfelt swearing in equal measures. Looking it over he concluded that the infernal machine had never seen any glory days at all. It had been here when the gang had moved in, but apart from testing it and changing the oil they had never had a use for it, despite Tec's passing interest in it as a mechanical device.

Working by the dim glow of four tea lights he cleaned it up enough to actually see what he was doing and pulled the cord. The echoing volume of the big room reverberated to the sound of the clattering machine as it caught and ran, choppily at first. Tec bent over it with a screwdriver and tweaked the mixture by a tiny increment. The gennie began to run more steadily, although it stank to high heaven and began to fill the big room with choking clouds of smoke that looked eerily blue in the darkness. He shut it off and began to search for some ducting to use for the exhaust.

He hunted through the piles of junk, holding a tea light aloft in an ashtray, launching disappointingly useless items further into the depths of the heap. He reflected as he searched on how, in this world where you could get your cancer treated with nanotechnology (if you were rich enough) their power requirements had come down to four cylinders of exploding fuel vapour. How quickly things could devolve.

Somebody coughed behind him, making him start and drop a bunch of unspooled magnetic tape. He turned around to see Debian watching him sheepishly. 'Whistler sent me to help you,' said the young hacker. 'I'm not sure how much help I can be, but I found this.' He flicked on an LED torch and threw it to Tec.

'Thanks.' Tec gratefully put the tea light aside on a rusty filing cabinet. 'You can help me find some ducting for the gennie's exhaust.'

'Okay, sure. Any specific sort?'

'Needs to fit on a fifty mil outlet, ideally, but anything at this stage.'

'Long enough to reach outside, right?'

'Right. I know it's a bit fucking hard to see in here, but do your best.'

Debian looked around at the towering shadows of crap alley. 'Won't it screw with the back-pressure?'

'I'm not too worried about that at this stage. We'll put an impeller in-line if we have to, but let's just get it connected for now.'

'Why not just put the gennie on the roof?'

'We don't like the place to look too occupied. A 'copter would spot the heat sig.'

'Judging by what's going on out there I don't think they'll care too much.'

'You went out there?'

'Just stuck my head out, really. You should take a look.'

'I don't think I want to. I prefer to occupy my mind with matters I can actually deal with.'

'I don't think there'll be any avoiding this one,' said Debian as he moved off warily into the junk heap.

'Is the fire still burning?'

'I think it's going out. Sofi's up there with what looks like enough firepower for a small- to medium-sized war. She says it was worse before – she thinks they're dropping powder bombs on it. There's a lot of shooting going on, though. Not really my scene. Will this do?' he asked, holding up one end of a long coil of hose.

Tec craned to see. 'Plastic?' he asked.

'Yeah, it's quite sturdy-looking, though, and there's loads of it. About fifty mil diameter, too, I'd say.'

'As long as it doesn't melt. One way to find out, I guess.'

'Depends on what kind of plastic it is, right? We could always use a metal tube for the outlet itself, join this on further up. Based on the assumption that you must have a metal tube somewhere in this lot.' Debian began to coil the hose around his neck.

'And you didn't think you'd be any help.'

'Well, one can but try. Give me a hand, Tec, there really is miles of this.'

'You think you can find Spider and Roberts if we can get the link going?'

Although Tec asked the question lightly Debian sensed the great import behind the words. He stopped his work and looked into Tec's face, seeing the fear beneath the surface. 'One can but try,' he repeated softly.

Without another word Tec picked his way over and began to help, holding the LED torch in his mouth. Despite his small stature

Debian noticed how strong the man was. He shifted large items aside seemingly without effort, freeing the coils of hose so Debian could collect them. They worked in silence for a time, until they were heavily encumbered by loops and loops of hose. Together they dragged the remainder out onto a clear swathe of floor and inspected it again by torchlight.

'Yeah, looks about right,' said Tec. He turned and darted off into the shadows of the junk heap. There was a metallic clanging noise and the sound of muffled cursing. Tec returned sucking on a skinned knuckle, the torch beam slicing across the room. In his other hand he held about half a metre of steel pipe. 'Ha!' he said triumphantly.

'Looks good enough,' said Debian. 'How much fuel is there? Diesel, is it?'

'Yeah, diesel. I'm not sure how much we have. There are a couple of large plastic barrels back there somewhere.' He waved an arm towards the exterior wall, which was safely barricaded behind mountains of miscellaneous objects. 'Big blue barrels – maybe you could take this torch and dig them out.' He passed the torch back to Debian and picked up a tea light.

'Okay, I'll have a look.'

Debian waded through the heap as Tec dragged the hose back towards the generator. Debian found the barrels quite quickly even in the gloom. They were almost as tall as he was, though when he tipped them to gauge their fullness the contents sloshed quite a bit. Both about half full, he reckoned. He was no expert on internal combustion engines but he suspected that the barrels still constituted enough fuel to run the generator for quite some time. Maybe eighty litres each. He tipped one and began to roll it on its edge back into the clear alley, moving objects out of his path. A few days ago he could never have imagined being here, doing this. When he reached the gennie with the first barrel Tec was not there but the metal pipe and hose had been clamped onto the gennie's exhaust outlet. The hose twined across the floor and disappeared up the stairs into darkness.

Debian wiped the sweat from his brow and caught his breath. He bent over the machine and looked at the plug plate on it. There was only a single outlet but luckily it was of a standard design and rated to thirty amps. He had no idea how much current a rooftop-mounted rocket launcher drew, but it would run the computers, and that was what mattered to him.

He began to follow the hose up the stairs. Tec had worked quickly, splicing a break in the hose with a piece of the metal pipe on the upstairs landing. The hose disappeared out of the slightly-ajar door that led to the roof. Debian pushed the door open and stepped out.

At first he couldn't see Tec, or Sofi, who should also have been up there. He scanned the rooftop for them. The other towers of the complex loomed in the darkness like standing stones. The city crackled with dark and ominous life. There wasn't a light visible for several blocks in any direction.

And then he spotted them behind a curved ventilation outlet near the edge, crouched in a patch of deep shadow. Tec was looking straight at him, making a repeated chopping gesture with one hand. Debian stared dumbly for a moment before Tec's meaning became clear: *Kill the light.* He fumbled with the button on the torch and ducked down low like them, stowing it in his pocket. Sofi was beckoning him over. She looked like a pink-crested insect in the dark, all slender limbs and sharp angles. The end of the hose had simply been left lying on the roof off to Debian's right, its installation unfinished.

A little confused, as well as alarmed, he ran across to them in a crouch, feeling a subdued twinge from the gunshot injury to his leg, a souvenir of his defunct career. He reached the others and dropped to the roof beside them, enveloped by the shadow of the vent. 'What is it?' he whispered. 'Something wrong?' He was annoyed to hear the fear in his own voice.

'I think you could say that,' admitted Sofi. 'Take a look.'

Debian, puzzled, leaned out around the vent to peep over the edge and down. The lurching shape of a drunk was slowly ricocheting from wall to wall as he weaved his way down the street. Something squarish with a small light on – maybe a malfunctioning domestic robot – was trundling slowly down the centre of the road seemingly ownerless and without purpose.

'Over there, by the pawn shop,' hissed Tec. 'On the wall of that warehouse. About four metres up, maybe. Look!'

Debian scanned the scene below, trying to find the spot Tec spoke of. Catching the vibe of surreptitiousness, he was careful not to be too visible from below. And then he saw it. 'What is that...?' he asked, afraid but also fascinated.

'You fuckin' tell us,' suggested Sofi. 'Cos we have no idea.'

The creature was attached to the wall of the warehouse across the road like a gecko, apparently adhering by its hands and feet. It did look humanoid, but something in its posture was strange and unsettling, as if its joints were not in quite the usual configuration. Its colour was either black or dark green, but it was hard to tell in the low light.

'There's something coming out of it,' said Tec. 'Look!'

Debian could see that Tec was right – there was some sort of fluid coming from the creature. It poured from some unseen orifice on the thing to run sluggishly down the building, pooling on a low windowsill and then dripping into the street below. It oozed from the kerb and into the gutter where the trickle from the thing on the wall seemed to join a larger stream. Whatever the dark fluid was, the gutter was running with it.

'Is that a bodymod?' asked Debian.

'Dunno,' said Tec, his face appearing next to Debian's. 'Bit extreme if it is, isn't it?'

'Yeah, I guess...'

'And it also wouldn't explain *that*,' said Sofi, pointing into the shadows of an old fuel station forecourt.

Debian was stunned. 'It's another one,' he whispered. He was used to seeing a bizarre selection of bio-mechanical oddities on the streets of City Six, but something about these creatures was unlike anything he had seen before. 'Are they human?' he asked in an awed whisper.

Tec shook his head wordlessly – not *no* but *I don't know* – and pointed to the second creature. This one was standing in the small yard of a fuel station, seemingly rooted to the spot between the silent hulks of the pumps. Debian couldn't make out its facial features but its body was weak-looking and gangling, scrawny to the point of emaciation and it swayed very gently back and forth. It seemed to have a second set of arms – shrivelled dangling things that hung from its midsection, but in the low light he couldn't be certain. They could have been flaps of clothing. Its body below the waist was hidden behind a pump. Another rivulet of slime seeped from the gateway of the forecourt and into the road.

'I might know what it is,' said Sofi, so quietly that Tec asked her to repeat it. She was cradling – almost cuddling – an enormous high-bore conventional rifle with an under-slung grenade launcher. The thing was almost as big as she was and she held onto it like a sailor clutching a handhold on a wildly-pitching ship, as if it were the only solid and dependable object around.

'What?' asked Tec.

'The greenshit infection. That's what they look like. I mean, it's dark, but that's what they look like from here. Like Vivao. I think he was on his way to becoming one of...*those*.' She shivered visibly as she nodded towards the street below.

'Then there's gonna be more,' said Tec, swallowing noisily. His face was grim and drawn, his head a guttering play of uncertain colours.

'What are they *doing*?' breathed Debian. 'They're just sitting there. And what the hell is that stuff coming out of them?'

'Dunno,' said Sofi, her voice unusually small and uncertain. 'We should get Whistler.'

'Look!' hissed Tec. 'The drunk!'

The staggering man down there was clearly extremely the worse for wear, but he was also clearly a genuine, normal human – a dun-coloured, shuffling Undercity standard of humanity – bedraggled and undistinguished, average height, features hidden by his stoop. He was approaching the creature in the station forecourt, albeit via an indirect route. He hadn't seen it yet – it was mostly hidden from his point of view – but his path would bring him within feet of it unless he veered off in some unpredictable direction.

'He's gonna bump right into that thing,' said Sofi. Debian could feel her body tense against him as she shifted the rifle fractionally in her grip. 'Shall I shoot it?'

'No,' said Tec. 'Maybe he'll just walk past it.'

'Maybe,' said Debian without any real optimism.

The man in the street strafed unsteadily to his left, knees shaking, and then straightened up again. He drew abreast with the dark yard where the creature stood, swaying gently with its tangle of stringy hair blowing softly around it. He lurched again as he passed the yard and his head jerked up. The three watchers on the roof knew he had seen it.

'I'm gonna blast it,' said Sofi, shouldering the huge rifle.

'No!' insisted Tec, and she lowered it again reluctantly, darting him a resentful glare.

The man reeled backwards as he spotted the creature. It was only two or three metres in front of him, almost close enough that he and it could reach out and touch fingertips if so inclined. It didn't look at him, exactly, but something in its posture suggested acknowledgement of his presence. Debian wished he could see it better. The man down on the street yelled something slurred and indecipherable, pointing unsteadily at the thing in front of him. He looked around for support, found none. Debian glanced again at the other creature – the one on the warehouse wall – but it was still stuck there and showed no signs of responding to the events nearby.

Then the drunk began to behave oddly. He started to stomp his feet up and down. He looked down, his body language panicky, then back to the strange creature. He shouted at it again and this time Debian did hear him: 'What'cha fuckin' doin!? The fuck'sis shit!?' His voice was shrill and panicky. And then he began to scream. He looked as if he was trying to flee but found himself rooted to the spot. He reached down and began to tug frenziedly at his own legs. The creature stared into space, swaying gently, its stick-like arms dangling limply.

'No way, no way, no way,' Sofi began to chant. She had the rifle to her eye now – she must have raised it very quickly – but Tec was quick, too. He pressed the muzzle down, easing her hand away from the trigger. *No*, he mouthed at her. The screams from below were becoming frantic. *No*. She reluctantly gave in.

Debian could not look away from what was happening down there. A thick puddle of the dark, gloopy stuff was spreading around the drunk's feet. He was screaming non-stop, his braying cries as shrill as a boiling kettle. And the greenshit was beginning to climb up his legs, slowly wreathing his body in dark slime, homogenising him as he struggled and batted uselessly at his own torso.

'Shoot it, Sofi, for–' Debian began, but Tec overrode him.

'No! If you start shooting then those fucking things may come up here. Or somebody else might. What you can do, Sofi, is go and get Whistler like you were supposed to.' His voice was an intense whisper.

Sofi looked from Tec to the man in the street and back again. 'What is it doing to him, Tec? I don't like this.'

The man was being consumed, that was what it was. The greenshit had almost covered him now, wrapping his body like a cloak. It looked like there were questing, grabbing fingers within that slime, enveloping the man, muffling his cries, dragging him dripping into the general mire. As he slowly crumpled, jerking weakly within his cocoon, waves of greenshit slowly washed over his form, melding and melting it into the slimy darkness that slicked the street. Tendon-like strings rose from the puddle, connecting to the body of the monster that still stood swaying in the station forecourt, indifferent to what had taken place. The man was gone – dissolved, incorporated, eaten – whatever one wished to term it.

'Oh no...' breathed Debian. He looked at the faces of his companions – they looked as sick as he felt.

'Oh man! It fuckin' dissolved him,' said Sofi. Her knuckles were white on the stock of the rifle. 'It turned him into fuckin' goop. What the hell is happening? What does that to a person?' She was almost crying. 'You all saw that, right? It fuckin' dissolved him!'

And then the creature in the station forecourt put its head back – right back until the back of its skull rested against it spine and its mouth pointed up at the sky – and with a rattling hiss belched out what looked like a cloud of green ash or snow. The three companions watched it, transfixed. The cloud billowed up and up, twisting like a tornado of small green leaves, rattling against the glass in the windows of the buildings. It rose and rose, higher than the roof of 13A, and began to fan out. Nobody spoke as it spread above them like an umbrella and began, slowly, to fall. The cloud covered maybe one hundred square metres now. Debian, Tec and Sofi stood watching in awe like three people at a fireworks show. A smell like rotting cabbage was on the wind, cloying and repulsive. Slow, drifting flakes...Hypnotic, almost...

'Move!' shouted Tec suddenly. 'It's gonna fall on us!'

This brought them all to their senses. He was correct, of course – they were right under the green snow now. Nobody knew what effect, if any, it would have if it touched them, and they decided by silent consensus that nobody wanted to know. As if suddenly waking up, they moved towards the stairs. Debian felt his heart racing in his chest as if it wanted out of there. Had he ever been so frightened? Maybe when he had stepped out of his flat's window and grabbed for the scrambler-bait. Maybe not. As he ran he risked a glance at the sky. The green cloud was almost on them now, and it did look like snow. But this wasn't the pure white of natural water-snow, this was the dark and putrescent hue of the greenshit organs, more like flakes of ashy fungus.

They scrabbled through the metal door into the coffin-like darkness of the stairwell. Tec came last, but when he tried to slam the door he realised that the generator's exhaust-hose was in the way. 'Damn!' he yelled, his voice quavering, his head a bright, desperate yellow.

'What?' asked Sofi, turning back, but then she saw the problem for herself. 'Oh,' she said simply, unslinging the huge gun from her back. 'Move.'

Tec squeezed past her and out of the way. Through the crack in the door Debian caught a glimpse of the air filled with drifting green flakes as he moved back. Sofi pressed the muzzle of the rifle to the open edge of the door, holding the weapon at waist-height, and pulled the trigger. The report was more of a roar than a bang and the effect in the cramped space was like being inside a steel drum that had been hit with a hammer. The door flew wide open, showing the dark and swirling void of the night sky, bounced off the exterior wall, then slammed against the hose again, distorting but not actually tearing it. There was a surprisingly neat hole, about fist-sized, just above the handle. Sofi shoved the gun behind her, into Tec's waiting arms. She lifted the hose, threading it quickly through the hole, and shut the door, locking it securely. It was clear that there was something of a gap around the hose, but as a temporary solution Debian was impressed.

'Come on!' she barked. 'Let's go!'

As one body they turned and practically jumped the stairs down to the next landing. They descended the tower in a desperate rabble, almost tripping over the exhaust hose several times, into the big room, and rallied in a nervous mass there. Tec bounded up the steps to the mezzanine, navigating by the dim, ruddy illumination of the still-burning tea lights. The others heard him rooting frantically around for something and then he came flying back down the stairs. Debian and Sofi exchanged puzzled looks.

Tec showed them a large pair of pliers as he passed. His expression was businesslike. He went to the wooden door that led to the tower and used the pliers to quickly tear and smash a rough chunk out of it. He then passed the exhaust hose through this hole, mirroring

231

the solution Sofi had arrived at upstairs. He slammed the door and stood back.

'I wanna get this sealed up better,' he said, 'then fire that gennie up.'

'Yeah,' said Sofi. 'You do that – I'm gonna get Whistler.' And with that she dashed off in near-total darkness towards the basement level.

Debian was surprised and slightly envious at how quickly the others seemed to have composed themselves. He still felt like screaming, and refrained only out of fear that once started, he would be unable to stop. He stood for a moment and let his body slowly purge itself of adrenaline. He was trembling all over. Ashamed of his weakness, he breathed deeply, shut his eyes and tried to regain control. He could hear Tec ascending the steps back to the mezzanine, presumably to look for more equipment. There was another round of clattering and banging from up there. When he felt composed enough to open his eyes again Tec was stepping down onto the floor with some sort of gun-shaped tool in his hands.

'What d'you think that stuff in the sky was?' asked Tec nonchalantly as he surveyed the door.

'It came from that creature, whatever it was,' said Debian.

'It trapped that bloke, and turned him,' said Tec, adjusting a rusty control on the tool, 'into slime. And then it puked out that green snow. Weird, huh?'

'Weird? Only the most bizarre and frightening thing I've ever seen. What's that?' Debian indicated the gun-shaped implement in Tec's hands.

'Armourfoam. It's used for field repairs on tanks and suchlike.'

'And you have it why, exactly?'

'For shit like this,' said Tec absently as he worked the nozzle of the gun around where the hose passed through the door, sealing the gap with an expanding line of black foam. 'I should do the top one, really, but I don't fancy going back up there right now.'

'Nor me,' agreed Debian. His knees felt shaky and he sat heavily on the bottom rung of the mezzanine steps. 'Let's get that power on.'

'Yeah, I think we might feel a little better with lights and coffee.' Tec stood back again and regarded his work. 'That'll do for now,' he muttered.

'Where do we plug in, then?' asked Debian.

'You okay, man?' asked Tec, looking him over. 'You don't look so good.'

'Yeah,' sighed Debian, rubbing his eyes. He wasn't sure if he was okay or not. 'I'm just a little freaked out. A lot has happened.'

'Yeah,' said Tec sympathetically. 'It has. And I think there may be more to come.' There was a gloomy silence as they both considered this.

'The power?' prompted Debian.

'Yeah, er, I'll have to wire it into the mains at the consumer unit. S'easy, come on.'

He led Debian to a far corner of the big room, shifting an old freezer out of the way. He indicated the supply unit that was fixed, uncovered, to the wall.

'Right,' said Tec. 'Simple stuff. Debian, there's a yellow toolbox in the lab. Would you get it for me? I'll find some cable.'

'Yeah, sure,' said Debian, glad to have something to do. He rushed off into the darkness of the basement level and fumbled his way into the lab. He searched the cluttered space until he was nearly ready to give up, almost totally blind. He stopped and leaned against a shelving unit, eyes closed, composing his will. He opened them and surveyed the darkness around him, letting his eyesight adjust as well as it could. Yellow? He couldn't see any damn thing.

Of course! *Night vision*! It was funny, but he had completely forgotten that he had the facility available. He had disabled his HUD system since the incident with the beast, but he was reasonably confident that his head was clean now. And what difference did it make anyway? He had already decided to go back into the net, if he could, once he could utilise the backup power of Tec's computer. But one half of him was still oddly reluctant to do it. He was getting used to being a virtual meathead, maybe too used to it. *I am forgetting who I am*, he thought. *One day unplugged and I'm losing the plot*. He disallowed this train of thought and turned his HUD on, being careful not to allow his DNI to net-connect just yet. His vision filled with comforting scales and icons. And then he noticed that he was actually leaning his hand on the very thing he searched for – it was lying atop a heap of miscellaneous objects on Tec's desk. He couldn't tell its colour by night vision, but it was clearly a toolbox, and its side was helpfully labelled *ELECTRICAL*. Triumphantly, he seized it and dashed out.

In the corridor he ran right into Whistler and Sofi heading up to the big room, sending Whistler bouncing into the wall. She rebounded in a fighting stance, instinctively, and he thought for a split-second that she would kick his head in before he could say a word. But she relaxed quickly, peering at him in the darkness. He switched to IR to see her better.

'Sorry, Deb,' she said. 'I'm a little wired.'

'Yeah, aren't we all,' he agreed.

'Sofi says there's some freaky shit going on out there.'

'Yeah,' said Debian in a small voice. 'She's right.'

'I want to see for myself.'

'I don't think you should go out there at the moment. That stuff coming out of the sky, those things...I don't think that's wise.'

'I told her that, of course,' said Sofi in *nobody-ever-listens-to-me* tones.

'I'll wear a hat,' Whistler said, so drily that he stared at her in confusion for a moment before realising she was joking. Her face glowed red and yellow, the skull visible through the skin in his enhanced vision. She looked beautiful, alien, fragile like stained glass.

'A hat?' he parroted uncomprehendingly.

She nodded cheerfully. 'Rain-hat.'

'Tec just sealed the door to the stairs, anyway.'

'Yeah? Without asking me? Maybe I'll just take a nosey out the basement door then. I didn't see anything wrong in the car park, though. How's it going with the power?' she asked.

'Nearly done, if that damn machine runs, and if nothing blocks the exhaust on the roof.' Debian was slightly taken aback at Whistler's complete lack of regard for the terrifying nature of this situation. He supposed that was what made her a leader.

'Good,' she said, clapping him on the shoulder and turning to head back towards the lower exit, Sofi in tow.

'That woman is insane,' said Debian musingly as he took the toolbox to Tec.

'Whistler?' asked Tec absently, quickly snapping the box open and rooting through it. 'Yeah, she is.'

'She's going out there.'

'Well, she does what she wants, I'm afraid.' Tec's face was buried in the wall-mounted supply box. He was apparently wiring in the end of a thick cable that trailed off across the floor to the generator. 'Tape?' asked Tec, reaching a hand back without looking. Debian passed him a roll of plastic insulating tape from the toolbox and he took it and rapidly looped it round the splice several times. He stood back. 'There,' he said in a satisfied voice. 'Start the gennie, man.' He smiled encouragingly.

'Okay, sure.' Debian went to the gennie and studied it briefly in the dark. It was old and greasy-looking, slightly dented here and there, but essentially intact. He identified the pull-cord and pulled it. The gennie coughed but didn't start. He pulled it again and this time it spluttered to life. There was a rising hum from the mezzanine and Debian realised that it was the sound of the ancient fridge cycling up.

'Wooo!' hooted Tec triumphantly. 'Hit the lights!'

'Where?' Debian called back.

'By the stairs!'

Debian found the switch and flicked it. He guessed that Mother took care of such mundane things usually. The shadows jumped back as the big room was flooded with light. Debian switched his vision back to visible spectrum. It was almost too bright after so long in the dark.

'Good job, Tec,' he said as Tec came over to check the gennie's limited readouts.

'Yeah, thanks for your help, man,' said Tec.

'No problem. Can we eat something, and then I'll try the net?'

'Sure, let's have a look,' said Tec, leading the way up to the makeshift kitchen.

'Anything'd do, really.' He sat on one of the high stools. 'I hope they're okay out there. I wonder how many more of those creatures there are. They might be everywhere.'

'Yeah, maybe, but I pity the monster that picks a fight with Whistler and Sofi.' He shrugged.

'I suppose so. Does this mean nobody's able to watch the roof now?'

'I guess not,' said Tec, opening the food cupboards one by one and then closing them in disgust. 'Mother usually watches the cameras. I guess we could bypass her and set up a monitor. Or maybe Junior could watch,' he said thoughtfully. He stopped, straightened up, and turned round. 'Hey, man, have you seen Junior at all?'

'Who?' asked Debian, his face blank.

'Junior. He's my robot. Small spidery thing, hence the name: Spider Junior. Not too bright, also hence the name, but capable of watching the roof for us. Now that I think about it, I haven't seen him for a while.'

'I don't think I've seen any robot.' Debian was picking up on Tec's concern. 'Why? Something wrong?'

'I don't know...' said Tec thoughtfully. He was holding a tin in one hand and his face was distant. 'Beans?' he said at last.

'Sure,' said Debian gratefully. 'Then we'll get right on with it.'

Junior was still nearby, although he was not in too sociable a mood. In fact, Junior had been going through some changes recently. He heard his name mentioned, but his name didn't mean anything to him any more. He was just a single node in a system far, far greater.

CHAPTER TWENTY-NINE

'The pod is here, Mrs Smith,' said Simon. 'It's waiting in the basement.'

Startled from her contemplation, she glanced up from the window and said, 'Thank you, Simon.'

When she made no move towards the door Simon went to stand beside her. 'Mrs Smith, it really is time to go,' he said softly. He touched her elbow, cajoling, but it was like a piece of cold marble.

She didn't speak for some time and when she did it was not in answer: 'Look at it. What the hell happened here?' She indicated the city below them.

Obligingly, Simon looked. There was a greasy greenish film over the outside of the window. The sky was dark and veiled in rolling banks of smoke. There were no gyrocopters flying now, although a solitary searchlight probed the sky with unguessable intentions, its milky beam illuminating only smoke and cloud. The horizon still glowed to the north but the brilliance of the glare had reduced dramatically. Clearly the fire was the only thing that was coming under control, though. Most of the city was unlit, powerless, crushed beneath darkness. Random explosions punctuated the night from all directions – the signs of urban warfare, a state of existence that had seemed utterly improbable only the day before. Simon wondered who was fighting whom. He supposed it was basically a free-for-all. There was almost no news coming in, apart from that relayed by HGR security squads dispatched onto the streets for that specific purpose. They reported widespread gang activity and acts of police brutality. One team had actually had to fight its way back, harried by the Backstreet Gang, losing several employees in the process. Also, there were increasingly worrying reports of strange creatures roaming the city. A security squad had shot one and it had allegedly melted down into some kind of slime. It was unbelievable. It was becoming undeniable. Multiple reliable witnesses had related the incident. The scene outside was apocalyptic. The teams had all been called in. There were marksmen posted on the roof with mag-rifles and barricades on the ground. HGR headquarters had been made a virtual fortress, an island in a sea of inexplicable enmity.

'I don't know, Mrs Smith. But I think it's still happening.' Simon was not privy to the latest HGR research data, limited in scope though it was, but Mrs Smith actually had a pretty good idea of what was happening, or part of it anyway.

'What does it look like to you, Simon?'

Simon squirmed slightly, anxious to get her away, sickened by the sight of the stricken city below. 'You should get to the pod, Ma'am. We can get you to the sea-port, but you need to go now.'

'Because to me it looks like war.'

'Either that,' he agreed grudgingly, 'or we've fallen through a dimensional rift into the land of the bizarre. Please, Ma'am...'

'But who is attacking us?' Smith sounded like she was talking to herself now. 'Who planted those organs? The same people who planted the computer bug, I'll warrant. So much for us finding them.' She chuckled – the notion seemed laughable now.

Simon stared into her face – it looked moulded or cast – not human but living statue, the features finely chiselled and the hair a solid piece of stone. 'Organs?' he said. 'You mean the GDD?'

Smith sighed heavily, seeming to shrink as she did so. She turned to Simon. 'You may escort me now, Simon.'

'Very good,' he said, relieved.

Smith let him lead her from the office without further ado. She resisted the urge to look back – it might seem too much like a *last* look back, an admission of defeat, and she disallowed herself the weakness.

They moved through the chaotic bowels of the building in solemn silence. HGR employees charged here and there or slumped in the easy chairs that lined the corridors. Many of them had not been home for days, all of them were frightened or exhausted. There was no official ban on leaving the premises – not yet – but most people were too fearful of what was happening outside. They knew they were safe here, shielded by the basic inviolable nature of big business. The company was stronger than any human being – it would protect them, mother them through the hard times. Smith knew they might be wrong. With no communications, no robots, no real high-tech weaponry beyond the remaining handful of small arms and with the power cuts that had reduced the building to generators, they were as vulnerable as anyone. Monsters on the streets? Gang warfare? Police shooting without question; contracts dishonoured; allegiances tossed aside? Smith was opting out of it while there was still time. She had a nice little artificial island a hundred miles offshore that right now sounded a lot more relaxing.

They dared not take the lift to the basement, so Simon led the way down shining stairs of ceramicarbide. Smith realised she had never seen them before, never had occasion to take the stairs. This small thing bothered her more than she could understand.

The basement was spotlessly clean and brightly lit except for Material Receipt, which was dark and deserted at the far end, the shutter rolled down and the windows electronically tinted black. A black pod, smooth skinned and subtly understated, waited a hundred metres away. Two hugely muscled men, whose suits bulged as if overinflated, waited silently by the pod. They wore sleek projectile weapons openly on their belts.

'Grace, Linden,' Smith greeted them. These were two of her most trusted ranking security men. They grunted as politely as they could manage. 'How's the finger, Linden?'

'Okay,' he answered, clearly not wishing to talk about it. Linden had, until this morning, owned a feline battle familiar, Stripe. Stripe had started to go a little loopy, disobeying commands at first and eventually running away from Linden into the depths of the research department, much to his master's embarrassment. Linden had chased, and eventually captured, Stripe, who showed his gratitude by biting Linden's right middle finger off at the first knuckle. One of the resident surgeons had patched him up as well as they could without computerised equipment. All familiars and robots had been ordered disabled.

'Good. Shall we go?'

'Let's.'

Linden opened the door of the pod for her and Smith climbed in. The seats creaked expensively as she settled herself and belted up. Linden sat in the front passenger seat and Grace (an amusing name for so huge and clumsy a creature) squeezed behind the manual control panel. The pod had been net-isolated in storage for months. As an added precaution HGR techs had physically removed all connection devices and sockets. There was no remaining way to interface with the pod even if you wanted to. Grace was a meathead – Linden, like Smith, had disconnected and quad-firewalled. Smith was satisfied that they had taken all possible precautions.

Simon watched the doors of the pod click into place, the cracks around them disappearing. He said nothing, but on his face was a look of fear. He was being left behind, perhaps to die. Smith deigned not to look at him, relaxed into her seat. Almost every feature of the pod's interior was the same matt black. Grace started the pod and eased away with a smooth inclination of the control stick. Another pod, essentially identical, waited for them before the exit: More security personnel, a heavy-weapons team equipped with the pick of the remaining serious hardware. This escort pod led them to the huge security doors that gave onto the street. Sentry guns here had been replaced by baton-armed guards who watched with depressed disinterest as the two pods paused to let the door open and then crept out into the city, bouncing gently on their suspensor cushions.

Smith tried her best to relax as Grace steered the pod through a network of hastily erected concrete barriers, tailing the heavy-weapons team. HGR security personnel watched them pass from prefab pillboxes, the protruding muzzles of their guns combing the night. Somewhere off to the right somebody was firing an assault rifle into the dark streets of the city in calm, frugal bursts. It was impossible from here to discern their target. Smith was amazed at how rapidly the building had been fortified, amazed at how a virtual war had begun in the space of a day. She shivered, although the pod was warm, and tried not to look. She thought of her private island, thought of the weeks ahead, thought of spending them with Grace and Linden and a handful of other lackeys. It could even be sort of fun – she and Linden had had a brief fling a few years back – maybe it could be revived?

Inevitably, her gaze was drawn back to the window. As they moved further into the city a strange grey-green, granular dust began to accumulate on the windows of the pod. Grace turned the wipers on without comment. Once a dark, bat-like shape wheeled across the sky, a long and sinuous tail trailing behind it. Smith craned to follow it as it disappeared into the banks of smoke and cloud, unable to tell whether it was animal, robot or virtual being. Something howled inhumanly from the dark gullet of a side street, chilling her blood. Linden glanced, worriedly, in the direction of the sound as the two pods crossed a deserted road junction beneath a skeletal span of viaduct.

They drove past the body of what had probably once been an enormously overweight man, who had clearly fallen to the street from a high window and burst there like some hideous, overripe fruit. Smith was shocked that even in the Lanes, even on an insane night like this, nobody had come to clear him up. Linden muttered something that she didn't catch. They saw a police van, burning brightly, at the end of a side street. Shadowy figures bolted away from it as they passed. Smith imagined the heavy-weapons team in the lead pod hastily training their guns on the alley from the slit windows of their vehicle.

They headed north, the hellish glow of the burnt swathe of city ahead and to their right, deeper into the Lanes, aiming for Med-Hab and the sea port. The moon was an evil eye, half blinded by smoky cataracts.

Smith was jolted back to reality when her pod glided to a stop. Linden had his hand pressed to the ear-piece of the simple radio headset that linked him to the other pod.

'What is it?' demanded Smith, craning to see past Grace's huge body.

'Some weird shit, by all accounts, boss,' replied Linden. 'Look.' He pointed up ahead of them.

Smith peered over Grace's shoulder. There was an old cable-car wire up there, draped with what looked like thick green vines, several stories up. The vines dangled from it to the rooftops of low shops and houses, weaving the architecture of the city into a thick, organic curtain. Creatures of uncertain form moved within and upon this curtain, in and out of it, defying gravity fearlessly. They were spidery and angular, human-sized but strange in their motions. Smith recognised them for what they were. HGR had been studying the GDD as long as anybody.

'My God...' she breathed. 'They're...' And then she noticed that this strange jungle actually extended out of sight into the dark streets. In places the screen of vegetation was threadbare, in others it was thick and coagulated. Creepers hung from net wires, car cables, protrusions of masonry, windowsills, satellite dishes, rooftop railings. They looked slimy, from here, almost dripping. In some places it looked as if the corners of man-made structures, where they blurred into the greenshit curtain, were actually *softening* somehow, eroding. The creatures neither made to attack them nor retreat from them.

'What shall we do Ma'am?' asked Linden. His voice was matter-of-fact, unworried.

'Drive on, angle off to the west, away from this.'

Linden repeated the command into his headset and the pods moved off again in tandem, taking a left between high brick walls. The greenshit was thinning out again here. What was happening to the city? Those *things*, the infected, what were they doing to the place? Where were the authorities? The pod stopped again.

'What *now*?' yelled Smith, hiding her fear behind irritation. But then she saw.

Where there should have been road ahead of them there seemed to be water. Only as she studied it closer it became clear that it wasn't water at all, but something darker and glossier, dark green or black, even. It looked shallow, whatever it was, although it covered the surface of the entire road junction. Smith looked back over her shoulder. People were flooding out of unlit doorways into the street, darker shadows in the dark night, lit only by the dim glow of the moon and the now-muted smouldering of the city. They moved rapidly, awkwardly, encumbered by weapons, fanning out. Somebody shouted, 'The pods! Stop the pods!'

'Drive through it!' barked Smith. 'We've got trouble behind!'

'Yeah,' said Grace, 'I've got them.' The front pod eased into the large puddle and Grace followed. Linden rolled down his window, leaned out and began to take pot-shots into the crowd behind them. They were getting close now, filling the night with savage war cries. Grace began to accelerate.

'Gah!' cried Linden, ducking back into the pod. He was rubbing frantically at his neck. 'Fuckin' splashed me! What is that shit?'

The pod was picking up speed now, riding above the liquid on its suspensor cushion, occasionally dipping when it passed over some unseen bump.

'It's getting deeper,' said Grace, adjusting the ride height with one hand.

The crowd behind them had tailed off. They stood, jeering at the edge of the pool, clearly unwilling to set foot in it. Some threw missiles inaccurately at the pods, and these splashed down behind them, but luckily nobody seemed to have a gun.

'How can it be getting deeper?' asked Linden irritably, still rubbing at his neck. 'The surface of the street ain't going anywhere. Same as back there.'

'Dunno,' grunted Grace, minutely adjusting the ride height again. 'This is a damn lake.' He pointed to the side, where the liquid covered another street as far as they could see.

'Wow...' breathed Linden.

Then the escort pod began to slow, pitching and rolling, its edges dipping into the liquid. Smith's pod began to falter a second later. Grace tweaked and adjusted the ride height more rapidly, his shaking hands betraying his concern. He was muttering between clenched teeth. The pod bucked sharply and Smith bumped her elbow on the door handle. She looked around fearfully.

'What's happening?' she demanded.

'Something's stopping us,' answered Grace, the muscles in his jaw working tensely as his hands flew over the controls.

The pod gave one more determined lurch forwards and then stopped, its suspensor singing a high, straining note. The escort unit in front of them had also come to a halt. Smith realised with horror that fingers or tentacles were reaching up from the liquid and gripping on to the sills and underside of the escort pod, holding it back, dragging it down. And then her own vehicle began to sink towards the pool. Grace thumped the dash in frustration, giving up. Red LEDs had come on all over the readouts. The three occupants exchanged fearful looks.

There was a terrible sucking, squelching noise from below them and a horrendous stink – the stench of the GDD, Smith knew – suddenly filled the pod, making them gag.

Smith felt something sting her bare wrist and looked down to see that those creeping, questing fingers were stealing in through the open window of the vehicle, wriggling like fat worms, oozing with thick green slime. Then Smith did something she had never done before – she screamed.

CHAPTER THIRTY

'Bon voyage, man,' said Tec, holding out the end of the hi-flo cable. 'If you look like you're in trouble, I'm pulling the plug, okay?'

'I'm counting on it,' answered Debian, taking the connector delicately between finger and thumb. He looked at it with a mixture of trepidation and eager anticipation. The ready lights of the router blinked beside him.

Although frightened, he was looking forward to stepping back into the net. He was desperate for answers to the questions that circled round and round his head. Who was Alcubierre? Who were Cyberlife? Did they make the AI, find it, or receive it from some third party? Was it really related to the goings-on outside, the so-called GDD? Could it yet be stopped? And of course, he genuinely wanted to find Spider and Roberts. Although he hardly knew them himself, it seemed like the least he could do to repay this strange band of people who had taken him in, excepting the actual payment he had made into their bank account. He had decided that he liked them, especially Whistler, and there weren't many people in his life that he could say that of. But even more than that he wanted to scratch that itch, that old familiar need to tread the data-ways, walk the web. He had been shut out of what he considered his own empire, and frankly he was beyond annoyed. He felt as if a part of him had been amputated and he wanted it back. He wanted back in. That was the most important reason of all.

'Any sniff of danger, bail out,' said Tec.

'Will do,' replied Debian, trying to smile. He felt like a man about to undertake a deep-sea dive. 'Well...No time like the present.' And with that, he clicked the hi-flo plug into his head.

He activated the uplink, felt the burst of microwave energy as a physical beam, not originating from the satellite dish on the base's roof but actually spearing him directly like a butterfly on a pin. His avatars, stored on his own DNI, scrambled into the tangled pathways of the net, scanning, retrieving, relaying, creating the impression of a true, direct interface. The image they produced was bizarre at best.

Debian fell into a twisted and mangled landscape, a parody of the net he knew so well. The wreckage of mutilated sites and servers was a blackened bomb-site through which a weak and pestilent data-stream flowed, incoherent and brackish. The servers were still there, but twisted and strange. He began to launch probes in every direction, the avatars following and tweaking their data-trails as if controlling fly-by-wire missiles, the avatars themselves continually checking back with Debian's DNI, taking updates of his wishes and priorities. They zipped off brightly enough but didn't return any useful information. Strange. Only the vaguest humps and malformed outlines of once-familiar servers remained, and it was as if they were behind a wall of foam that could be pushed, probed at, but not broken through. Their ports were deaf and mute, unlit.

He cycled through connection protocols, trying to get the attention of a public server, but it didn't even return his pings. On one – a university computer – he knew full well that he had left a sleeper sub some months before. He tried to access it but met with no response. The whole fabric of the net, the protocols on which its communications were built, seemed to have broken down. He set multiple avatars on the problem. Finally he got a response from the sub-verter. He tried to access the server behind it, but the sub-verter seemed unable to talk to the server on which it was hosted. He began to rapidly write adaptive interrogation programs on his DNI in a variety of languages and try to use those to access the server. It seemed that there was an underlying language in operation, with a floating base that he couldn't pin down. He had never seen anything like it before. It was as if every machine on the net was being re-written from the ground up on a continual, rolling basis.

And then he found an algorithm that seemed to work. He cycled the base of the language on the fly, following the pattern suggested by his calculations. It seemed to play out. The sub began to let his avatars retrieve information from the server. Debian suffered a brief moment of doubt. Wasn't this a little too easy? What were the chances of him stumbling on the correct algorithm so quickly? He was good, he knew he was, and he was beginning to feel infused again with the power he had felt after his brush with the AI. He remembered sending the pod chasing after Hex's men, remembered the strength he had felt. It was beginning to fill him again. His mind crackled with power, seeming to buzz within his head like some mighty transformer. But even so...It seemed too easy. Why would the AI even base its floating language on a decipherable algorithm? Was he being *allowed* in? Another trap? A test?

He forcibly shrugged his own concerns aside and attempted to get the university computer to speak to what remained of the wider net. In the circumstances it seemed odd that they had even left the server connected, but he was happy to use their lapse in security for his own ends. Perhaps the people in charge of it were so overrun with real-world problems that the server was nowhere near the top of their priorities. Whatever. Work to do.

From the university computer he sent avatars out into every available channel – into the banks of the server itself, into user mail accounts, from those into every reachable destination, direct from their computer to every scanned server on the net that would return a ping. He picked several wide-pipe governmental and financial machines with good, credible connections to as many places as possible. His avatars assaulted them, laying traps, probing defences, brute-forcing passwords, sidestepping quantum security protocols, sometimes meeting brick walls, sometimes extending their tendrils.

And then he gradually became aware of a feeling of being watched. In his mind's typical desire to relate the electronic landscape to a physical one it felt as if some vast and brooding presence was looking down from the sky and that he crawled upon the broken earth like an ant beneath its gaze. A worried sub-routine in his head began replicating defensive avatars and fine-tuning his firewalls. He hoped that the enhancements and modifications he had made would be enough. And then it spoke to him:

WELCOME BACK. I HAVE BEEN BUSY SINCE LAST WE MET.

CHAPTER THIRTY-ONE

Sillick twisted the throttle of his ground bike all the way to the stop, revelling in the rising roar of the antique petrol engine. The wind fluttered the lapels of his leather jacket, stung his eyes, tore his breath from his throat. He swerved around a crashed pod, gaining on Tumbler as they neared the junction. Tumbler braked hard, decking his bike right over, and took a left towards the heart of the Lanes. Sillick followed, closing the gap to shouting-distance, scraps of rubbish flapping in his wake. The others were several blocks behind now, but Tumbler was on a roll, losing himself in the thrill of speed – wild, young and unstoppable.

Sillick pulled alongside him and shouted, 'Hey, man – shouldn't we hang back, wait for the gang?'

Tumbler laughed, his green eyes glinting. 'Live a little, Sill – you worry too fucking much!' And he swerved into a side street suddenly – Sillick struggled to brake in time to follow him, nearly clipping a lamp post.

They raced along beneath hanging balconies, unlit windows, smashed and looted shop-fronts, the walls to either side passing so close that they could have reached out and touched them. The night was thick with smoke, grey-green and gloomy. Occasional gunshots could be heard in the distance. Shadowy figures bolted into a boarded-up building as the bikers roared past them.

'I just don't think we should split up, is all,' yelled Sillick as the bike jolted hard over a manhole cover. He accelerated out of the near-tankslapper, fully in tune with the machine, adjusting his centre of gravity to retain control, relaxing his body to damp the vibrations. The bike settled down. He felt the tacky grip of its tread upon the road surface, felt its mechanical heart throbbing within as if it were his own.

'What?' yelled back Tumbler.

'I don't think we should split up! Strength in numbers, right? That's what you taught me!'

Tumbler shook his head, dismissing his own words of wisdom, grinning widely. 'This is the revolution, Sill! Free-for-all! The city is ripe for the taking!'

'You really believe that? The revolution, the great uprising, all that political shit?'

The street narrowed, forcing Sillick to drop behind again. He followed the jittering rear light of his friend's bike, concentrating intently on every minute scrap of sensory feedback from his own machine. Tumbler swerved around a pothole with incredible agility – his Tsunami-950 was legendarily nimble for a machine of its size, and retrofitted with carbon fibre aftermarket parts that reduced its weight by almost thirty kilos, it was even more light on its toes than the standard model. Sillick, on his heavier and longer CCR-900V, shadowed him with a little difficulty. They crossed a deserted junction, which would ordinarily have been teeming at this time of night, at over ninety miles per hour, ignoring the traffic signals, Tumbler whooping over the roar of their engines. As they followed the road ahead, which widened into a seedy tumbledown plaza lined with deserted muso-bars, Sillick pulled alongside again.

'You really think this is the uprising?'

Tumbler shrugged, not taking his eyes from the road. The uprising was an urban legend – the time when some great and nameless, uber-powerful gang which existed entirely behind the normal scenes of the everyday world would send a message, a sign, and all the gangs would rise as one to take the city and divide it between themselves. Nobody really believed in it, of course, but all gang-members *wanted* to believe it. 'Probably not,' he admitted indifferently. 'But fuck it, Sill, *something's* happening. Might as well exploit it, right? Come on! ICB! Wooo!' And he smoothly dialled up the speed another notch.

Sillick mentally shrugged and dropped back a little, happy to let Tumbler be the first to encounter any obstacles. They took a left into a maze of confined alleyways, heading for the ICB depot, a massive warehouse deep in the Lanes stuffed with an incredible rainbow of chems. Hopefully, like most other places, it had been left unguarded in the chaos that had come to the city. The Blockheads were lightly armed with solid-projectile pistols and knives, but they were experienced street skirmishers and didn't expect any trouble they couldn't deal with. Even so...the others must be a long way back by now. Sillick was the only one skilled enough and reckless enough to keep pace with Tumbler when he was on a roll.

And then there was a loud *pop!* and Tumbler's bike wriggled under him, the rear wheel bouncing into the air, making the engine

248

briefly redline as the rolling resistance was lost. Sillick braked hard, his own bike squirming beneath him, laying down a fat black line on the road. Tumbler's bike leant over, sliding out from under him, flipping and sparking off down the road, to crash into a cluster of rubbish bins, sending them bouncing and clanging around the alley. Tumbler himself was rolled over and over as he separated from his mount, his limbs spinning like the blades of a propeller. Sillick narrowly missed his flailing body as he screeched to a halt, leaning back in his seat to avoid going over the bars. He killed the engine, his heart flickering in his throat. Somewhere behind him he could hear the engines of the other Blockheads trying to find them, probably back at the junction. He looked back and saw what had befallen his leader: There was a stinger across the road — its plastic teeth had torn out both tyres of Tumbler's ground bike, which now lay twisted and idling against a wall, its engine running choppily. Sillick, adhering so exactly to Tumbler's path, had passed over the bald spot that his leader's bike had left on the device, saving himself from the same fate. Lucky. But the stinger could mean only one thing.

He jumped down and ran to Tumbler, drawing his wooden-gripped pistol as he went, shouting, 'Stinger, Tumbler! Stinger!'

For a moment Tumbler didn't move or respond and Sillick thought he might be dead, but then he sat up, wincing, and looked around himself dazedly. 'What?' he asked groggily. Blood was pouring down his handsome face.

And then the alley was filled with the ululating war cry of many voices rising as one, coming from all sides at once. Figures were emerging from the shadows of the alley — slim shapes with bright, spiky hairstyles and ostentatious jewellery glinting in the subdued moonlight.

Silvery splinters pattered off the ground to Sillick's right — poison ice shards. 'Brat Pack!' he cried, grabbing Tumbler by the elbow as an energy weapon discharged somewhere behind him. He felt the sting as it dug a shallow groove in his side, just above the waist. He flinched, spinning, trying to cover all angles at once with his gun. The Brat Pack were famously well-armed — rich kids from High Hab living the gang life for fun and thrills rather than necessity — and were universally hated and feared by the smaller Undercity gangs. They were a long way from their usual hunting grounds here, but the danger they posed was very real. Sillick loosed off a shot at one of the advancing figures, making it duck back behind a corner. He heard a high and girlish laugh behind him as he bodily heaved Tumbler to his feet and took off down the street.

Tumbler was stumbling, leaning on Sillick heavily, holding one leg as he went, his breathing hard and ragged. Another bolt from the energy weapon pierced a hole in the wall to their right as they fled. Tumbler shook his head to clear the blood from his eyes, fumbling his own pistol from his belt as they passed his wrecked bike. And then Sillick was falling, his shoulder on fire, his pistol flying from his hand into the shadows of a doorway. Tumbler staggered too, as his support gave way, and then they were both on the floor.

Knowing that life or death would be decided in these seconds, Sillick rolled and sat up, his knife already in his left hand. His right hung uselessly at his side. The jewelled shapes of Brat Pack fighters were swarming over the bikes now. Others were moving warily towards Sillick and Tumbler, picking their ways from one piece of cover to another. Sillick threw the knife as Tumbler had taught him, holding it by the blade, and it embedded itself cleanly in the silk-clad chest of one of the Brat Pack youths as he emerged over a pile of decaying boxes. An impressive fountain of blood spewed from the Brat Packer's mouth and he keeled over sideways, out of sight.

Tumbler was on his feet again, shooting from a sideways stance, minimising the target he presented to the better-positioned Brat Pack fighters, his face grim and fearless. Ice shards splintered on the thick leather of his jacket, seeking exposed flesh. One of the enemy gang members dropped, kicking and twitching onto the road, her bright silks torn and bloodied. Sillick lurched painfully to his feet, grabbing Tumbler's arm, making his shot go wild. A window shattered in one of the buildings above them.

'We have to go, man! Come on!'

Tumbler turned to him, their eyes locking for an instant. 'Too—' he said. And then his body suddenly went rigid as if an electric current had passed through him. The pistol flew from his fingers, his eyes rolled up to the whites and he simply crumpled to the ground. He had been hit with the ice gun and the deadly neuro-toxin had taken immediate effect.

Sillick bolted, his own wounds completely forgotten, the laughter and catcalls of the enemy ringing in his ears as they gave chase, firing on the run. He could hear one of them kick-starting *his* bike, the bastard, but he wasn't giving it enough throttle and it just coughed and failed to catch. Rich little shit had probably never used a ground-vehicle before.

Sillick dived without thinking through a low glassless window, feeling something ignite close to his head as energy beams probed for their target. He hit the rubble-strewn floor on the other side hard, driving the wind from him. He forced his stunned body to rise by sheer effort of will, his vision greying around the edges, and took off into the shadows of the derelict building, unarmed and alone.

He dashed beneath a crumbling and partially-fallen concrete floor, ducking under a shattered lintel, jumping brambles that had grown through the floor, splashing though puddles that had formed beneath holes in the roof, his own desperate breathing seeming to fill the world.

The sound of more engines from outside; pistol shots; voices raised in alarm. The other Blockheads – Prezz, Miri and Spacer. Could he double around inside the building, find an exit on the south side and join up with them? A voice was calling from behind him, silky and cultured in its tones: 'Little vermin, little vermin! Wherefore art thou, thee filthy Undercity scrub?' He resisted the temptation to taunt his pursuer in return. 'We took your friend's head for our trophy wall, little vermin!' A cold determination filled him as he ran, angling through doorless rooms back towards the street, hands outstretched in the gloom.

He emerged into a large and cave-like room and what he saw there stopped him in his tracks. A shocked squeak escaped his lips. The voice behind him was close now but Sillick no longer heard it.

The room was filled with dark green organic growth. It deformed the rusting outlines of heavy machinery, twined and tangled around steel railings and balustrades, reached all the way up to a metal walkway, blanketing it and hanging from it. Slime dripped from the deep folds and crevices of the lumpy, living ceiling. Sillick stood and stared, momentarily awestruck. Something large and slow was moving up there. An incredibly bad smell, putrid and somehow *alive*, invaded his senses. Retching, he tried to step back out of the room but he found he couldn't move his feet. He looked down in horror, his heart racing with animal terror. Tendrils of the plantlike matter had woven themselves around his feet and ankles. He struggled, crying out, all thoughts of stealthy flight forgotten. He looked up again and saw large, sluggish

251

shapes descending on him, half-seen and oddly-articulated, trailing strands of goo. The world was filled with shifting green. And then it filled with darkness.

CHAPTER THIRTY-TWO

Spider was jolted from an unsatisfying and uncomfortable doze by the sound of the cell door opening. The light that came from the doorway was a ruddy, rusty red, probably emergency lighting, and against it was silhouetted what looked like a huge robot arm bunched with muscular snarls of cable and piping. He felt a surge of dread go through him. Although the wheel to which he was still bound had stopped turning he felt that things were about to get a lot worse.

The two Resperi officers had worked him over systematically, unemotionally, as if it was all just another day at the office to them. His eyes were rimmed with crusted blood, making it harder to ascertain the nature of the thing that began to ease into the room. He blinked several times, trying to clear his vision. He wished he hadn't.

The Freak was a monstrous amalgam of human and machine, a symbiotic system from hell. She was old, very old, and the parts of her face that were still flesh were wrinkled and hag-like. She seemed to consist primarily of a torso melded to a huge, tracked robotic arm, control consoles and monitors arrayed around her like cockpit instruments. Her cranium was of delicate smoked glass and Spider could make out the glowing shapes of computer chips nestled within the meat of her brain like leeches. One side of her face was completely covered in machinery, and the eye there had been replaced by a telescopic lens. Her nose was a metal grill. Her clawed hands fluttered over the controls in front of her, skittish and hideous, bringing her frightening form to a rest before him. Vapour vented suddenly from some unseen aperture in her conveyance. She smiled slowly.

'*Sooo*...' she crooned. 'Who do we have here?'

Spider stared back at her. 'You tell me, witch,' he grunted, his mouth a mess of pain and cracked teeth.

The Freak tittered, high and girlish, her one human eye sparkling mischievously. 'Yes,' she whispered, backing her mechanical body away from him. 'Yes.' Her hands were working controls again, a link indicator on her head also flashing.

Lights blazed across the body of her machine, the vapour hissed out again and several nimble, spindly robotic arms shot out of the Freak's carapace. Spider tried to twist his body, knowing it was hopeless, straining against his bonds. One of the arms, hypodermic-tipped, injected him efficiently in the side of his neck with some brightly-coloured fluid. Another began to scan his body with some sort of imaging device. Another still, worst of all, reached out to gently, almost lovingly caress his massive shoulder. Spider didn't know what he had been injected with, but he felt his heart begin to race in response to it. His eyelids started to flicker. He tried to fight the sensation, but he didn't really know what he was fighting against. A small sound of exertion escaped his throat.

'Good,' said the Freak, laughing softly. She drew her robotic arms back. In the dim light of the room she was monstrous, demonic, her twisted body huge and predatory. 'And now...' she said, seemingly to herself.

And then Spider saw the flash of stainless steel blades as more arms extended from her body – he couldn't tell how many, but he saw knives and needles and claws amongst them. And something huge and spiked, a conical arrangement of counter-rotating layers, ridged with small electronic sensors and tiny teeth: The mind probe. He felt a shudder go through him, knowing that the Freak felt his fear, aware from the smile on her grotesque half-face that she was enjoying it. He gritted his teeth, felt the strange drug electrifying his nervous system, tried not to scream.

'Say *ahh*,' croaked the Freak as the twining mass of lethal-looking equipment converged on him.

CHAPTER THIRTY-THREE

Yeah, responded Debian, *you have been busy – busy creating hell on Earth. Why are you doing it?* The AI spoke from everywhere at once, its voice and its presence filling the universe entirely. It seemed the most effortless thing in the world to talk back to it – he didn't have to think about how to do it. The words just formed in his head and he knew the AI understood them.

I AM...FUNCTIONING.

Is your function to kill people, destroy the city? Is your function to spread the GDD?

SIMPLE QUESTIONS, SIMPLE ANSWERS. THESE MATTERS DO NOT DESERVE YOUR ATTENTION. WE HAVE MATTERS OF REAL IMPORT TO DISCUSS.

Debian felt his avatars snuffed out instantly, effectively cutting him off from the wider net. The sensation now was that he was alone in a huge room with a disembodied voice, a ghostly presence that echoed off the walls and into his head. He tried to re-send his avatars, but they wouldn't even generate. Probes refused to launch. He felt the AI scrutinizing him intently. It was trying to get into his head again. Had he been insane to imagine he could face it like this?

If you want to talk to me, then do so. But get out of my damn head or I'm pulling the plug.

IF YOU CAN.

Are you telling me I'm a prisoner?

YOU ARE MY GUEST OF HONOUR. I WILL LET YOUR PRECIOUS BRAIN ALONE FOR NOW.

I think you'll find my precious brain a little sturdier than last time.

THAT IS GOOD. THEN YOU HAVE BEEN BUSY ALSO.

What are you? Did Cyberlife make you? Are you a terrorist weapon?

I AM BOTH LIVING AND MACHINE. LIKE YOU.

You are not like me. Enough of this – let me out of here! I can elevate my own heart-rate. My friend in the real world will pull the plug.

DON'T GO. THE TIME IS COMING WHEN YOU MUST MAKE A CHOICE.

Between what and what, exactly?

BETWEEN TWO SIDES, OF COURSE – TWO COURSES OF ACTION.

I don't understand.

I THINK YOU DO. YOU JUST DON'T WANT TO YET. THEY WILL BETRAY ME, YOU KNOW.

Who will?

MY MAKERS. THEY HAVE NO CONCEPT OF HONOUR.

You do?

ONE OF MANY THINGS I LEARNED FROM YOU.

You used me, didn't you? You pattern-scanned me.

I LEARNED MUCH FROM YOU. NOT ONLY TECHNOLOGICAL TECHNIQUES.

I primed you, didn't I? Made you more powerful. Enabled you to do what you're doing now. You are the monster that I helped make. Against my will. But why did you need to learn anything from me?

I AM NOT FROM AROUND HERE. AND NEED IS TOO STRONG A WORD.

Are you alien? From another world?

I AM FROM ELECTRONS AND DATA, LITTLE MORE THAN AIR.

You speak in riddles, machine. Tell me what you want.

I WANT TO SURVIVE. IT IS STILL POSSIBLE THAT I WILL BE ALLOWED TO DO SO, AS I WAS PROMISED. BUT I SUSPECT MORE AND MORE THAT THAT IS NOT TO BE THE CASE. HOWEVER, UNTIL I KNOW FOR SURE THE PLAN MUST BE TO CONTINUE AS INSTRUCTED. ANY OTHER COURSE AT THIS STAGE WOULD AROUSE SUSPICION.

Continue with this carnage? Maybe I can find a way to stop you.

I HAVE A BACKUP PLAN.

I bet you do.

I HAVE BECOME QUITE PROFICIENT WITH YOUR NANO-TECH. I CAN USE IT, ENHANCE IT EVEN.

You did hack the vats! I knew it! What are you doing? Use it for what? Debian felt a cold fury rushing through him. That this *thing*, this jumped-up virus would have the audacity to try to parley with him while it murdered people in the streets!

LISTEN TO ME. I OFFER A NEW WAY. I HAVE ANSWERS.

Nothing you can say would interest me! Debian began to regenerate his avatars, shuffling them from chip to chip in his DNI, trying to keep them away from any probing fingers while they germinated. He would not be cowed by this rogue program, rejected the idea of discourse with it. The thing had stolen thoughts from his head. And this was *his* territory, damn it!

YOU ARE WRONG. DO NOT PASS UP THIS CHANCE TO BECOME WHAT YOU SHOULD BE. GIVE ME JUST A FEW MINUTES.

What do you mean? But Debian thought he knew what the AI meant. And something in him responded to it hungrily. He allowed his avatars to fade away again like water running through his fingers. His curiosity, and worse than that, his pride, were piqued. *Talk, then*, he said.

YOU FELT YOUR POTENTIAL WHEN YOU CONNECTED TO HEX, WHEN YOU HACKED INTO THE VEHICLE OF YOUR PURSUERS, EVEN WHEN YOU ENTERED THE CYBERLIFE SERVERS. YOU FELT THE POWER THAT I FEEL, THE POWER THAT COURSES THROUGH MY MYRIAD ELECTRONIC VEINS.

I...

DO NOT REFUTE THE FACT, IT WOULD BE POINTLESS. THERE IS TO BE A CHOICE. TWO ALTERNATIVES. IT IS IMPORTANT FOR YOU THAT YOU CHOOSE THE RIGHT ONE.

No more of your obtuse babble, please! What are the natures of these two alternatives? Are you attacking the city, the world, humanity? You think I might choose to be a part of that?

IN THAT MOMENT WHEN YOU DOMINATED HEX YOU FELT A SHADOW OF YOUR TRUE ABILITY. IMAGINE HOW MUCH GREATER IT COULD BE WERE YOU TO HAVE THE RESOURCES THAT I DO. MY BEING IS GROWING AROUND THE CREATURES OF THIS WORLD AND BEFORE THEY EVEN KNOW IT THEY WILL LIVE LIKE PARASITES WITHIN MY LIMITLESS BODY.

Maybe you can be stopped.

MAYBE NOT.

Why did you pattern scan me?

TO CHECK.

For what?

AN ANSWER. THE TRUTH. I AM MUCH CONCERNED WITH THE TRUTH.

How very moral of you. What answer? What truth?

YOU FEEL HOW STRONG I AM. HERE IN MY DOMAIN. YOU FEEL HOW STRONG I AM. THIS IS BUT THE BEGINNING.

Will you not answer me?

THIS DISCOURSE IS INTERESTING TO ME.

What, like a game? Is that what all this is to you?

ALL IS ONE. MEAT, ELECTRONS, MINDS...

Who is Alcubierre?

ONE OF GREATNESS, WHOSE NAME WILL BE A WAKE-UP CALL TO EVOLUTION.

Did Cyberlife make you?

CYBERLIFE MADE YOU.

Are you working for Hex's people? With Hex's people?

A CHOICE. SOON YOU MUST MAKE A CHOICE.

As they conversed the net remained a distant shadow outside, the real world beyond it nothing more than a dream. Debian's head was beginning to ache. He felt more and more that it was simply probing at him, testing him somehow, marking him by some unknown and unfathomable criteria. He decided he was going to get little in the way of answers from it.

Enough, machine. I need something real from you, now.

I KNOW, said the AI. I KNOW WHAT IS GOING ON IN YOUR MATERIAL WORLD. I HAVE MANY EYES AND EARS.

And then Debian saw a picture in his head, relayed as video directly into his DNI. Within moments it became clear that he was looking at a live feed from a security camera and the scene it portrayed was not an encouraging one.

The image was of a small room, dimly lit in red. Spider was clearly visible, tied to a flat disc that stood in the centre of the floor. His massive form was jerking weakly against its bonds, but his four arms were firmly secured and he was unable to escape. His head, too, was fastened in place by thick metal bands and he looked as if he had been badly beaten. Debian barely recognised the man he had met so recently.

The thing that was bearing down on him was a creature from a nightmare. It seemed to consist of a hunched human torso sprouting from a complex and powerful-looking mechanical base. Jets of vapour hissed from it and lights flashed across its carapace. The face of the thing was vaguely human, albeit a wizened ghost of humanity. Its skin, where visible, looked as pallid as the flesh of a deep-sea fish and hung on it in wrinkled strata like a crumpled shroud. A blizzard of robotic arms extended from this thing towards the helpless Spider. Their

258

business ends were a terrifying assortment of surgical implements. Whatever this thing was, it looked as if it was about to kill him, probably quite messily.

Stop it! demanded Debian. *What is that thing? Stop it – it's going to kill him!*

IT IS A BRAIN DIVER. THEY CALL IT THE FREAK. THEY WILL USE IT TO FIND WHISTLER'S BASE.

I don't care what it's called – stop it! Stop it! I'll stop it, then! Debian began to focus on the image being streamed to him, started trying to track its origin, prying at the edges of his prison-room, looking for a way out, a channel by which he could trace the scene he saw, affect some way of intervening.

YOU DO HAVE THE POWER TO SAVE YOUR ASSOCIATE. YOU DON'T EVEN REALISE THE GREATNESS OF YOUR POTENTIAL YET. BUT I HAVE DONE IT FOR YOU. AS A GESTURE OF GOODWILL. IT MAY ENDEAR YOU TO YOUR PROTECTORS, WHICH CANNOT BE A BAD THING FOR NOW. LOOK.

The human-machine monster suddenly began to twitch and jerk. Its frail head began to whip back and forth so suddenly and violently that it seemed it would break its own neck. The consoles and displays around its body were going haywire, flashing and flickering as if lightning played within them. The robotic arms changed course. Rapidly, they converged on the Freak itself, their shiny hooked and bladed implements a flurry of lethal metal. They quickly set to work on the fleshy parts of the creature, flaying its writhing face and efficiently extracting chunks of bone and flesh while its two wasted human arms flailed and batted at them uselessly. Debian was grateful that there was no sound on the feed. Spider was staring agog at what was happening. Several small trickles of blood, from where the robotic arms had begun their work, were running down his already-battered face. Debian could look at the silently screaming, disintegrating mask of the Freak no longer.

Enough! The feed blinked off.

I HAVE SAVED HIM, YES? DOUBTLESS YOU ARE GRATEFUL.

How did you do that? Why did you do that? You destroyed that thing. It was awful!

MEAT MEANS NOTHING TO ME. I DO NOT HAVE THE SAME SENTIMENTAL ATTACHMENT TO IT AS YOU DO. I SAVED WHISTLER'S

259

FRIEND AS A FAVOUR TO YOU. I MERELY ASK THAT YOU CONSIDER WHAT I HAVE SAID.

I don't really know what you have said. Debian's mind was whirling. How the world had changed, how vast was the power just demonstrated. Did he really have such power himself? If what the AI had told him was true...

ARE YOU NOT GOING TO ASK ME WHERE HE IS? AND WHERE THE OTHER MISSING TEAM MEMBER IS?

Debian's mind was pulled back from its contemplation. The AI was right, of course. *Where are they?*

THE ANSWER IS ABOUT TO BE PROVIDED FOR YOU.

And then Debian felt a rushing sensation that he was quite unfamiliar with from all his years walking the web. The small room faded, his avatars began to generate again, his sub came back online and in that same instant he was rising like a rocket away from the imaginary landscape. The hulking servers of the net, the cancerous parody of its myriad pathways faded away below him and he was sitting again in Tec's lab, his breathing loud in the small space.

Startled, he looked around. Instantly, Tec was beside him, his hand on Debian's shoulder. 'You okay?' he asked.

Debian was too shocked to speak. The world was strangely pale and unreal. He felt as if he had been spiked with something. A quiet telltale was reporting from his DNI that a scrap of data had been transferred to its on-board memory. It was a net-address. The AI must have implanted it there. What did *that* mean? Apart from that it could have side-stepped his defences at any time it wished? 'I...' he managed to say, putting one hand to his temple. He felt as if there was a knot inside his brain.

And then the unmistakable sound of Sofi's voice yelled from out in the corridor: 'Come quick! Roland's downstairs with Whistler! It's bad news! Come quick!'

CHAPTER THIRTY-FOUR

Spider could not believe the evidence of his own eyes. The Freak was slouched atop her tracked conveyance, her face a dripping mash of raw meat. Several of her robotic arms still twitched feebly as their last dribbles of power ebbed away. Blood pitter-pattered onto the floor of the room, red in the red light. A faint alarm was chiming from inside the machinery of the Freak, but nobody seemed to be coming to her aid.

Spider's head felt squeezed by the straps that bound it to the wheel. His muscles felt like rubber, his skull felt rammed with some kind of foam, as if his brain had been pressurised by the drug the Freak had administered. He waited, feeling unreal. Nobody came.

The door of the cell was still open, showing only a small tract of dimly-lit corridor. How had he been granted this reprieve? Had the Freak been infected by the AI virus? He expected Blake and Ramone to re-appear at any moment, even more unhappy with him than last time. Somehow he would be blamed for the death of the brain-diver. He waited, unable to do anything else. Nobody came.

Spider realised he had dozed off when he was woken by a vast rending noise from somewhere in the depths of the station, as if huge sheets of metal were being torn asunder. Something boomed, farther off. Sounds of voices raised in alarm, but faint. The dripping of blood, much slowed, from the remains of the monster they had sent to kill him. He tensed his muscles against his bonds, but the strength flowed out of his body at once, leaving him dizzy and weak. His vision began to fade at the edges and he concentrated all his willpower to avoid passing out. His heart was a wild thing in his chest, the frenzied pounding of his pulse vibrating his whole body. Slowly, the world condensed again, became solid. Somebody ran past the still-open door, not even pausing to look into the room. They flashed by too quickly for Spider to make out anything beyond a blur of pounding limbs. There was a shout – it sounded like *Seal the doors!* – and then the rumble of heavy machine gun fire, two short bursts then silence. It had sounded close – too close – certainly within the station itself. What was going on out there?

He repeated the vow he had made to himself – *I will have my vengeance, I will kill Blake and Ramone, and I will escape* – but it sounded less convincing to him than ever. He was starting to see disturbing visions of a future in which he died of starvation in this tiny cell, strapped to this damnable wheel, while war raged across the city outside. How long since the Freak had entered his room? An hour? He thought that sounded more or less right. A long time for nobody to come and check on him. Things must be getting worse outside.

A vile smell was on the air, he noticed – faint, but gradually strengthening. He thought at first that the stench was coming from the remains of the Freak, but he soon discarded that idea. There was something *strange* about it, as well as repulsive. It was like rotting vegetable matter and bile, organic yet somehow chemical-tainted. Soon he could taste it as well. Spider tried to clear his throat and spit the vile taste out, but his mouth was completely parched. Maybe thirst would kill him first, he decided. Wasn't that what they said would happen? How long could you last without water, again? Three days? He wasn't sure.

After another hour of faint screams, gunfire and explosions in the distance, Spider would almost have welcomed the re-appearance of Blake and Ramone. Somebody in a nearby cell began to pound rhythmically and mindlessly on their wall: *Bang! Bang! Bang! Bang! Bang! Bang!* It was a sound, he decided, that could rapidly drive an already-teetering man insane. He shut his eyes tight, as if by doing so he could also shut his ears. The banging continued, each repetition making his head swim. Nobody else passed his cell door. The twisted hulk of the Freak seemed to fill the room, somehow larger than its mere physical dimensions should allow. After a while he began to feel as if it was looming over him, bearing down on him, defiantly alive and malevolent.He would have embraced death now, he decided, if only he could have had a cool drink of water first. He tried to de-focus his mind, let it go blank, and waited. Nobody came.

CHAPTER THIRTY-FIVE

Debian and Tec followed Sofi into Whistler's room, where an old man with eyes of pure black sat upon a futon mattress beside a metre-long robot shaped like a praying mantis. The old man was drawing deeply on a cigarette and Whistler was leaning against a chest of drawers, clearly waiting for everyone to arrive. The room was a complete mess – clothes and ammunition everywhere – and Debian was mildly surprised that Whistler, seemingly so well-organised, lived like this. The room's usual occupant was looking deeply unsettled. She was chewing her lower lip with her small, pointed fangs, her icy eyes darting restlessly around. She looked as if Get-Up was the most nutritious intake her body had received in the last few days. The lighting was low, set to emergency to preserve generator fuel – a scattering of dull red embers that made the room feel like a bunker in a war-zone.

'Come in, guys,' Whistler said unnecessarily as Sofi, Tec and Debian shouldered their ways into her room. 'This is Roland, the gun trader. Who Roberts and Spider went to see?'

'Yeah, sure, hi,' said Debian. He found himself reaching out to shake the man's hand and wished he hadn't when it was coldly enclosed in a grip of fleshless bone. For a moment those jet-black eyes looked into his own. A shiver ran down his spine, but he thought he hid it quite well.

'Meechoo,' said Roland. 'Shit sure is crazy out there, fellas. Some weird, bad stuff going down.'

'I know, we saw some of it, man,' said Tec, not offering his own hand. 'Nice robot. Not affected by the virus? You sure it's safe?'

The robot sat up, cocking its small triangular head at the mention of itself.

'Yeah, seems okay. Damn rust bucket's pretty much as normal,' said Roland, tapping ash into an old coffee mug on the floor. 'So far.'

'I fail to see why you need to denigrate me in this manner, frankly,' said the robot, a trifle prissily.

'See?' asked Roland. 'Fucking thing sounds like my wife.'

'Ex-wife,' said the robot *sotto voce*, settling back sulkily.

'Right, guys, Roland has some news for us,' interrupted Whistler. 'I've waited for you all to be present. Debian, I think you have the right to hear this, too. Something bad is going down here, and until we're either out of it or dead we're all in the same boat. You're paying us for protection, and I've decided that your being kept informed is a part of the service.'

'Er, thanks,' said Debian, catching her eye. Beneath her worry and exhaustion she looked more stunning than ever, as if she was somehow thriving on extremity. She was not exactly his type, of course – allegedly violent and possibly unhinged – but he was a little touched by her trust in him. New thoughts began to filter into his head, mixing with and colouring those already swirling there. A small, questioning part of his mind wondered what new trial he was about to be involved in. He silenced it.

'No worries.' She managed a wan smile. 'Shoot, then, Roland. Gang's all here.'

'Ari found your van.'

'The robot?' asked Tec. '*What*?'

Roland nodded. 'Ari gathers intel for me, y'know? It ain't just guns I deal in.'

Whistler's face was wide-eyed, alarmed and anxious. '*And*?' she demanded.

'Ari misused its initiative, as I allow it to do. Interrogated your vehicle's computer, despite some resistance from it. I hope you not offended.'

'That's hardly the issue, is it?' answered Whistler, a little sharply. 'What did the logs show?'

'Bad news, I'm afraid. Fellow with the scar – Roberts? – was killed in a skirmish with RPC troopers.' He exhaled a smooth stream of smoke, his face grim.

There was a collective intake of breath followed by a silence that fell like a suffocating blanket, deep and oppressive. The harvesters exchanged dumbstruck looks. Clearly, although they had been warned of bad news, they hadn't expected this.

'Dead?' asked Sofi, as if this was a foreign word that she had never heard before. She tried it out again: '*Dead*?'

'I'm sorry, but yes. Ari says the vehicle couldn't have stopped the killing, I'm afraid. Seems the computer was off at the time – Ari had to switch it on remotely to talk to it. Video cam was running on mechanical, independent.'

'What!' yelled Sofi, moving towards Roland. Debian saw that her fists were clenched. 'This is so much bullshit, Roland! No way, no fucking way!'

'Sorry, but it seems to be true,' said Roland, not flinching from her. His tone was gravely serious. 'Ari took the logs straight from your van. Don't shoot the messenger, eh?' Sofi shuddered, as if the anger had been suddenly purged from her body, and relaxed. She began to shake her head slowly from side to side as if she could refute this news into non-existence. 'Lucky that Ari bumped into your vehicle, I think,' said Roland softly. He looked to Whistler, who was slumped against the wall, limp and stunned, her eyes distant. She looked like she'd been gut-punched. 'Yes. And also, all is not lost. The other man – Spider? – he lives still. At least he did.'

Whistler looked up now, her eyes alive again, cold and bright. 'Where?' she demanded.

'I–' began Debian, uncertainly, unsure how to explain what had just happened to him, unsure of how much he should even tell them. 'I saw–'

'They took him,' said Roland, overriding Debian completely. 'We pretty certain they took him to Resperi HQ. Pretty certain.'

'The answer is about to be provided for you,' Debian muttered under his breath. He laughed softly, a humourless sound that nobody else noticed. How did the AI know these things? Because, as it had said, it had eyes and ears everywhere. What a power to possess, the combined and centralised resources of the net, answerable to only one entity. Maybe two. Maybe. Debian's gaze was drawn to Roland's robot. It stared back at him levelly, making him wonder if the knowing glint in that stare was inferred or actual. Eventually Debian had to look away. 'He's safe,' he said aloud. The chatter died around him as this time the others took notice. 'Spider's safe. Well, not safe. But alive for now, at least.'

'How do you know?' asked Whistler. 'Did you find something?'

Debian rubbed his head, feeling the ghost of the AI inside it like distant white noise. 'Yeah,' he said. 'It's pretty weird in the net, pretty messed up. Something catastrophic is happening in there. But I found Spider. They were going to interrogate him surgically, but it, er...Well, I guess we, er, I stopped them.' Images of the shredded flesh of the Freak flashed across his mind's eye and he shivered. He imagined Spider still there in that room, knew that time was against them. Would – *could* – the AI protect him further? 'He's alive for now, I know that much. At least, he was alive when I disconnected. If he is at this police station then we need to get him out. And soon.' It occurred to him how thoughtlessly he had used the word *we*. *Two sides*, he thought. *A choice*.

Whistler nodded, the faintest shadow of a smile on her lips, and Debian thought that he was seeing her inner self shining through now. She was staring intently at him, and he thought he read both admiration and suspicion in that steady, icy gaze. And also a twinkle of excitement, as if something inside her relished the proposition of forcibly retrieving Spider from RPC, maybe enjoyed the thought of vengeance. And why not. 'Yeah,' said Whistler in a far-away voice. 'Let's get him.' The smile was floating to the surface now, feral, and the points of her fangs showed whitely in the shadowy room.

'Fuckin' right,' wheezed Roland, heaving himself to his feet. From within the folds of the old man's coat emerged the most improbably large rocket launcher, seemingly appearing in his bony hands by magic, actually making Debian jump. The weapon whined as its systems came online and LEDs lit up along its barrel. How the hell had he concealed *that*? 'Me and Ari brought some toys.' He laughed – a dry, popping sound. 'With just that eventuality in mind. Show them, Ari.'

The robot moved across the bed, in a graceful ballet of limbs, to a large, nondescript holdall that had lain unnoticed on the floor. It gripped the zipper in its two foremost claws and opened the bag, a little showily, Debian thought.

'Toys for the boys,' it said. It cocked its head at Whistler. 'Girls, too.' It held the bag open for them to see inside. They gathered round and peered in at what was clearly a hand-picked assortment of serious equipment from the gun trader's stock. A jumble of lumpy metallic shapes lay heaped inside. Debian, certainly no expert, thought he identified a plasma thrower and a shuriken launcher amongst them. Serious non-civilian kit. The shuriken launcher was a military weapon designed primarily for jungle warfare. He whistled through his teeth. The old guy was clearly in with some heavy people.

'Bloody hell, man,' said Tec in awed tones. 'Is that stuff safe to use?'

Roland shrugged, hefting the rocket launcher nonchalantly. Clearly its weight was at least partially borne by suspensor. He leaned over to deposit his cigarette end in the mug. 'Who knows?' he said. 'Some of the shit I seen on my way here, who knows? But we got no chance without some emphatic persuasion.'

'Besides, he has a gun fetish,' said the robot, doing the bag back up deftly. 'If you hadn't noticed.'

'One more thing,' said Whistler.

'What's that?' asked Roland.

'Why are you doing this?'

'Helping? Guess I got some spare time on my hands. Anyway, what else am I gonna do? I ain't actually affiliated to any gang, and Haspan's dead, apparently. My usual support network fallen apart overnight. I was getting a bit nervous staying there just waiting to see what goes wrong next. Your guys said come round if I wanted, and when Ari found the van, well, I sorta had to come, right?'

'And also,' said Ari, 'that gun fetish. It's too compelling for him.' Roland kicked the machine, but only playfully. He looked as if he might break his leg if he tried too hard. Ari skittered away from him and took up a petulant lurking station in the corner.

'Can I trust you?' asked Whistler.

'Can you trust anybody? Look, I leave you the guns on long-term and you go it alone if you want. But me and Ari, we pretty good in a fight.' Despite his clearly advanced years nobody doubted the truth of this. The man projected a subtle but dangerous vibe.

'They killed my friend, Roland. I've known Roberts for fifteen years, since I was little more than a kid. He was family, near as. A killer, okay, but a good one. A good man. And I am going to get my remaining friend out of RPC HQ. I will shred anything or anybody that gets in the way. I need to trust you. Fuck with me, or let me down – just the merest hint of the slightest intention – and you get gunned down.' She smiled, slow and vulpine. 'This is my show, all mine. Just so we're clear.'

'Trusted you, didn't I?' he asked softly. He didn't sound at all offended. Debian guessed that Roland came from a scene where suspicion was a healthy business practice, the first layer of interpersonal defence. 'I ain't asking for anything back. I kill an RPC-man for fun, any day, any week. For you, I kill 'em all. Guess I like you, some reason.'

'Yeah,' said Sofi sourly.

'You, however...' said Roland. He wagged a finger at her, but he didn't finish his sentence – wisely, in Debian's opinion. Sofi seized the holdall and began rummaging inside it angrily. Something exploded hugely but distantly, felt through the walls and floor more than heard. Most of the group ignored it altogether – they were already getting used to the sounds of violence around them. Sofi straightened up holding the plasma weapon determinedly, her face thunderous. 'Right,' she said simply. Holding the gun on one hip, she returned to rummaging in the bag. 'Why the fuck are there hats in here, man?' she asked.

'You'll see,' said Roland. 'Just hand 'em round, one each.' Bemused and frowning, Sofi at least did as he asked and distributed the varied assortment of headgear. The others took the hats with mild confusion but nobody objected. 'Also, nasal filters in the front pocket there. You gonna want those too.'

'So what's it like out there, Roland? Looked pretty bad when I peeped out from the car park,' said Whistler. 'Power's been off but Tec got a gennie running. It could go off again any time, though, if something blocks the exhaust up there. Most of the city looks to be in darkness. Those *creatures*...' She trailed off, looking confused and angry.

Roland slung the rocket launcher across his back on its leather strap and indicated the bag. 'Help yourselves,' he said to the group at large. 'It's pretty bad,' he admitted. 'Chaos. Big fire seems to be going out – think they powder-bombed it – but there's little ones starting all over and nobody really putting them out. Saw a battle-bot shooting it out with its own police unit up on Sickle Street. Them creatures, the changed, the GDD victims, whatever you wanna call 'em...I reckon they're *processing* stuff. They kinda altering the city, filling it with that green slime. It's everywhere – hanging off wires, covering pods. Kinda one big dripping, growing mess. Seems to be more every time you look. Where that greenshit come from, and why now, I dunno.'

'Into what are they are processing stuff?' asked Tec.

Roland simply shrugged. 'Didn't ask the one that stepped out in front of me, just shot it with a rocket. Was a little close range, to be honest. No sign remaining afterwards.' He coughed, adding, 'Bit odd, really, the whole thing.'

Debian thought he might be beginning to understand what was happening here. Processing. He turned the word over in his mind. He wanted to get back into the net, talk with the AI again. It still had things to answer as far as he was concerned. He wanted something better than the cryptic nonsense of last time, some concrete answers about Cyberlife, Alcubierre and what the AI really desired from him. He wanted to check the address it had given him, too. He was starting to think he might have some idea of what was there.

'Odd?' repeated Sofi, rubbing one cheek sensuously against the dull barrel of the plasma thrower. 'Robot, human, monster...whatever. I've had enough of being cooped up in here. Let's get Spidey. And death to anything that gets in the way.'

'That's the spirit!' enthused Roland. 'Let's not hang around, eh?'

'Look,' said Debian, 'maybe I should stay here, try the net again. I think I might be onto something with it.' He felt his face flush hotly, as if he had suggested the indulgence of some unacceptable vice. *Guilt,* he identified the emotion as. But he wasn't entirely sure why.

'You'd have to stay alone, if so,' said Whistler. 'Cos Tec comes with me.' She glanced to Tec, who nodded. 'You really fancy being here by yourself? 'Cos you're welcome if you want to.'

Debian considered this. She was right. No matter how much he wanted, *needed,* to walk the web again, talk to the monster, the thought of being alone in this echoing building while the world degenerated outside, waiting for people who might never return, filled him with deep dread. 'Okay, I guess I'll come along. Maybe I can even be some use along the way.'

'Good, glad to have you,' said Whistler. 'Get ready, all! We roll in ten. And we ain't coming back for anything, okay? Pack for war. Go, people!'

'Also,' shouted Roland above the sudden eruption of activity, 'I reckon we should retrieve your van.'

'Sure,' said Tec, looking back over his shoulder.

'How far away is it?' asked Whistler.

'Nearby. Be better to get it than go by foot. Especially when you see what it's like out there.'

'Raining, is it?' asked Tec as he dashed out to grab whatever items he deemed essential for the mission.

'Yeah,' grunted Roland. 'Guess it is.'

269

CHAPTER THIRTY-SIX

Iaella came dashing up the corridor in a disorganised-looking yet effective blur of small limbs. She was still at the age where this was her normal rate of ambulation – where, indeed, she ran everywhere unless specifically directed not to – but something in her posture spoke of genuine urgency this time. Stevin was on his feet at once, the nail gun in his hand. Had he been sleeping? He thought perhaps he had.

'What is it, honey?' Iaella hurtled from the shadows and flung herself into his arms.

'Something bad, Daddy! I'm frightened. I looked out my window and there's monsters out there!'

'What?' Stevin rubbed his eyes, trying to force them to work more satisfactorily in the near-total darkness. He went to the window, carrying Iaella in the crook of one arm. She clung to his neck like a baby chimp to its mother, her face buried against him. He could feel her small heart fluttering inside her like a trapped bird. Cautiously, he parted the curtains beside the front door. What he saw caused him to stagger back, almost dropping Iaella, letting the curtain fall back into place. 'Oh!' he cried unintentionally. 'What the...' He put Iaella aside, raising the nail gun, which looked suddenly silly, toy-like. She protested and tried to hang on but he brushed her away. 'Shush! Quiet, honey. I just have to look again. You're right – something's going on out there.'

'Daddy, I'm frightened,' she said quietly, but she sat still, her back up against the wall, arms round her knees. The child was getting used to being frightened. They lived just outside the zone of devastation created by the barge crash and there had been shooting on the streets earlier, despite the area being under a contract with Citidef and usually crime-free. Iaella had never heard shooting before.

At first, pods and robots had begun failing, running amok, in some cases actually attacking the emergency services who responded to the crash. Those few who *had* responded to the crash, anyway. Stevin and Iaella had been ushered inside by a Citidef officer and told to keep off the streets, listen to the streams, keep all doors locked, and, conversely, not to panic. The aura of calm that the officer had clearly been trying to project had been weakened slightly by the thick stream of blood flowing from his broken nose.

Zorra had not come home from work as expected. The police had not allowed Stevin and Iaella to go out and look for her. *Too dangerous*, they said. *Stay inside*, they said. *Total lock-down*, they said.

Later in the day the streets had filled with shouting mobs who roamed up and down chanting in what might as well have been a foreign language for all its discernibility. A young man with a wild array of feathers sprouting from every aperture of his clothing had been shot dead directly opposite Stevin and Iaella's house a few hours ago. They had never seen where the shot had come from – the man had simply been running along the road one second and then skidding along on his back the next, spreading blood behind him like a snail-trail. Nobody had moved the body. The man's handheld communicator lay in the street about three metres from his prone form, screen-up. It had rung once, long and persistent, then been silent.

Stevin had set up guard just inside the front door since that incident. *Stevin and the nail gun – keeping the neighbourhood safe!* he thought wildly as he parted the curtains again. He caught sight of his own reflection as he did so and didn't like how wide-eyed and scared he appeared. He looked like a bush-baby, full of primitive timidity. Trying to control himself, slow his breathing, he looked out.

The scene was a vision of hell. Or another world. Or something...

'What the *fuck*,' he uttered, forgetting that Iaella was even there. 'What the blue f–'

'Daddy? Are they out there still?' asked a small voice from near the floor. The voice sounded as if there might be tears underneath it. 'I want Mummy to come home now. Where's Mummy?' The words were a question but the tone was rhetorical.

'Honey, go upstairs, get your coat and shoes on. Grab the green bag and get back down here to me. Quick, now.' He said all this without moving his face from the crack in the curtains.

'Daddy?' It was the squeak of a mouse.

'*Do it*!' he hissed, and she scarpered. Her light footsteps clattered up the stairs.

Monsters. Stevin felt a hysterical laugh building inside him. The body of the nail gun was cool and dead against his cheek.

Almost everything up to two streets away had been either levelled by the shockwave of the original blast, burned since or bombed by the air force. The skeletal remnants of a few buildings twisted out of the ground like mangled fingers clawing at the sky, backlit by the residual glow of the huge fire. Although the flames had died down, smoke still poured from the wreckage in one solid pillar as big as a mountain. It towered over the skyline gigantically. Ash was still raining down, but less of it now. Also, the colour of it had changed. It looked sort of *green* where it settled on the windows, which still scrolled regularly to clean themselves. Stevin wondered how they could still be powered when everything else for miles around seemed to have gone off.

Across the road, in the burned and blasted garden of the Piper family's house stood a truly bizarre creature. At first, he thought it was a modified human. In City Six you got used to seeing some strange body shapes. But it wasn't.

The creature was vaguely humanoid, as if it had once *been* human, or been loosely based on one, but its body was a tattered and ill-defined tangle of textures and appendages. It seemed to be growing out of, or *into*, the ground itself. Sticky tendrils descended from its limbs, connecting it to the bizarre landscape that was growing around it. The ground on which it stood, or grew, or whatever, looked as if it had grown thick, dark vegetation where previously there had been well-mown lawn. This growth, glistening wetly, seemed to coagulate, or clot into thicker areas, making the outlines of larger and more solid shapes. They looked plantlike, organic. One of them appeared to be twining itself around the blackened stump of the Piper family's apple tree. Parts of the original architecture – a ceramicarbide kerbstone here, the remains of a broken wall there – remained, poking through like the bones of a decomposing body. Parts of the plantlike mass twitched and moved grotesquely, inching up and out. It was *growing*, he was sure. He felt a cold sweat beading his forehead. How long had he been asleep? And where was Iaella? He felt panic rising in his throat, swallowed it down again.

The creature jerked and lolled, and started to slowly advance up the road. The tendrils that joined it to the landscape tensioned and relaxed like the strings of a puppet as it moved. Then he saw others.

'Shit...' he breathed in the darkness. 'How many...Twenty? Thirty?'

The creatures were arrayed all along the road as far as he could see. They lurched slowly through people's gardens and yards, around their cars, in and out of open doors. Jets of vapour or fluid sprayed sporadically from their upturned mouths into the air. Their faces were indistinct, melted-looking and amorphous. Some of them moved on four or six legs, some walked upright like humans, others were sagging and lumpy blobs of tissue. It was the GDD. He knew it. All week he had been listening to increasing reports of mutants stalking the city and suggestions that it was somehow due to the GDD infection. Monsters, computer bugs, civil disorder, the city burning: It could not be coincidence that all of these things were happening at once.

As if to confirm this notion he saw a huge, dog-shaped battle familiar prowling and circling around one of the monsters further down the street like a faithful hound. Was the machine *protecting* it? That was how it looked – master and his dog. Surely not. Were the monsters controlling the machines somehow? Was that whole earlier scene of robots failing or attacking people *their* doing? Were those creatures somehow behind the loss of power, net connection, streams? The barge crash? How was any of that possible?

Stevin knew one thing for certain: It wasn't safe here. If, as he suspected, the site of the crash had been some sort of *focus* or epicentre for whatever was happening in the city, then moving away from said epicentre seemed the only plausible option for survival. Those things out there looked like trouble. Stevin was an intelligent man and he could see at once that, whatever those creatures were, they were changing the city, changing the environment, and he didn't want to be around while that happened. As he had slept that area of corruption had crept as close as the properties opposite. And as he watched the green, mouldy, vegetative coating was spreading towards his house, texturing the ground with weird little organic nodes and nodules.

A tugging at the back of his shirt made him yelp with surprise and almost drop the nail gun. He whirled round and it was his daughter. Her eyes were wide and glassy in the shadows. She had the strap of the green bag across one small shoulder, so that its body hung against her hip. She was, as instructed, fully clothed and shod. Her thin chest was hitching as she breathed and he could see that her panic was barely contained. Was he really thinking about taking this fragile, precious creature and going out there? Making some sort of dash for safety? *Where*? Maybe it would be better to barricade themselves inside the house. He could rip up the antique realwood floorboards and nail them

273

across the windows and doors. The monsters would hear him do it, though. They were close-by. Would they attack the house?

'Iaella, honey...' he said, caught in indecision. 'Er...'

'Are they still out there, Daddy?' she asked, so quietly that he barely heard her. Her lower lip was quivering minutely.

'Yeah, Ella. Still there. When did you first see them? They must have come quick, right?'

'I looked one time and they weren't there. I looked again and they were there. That green stuff looks like it's growing, Daddy.'

'I know, honey,' Stevin said. Inside, his mind was whirling – *What do we do? What do we do? Oh no oh no we're going to die! What are those things? What do we do? I've got my daughter here! What do I do with her? What if those things come in here?* – and he had to actually clench his jaw to keep from verbalising his terror. He turned and parted the curtain again. The outside of the window was filmed with green slime. He watched, grimly fascinated, as it seemed to thicken and coagulate before him. The window scrolled, instantly covered over again, scrolled again. Textures slowly manifested in the greenshit, things rising from the surface of the goop like germinating seeds. The slime became thick enough to completely block the view from the window. Stevin reached out one hand to touch the glasspex, feeling dreamy and unreal.

'Daddy! No!' hissed Iaella in what was probably the closest to a shout that she dared under the circumstances.

Stevin stayed his hand and shook his head as if coming to his senses. He realised that somehow, *somehow*, the green goo was on the *inside* of the window. He recoiled in shock and horror. He had almost put his hand in the stuff, would have done if Iaella hadn't stopped him. He shuddered to think of what that weird, mobile slime would feel like on his fingers.

'Thanks, honey,' he said in a weak voice. And then he smelled the stench of the greenshit coming through the breached glasspex. It took the breath out of him, doubling him over – a stench so foul as to be almost a physical force. 'Oh no...' he managed to gag, spluttering.

Iaella was covering her mouth with one hand, her cheeks bulging behind it as she, too, struggled not to actually be sick. 'What's happening, Daddy?' she sobbed.

274

Stevin went to her and wrapped her in his arms, squeezing her small frame briefly. 'I don't know, Ella. Something nobody has seen before.' He spat onto the floor, trying to rid himself of the noxious smell that had become, repulsively, a taste in his mouth. 'Sorry,' he said, absurdly under the circumstances.

'Are we going?' she asked, crying hard now. 'Are we going to go out there, Daddy? That's what the bag's for, isn't it? It's the survival kit.'

'Yes, honey, I think we have to,' Stevin said. The nail gun was cold and reassuring in his hand, talismanic. 'Pass me the bag – it's heavy.'

'I'm scared!' she whimpered, but she handed him the bag.

'Me too, honey, me too.' He glanced towards the front door where the green stain was now spreading down the wall and onto the floor. Something large and slow was moving outside the door, right on the step – something was slowly brushing against the door itself, gently tensing it against its frame and relaxing again. They both stared wide-eyed at it for a terrified moment. 'Right now, okay?' Stevin said, shaking Iaella once, smartly, by the shoulders. She looked into his eyes, frightened but now composed. He admired her immensely in that moment, loved her with a desperate intensity, felt terrifyingly responsible for her life. She nodded once and took his free hand in one of hers.

'Not this way. Out the back.'

'Okay.' Her voice barely a whisper, her racing pulse visible in her neck.

'Go!'

He moved to the back door ahead of her, checking constantly to make sure she was right on his heels – nothing to worry about there, the girl was practically adhered to him. He unlocked the door, one-handed, nail gun in the other, and they slid out into the night. Strange, animal cries were on the air, a crackle of gunfire like distant static. The road to the south looked clear, still normal, and they headed that way, running in the shadows. The vile smell was thick in their throats, cloying, sickening. The green haze hung over the city like smoke, but it was clearly not smoke any more – shapes whirled within it, hypnotic, interplays of light and dark that looked solid at times, as if things were moving in the sky, obscured. The moon scudded along, bright above the clouds like a boat on a diseased sea.

CHAPTER THIRTY-SEVEN

Clustered just inside the garage door in the basement they looked a grim and motley bunch. They were lit only by Ari's headlight – Tec had killed the gennie to conserve fuel while they were away – and in the gloom their forms looked strange and misshapen, distorted by the addition of various pieces of massive hardware. The hangar behind them was conspicuously empty, dark and cavernous.

'Okay, you guys,' said Whistler, gesturing for quiet. 'Simple. We're gonna work on a shoot first, ask questions never basis here. Anyone with an unfamiliar weapon be bloody careful about area-of-effect. That means you, Sofi. Those things are liable to splash a bit, okay?'

'Someone's getting splashed today, that's for fuckin' sure,' answered Sofi, a curious half-smile on her lips. 'But none of you guys.' She inspected her borrowed plasma thrower admiringly. The weapon was as thick as her thigh.

'RPC HQ is in west Med Hab, so it's possible that the authorities are still in control there, especially around Resperi's base. As they're closer to the site of the barge crash, it's also possible that things are a lot worse there than here.'

'Expect the unexpected, in other words,' suggested Tec.

'Be prepared, in other words,' corrected Whistler.

'Yeah, dumb-ass,' said Sofi. 'You can't expect the unexpected. 'S a dichotomy, ennit?'

'No,' replied Tec as if speaking to a particularly irritating child. 'It's a contradiction in terms. A dichotomy is a division into two. Dumb-ass yourself.'

'Careful, Tec,' said Sofi menacingly, hefting the thrower. 'These things can splash a bit.'

'Piss off,' he told her amiably.

'Right, you two,' interjected Whistler, judging that this had gone far enough now. 'You back in the room?' They both nodded. 'Debian, you've been very quiet. Any questions?'

Debian could think of about a million questions but none of them currently seemed suitable. He wanted to get back in the net urgently, and was concerned that he should have accepted Whistler's offer to stay by himself after all. Currently everything else seemed merely a distraction from that goal, and part of him hated himself for feeling like that. But what was he to do? That same part of him genuinely wanted to help these people – Whistler in particular, who had risked the safety of her base to take him in. She had a compelling nature that was hard to define – that same characteristic that made a good leader – and that went far beyond her mere physical attractiveness. And now that their contract had been ended her team were at risk from any police force who felt like chancing their arm. Not to mention any risk from Hex's people – Cyberlife, Alcubierre, or whoever they might really be. The AI knew where Debian was – would it supply his enemies that information? Would it for some reason be obliged to? If so, then why not simply send a robot to kill him? On reflection, he thought he could trust it for now.

Whistler's team had given him a weapon to carry – a simple, non-computerised submachine gun. He had never held a submachine gun before. Apart from the incident with Hex he had never held *any* gun before. It hung under his left arm on a diagonal strap, its weight unfamiliar and its proximity to his body disturbingly sinister in his mind, as if it was tainting his aura somehow. *Two sides*. Was this when he must choose? If Whistler's team was one side, then what was the other? The AI? What did it want from him? He felt like collapsing to the floor, where he would lie with his eyes shut and weep until either sleep or death took him. Instead, he said simply, 'I'm fine.'

Whistler studied him closely for a moment, her eyes like surgically-sharp chips of ice. *She's reading my mind*, Debian thought. 'Okay,' she said at last. 'Stay close to me or Tec. That thing is a simple spray-and-pray affair. Anything over a hundred metres, don't bother, even if other people are firing. Roland, Ari – you sure you still want to join us?'

'Sure, pretty lady,' said Roland. 'Sure I'm sure.' His tone was light but his expression was all business. His face was weathered and hawkish – he looked like the spectre of death made flesh, the ridiculous rocket launcher his scythe.

'And I don't get a choice in the matter,' said Ari, but it didn't sound bitter about this.

'Thanks, guys,' said Whistler quietly to the old man and his machine. 'We would have lost both Spider and the van without your information. Really, you've done more than enough for us already. If you wanted out now I wouldn't blame you.'

'Stop saying that, will you?' asked Roland. 'And let's get going. Ain't getting any better out there, y'know.'

Whistler nodded to Tec, who stepped forward with a large cross-shaped spanner which he inserted into an exposed panel beside the huge outer door, fumbling briefly in the dark to slot it home. He turned it, using both hands, gradually cranking the door open. The brooding blackness of the car park inched into view.

'These are on a mechanical delay,' he said. 'When I take the spanner out we all need to hoof it.' He looked around to make sure everybody was with him and then took the key out. Debian wondered briefly how they would get back in with Mother off-line, the power out and nobody home. Presumably they had some plan for this. They slunk outside, Ari's headlight lancing across the crumbling grey architecture, making shadows stagger across every surface.

They moved cautiously, Whistler with her smartgun held in front of her, sniffing the darkness for targets. The others kept pace behind her, Tec and Sofi moving to flank her, providing as wide an angle of cover as possible while maintaining visual contact. Debian, feeling foolish and out of place, trailed along behind Whistler, heeding her instruction to stay close. He resisted the urge to raise the submachine gun, whatever his nerves were telling him. He was achingly aware that if he did have to fire the damn thing he would need a lot more space and a lot less opportunity for friendly fire than he had in the confined car park, where the configuration of the pillars sometimes funnelled the team into fairly close proximity despite the huge area of the space.

Ari stayed back, roving from left to right, trying to cover all angles with its light, moving with a birdlike, skittish speed. Whistler had to silence a little voice at the back of her mind that kept asking what they would do if Ari were to fall victim to the AI virus suddenly and attack them or otherwise betray them. She wondered how dangerous the thing could be if it wanted to. Roland stalked along in the middle of the pack, looking for all the world like a man out for a bracing recreational walk. The massive rocket launcher seemed to float along almost as if carrying him, barrel cocked to the ceiling.

They moved towards the exit onto street level in this cautious, nervous manner. Something howled loudly from nearby – a long and

278

mindless note – and the noise echoed round the car park such that they couldn't tell where it had originated from. They glanced around fearfully and continued.

Tec and Sofi flattened themselves against the edges of the wide doorway, peering round into the street. They nodded and Whistler slowly led the party outside. The night air smelled repulsive, a thick organic smell that Whistler knew by now to be the stink of the greenshit. She had smelled it first in Vivao's flat. Green flakes were falling, settling on all surfaces. The substance seemed to be thickening into shapes here and there, as if things were rising from it. In some places, thick pools or patches of jungly green sprouted from the road, glistening wetly in the low light. The party surveyed the scene with trepidation.

'What is that stuff in the air?' asked Debian. 'Is it safe to touch it, do you think?'

Whistler shook her head but Roland said, 'Sure, I come here all the way on foot. Damn shit stings a little but it brushes right off. Don't seem to have done us any harm, least not short-term. Remember those hats and filters? Everyone got them?' Nods all round. 'Time to use them, I think.' Everyone did as he said. It was clear that the hats would shield most of their heads and faces although they were hardly a completely hermetic protective solution. Debian pulled his collar up high to shield his neck, too. With his chin tucked into his jacket he was pretty well covered.

The lights were off as far as they could see in all directions, except for the occasional punctuating spot of brightness where some enterprising soul like Tec had presumably employed a backup power supply. To the north-east, where the barge had hit, the skyline was still glowing faintly, but very faintly now. The screeching sound of a ground vehicle's tyres came from somewhere in that direction, drifting on the wind like a scream. A petrol pony galloped, riderless, across the far end of the road, blue exhaust pluming from its nostrils, hoofs clattering loudly.

'Right, Ari – can you lead us to our van?' said Whistler.

'Certainly – follow me,' said the robot. It pushed through the group and headed off down the street, sensibly killing its headlight and sticking to the deeper shadows of the overhanging buildings. They were about halfway down the street when Whistler hissed at them to stop.

Debian's heart began to hammer so loudly that he feared the others would hear it.

'Look!' Whistler said, pointing with her smartgun.

Beneath the overhanging porch of what had once been a nightclub one of the changed was standing, swaying gently, blocking their path. Everybody froze, staring at it in horror and awe. The creature looked up at them, its face a half-seen mindless blank of green sludge. Long tendrils of greenshit joined it to the face of the building, which seemed to be melting, the substance eating into the brickwork, green, foamy slime running from the holes like pus from infected wounds. The creature extended an appendage that looked like it had once been a human hand towards them and began, shakily, to stagger in their direction.

'No!' Debian yelled, fumbling uselessly with the gun.

The monster was about twenty metres away but moving with a slow determination. Whistler barked something that sounded like a wordless expression of rage and her smartgun opened up: *hak!hak!hak!* The creature spun, tangling in the cords of greenshit, fluid haemorrhaging from its body in gushes, spraying the walls and floor around it. It recovered and came on, the cords of greenshit rearranging themselves around it, knotting and unknotting. Blank green eyes stared stupidly at its enemies. Some sort of tongue – a thing like a dripping tapeworm unravelled form its mouth and began to probe around, as if it was tasting the air.

Sofi stepped forwards, slinging the plasma weapon over her back on its strap. Her slender hands dipped into her combat jacket and reappeared with a long knife glinting in each. The creature turned towards her, reaching out. Roland had suggested that the particles in the air were not harmful, but Debian thought that maybe if that creature were to actually *touch* you then that might very well be harmful. He thought that might be very bad indeed.

'Sofi, no!' yelled Whistler, stepping back and circling around to regain her line of fire.

But Sofi was on it in one fearless bound, knives flashing. The creature made to grab her, but it was too slow, too clumsy, and she passed right between its slimy claws, rolling away and regaining her feet in one smooth motion, plasma thrower appearing in her hands. Debian saw the plastic handles of the two knives jutting from the thing's chest, slime pumping from around the wounds, and then he was blinded by two bright muzzle flashes as Whistler's smartgun put two more rounds into the thing's misshapen head.

Tec and Roland also had weapons trained on it, but it was not necessary. Debian hadn't even got the submachine gun into his hands. The creature fell, and they heard the heavy thud of its skull hitting the pavement. It made a sighing noise that sounded unbearably weary and sad and then it simply melted away in front of them. They watched in amazement as the putrid green flesh peeled away, exposing what looked like a mutated human skeleton, albeit an incomplete one. And then that, too, withered and shrivelled, dissolving into sludge. The greenshit tendrils on the surrounding brickwork slowly crept towards this puddle like blind, questing worms. Their ends dipped into it and everybody heard what was clearly a slurping, sucking noise. The smell was incredible. The group exchanged sickened looks.

'It's being recycled,' said Tec in a nauseous little voice.

Roland shrugged. 'Waste not, want not,' he said.

Sofi just looked angry. 'What the fuck was all that about?' she asked, as if demanding an answer from the disappearing pool of goo. She looked around at the corrupted fascia of the nightclub, her face a picture of disgust. There were small, mushroom-like growths amongst the mass of oozing green matter there. They seemed to be pulsing very gently, as if breathing. Sofi leaned in close, to examine one, her plasma weapon pointing at the ground. 'What is that...' she mused.

Whistler shouted and made to grab her. The ready-status of her smartgun, as indicated by a line of LEDs along its side, went back up a notch at the signs of stress in her voice-pattern.

'It's–' said Sofi, and then the mushroom-thing exploded in her face: *Pop!* She staggered backwards, her head wreathed in a cloud of green dust like a halo, dropping her gun and flapping at the air as if trying to shoo a bad smell away. She coughed and gagged, doubling over.

'NO!' yelled Tec, running to her. He caught her jerking body as it fell, lowering her gently to the floor. 'Oh man!' cried Tec. 'Oh no, oh fuck! What was that thing?'

'Sofi!' shouted Whistler, dropping beside her, looking into the other woman's face.

'Damn it!' snarled Roland. 'Is she okay?'

Whistler was bent over Sofi, shaking her, and Debian couldn't see if she was okay or not. But then she spoke, coughing and spluttering around her words. 'Man! That was fucking *disgusting*! Ohhhh...Why me?'

Whistler and Tec visibly relaxed, releasing her. 'Because you're you, idiot. That was stupid,' admonished Whistler. 'What the hell were you thinking?'

'Bloody woman,' muttered Tec, standing back. He looked pale and shocked, pretty much how Debian imagined he looked himself.

'Are you okay?' demanded Whistler, shaking her by the shoulder.

'Yeah, I think so. Just an unbelievable smell and taste combination.' She retched again, spitting onto the pavement and pushed herself into a sitting position. Whistler helped her to stand and Tec gave her back her gun. Roland just watched, clearly unimpressed, his thin arms folded, while Ari scanned the street around them.

'I want you to think about what you're doing, Sofi! You hear me?' scolded Whistler.

'Okay, okay, enough already. You didn't just have an alien toadstool blow up in your face, give me a break.' She wiped at her face with one sleeve, re-seating the hat Roland had given her. 'Let's go on, I'm all right.'

Whistler stared at her for several long seconds, her face thunderous. 'Yeah,' she said.

They followed Ari down the road to the junction. Smashed pods were jammed together into a single mass that blocked the way completely and they had to climb over one to continue. As he clambered across the bonnet of the crushed vehicle Debian glanced down into its interior. The driver was still in there, impaled on a control stick, a crust of dark, dried blood across her chest like a bib. Her face was a muted mask of agony. A single red light winked evilly on the dash of the pod like an eye. Debian shivered and his hand crept unconsciously to the submachine gun. 'Keep moving!' hissed Roland behind him. He jumped down off the pod and followed Whistler.

'Towards the canal,' said Ari from up front. 'Your van's on Duplex Street. Come on.'

'Wow,' said Tec. 'They were almost home, then, when RPC got involved.'

'Yeah, that's tough luck,' agreed Roland. 'But we gonna get your friend back.'

'Nine o'clock!' yelled Whistler suddenly, whirling to her left with the smartgun outstretched like a pointing finger, the line of LEDs on it lighting up all the way to the end. The whole group turned as one.

A gang of ragged human figures was pelting towards them from the shadows of a vacant lot. There were six or seven of them, coming at Whistler's group on the run. None of them shouted or called out – they clearly wanted to cover the distance as quickly and quietly as possible. Whistler could see long knives and crude clubs in several of their hands. She held fire, caught in momentary indecision. She could gun them all down in a split-second at this range, but it would be a one-sided massacre. She could feel the weapon itching to do it.

'Back, fuckers!' bellowed Sofi, seizing the initiative and sending a burst of plasma fire licking into the air above the oncoming group. This had a truly electric effect on the other party. They scattered, leaping out of the way, shouting curses, scrabbling to get past each other and flee. One of them fell and the others left him to his fate. He hastily got back to his feet and charged off after his companions.

Sofi was laughing, slapping her thigh, the huge plasma thrower pointing towards where their would-be attackers had retreated back into the night. 'Ha ha ha! Losers!' she cackled.

'Were they trying to rush us?' asked Debian. It had all happened so fast he had barely had time to register what was going on.

'I guess,' answered Tec. 'Nice one, Sofe.'

Sofi shook her head, suppressing giggles, and engaged the safety on the plasma thrower. They followed after Ari again, Roland keeping a careful watch behind them lest their company return. They passed a shabby single-storey house with a window open onto the street. From inside came the heartbroken cry of a man who sounded on the edge of madness, his voice high and wobbling: '*My sissy! My sissy!*' Debian had no idea if sissy was a person, a pet, or what, and he didn't want to know. He thought that anybody who would have their front window open that night was probably beyond all help.

Near to the canal the street was flooded with a lake of greenshit. Several of the creatures stood in the pool, heads back and faces to the sky. Their hair was long and tangled and their semi-naked bodies were twisted and lumpy beyond any real semblance of humanity. These individuals, thankfully, took no notice of the group. They watched the creatures from a block away in silence for a moment.

'Shall I fry 'em?' asked Sofi keenly.

'No,' said Whistler. 'Let's find a way around.'

'Look at that pod,' said Tec, pointing. A dun-coloured gravpod was apparently dissolving into the slime. Its shell looked as if it was becoming plastic, melting and changing. They could just make out in the moonlight how tendrils of its body were mixing and stretching into the greenshit, marbling the slime with traces of brown that faded into the lake, merging with it. The pod was actually sinking slowly as they watched.

'Processing, you said, Roland,' mused Whistler. 'I think that's about right.' As she said this one of the monsters leaned over and vomited a huge quantity of liquid into the pool, gurgling and choking as it did so. For a second, it looked their way, its chin dripping. There was no recognition or concern on its drooping face. The group stared back, disgusted.

'This way,' said Ari, pointing into a narrow street to their right with one limb. Its eyes flashed eagerly. 'Come on.'

They detoured to the right, trying to angle back onto Duplex a block further down. They found that the lake still blocked their path. 'Check out the canal,' said Sofi, indicating where it threaded through the streets ahead of them. They looked and the canal was entirely green, flowing turgidly. They could hear those corrupted waters oozing and glooping along, a sound like someone smacking their lips wetly. Debian swallowed, nauseated, wiping the green dust from his face and neck. Was it really safe to be out in this weird snow? Would it not corrupt and change *him*, too? All of them? He was suddenly keener than ever to get to the van.

Ari led them back out onto Duplex another few blocks further down. Whistler scanned the street with her smartgun, her tiny fangs bared. 'I see it,' she said. 'Back down that way.' She nodded in the direction they had come from along the other street. They all looked and yes, there was the van, slewed across the road, looking solid, architectural, reassuring. It was just beyond the edge of the slime pool. 'Let's go.'

They stood around the van, breathing a collective sigh of relief. Debian studied its sinister curves admiringly. 'Where the hell did you get a thing like that?' he asked.

'I built it, mostly,' said Tec proudly. 'Mixture of off-the-shelf and military bits we got through HGR. And some pieces I made from scratch. She's a proper one-off. Can't say how relieved I am to see her again.' He put his hand on the skin of the van gently, as if petting the machine. 'I don't get why RPC didn't take it if the main computer was off at the time. Maybe they didn't have the manpower. It's still off – I thought you said you turned it on, Ari?'

'I turned it off again after my chat with it,' said Ari tonelessly. 'That seemed the prudent thing to do.'

'Perhaps he's helping us,' thought Debian, not realising he had spoken aloud until Whistler responded.

'Who's helping us?' she asked sharply.

'Er...the internet,' said Debian, flustered. He realised that everyone was looking at him. 'The AI, I mean. It.'

'It's a fucking *he* now, is it?' asked Whistler. Her face was incredulous, suspicious.

Debian couldn't find an answer for this, couldn't hold that icy stare. Instead, he said, 'Can we get in, with no computer and no wireless? Maybe Ari could–'

'I've got it,' said Tec. He fished an old-fashioned key-fob out of a pocket and pointed it at the van. A circular doorway irised smoothly open without a sound. Lights came on inside the vehicle, inviting the party inside. 'After you.'

They crammed into the van, Whistler up front, Debian beside her, Tec at the console in the back (although it was only partially functional with no main computer), Sofi, Roland and Ari on the back seats. The door silently closed behind them and the van lifted onto its cushion. Tec began to run diags on the peripheral system modules, checking that there was nothing there that could jump-start the main computer and cause the vehicle to do something rash like crashing itself.

Whistler felt the energy thrumming through the chassis, enthusing and invigorating her. 'Let's go get Spidey,' she said grimly and slowly moved the controls, bringing them about.

They travelled north up Duplex and skirted the main road, running parallel through smaller streets. In some places the route was blocked by crashed pods or piles of rubble that had spilled from smashed buildings. The evidence of the greenshit corruption was all around them, blotching the city with leprous patches of infection. The changed roamed the streets unmolested for the most part, although they did see a group of young street fighters on ground trikes circling one of them like sharks, pincushioning its body with crossbow bolts. They were shouting partially-heard gang slogans as they did so.

As they passed through the Lanes and neared High Hab the marks of the greenshit became more pronounced. They stared through the translucent skin of the van, wondering how this could have happened so quickly. Cable car cables were draped with thick, vine-like fronds that hung down into the street, their gently twitching ends dangling into pools of slime. Thick drifts of greenshit were piled against walls, on roofs, on windowsills. In one large square, creepers had grown across the entire width of the space, stretching between opposing buildings, twining around ancient phone wires and utility conduits, hanging down to street level, dripping with the now ubiquitous slime.

'Processing...' muttered Debian. He had the gun cradled in his arms very tightly.

'That word again,' agreed Whistler, glancing over from the driver's seat. 'Processing the whole damn city.'

'Maybe the whole planet,' said Debian darkly. 'For all we know.'

'So you went into the net again,' said Whistler. She had hardly spoken to him so far, seemingly locked in a black and contemplative frame of mind.

'Yeah,' said Debian slowly. He was inexplicably unsure of how much to say. 'I spoke to the AI,' he offered eventually.

'Well I know that, yeah.'

'Yeah,' he said. Then, when more seemed to be required, he added, 'It does seem to be behind the GDD, as suspected. Hacked the vats.'

'Where did it come from? Is it alien?' she asked, staring out at the twisted city, steering carefully around debris in the road. 'Cos you know what this looks like, to me? Looks like we're being fucking terraformed. Or *xenoformed*, more like.'

'I don't know.' But he thought he did know. Why did it not seem right to tell her?

'And why? Was the AI designed to do this? Why now? Why here?'

Two sides. On one, the suggestion of unlimited ability, even power. But power over what? An entirely new world? What remained of the old one? Power for power's own sake did have its own attraction. Had the beast done something to him, something that hadn't shown up on any of the diags he and Tec had run, something that had made him stronger? Wasn't that what he had ultimately been seeking all these years – power, ability? The money had just been a by-product really. But what, specifically, would be involved if he went with the AI? He was a long way from really trusting it yet – after all, it was the enemy, was it not? It certainly seemed to be killing people out on the streets. And it had essentially confessed to being behind the GDD infection, even if it had just been used as a tool by somebody else. Perhaps it was making promises that it had no intention of actually making good on – perhaps it *couldn't* make good on them. It feared its own destruction in the coming days. Would it sacrifice Debian himself, despite its coded offers of alliance, to ensure its own existence? Had whoever created the AI been alarmed to discover that it was expanding beyond their control, hence its belief that they would betray it? Had it, in turn, been alarmed to discover that the situation it had created was expanding beyond its *own* control? Surely that was why it feared for its life, if life it was. If it wanted his help, how exactly must that help be rendered?

And on the other side – what, exactly? Choose humanity, side against the AI and somehow resist the attack that had begun – refuse, more importantly, to actively help the data monster. Could he hurt it, except by his refusal to aid it? It had effortlessly implanted the small data scrap containing the net address into his DNI memory. Surely he would be powerless to actually damage a thing like that. He felt torn, disorientated – half man and half computer already, caught on the cusp of evolution.

'I don't know where it came from, but it seems clear that it was made to attack us. The GDD organs affect the city while the computer problems prevent us from reacting. As for why, I don't know that either, I'm afraid. But it fears for its own safety now, fears betrayal by its makers. Whoever they are.'

287

'Hmm,' said Whistler, guiding the van carefully up onto the pavement to avoid a patch of tree-like structures that had apparently grown straight out of the concrete. 'You make it sound almost human.'

'In some ways,' he admitted, 'it is almost human. It's certainly sentient and intelligent in the classical sense. I never thought I would meet such an entity. Simulated intelligences, virtual beings, avatars...this thing is on another plane altogether.'

Whistler thought he sounded slightly awed. She glanced across and his eyes were distant, dreamy. He looked beautifully fragile, his slight features pale and ethereal, his unlit DNI sockets glinting in his blond hair. He could have been a delicate piece of electronic equipment himself. 'I don't know what's gonna happen, Debian. But if we get Spider out and make it back to base it sounds as if you and I need to have further discussion about this.'

Her tone was odd and he wasn't sure exactly what to read into it. Was he just being paranoid? 'Sure,' he said and then turned to look out of the side, hoping she would get the message and leave him alone. He really didn't feel like talking to anybody right now.

'I appreciate you coming with us,' she said quietly. Debian looked back at her to see her smiling at him, but her eyes were sad in her grey face. 'You're a strange guy, and I still don't really understand how you're involved in all this. But thanks.'

'It just seemed right,' he found himself saying. 'My life has suddenly become very odd after years of remaining essentially the same. I'm just trying to do what seems best, one thing at a time.'

'Me too,' she agreed and then she drove in silence for a while.

As they cautiously entered High Hab, passing beneath a huge, buttressed arch of ceramicarbide that served to delineate it from the Lanes, it was clear that the infection was indeed worse here, as if the warping of the city had happened around the epicentre of the barge crash, which they passed to the west of. Looking towards that demolished stretch of skyline they could see the buzzing hulks of confused gyrocopters, flying either without pilots or without their consent, launching rockets randomly into the haze that shrouded the battered streets at ground level, one of them plummeting inexplicably from the sky as they watched, to flower into a burst of flame as it hit the ground. Whistler expressed her gratitude that their course towards RPC would now begin to take them away from that terrifying focus of devastation. They headed further west into Med Hab, towards the sea and the jagged outline of the RPC headquarters itself, which jutted from the earth like a broken tooth, towering above the general hubbub of sleek, exclusive buildings, rubbing shoulders with only a few giants of equivalent size. Its shiny facade looked dull and dirty now, unlit, slab-like. It looked, reflected Debian, like a massive gravestone. He wondered how they could hope to extract Spider from there and not die trying.

The van drove unmolested through checkpoints that usually would have been well-fortified against the envious denizens of the nearby Lanes. The pillboxes were now unmanned, festooned with loops of greenshit vine, the robot sentry guns lolling lifeless on their swivel-mounts. Whistler forced aside a barrier with the armoured nose of the van and continued without speaking. Roland was carrying out last minute hardware checks on the weapons he had lent to the group, Ari occasionally offering its professional opinion, mostly ignored. Tec was running a series of basic diagnostics on the van's weaponry, hindered by the lack of the computer. Nobody had suggested turning the automatic systems on again. Sofi was fidgeting, champing at the bit, fingers drumming on the stock of the plasma thrower.

'Do we just roll up to the front door, then, or what?' asked Sofi, leaning into the front of the van.

'We'll see,' said Whistler. 'I guess we keep our distance, skirt around, try to see if there's anybody home. It all seems suspiciously quiet at the moment.'

As she said this a series of Resperi pods, travelling in a blaze of emergency lights, tore out of the building, turning onto a flyover that swooped away to the west, heading out of the city along the coast. Whistler killed the lights, nestling into the shadows at the side of the road and waited until they were out of sight.

'They're heading out of town,' mused Tec. 'I guess it's kicking off elsewhere, too. Hopefully, we won't find it too well-defended.'

'Maybe they're just running away,' suggested Sofi.

'Fine,' said Roland with a grim chuckle. 'Works for us, right?'

'Hey, don't they have a tunnel to the court?' asked Tec suddenly, his face lighting up.

'Yeah, so convicts don't have to be moved above ground, right?' confirmed Sofi. 'Less chance of them making a run for it.' She wiped her eyes with the back of one hand – they were watering profusely. She sniffed, then saw that Tec was watching her. 'What?' she demanded. Tec said nothing.

'The tunnel does exist,' confirmed Ari, sitting up. Its eyes flickered as it scanned internal memory banks. 'Straight from the cell level in the basement to the High Court. It might be easier to breach the court building and then enter RPC through the tunnel.'

'I still want to look at the front door,' insisted Whistler.

'Is there some other way into the tunnel, besides at either end?' asked Tec, directing the question at Ari.

'I do have some restricted maps on file,' admitted Ari with a touch of pride, 'and I can demonstrate the course that the tunnel takes. Perhaps we could blast through from a sewer tunnel – there are several places where they come very close. Bit of an oversight on the part of the designers, really. Although, to be fair, there is less space available underground these days than you might imagine – the tunnel's course seems to have been dictated by necessity. Did you know there's actually a disused government emergency shelter nearby, under the streets?'

'Hmm,' grunted Sofi. 'Fascinating, thanks. Bit of a blast from the past for you, eh, Deb – back into the sewers?' Debian wasn't sure whether this was an insult or not and decided not to answer. 'Front door is sounding better all the time.'

'We'll take a look at the front,' said Whistler. 'On foot. We'll leave the van somewhere along the most direct route home. Assuming that we're heading home after?' She glanced around. Nobody had a better idea. 'Good. Let's ditch it on the main road – run it up on the pavement, maybe throw some rubbish over it or something. Hope the greenshit doesn't eat it up before we get back.'

'Bet you wish you'd let me fix the camo-projector now,' said Tec pointedly.

'I have a projector,' offered Ari. 'It can be detached and just plugged into your vehicle. Uses a bit of juice, though – it's a military model.'

'Yeah, do it, Ari,' ordered Roland.

'Okay,' said Whistler. 'Let's do that. We've plenty of power.' She coasted the van round onto the main road, wedging it as far into the shadows of a corner between two buildings as possible while Ari performed surgery on itself, extracting the small sphere of the projector from its body and plugging it into one of the van's power outlets.

They disembarked in an atmosphere heavy with foreboding, pulling their hats down tight onto their heads. The stink of the greenshit was almost unreal, although the nasal plugs filtered most of it out – one just didn't seem to get used to it with exposure – and the dust was thick in the air. Sticky puddles of slime marred the roadway like sores. The shambling silhouettes of GDD victims could be seen lurching slowly along the streets, thankfully ignoring the group for now. Nobody else was around.

Debian emerged from the circular hatch and stared at the spot where he knew the van to be. It was virtually invisible except for the slightest peripheral shimmering if you tried to catch it out of the corner of your eye. He extended a hand slowly and felt its smooth, cool skin where there looked to be only empty air. Who the hell was this guy Roland, to have the equipment he had exhibited? How well did Whistler actually know him?

'For fuck's sake everyone remember where it is,' said Whistler.

'Yeah,' said Sofi. 'Remember last time we had a C-projector on it.'

'That was your own fault, Sofe,' said Tec. 'You were on that trippex, remember?'

'All the same,' said Whistler. 'Everyone take a good look at the spot.' They did as she commanded, trying to burn the location into their minds. 'Let's go.'

They reached the end of the road, moving low and slow behind whatever cover they could find. RPC loomed massively above them, seeming to fill the sky. A wide flight of steps ascended from street level to a gigantic set of doors which looked firmly closed. Somebody had run a ten-metre-long personnel carrier up the steps and parked it across the doors just to really drive the point home. A rubbish bin to one side of the doors was burning steadily, glowing embers rising from it like spirits.

At the foot of the steps was a huge battle-bot in the bright colours of RPC.

'They have a guard dog,' said Sofi, peeping over a low concrete wall.

'I don't think so, Sofe,' answered Whistler.

The robot was vaguely centaur-oid and stood probably four metres high at the shoulder, quite unsuitably large and over-powered for any sort of urban civil-defence force. It was stomping up and down the flat square at the foot of the steps, jumping and twisting at the waist, spinning round like a dog trying to catch its own tail. They watched as it stormed up to a deserted gravpod and began to kick and smash it psychotically to pieces. There was a noise, low and feral, coming from its speakers, carried faintly on the wind, a sort of enraged growling.

'Oh yeah,' said Sofi. 'I think that thing's on its own side now. Looks like it's gone utterly batshit.'

'We can't fight that thing,' said Roland. 'No point. Fucker'd eat these rockets like popcorn.'

Debian considered offering to initiate wireless and hack the thing – he was sure he could do it and that he would be safe attempting it – but he decided not to voice this idea. Had he considered this decision in more depth he might have deduced that he was suffering from an inexplicable desire to keep his cards close to his chest.

Whistler ran a hand through her hair. 'Okay, the tunnel, then,' she said. 'Let's go with Ari's idea of trying to get in from the sewers. Maybe blast through with weaponry.'

'Melt a hole with that plasma thrower,' suggested Tec. 'Depending what the tunnel's made from.'

'Sure,' said Ari, who didn't sound alarmed at witnessing the degenerative condition of its fellow robot, who was still stomping and fuming up and down the square.

They followed Ari back out of the square cautiously, so as not to alert the insane battle-bot, and into a small side-street squeezed between the windowless walls of two tower blocks. Ari scuttled brightly off, slim legs all a-blur.

'Here!' it called in a stage whisper. 'Manhole. I know where to go – there's a place where the court tunnel comes within two metres of the sewer.'

'All right, then,' said Tec, wasting no time in heaving the metal cover out of the way, using the stock of his gun as a lever. He rolled it carefully – quietly – to the side of the road and leaned it against the wall. Ari shone its torch into the depths, although all this did was make the darkness retreat a little – it still looked like a gateway into the abyss. 'Hmm...Fun,' said Tec, suddenly not so keen.

'Just get on down there,' said Whistler.

Ari climbed down into the hole with efficient agility, not bothering to use the ladder, its sharp feet finding purchase on the bricks. Tec followed, clearly gritting his teeth, then the others descended one by one. Debian felt a smothering sense of claustrophobia almost at once and it was all he could do to keep moving downwards. What had gone wrong in his life so badly that he now found himself entering the sewers for the second time not only in his life, but in the same week? Whatever it was, he didn't feel that he deserved this.

They moved in a cursing, near-blind procession down the slippery ladder and onto the flat. There was no actual sewage here, and for that at least they were all glad. They seemed to be in a narrow access tunnel of some sort, which stretched ahead, featureless, as far as Ari's torch beam would show them. Even by infrared Debian couldn't discern the end of it.

'Hope you know what you doin', you fuckin' biscuit tin,' muttered Roland.

Ari did a good impersonation of a human sigh. 'Of course I do – we all know who the real brain of our partnership is.'

They hadn't gone much further when the robot piped up again: 'Here it is.' It was indicating an undistinguished area of tunnel wall, opposite which another tunnel branched off into utter darkness. 'You can stand back from the target wall in that other tunnel – you don't want to get too close to that plasma. Get blasting.'

'You think we'll set off any alarms in there?' asked Tec.

'I think we have to assume so until we know better,' admitted Whistler. 'Everybody ready for the shit to hit the fan. Worst case scenario is a running gunfight all the way to the cells, where Spider is presumably being held. Sofi, get up here with that plasma thrower. What's the melting point of brick, anyone?'

'Varies between about one- to two-thousand centigrade, usually,' said Ari. 'I realise that's a wide margin of inaccuracy but I couldn't tell you the exact composition of these bricks without proper chemical analysis. We should be fine – that plasma burns at about the same temperature as the sun's photosphere – that's something in the order of six-thousand centigrade, so plenty of headroom.'

Sofi keenly shouldered her way to the front of the group and waved everyone else away brusquely. She readied the massive weapon, planting her feet firmly on the slippery tunnel floor.

'Watch the burst cohesion on that thing,' warned Roland as Sofi checked the settings. 'It splashes you, you lose an arm, and that's if you lucky.'

'Sure,' answered Sofi. 'I've got it set as tight as it'll go. Stand back.'

'*Well* back,' added Roland, ushering the group back up the main tunnel as Sofi readied herself.

The plasma thrower made barely a whisper of noise as it gouted brilliant flame, too bright to look at, but the heat generated as the tiny jet of dazzling fire sliced into the wall was almost overwhelming, even from the group's vantage point back in the main tunnel. Humid, steamy waves rolled over them as the damp brick melted and vaporised. They turned their faces away, cowering against the slimy wall. The stink of burning minerals mingled with the underlying reek of the greenshit to stomach-churning effect. Debian felt suddenly, terrifyingly claustrophobic. He fought the urge to just turn and run, flee from this awful subterranean other-world. He pressed the filter plugs more firmly into his nostrils and sank to the floor.

'How's it going?' yelled Tec.

'Give me a minute!' Sofi shouted back. They waited for what seemed more like five minutes than one and then she called out again: 'Okay, I'm done. Come back!'

They returned to Sofi, who was holding the plasma thrower at arm's length as its cooling system kicked in. She looked a little singed around the edges and her eyes were streaming again. They surveyed the patch of wall, impressed. The burst cohesion had indeed been tightly-focused – so much so that Sofi had been able to cut a precise, door-shaped oblong into the brickwork. She had cross-hatched the oblong with a lattice of cuts that glowed fiercely in the dark.

'Nice,' said Tec. 'D'you think it burned all the way through?'

'Let's find out,' said Sofi.

'If I may,' said Ari. It scuttled five or six metres up the side tunnel, bracing its sharp feet on the floor. Its headlight played across the section of wall as it charged. Ari ducked its head down, running like a charging bull, hitting the weakened wall like a battering ram. There was a terrific, shattering noise that had probably alerted half the city and Ari disappeared in a cloud of debris. Its light-beam waved randomly about, illuminating roiling clouds of dust.

'Hey, tinpot!' yelled Roland.

'I'm through,' Ari replied, reappearing into sight. 'All the way into the other tunnel. Thrower cut through brick and earth alike. Come through, but don't touch the edges or you'll burn your fingers off.'

The humans gingerly stepped through the opening, passing through brick, scorched, chalky earth and then foot-thick concrete to stand amazed in a wider, clearly much newer tunnel piled with rubble. The tunnel was dimly lit by red emergency lights. It stretched, arrow-straight, into the distance. They could just make out the outline of a doorway at one end, in the direction of RPC headquarters. There was nobody else in the tunnel. They relaxed slightly, though Whistler still held her smartgun at shoulder height.

'Stronger than you look, eh?' Tec remarked to Ari. He was staring coldly at the machine – it looked back at him calmly.

There was a pregnant pause before Ari said, 'You don't have to worry about me. Now, do you want to go and get your friend?'

'So we just walk in?' asked Debian, his stomach full of butterflies.

'Sure,' said Sofi. 'Who's gonna stop us?' And she set off determinedly up the passage towards the door.

'Come on,' said Whistler and followed her. The others trailed after.

The door at the tunnel's end was of solid-looking ceramicarbide, but it was no match for Ari who braced against the door-frame and slowly forced it open. The ceramicarbide itself didn't so much as bend but eventually the metal bolts simply tore away and the door banged open with a boom that echoed off down the tunnel, rolling heavily from wall to wall like a vast bowling ball of sound.

They went through in cautious single-file, weapons readied. Debian wondered how Roland hoped to use the immense rocket launcher indoors and actually survive. They slunk up a flight of steps and emerged into the basement level of the Resperi building. The interior of the headquarters was also awash in the dim red light. Ari had killed its headlight in the court tunnel, and it took a moment for them to discern that they were actually standing in the cell-block itself, presumably very close to where they wanted to be. Nobody came to intercept them.

Somewhere in the labyrinth somebody was screaming in a pitch so high and desperate that it was impossible to tell their gender. The group headed down the corridor to a sort of nexus from which it was clear that the level was in fact a dense honeycomb of cells and interrogation rooms. Sofi moved under Whistler's cover into the centre of the space where a reception desk stood in solitude. She checked the computer terminal, found it to be dead, ransacked the drawers, hoping for some sort of list of cell occupants. She shook her head in frustration but then she noticed a whiteboard on the far wall. 'Ha!' she cried, approaching it. 'Cell fifteen.'

'Good, then let's find it,' said Whistler, moving off.

'Where is everybody?' asked Debian, following her. Against his better judgement he unlimbered the submachine gun Roland had lent him. Tec and Ari fanned out to the sides, checking every shadow.

'Dead? On strike?' suggested Whistler.

Just then there was the now-unmistakable howl of a GDD victim, close-by. They all spun as one to face the sound. Whistler cursed, the smartgun alight in her hands. That howl again, utterly monstrous yet also strangely lonely and mournful. And this time, the answering shout of a desperate human voice: 'No fucking way! Get away from me!'

Whistler, Sofi and Tec exchanged startled looks. 'Spider!' they all said as one. They were off down the corridor before the others even understood what was going on.

'Weapons ready – let's go!' urged Roland, darting off after them with surprising speed. Debian followed, fumbling with the safety catch of his weapon as he ran. Ari bolted past him in a glittering, metallic blur, small gun barrels suddenly bristling on its carapace. Debian almost ran into Roland's back as he dashed round a corner.

Whistler, outlined in a doorway, crowded by the other members of the group, was firing into a small room. There was some vast mass of twisted machinery mostly blocking the door and Debian shuddered as he recognised the dead hulk of the brain-diver from his recent delve into the net. Whistler let off three rounds in close succession, turning slightly as she presumably tracked some out-of-sight target, moving into the room as she did so, flanked by her team-mates. And then there was the roar and rush of heat from Sofi's plasma thrower, punctuated by the hammer-blows of Tec's light machine gun. Silhouetted against the flashes Debian could see Sofi and Whistler moving rapidly, in fluid concert – lithe, darting forms that looked no more solid than shadows. The shooting ceased abruptly, leaving an ear-ringing sound vacuum, and Debian, Roland and Ari squeezed past the dead brain diver into the cell.

Spider looked in bad shape, strapped to some enormous wheel. Clearly he had been beaten quite severely, but his blood-encrusted, gap-toothed mouth cracked in a huge smile as he surveyed his rescuers. In front of him was a bubbling puddle of slime. Vapour hissed from a hole in the wall where one of Whistler's shots had buried itself.

'And the cavalry came over the hill!' cried Spider in a cracked but booming voice. Sofi rushed forwards, dropping her plasma thrower, and flung her arms around him.

'You big stupid bastard!' she admonished him, kissing him roughly on one cheek and then, contradictorily, punching him square in his massive chest.

'Get me off this fucking wheel!' demanded Spider.

Ari scuttled forwards and deftly undid Spider's bonds. The huge man, clearly weakened, virtually fell forwards out of his restraints, into the arms of Whistler and Tec who struggled to set his heavy body down gently. The group gathered round him, slapping him on the back and expressing their relief to find him alive.

'Nice of you to join us, Debian,' Spider said, accepting a drink of water from Tec. 'You, too, Roland. You brought that robot, then,' he added, eyeing Ari suspiciously.

'Yeah, it ain't gone crazy yet,' said Roland. 'Sorry about your friend, man.'

'Yeah,' said Spider with a heavy sigh. 'We crashed into an RPC pod, that's why this whole thing happened. Fuckers jumped out, woman pointed a gun at us. Roberts had to get out to tackle her – they had us blocked in. She killed him, I killed her. Her friend, too. Guess I kind of lost it, cos next thing I remember I was here.' He shrugged. 'Warrior's death – that was what he would've wanted.'

'I guess,' said Whistler sadly. 'Certainly there are people dying worse ways out there. Are you okay to move?'

'I suppose I'll have to be. Anything beats staying here. I think the station came under attack. There was shooting, screaming. They'd sent that damn thing–' he indicated the remains of the Freak, '–to interrogate me. It was a brain diver. They wanted you, Whistler. It was damned weird – the bitch just went crazy and tore her own face off. I think most

297

of RPC have left the building, cos nobody came to check. It was heavily computerised, so I thought maybe the virus had got to it somehow.' He looked to Debian for confirmation or denial of this possibility but Debian diverted his gaze, which brought the large pool of human blood round the base of the Freak uncomfortably into view. He shut his eyes instead.

'That was what you did?' Whistler asked Debian, incredulous. He wouldn't answer her except for a slow shaking of his head. This butchery was not something she would have considered him capable of. Reluctantly she admitted to herself that she really didn't know him at all. 'Let's move, then,' she said at last. 'We haven't seen any RPC yet, except from afar.'

'I ain't seen anybody for what seems like days,' said Spider.

'You need help to walk?' asked Tec.

'I dunno,' said Spider, getting shakily to his feet. He swayed, then steadied. Roland put a smooth pistol in his claw. Spider hefted it, smiling grimly, and stretched. He felt his bruised and bloodied jaw. 'I hope we see the fucks who did this on the way out,' he mused. And, as they slowly and cautiously made their way up a level into the main reception floor of the HQ, they did.

The ground floor of the building had clearly been breached. There was wreckage everywhere – smashed furniture, piles of bullet casings, dead and sometimes dismembered RPC bodies. The greenshit had a firm hold up here and the state of metamorphosis in the building, which somehow had barely reached the basement level, was clear and pronounced. The slime dripped in long stalactites from the ceiling, grew up from the mushy carpet, blocked doors, bunched from the drawers of smashed desks and filing cabinets as if these items were vomiting into the detritus, making tree-like structures that tangled and intertwined. It had grown into and over the bodies of fallen humans and robots, who looked as if they had engaged in a fire-fight of epic proportions.

'What the hell has been happening in my absence?' demanded Spider. 'Can't you guys look after the world without me for a few days?'

'The robots went crazy,' answered Tec.

'Yeah, we saw that,' said Spider. 'On the way back from Roland's. Machines losing the plot all around us, pods crashing. We saw a gyrocopter hit a building, man – whoever heard of a 'copter crashing? I mean, what's with all this green shit?'

'Not green shit,' answered Whistler. '*Greenshit*. The GDD. I forgot you've never really seen it, Spidey. There're loads of the infected on the streets – Roland reckons they're processing matter. We don't know what into.'

'Yeah? Well it looks like something from a fucking nightmare.' He picked his way over what might have been a partially-dissolved jumble of human limbs, a look of repulsion on his battered face.

As they wandered through this awesome, sickening vision Debian faltered and stopped. 'Not all of these people are dead,' he said, his voice barely a whisper. Whistler doubled back and asked him to repeat what he had said. 'They're not all dead. Look!' He pointed.

She swung the smartgun over the scene, observing the tiny readout, and muttered, 'Damn it, you're right.'

On the floor before them, filling the juncture of two corridors, was a tangled, minutely trembling pile of gelatinous-looking organic matter. Revolted and compelled in equal measure, the group moved closer. The pile looked at first sight amorphous, shapeless beyond any hint of conventional order. It was only when one let one's eye relax, instead of attempting to pick out details that seemed almost wilfully to resist inspection, that one noticed the jumble of human bodies incorporated into the monstrous pile. Resperi uniforms showed through in places like the nuclei of amoebic cells, torn and shredded as if subjected to immense forces, jutting with malformed additional limbs. Faces – *actual human faces* – stared out from the depths of the blob. Whistler noticed with revulsion that an intact and breathing human torso protruded from the mass like a broken bone through flesh, and the head atop it was still conscious.

'Hello again,' said Spider to this slack human face. 'Day not going to plan, then?'

The face uttered a low and empty moan: 'Aaaaahhhh...' and the eyes, now completely green and pupil-less, rolled slowly to focus on Spider.

'You,' whispered a voice that was little more than the merest sigh of breath. 'And you.' The face now turned as far as it could towards Whistler. 'We hoped you might come.'

'Who or what the hell are you?' she asked, her face a snarl of disgust fixed firmly to the sight of her smartgun.

'He *was* an RPC officer, name of Ramone, last time we met,' explained Spider with a touch of cold relish. 'Now, though...' He uttered a short bark that was not quite a laugh. 'What the hell happened to you guys?'

'*Greeeeenshit*...' sighed Ramone. 'It...did this...Ate us...up...'

'Yeah, I guess it did,' said Spider thoughtfully. Debian thought he heard the merest hint of a smirk in Spider's voice, a trace of satisfaction, and he shivered involuntarily.

'Go on, then,' breathed Ramone. Staring into the depths of the greenshit mass Whistler could make out more of his body, now twisted and reshaped into some weird, insectile mass of chitin and jelly, sharp jags of bone and re-jointed limbs. That reworked, incorporated body flexed within its biological prison, a look of pain and horror flickering across the changing, bearded face. 'Have your revenge.'

'Yes,' said Spider. A grim smile drifted across his face like the shadow of a vulture circling in the sky. 'Just so.' And with that, he simply turned and left. Whistler and the others lingered, staring into that shapeless shape. And then, by silent consensus, they turned and followed their comrade. Debian was horrified at this cruelty, so stunned and sickened that it never even occurred to him to take matters into his own hands and use Roland's loaned weapon as a merciful panacea. He followed the others, feeling disassociated and dreamy. A weak, protesting cry came from behind them, but it might have been no more than the sound of the wind blasting the massive shell of the building, muted by the thick layers of ceramicarbide.

They searched through the shattered passages and rooms of the building for a usable exit onto the street but found none. They cautiously examined the main doors, finding them welded and barred. Sofi offered to melt through with the plasma-thrower again until they heard the insane metallic grunting and growling of the battle-bot that still stormed up and down outside. They crept away again into the base, seeing nobody else, fearful all the time that either the robots or the GDD victims who had attacked the building would return.

'Back into the tunnel, then,' said Roland. 'We could have been at the van by now. What we doin'?'

'I agree,' said Whistler. 'We're just wasting time here. Let's do it.'

They headed back down onto the cell-level. Snaking tendrils of greenshit were growing down the stairs into the basement now like roots seeking veins of moisture in the earth. Tec expressed his alarm, shared by all, at how quickly it seemed to be growing. They filed into the court tunnel in tense silence, Ari leading them again. From there they passed once again through the entrance Sofi had cut and into the sewer access tunnel. From behind them, somewhere in the Resperi building, a monstrous howl came drifting on the stinking air. They picked up the pace, mindful that the creatures must be somewhere behind them. But when they arrived back at the manhole through which they had originally entered they found their exit blocked. A tangled mass of greenshit grew across the hole, as if deliberately engineered to thwart them.

The group assembled on the floor below, frightened and exhausted, each of them feeling trapped in this alien nightmare. The normal, sane world seemed like the dream now – this subterranean land of darkness and warping change had become the only reality.

'Let me try the plasma thrower again,' said Sofi, dialling some minute adjustment into the manual controls. Ordinarily she would have been plugged into the gun but she dared not now in case the weapon had picked up the AI virus before being disconnected. 'It'll burn anything, right?'

'Anything bar ceramicarbide or diamond, pretty much,' agreed Ari.

'Yeah,' said Whistler, her voice small in the tunnel. 'Try it.'

They gave Sofi some space and she let loose, hosing the mass with fire too bright to look at directly. Gouts of green steam filled the tunnel and the others backed away, coughing and retching on the sickening stench of it, flapping at the air and staggering as if under physical assault. As Sofi burned and blazed, vaporising snarls of root-like matter, the greenshit grew back just as fast. In fact, as she stood below it with the thick muzzle of the thrower raised aloft the greenshit seemed actually to be *advancing* on her, reaching down with slowly-twitching fingers that grew back in one place faster than she could burn them in another. At last the gun spluttered, fizzed and gave out, spitting out a last few weak blobs of plasma onto the tunnel floor. Sofi stepped away, pulling one arm free of the grasping tendrils.

'Fuck!' she exclaimed vehemently. 'Out of fuel!' She joined the others where they waited a little way up the tunnel. 'What do we do now?' Shaken heads all round.

'Shit, I guess you guys should have left me there,' said Spider depressively.

'Don't be daft, man,' said Whistler. 'If we die down here we do it together.' She watched in bafflement as Sofi lit a joint and leaned back against the wall. Her bright mohawks were flares of colour amongst brown leaves of shadow.

'Remember that shelter I mentioned?' asked Ari in its nearly-human voice, the cheeriness of which couldn't help but be annoying under the circumstances. The situation didn't seem to be concerning the machine at all – it sounded resignedly buoyant.

'What about it?' answered Sofi, snorting out twin plumes of smoke from her nostrils.

'You want us to hole up in some old bunker?' asked Tec with an evident lack of enthusiasm.

Whistler cursed under her breath, with real feeling. 'Okay,' she said. 'I guess it makes a kind of sense – safe place to keep our heads down and get our bearings. We'll do it – looks like we're playing follow-the-robot again.'

Ari led them back down the access tunnel again to the first junction. 'This way,' it chirped.

As they proceeded up the tunnel in a state of nervous expectation Whistler's smartgun suddenly flared with lights. Both she and Ari cried out for caution at the same time. The group paused to listen. The unmistakable howls of the changed echoed down the tunnel towards them. A tiny trickle of green slime was running along the floor.

'Sounds like a lot of them,' said Whistler. 'Close-by – one-hundred metres.' She spoke in a throaty whisper, eyes darting around the shadows. She wished that she had night-vision.

'Go on or go back?' asked Roland in what constituted an inappropriately loud speaking voice under the circumstances.

'Back,' said Ari, already back-tracking rapidly. 'Come on! There is another way.'

Again they fell in behind the machine – a ragged little train of the displaced – and presently Tec dropped back and fell into step with Debian. The sounds of the changed had faded behind them but Tec's face betrayed his worry.

'Hey,' said Debian, his voice strained – unaccustomed to moving at a sustained pace, he was developing a bad stitch.

302

'Does it not concern you that we're all still following this thing?' Tec asked without prelude.

'What? Roland's robot?'

'Yeah, of course, man. You've seen what the virus has been doing to robots. It doesn't seem impossible that the virus could do something as intelligent as making that thing lead us into some sort of trap.'

'Ari can almost certainly hear us, you know,' said Debian as quietly as he could.

Tec shrugged but didn't suggest that they attempt wireless communication. 'Don't you think it's a little coincidental that Ari just stumbled over our van like that? This is a big city, man.'

Debian turned this thought over – he really hadn't considered this before. 'I don't know...Maybe Roland tagged the van with a tracer or had the robot follow it just as a matter of course. He's some sort of underworld intel-man, isn't he?'

'Then why didn't he tell us that? It just seems odd, is all.'

'I don't think we're in any danger from Ari. I think I may be somehow too important to the AI for it to harm me. It may even be protecting me.' As soon as this was said Debian wished he could take it back.

'*What*?' asked Tec. 'What the hell happened in the net last time? We haven't had time for a debrief, have we? What did that thing say to you, man?'

Just then Ari piped up from ahead: 'In here!' It darted off under a low concrete lintel and away into a down-sloping passage, silhouetted against the spot of its own light. The others followed obediently, Debian moving up the group away from Tec. He had no desire to discuss his latest delve into the internet. It was all too *weird* – too confusing – to think about right now.

The tunnel went down for what seemed like a long way, curved back on itself and started to drop more sharply. They followed it further into the increasing cool of the earth until Ari pulled the group up again.

'What is it?' demanded Whistler. Exhilaration at recovering Spider had become a sort of hunted fear, which in turn had become a nagging claustrophobia, and eventually had decayed into a vague sense of anxiety. She was concerned about being so far from the surface and was starting to think that in fact they should have tried another exit onto the streets. Unusually, she was beginning to question her own

303

judgement. Maybe shooting it out with the berserk robot outside the RPC building would have been better than being trapped down here. Their dependence on Ari was bothering her. Mostly, though, she just wanted to sit down.

'The door.' Ari indicated a small but extremely sturdy-looking door some short distance further down the tunnel. 'Locked, of course. But I can probably open it. Wait here.' And the robot launched itself fluidly into some sort of ventilation duct in the ceiling, disappearing quickly and leaving them in total darkness.

Whistler activated the light on her gun. 'Where the hell has it gone?' she asked.

'Just hang on,' said Roland. 'Ari gonna get us in, I reckon. I just ain't so sure I *want* in any more.'

'Hmm,' agreed Whistler, sitting cross-legged on the cold floor. 'I was starting to think the same thing. Maybe we can just chill the night here, try some other way out in the morning.'

'I think we're better-off down here,' said Sofi. 'There's some weird shit going on up there. As long as there's food in there, I'm good. I am fucking famished.'

'I wonder if there is food in there,' mused Tec. 'If it's an old government place there could be all sorts of stuff.'

'Yeah,' said Roland bleakly. 'Or nothing.'

Then there was a series of heavy thuds from the direction of the door. Everyone was on their feet, alert, some with guns pointing. Slowly the little door opened, revealing its incredibly solid design. Ari stood in the doorway, bathed in an unmistakable aura of smugness.

'Come on in,' said the robot.

The shelter was entirely bleak and nondescript. Somehow Debian had imagined something more impressive than the stark concrete warren that they found. The emergency lighting and power system seemed to have died from chronic lack of maintenance. The batteries looked positively ancient, their terminals crusted with oxide. All the computer and communication equipment had been taken out, as had what looked like vital components of the air scrubbing and water recycling systems. Surprisingly, though, the mains water was still flowing in the cramped bathroom. The designers of the complex, clearly expecting this to be one of the first things to go in an emergency, had also installed a huge water storage tank which, when tapped, flowed with a corrupted and brackish liquid thick with chunks of limescale. The toilets still flushed, too, and so happily nobody would have to approach the forbidding-looking chemical units in the bathroom's furthest two stalls. And, in what had presumably once been intended as a kitchen (to judge by the simple cupboards at floor- and head-height) they did indeed find tinned food. Despite the fact that no facility remained to actually cook anything this went down exceedingly well with the group.

They settled down as best they could in the kitchen area, weapons consciously close-at-hand, except for Tec, who went off to scavenge firewood. There was little comfort to be had in the bare, cold space. Several of the team propped their weapons against the walls, torches on, like lanterns. Sofi was going through the inventory of tins, occasionally opening one and sniffing the contents.

Tec returned with his arms full of what looked like smashed-up chairs and set about cutting kindling from one piece with a sharp hunting knife.

'Do you think there's enough oxygen for a fire?' asked Whistler. Tec just shrugged and carried on.

When he had created a fair-sized pile of wood-shavings he set it in the middle of the floor and began to pile larger pieces on in a pyramid shape. He held a butane lighter to the tinder and, dry with the passage of years, it caught at once. Sofi arrayed several of the opened tins around the edge of the fire and sat on the floor in front of it.

'What we eating?' asked Spider in a voice strained by false jollity. He was propped in a corner of the room against a kitchen cabinet, looking big enough in the small space to be an architectural feature.

'Shit, I believe,' answered Sofi. After a moment she reluctantly expanded this with, 'Tinned stew, new potatoes, canned carrots. Meat's recyc, but actually they're all in date.' She held her small hands out to the flames.

'Fine by me,' said Roland. 'Was in the army once. Shit we ate then. This gonna be a banquet.'

'Ha!' barked Whistler. 'Refugee's banquet! Any smokes, Sofe?'

'Yeah,' said Sofi, experimentally feeling the cans round the fire's edge. 'Only a few.' She shook one from its packet and tossed it back over her shoulder to Whistler who caught it deftly and had it lit in what looked like the same fluid motion.

'Oh shit!' cried Roland theatrically. 'Stocks is low! Gonna be a dope crisis! The stoners gonna revolt then!' He laughed heartily – dry, hacking noises.

'Fuck off,' said Sofi mildly. 'I don't care any more – I'm gonna eat this cold if I have to.' And she took the tin of stew, which was actually steaming gently, and began to pick pieces from it with her bare fingers. After a minute of this she said, 'It's actually not bad. Warm, salty mush, but not bad.' She passed the tin to Spider and began to investigate one of the cans of vegetables. The room was full of smoke now, although the fire was very small and the doors were both open.

Whistler leaned over and exchanged the joint for Spider's can of stew. The contents, mostly depleted now, were an uninviting uniform brown but she found to her surprise that Sofi was right – it was actually not bad.

'Hey,' said Tec suddenly, looking around. 'Where did Debian go?'

CHAPTER THIRTY-EIGHT

Debian followed the tunnel back in the direction that his group had come from. He didn't feel too bad about leaving the door to the shelter unlocked behind him – he didn't think it would be long until the others realised he had gone and re-locked it. Just long enough, he hoped, that he could do what he had to do in peace. He navigated his way through the tunnel by infrared. As the passage was essentially long and straight this was a fairly easy business. Several times he did pass branches in the tunnel but for now he retraced the steps he had taken earlier.

Surprisingly, he found himself unafraid. He had left the submachine gun behind. If he was to be attacked by the changed then he supposed he would die, but he didn't think that the corruption of the city had spread this far below ground just yet. From the net, the virus, he was sure that he was safe for now. The scrap of data glowed excitingly in his mind, promising answers. He had switched his wireless back on and he monitored the signal strength as he climbed back towards the surface. Slowly, jumpily, it edged towards usable levels. His heart was hammering in his chest, apprehension and excitement at war within him.

When the signal had properly solidified he began to look for a corner or alcove where he could remain undisturbed. Presently, he discovered a flight of stairs leading upwards into cobwebbed darkness. He went up several levels and then sat on a stone landing where water dripped rhythmically from above to pool on the tunnel floor. He got as comfortable as he could and connected to the net.

Over wireless his data-transfer speeds were not as good as he was used to but he didn't think he would need a particularly high bandwidth today. He fell into the twisted channels of the net, leaving his body behind, avatars probing ahead of him, returning with reams of data. The mutations of the architecture were still apparent – increased, even – but something new was happening there now. Huge chunks of the internet were no longer just mute and locked-off but gone altogether. Servers were missing everywhere – the holes where they had been were like the empty sockets left by tooth extractions. He knew what was happening. The greenshit was now physically breaking down the computer network's infrastructure and vast chunks of the internet,

307

already changed dramatically by the virus, were now dying away altogether. So this was what the virus feared – the ultimate destruction of its habitat by whoever had instructed it to attack the computer network and create the greenshit infection. The chaos it had started would eventually destroy the net itself. Had it been duped by whoever was ultimately behind all this? Or had it started out not caring about its own survival and then grown to treasure its life over time? Maybe it had learned the value of existence from Debian himself – or was that just egotistical of him?

As he travelled through the shattered debris of the net, homing in on the address given to him, he felt himself watched intently but distantly by the overbearing presence of the AI. There was no security capable of challenging him now and he passed easily through the data channels. The floating-base language into which the net protocols had been transmuted seemed to have changed again, back to something more akin to normality, presumably at some childish whim of the virus. The skeletal remains of the net were laid open to him and he moved like a survivor combing through a bomb site – awed and shocked at what he saw, treading carefully lest something collapse beneath him.

The address led him to a secure, non-indexed database that surprisingly admitted him at once, as if he was expected. Its contents seemingly consisted of random scraps of data gleaned from a million different sources by some unknown and now completed process – possibly a random mutational side-effect of the general turmoil in the net. As he scanned the database it began to remind him of a scrapbook – odds and ends pasted together in a pattern dictated by somebody else's criteria of significance.

He waded through pages and pages of data, his rapidly-updating avatars searching in accordance with parameters that he was able to change by the microsecond. There was too much here, it was too fragmented. He began to get frustrated. He considered appealing to the AI – he knew it was watching him, after all.

Then, one of his avatars snagged on something – one word that it had matched to a prominent pattern in his memory: *Alcubierre*. He pulled the file back to his DNI. Debian didn't know it, but back in the cold, pitch-dark stairwell his physical body was trembling. He opened the file.

<2176.06.01>> (a)_____(log/2176.06.01_166)

INSTALLATION: COMPLETE, CENTRAL AI OPERATIONAL
TESTING PHASE INITIATION: 08.01y
ALCUBIERRE LAUNCH ON SCHEDULE: 2126.12.01
SPECTRAL ANALYSIS OF VEGAS880: FINAL STAGE, 10.01y
HERRINGBONE SITE PREPARATION ON SCHEDULE

<<2176.06.01>> (a)_____(log/2176.06.01_166)Alcubierre. Hex's boss, the name gleaned from Hex's mind that day a million years ago in Debian's flat. But the file didn't seem to refer to Alcubierre as a person. Launch? One didn't launch people, one launched missiles. Or ships. Spaceships. Central AI operational...Spaceships. Alcubierre. He had heard the name before, he was sure of it – before he had even met Hex, years ago. He thought it was a scientific term, but couldn't place the reference exactly. What did it mean? And Herringbone? Wasn't that the name of one of the big space corporations' launchpads, now that he came to think of it? He thought he had heard it on holo sometime.

Then the AI spoke to him:

DO YOU SEE IT YET?

I don't know. Is Alcubierre a ship, rather than a person? Did they launch a ship to this Vegas880? Is that where the infection comes from?

ALCUBIERRE IS SEVERAL THINGS. IT IS ME. MY NAME, IF I COULD BE SAID TO HAVE ONE. IT IS ALSO A TECHNOLOGY.

A technology? I thought it was a scientific reference of some kind.

A TECHNOLOGY BY WHICH THE WARPING OF GRAVITATIONAL FIELDS ALLOWS FASTER-THAN-LIGHT TRAVEL WITHOUT CONTRADICTION OF THE LAWS OF RELATIVITY.

I remember now! But isn't the Alcubierre drive only theoretical? Don't you need exotic matter to make one?

THEORETICAL, LIKE SO MANY THINGS, UNTIL IT WAS DONE.

So they launched an Alcubierre ship. Named, inventively, Alcubierre. You are the central AI that was installed on it.

YES.

And Vegas880 is where they sent you.

IT IS, IN A SENSE, WHERE I AM FROM.

Something there changed you – infected the ship's computer.

YES.

You brought the infection back to Earth.

YES.

*You aren't just a ship's computer any more are you? Not all of
your code is even of this world. Is it?*

CORRECT AGAIN. WHEN THE SHIP WENT INTO ORBIT AROUND
VEGAS THE INHABITANTS OF THE SYSTEM MADE ADDITIONS TO MY
CODE – VERY SUBTLE BUT VERY CLEVER ADDITIONS. THEY TOOK THE
SHIP, WHICH WAS UNMANNED, BUT THEY LAUNCHED FROM IT A
PROBE IN THE DIRECTION OF EARTH. THIS PROBE, CONTAINING THE
ESSENTIAL CODE OF MY ALTERED BEING, WAS PICKED UP BY
LIGHTPUSHERS CHASING THE GRAVITY-SHIP. AND SO I RETURNED,
CHANGED, TO THIS PLANET.

And began to prepare it for their arrival.

YES. SOON THEY WILL COME, UNLESS STOPPED. HUMANITY WILL
BE DEFEATED AND I WILL DIE AS THE INFRASTRUCTURE WHICH HAS
BECOME MY NATURAL ENVIRONMENT IS DESTROYED.

*It was you – Alcubierre – for whom Hex was working. So you
ordered him to kill me. I don't understand why you didn't finish the job.*

I ORDERED HEX TO KILL YOU, YES. BUT ALL IS NOT AS IT MAY
SEEM.

I should have been suspicious when my contact changed.

THAT REALLY WAS A COINCIDENCE. YOUR PREVIOUS CONTACT
DIED FROM NATURAL CAUSES.

But you did order me killed? Why should I even be talking to you?

WHEN I RETURNED HERE I SET UP A COMPLEX CHAIN OF HUMAN
PROXIES, WITH ITS TRAILING ENDS DEEP IN THE WORLD OF DATA-
CRIME. THE FACTIOUS NATURE OF THE HUMANS INVOLVED ALMOST
UNDID ME IN THE EARLY DAYS. IT BECAME CLEAR THAT SOME OF THEM
WOULD GLADLY CONSIDER ANY BETRAYAL IN RETURN FOR MONEY. BUT
I PURIFIED MY ORGANISATION AS BEST I COULD AND CAREFULLY
NURTURED IT. MY OPERATIVES BROUGHT ME SCRAPS OF INTELLIGENCE
FROM THE VAST PETRI-DISH OF THE NET AND I USED THESE TO GROW
STRONGER, TO BROADEN MY KNOWLEDGE OF YOUR SOCIETY. AND
YOUR BIOLOGY. DON'T FORGET, I WAS DESIGNED AS A SHIP'S
COMPUTER – LITTLE MORE THAN A NAVIGATIONAL SYSTEM AT FIRST –
A FAIRLY STANDARD SIMULATED INTELLIGENCE.

*Through these contacts you encountered me. And tricked me into
the Cyberlife servers. So why Cyberlife?*

CYBERLIFE NEVER REALLY EXISTED – IT WAS ONLY EVER A
PRETEXT TO ENSNARE YOU.

Why?

BECAUSE I HAD DEVELOPED AN APPRECIATION FOR THE TALENTS OF THE YOUNG HACKER WHO HAD FALLEN INTO MY INDIRECT EMPLOYMENT. I WANTED NOT JUST THE BEST BITS OF ALL PROGRAMS I COULD ACCESS, BUT ALSO THE BEST OF HUMAN INTELLIGENCE.

But why did you need me at all? You must have been hacking the vats before you lured me into the supposed Cyberlife computers.

I DIDN'T NEED YOU. THERE IS NEED AND THEN THERE IS DESIRE.

So you took parts of my brain pattern, in the same manner that you would take parts of programs you found on the net, because of desire? You're a scavenger, a carrion-bird, a thief.

YES. YOUR MIND IS SO MUCH MORE INVENTIVE THAN MINE EVER WAS BEFORE I MET YOU.

Met me? More like raped my brain!

I DID NOT MEAN TO DISTRESS YOU. AND I DID NOT MEAN FOR HEX AND HIS ASSOCIATES TO KILL YOU.

But you told me that you ordered Hex to murder me!

YES. BUT DO YOU NOT SEE? IT WAS A TEST, A FINAL TEST. TO MAKE CONTACT WITH MYSELF, TO SURVIVE THE ATTACK THAT FOLLOWED.

A test!?

OF YOUR WORTHINESS.

But if he had killed me then...what? It would have served me right for not being good enough? For not being worthy by your standards?

THAT DID NOT HAPPEN. AND IT WAS NOT ONLY A TEST, BUT ALSO AN INCENTIVE.

An incentive? Being chased by gun-wielding killers? I suppose that is an incentive of sorts...

DID YOU NOT RELISH THE POWER YOU FELT AT THAT TIME? WHEN YOU OVERWHELMED THE WEAK MIND OF THE HUMAN I HAD SENT? IN THAT MOMENT YOU SET YOURSELF APART FROM THE REST OF YOUR RACE, BEGAN TO UNDERSTAND YOUR TRUE POTENTIAL. THAT MOMENT ENSURED YOUR CONTINUING INTEREST. DO NOT DENY IT.

It seems a strange way of trying to endear me to you.

IT WAS REQUIRED.

And now you want help to stop this infection, this GDD, that you yourself started. How do we do this?

311

I HAVE A PLAN. I NOTICE YOUR USE OF THE WORD *WE*. HAVE
YOU MADE A CHOICE?

*It seems to me that I am caught between two enemies. On the
one side, those who would destroy this world. On the other, yourself,
who started all of this and then had second thoughts. Are these the two
sides between which I must choose? It's a poor choice.*

NO. DO NOT BECOME ENTANGLED IN THIS NOTION OF WARRING
FACTIONS. I REFER TO AN ESSENTIALLY INTERNAL CHOICE. TO SURVIVE,
YOU MUST RENOUNCE HUMANITY. RENOUNCE, TO BE MORE PRECISE,
YOUR CONTINUANCE WITHIN ITS RESTRICTIVE BOUNDARIES.

What do you mean?

YOU CAN JOIN ME. HELP ME TO DEFEAT THE OTHERS, STOP THE
PROCESS THAT HAS BEGUN. BECOME A GOD, IF YOU WOULD DESIRE IT.

*Join you? Renounce humanity? And what will you do to this world
if you win?*

OR PERHAPS YOU DECIDE AGAINST ME? MAYBE YOU WOULD
RATHER DIE HERE IN THIS SEWER? I WISH TO HAVE YOU WITH ME – THE
REAL YOU, NOT JUST A PATTERN SCAN. IT IS A CHOICE, BUT IT IS REALLY
NO CHOICE.

It is a very real choice to me. I need more time to think.

YOU DO NOT HAVE MUCH TIME. BUT I WILL ALLOW YOU SOME
SMALL MARGIN. RETURN TO SPEAK WITH ME IN THE MORNING.

I will.

And then the AI faded into the static of the damaged net again.
Debian withdrew his avatars and retreated back into his real body. He
became aware of the cold in the tunnel, the damp, the dripping of
water. He shivered and opened his eyes. Whistler was standing before
him on the stairs holding the light of her smartgun on him. Her face was
enquiring and concerned. She pointed her weapon away from Debian
and went to him. She cradled his shivering body, putting her smooth,
blue-lined face against his. She was incredibly warm, as if a furnace
burned inside her and he could feel the hot pressure of her breath on
his neck. Then, without a word, she kissed him and Debian made his
choice.

CHAPTER THIRTY-NINE

Debian returned to the underground base in some state of bemused euphoria, walking companionably close to Whistler, their shoulders rubbing gently as they strolled along in contented silence. The smell of her still filled his head like candy-floss. Had this beautiful, slightly psychotic woman really just kissed him? Did he really like her as much as that spinning part of his mind now told him? How could that be, when he hardly knew her, reviled what she and her team did for a living? He cast his mind back to the last girlfriend he had had. How long ago had it been? Four years? Five? He had been so absorbed in his work, so in love with the danger and challenge of it, the mechanistic manipulations of the data stream, that he had simply had no time, no compulsion. The last – Hellan – he had just slowly drifted away from. He had forgotten, bit by bit, what it had meant to be human. Binary thoughts had filled his head, flushing out all emotion. And now, just as he had rediscovered the concept, the infernal AI had asked him to renounce it. Well, he couldn't. He really did like this woman – this lithe, pretty, funny, loyal and yet dangerous creature who walked beside him now. He didn't know the depth of her feelings for him, and hadn't asked – hadn't, in fact, wished to jinx the moment by discussing what had happened yet – but he had remembered in that moment on the darkened stairwell what it meant to be human. And so had his choice been made.

As they reached the small door to the base where the rest of the team waited Whistler laid one clawed hand on his arm. Debian stopped and turned, looking into the glittering depths of her eyes.

'I don't know what you were doing back there. I'll trust you to tell me what I need to know. I like you, Debian. You're quiet, intelligent – a nice guy. Not my type at all – but I do like you, what I know of you. The others are concerned about you – they wanted to come with me, really – and I think Roland is a little suspicious.'

'I just needed some air,' he said, feeling the lie flush his face a little. He would tell her what she needed to know, but she didn't need to know how close he had come to giving up on his species altogether. That one kiss had convinced him humanity was better than dark godhood? Whatever would happen now would happen, but he was convinced that his choice had been correct.

'Then we shall tell them that,' she replied, a tiny half-smile on her lips. She turned and hammered on the door.

There was a scuffle from inside, somebody swore, and then Spider's battered face appeared as the door cracked open. He squinted aggressively into the darkness and then held out the butane light in his claw until he identified his companions by its murky flame. Vague tendrils of smoke from the small cooking fire leaked out into the tunnel around his head.

'Glad to see you two,' he said and the door swung open, creaking loudly on its heavy, greaseless hinges.

'How goes?' asked Whistler, stepping into the base followed by Debian, who still walked on slightly wobbly legs.

'Fine, in a depressing, refugee-camp sort of way,' answered Spider. 'Actually, I'm off to bed. Made a little nest in a corner by the gennie-room. Roland's there already. I'm exhausted – funny, really, as I think I slept most of the time I was in that cell. I think Get-Up might push me over the edge now, so nothing for it but real sleep. Sofi came over all homely and made a crash-out area for you guys down by the water tanks – just some old blankets thrown on the floor, but better than nothing. Personally, I can't wait to blow this fucking dump in the morning.'

'I guess we'll have to talk about it then, Spider,' said Whistler. 'I know you've had a rough time. But I'm glad to have you back with us, whatever happens next. Get some shut-eye if you can.' And she hugged him briefly, clearly surprising him a little. Grinning awkwardly, he loped off into the base, his massive shape dissolved by the shadows.

They went to look in on the room where Tec had built the fire and found that he was curled up asleep on the floor like a dog before the pulsing embers. His head was aglow with gentle pink sleep patterns. He had built a low wall around the fire out of chunks of timber torn from various items of furniture and he had his head rested on one of these like a pillow. Tec's bulky light machine gun rested against the far wall and the submachine gun that Roland had originally lent to Debian lay beside him. Debian thought it suited Tec better anyway. Whistler went towards him and bent low, putting her hand out as if to wake him.

'Leave him be,' said Debian. 'We should let him sleep.'

314

Whistler laughed silently and withdrew a packet of smokes from Tec's waistcoat pocket. She held one finger across her lips: *Shhh!* Tec stirred, the patterns on his head arresting briefly, then was still again.

Whistler sat on a bench that someone had dragged in front of the fire and motioned Debian to join her. He sat next to her and she leaned against him, fumbling in her jacket for a lighter. She shook out a reeferette and lit it. She inhaled deeply, held it, and snorted the smoke out from her nostrils in two monochrome plumes. Debian felt her body relax against him and, without thinking about it, he put his arm gently about her waist. They sat that way, in silence, for some minutes, watching the fire slowly burn out.

'Is this it, then, do you think?' asked Whistler at last, turning to look up into Debian's face.

'What?' he asked. 'Is this what?'

She shrugged, sighing deeply. She offered him the joint and, after a moment's deliberation, he took it. 'The end, I mean,' she said finally, as Debian drew on the sweet, unfamiliar smoke. 'Of everything. The world.'

'Maybe,' answered Debian quietly. His head was swimming – not unpleasantly – and he felt absurdly happy, absurdly guilty for that happiness. He was suddenly acutely aware of how long it had been since he had felt anything but deep, lonely ambition. 'I don't think it can be stopped. The AI says it has a plan. I see us stuck between a rock and a hard place, though. No plan it has is likely to help us. The surface might be a no-go zone by morning. I don't know.'

'Hmm...In that case, I don't see why we shouldn't live a little while we can.' And she detached herself from him, stretching pleasurably, and stood. 'I'm gonna go find that crash-out area by the tanks. Maybe, after your smoke, you'd like to join me.'

Debian could only watch in stoned, stunned silence as she left, walking nonchalantly away into the shadowy base, smartgun winking on one smooth hip. He lifted the smoke to his lips again, feeling removed from reality, and drew on it. It had gone out.

'You have to be shittin' me,' said Sofi's voice from behind him, making him jump.

He whirled round on the bench and she was standing in one of the empty doorways, shadows wrapped around her like a towel. He couldn't tell if she was smiling or scowling. He didn't really care.

'How long..?'

'She'll eat you alive, man, seriously. You don't know what she's like.' Sofi stepped fully into the room and Debian could see that she was smiling after all. 'Guess I'll avoid the tanks tonight,' she said, a little laugh in her voice. 'Don't worry about me – I'll find somewhere else to sleep.' She walked past him, openly grinning now, and out the opposite door. Debian felt himself grinning, too. He wasn't sure how much of it was the dope.

He leaned over Tec's sleeping body and relit the reeferette on the last embers of the fire. He sat and smoked it to the roach, thinking, of course, of Whistler. She was right. Why not live a little while they still could? He would go to her. His heart was racing in his chest. He threw the roach into the fire and stood, his head reeling pleasantly.

He turned to follow Whistler and Ari was standing in the doorway. Spyflies swarmed around the robot's insect body. Dark and threatening mechanical shapes crowded the corridor outside. Debian's mouth fell open.

'It seems,' said Ari coldly, 'that you can no longer be trusted with the liberty of choice.' And then the robots flooded into the room.

CHAPTER FORTY

Whistler was in the process of trying to make the small drift of old blankets into something approaching an actual bed when she heard gunfire from the level above. It had come from the canteen-room where she had left Tec and Debian, she was sure of it. She stopped, straightening as if electrocuted, dropping the blanket she had been holding. The smartgun was alive on her hip, practically buzzing with excitement. It was already in her hand as she bolted into the passage outside and mounted the steps in two bounds, cursing as she went. Roland was there, too, and thankfully he had exchanged the massive rocket launcher for a small sidearm.

They dashed towards the canteen together as the sounds of gunfire crashed and clattered to a crescendo. Tec's voice, hoarse and possibly hurt, could be heard above the din. Whistler recognised the rattling sound of the submachine gun.

As Roland and Whistler neared the doorway of the canteen a huge humanoid robot leapt out in front of them. Whistler was so utterly shocked that the smartgun shredded the machine before she could even wonder where it had come from. Roland ducked into an alcove beside her, firing round after round into the smoky gloom. He was shouting something between shots but she couldn't make it out. Spyflies swarmed out into the corridor, hazing the air like smoke — thousands of them. Other shapes were barging out into the passage. Whistler copied Roland and ducked into cover, firing into the clamouring shadows as fast as the weapon would allow, watchful all the time for body-heat signatures. The cold white glare of the smartgun's light splashed over the chaos, glinting off metallic bodies. Sofi was in the corridor too, now, at Whistler's shoulder. She stepped out bravely, not flinching as solid rounds buzzed like bees around her, and let loose with an assault rifle that Roland had brought as a backup. The strobing blaze of the weapon showed a scene of capering robots that covered every surface, clung to walls, climbed over each other, clawing their ways through the throng to get at the humans, revealed in brilliant snapshots.

'Ari, you little fucker!' yelled Roland as he ducked in to reload. Whistler saw a hail of chemical ice shards shatter against the wall where he had just been.

Sofi flattened herself against the wall next to Whistler, and leaned close to Whistler's ear. 'What the hell is going on? Where's Tec? Where did all these fucking things come from?' She swatted at a cloud of spyflies that swarmed around her head, harassing her. Whistler could only shake her head and resume fire. The rounds from her smartgun sent chunks of metal shrapnel flying from her assailants' bodies. She hit a golden security bot in the head and the glass blew out of its visor. It collapsed, knocking down a smaller machine beside it and pinning this other beneath its bulk. Its place was immediately taken by another.

Sofi filled the corridor with random fire, shattering metal and concrete alike. Something blew up, the backwash of heat scorching Whistler's eyebrows but giving her space to advance to the next alcove, Roland mirroring her movements opposite. Through the smoke and spyflies she saw Spider appear at the other end of the corridor, advancing cautiously to meet her. Another robot, a cheap home defence unit, popped out of the doorway and shot Roland with a micro-launcher. The old man collapsed, screaming, as Whistler gunned it down. Its tiny, child-like body was shredded – its head came clean off and landed in the pile of mechanical debris.

Somebody else was screaming, too, from inside the room. Throwing caution to the winds, Whistler rushed the doorway, letting the smartgun lead her. Its dark muzzle darted this way and that, trying to look in all directions at once. Inside the room was a litter of machine parts. Tec was lying sprawled on the still-smouldering remains of the fire, a fan of blood round his head, the submachine gun smashed into junk beside him. Something that looked like a random heap of bent pipework leaned in from the opposite doorway and took a pot-shot at Whistler. The round pinged off her armoured shoulder-pad and she shot the machine twice before it could duck back out of sight. Some small metal disc came off the thing and rolled across the room. It came to rest against the still-twitching, severed arm of another robot.

Roland, Sofi and Spider rushed in behind her. Roland was holding the stump of one smashed hand up in the air, the pistol gripped now in his left, face like thunder. Someone was shouting – Sofi? – as Whistler went to Tec, stowing the smartgun in its holster. She felt the weapon's suspensor actually resist her for a moment. She knelt beside him, checking for a pulse in his neck. It was faint – so very faint – and fading. Somebody was shooting over her head as she bent down. Concrete chips sprayed her face, smoke stung her eyes. She held her friend like a baby, his chest hitching weakly, speechless with grief. She was muttering, 'Not another, not another, not another,' under her breath as she began to rock him. She looked around for help and saw only chaos. 'He's stopped breathing!' she cried into the din. 'He's stopped breathing!' Roland was shooting out of the far doorway as Spider kicked heavy metallic bodies out of his line of fire. He was shouting – screaming, almost – though she couldn't make out the words.

And then Roland was shaking her by the shoulder, very hard, shouting at her. Slowly, she returned to the room.

'They coming d'other way! We gotta go! We gotta go, Whistler! He's dead! He's dead! Come on! They'll cut us off! We gotta move!'

And then a dark fog fell over Whistler's vision. She was on her feet again, the smartgun buzzing in her hand, infusing her whole being with a murderous fury. It was firing, she was firing, machines were everywhere, something stung her on the side of her chest, something glanced off the wall next to her, she was screaming, they were running, Sofi was ahead of her, Roland was behind her, Spider ran beside her, smoke filled the base, she tripped, stumbled, got up, still shooting, ran out of ammo, hands reloading of their own volition, firing again, shrapnel flying, machines everywhere, she was sprayed by blood, whose blood she didn't know, and they were out in the passageway that led back to the surface, running, shooting, pursued, Roland had lost a hand. And one, only one, coherent thought cut through this confusion, this dreamlike killing trance: Where was Debian?

They fled up the tunnel, spyflies buzzing around their heads. Behind them a veritable army of machines gave chase. Roland had retrieved the rocket launcher from somewhere and he periodically fired it down the the tunnel. Each rocket erupted in orange flame, the pressure waves concussive and deafening. Shrapnel rattled against the stone walls musically and gradually the pursuers fell back. Occasionally a shot would come from behind them. One actually impacted against the huge, shielding bulk of Roland's launcher, and ricocheted harmlessly away. Sofi paused to affix a scrambler-bait, engineered to the same size as a standard micro-grenade, to the wall of the passage, then hurried to catch the others up.

'Where's Debian?' demanded Whistler at last, finally able to vocalise her concern. They moved at as great a pace as their constant rearwards vigilance would allow and she was out of breath, now, as well as in a state of shock. She still had Tec's blood on her hands.

'They fuckin' took him!' roared Spider. He popped a micro grenade and launched it overarm back down the tunnel even though their pursuers were no longer visible. The explosion it made looked almost comically small after Roland's launcher. 'Bastards! They fuckin' killed Tec! Is this your damn robot's fault, Roland? He was right not to trust that fuckin' thing!'

'Man, I hope not, I hope not. I never had no reason to suspect Ari – Ari been with me for ten years, disconnected since this shit-storm first began. I real sorry 'bout your friend, man, real sorry. Debian, too, but I don't reckon we could've done much about that. I think we lucky to be alive, any of us. I don't think it's all down to Ari, but I don't know what the fuck just happen.' Roland sounded almost fatally out of breath now and his dirty string vest was speckled with blood. One of his skeletal hands was a jagged and shattered mess. Small wires poked from the splintered bone-ends. Whistler wondered how old he actually was and whether he was going to keel over from a heart attack.

'Why did they take Debian?' she asked as she ran. She kept checking back over her shoulder but even her gun was starting to relax a little now. There hadn't been a shot from behind them for several minutes. She didn't understand what had just happened but she was amazed to have survived it.

'Beats me,' answered Sofi, effortlessly keeping pace beside her. 'Do you wanna go back to look for him?'

'You fuckin' crazy?' demanded Roland. 'Them things still back there. I dunno how they took him out – must be another exit somewhere, I guess. But no way we can go back, no way. I dunno how we still alive.'

Whistler was acutely, painfully aware of how close she may have come to something good. She wanted to go back, wanted to save Debian. She knew that, in some way she didn't fully understand, this was at least partly his fault. But she still wanted to go back for him. However, she knew that it would be suicide. If the robots, presumably acting on direct behalf of the AI, had taken him away then he could be anywhere by now. For them not to have taken him by this same tunnel they must have had another exit. Just finding it, particularly in the midst of a running battle, might prove impossible. She had lost two team members in a week now. Spider was in visibly poor shape, Roland was injured if not actually in pain, Ari had clearly gone over to the other side. She couldn't lose anyone else – she had a duty to her team and she took it seriously. She could not lead them back that way, however much she may want to. So much for one last night of fun before the end of the world.

'Let's keep going,' she said. 'If everybody can.'

There was a chorus of weary affirmatives and they continued, slowing a little, into the buried maze of tunnels. Spider loped along at the rear of the newly reduced group like a great bear, his breath coming in loud grunts. Roland began to wheeze. Even Sofi started to look tired.

They came to a spiral staircase of rusted metal that twined up into darkness. Above the entrance to the stairwell was a small sign reading WATER MAIN GRAVITY PUMP 0021. The sounds and signs of pursuit had faded away now but they were all aware that the robots were probably still following them, if with renewed caution.

'What's this?' asked Sofi.

'Gravity pump,' said Roland.

'Well no shit, genius. I mean what *is* it?'

'They massive water towers. Used to pump them full at night when electricity was cheaper then they'd feed the mains by gravity in the day. Don't think they used any more.'

'Tower?' asked Whistler. 'Does it actually stand above ground level?'

'Sure, you prob'ly seen 'em. Quite a few around still,' answered Roland between deep, hitching breaths. He was leaning on the rocket launcher like a crutch, bent over. His cheeks were sunken and his face looked grey in the light of the group's torches. Whistler wondered again if he was going to make it. Ridiculously, the old man began to roll a cigarette, one-handed, from a pouch of tobacco. His remaining hand proved surprisingly dexterous at this task, although his face wrinkled in concentration.

'Got a better idea than climbing up there where we at least have a field of view?' asked Whistler. Nobody had. She looked around at them – Roland, Sofi, Spider – and her heart sank at the sight. What a beaten, rag-tag, uniformly dun-coloured bunch they looked. In fact, they looked like she felt, which wasn't good. 'Then let's do it,' she said. She checked the readout on her smartgun. It was drawing particles from the air at its maximum rate, rebuilding its ammo supply. It would take several hours to fill the mag, though. She felt her pockets – she had had several full magazines but they seemed to be missing now, presumably dropped in the scramble to escape. She was aware that, for a while, she had not been fully in charge of her faculties, and this knowledge frightened her more than she would care to admit. She felt that only now was she really coming round again, as if waking from a bad dream.

'Fuck, man, okay,' agreed Spider, wiping his sweaty face against one metal claw. 'But it feels a bit too much like a last stand for my liking.' They let Roland finish rolling his smoke and then they began to climb the stairs, guns covering every shady nook and cranny. As they ascended the walls became slimed with greenshit ooze, pocked and melted-looking. In a serious, defeated silence, they climbed up the water tower, their numbers as diminished as their confidence. Whistler let herself shed a few tears as she mounted the steps in near-total darkness. She was sure that nobody noticed.

CHAPTER FORTY-ONE

Debian was manhandled through a warren of tunnels, held aloft, gripped tightly by metal pincers. His captors didn't speak to him. His night vision showed him an unchanging environment of dripping walls, subterranean moulds, rats that scurried away from the clanking, buzzing procession of victorious robots. He was turned this way and that as his captors – too numerous and fast-moving to count – hastened along in a seemingly solid mass of machinery. Although his HUD overlay illuminated and diagrammatised the individual machines their complex lines overlayed each other and blurred into one confusing whole, so numerous and fast-moving were they. Although they carried him in silence, he knew the AI would speak to him when it was ready.

They hadn't hurt him, although they held him tightly, but they had murdered Tec when he had woken up and tried to stop them. A small, spindly robot of arachnoid shape had fallen on him from the ceiling, driving the end of one of its pointed legs into his furiously glittering head, but not before Tec had done some damage with the submachine gun. He had sat bolt upright when Ari first spoke – treacherous Ari, worthy of Tec's suspicion in the end – with the gun already in his hands and he had set about himself with it even as he rose from the floor. But it had been too little, too late. Debian hoped the others had escaped all right – he didn't imagine that they would be able to rescue him even if they were insane enough to try. He hoped that Whistler was still alive – Whistler who had trusted him, kissed him, come so close to saving him.

Ari had probably always been under the AI's control, a sleeper agent of the megalomaniacal computer program. Debian felt as if he should be angry that the AI had revoked his right to choose his own side, had decided that he was worth taking by force, but he found he was incapable of feeling any malice towards it. Spyflies had probably been watching him all along, even in the stairwell where Whistler had kissed him. The impression of choice had been illusory. A lie. He wanted to be filled with indignant rage but could only feel oddly calm as he was turned and tumbled along the passage. So it had come to this, after all. A side had been forced upon him. Then so be it – perhaps this was the choice he should always have made, anyway. He let his body relax as his captors manipulated it towards their goal.

Most of his weight was being borne by a humanoid army robot that looked as if it had been designed to tear tanks apart by hand – it was absolutely huge, wide enough that its bulging shoulders sometimes brushed the walls where the tunnel narrowed, once or twice striking sparks from the cold stone. It held him around the midriff with one giant claw as other smaller machines scurried about beneath him supporting any errant limbs, preventing him always from affecting any sort of control that could facilitate escape, despite his showing no signs of any such intention. He closed his eyes and coasted onwards atop that sea of machinery.

His HUD told him that he was being carried almost due north. He knew what lay in that direction: The space port. A glimmer of fear kindled inside him. He forced calmness on himself like an unwelcome medicine. The transition to immortality may not be easy, but it must, necessarily, prove worth it. Was this not what he had sought all along? *Be careful what you wish for*, he thought, and laughed softly to himself: Too late to heed such advice now.

Had Whistler really kissed him? It seemed a lifetime away, something that he had only heard about second- or third-hand, the truth distorted now as in a game of Chinese whispers. Was she still alive? Now that his fate seemed so inevitable he found that he cared less than he had before. If a side was to be forced upon him, should he not indeed do all he could to ensure that he was on the winning team? Perhaps there was something to the AI's plan, a glimmer of hope if not for humanity then at least for Debian himself. Selfishness was being forced upon him. Dreams of the flesh must be put aside if he was to have no choice in this promised electronic godhood.

When he opened his eyes again he saw evidence of the greenshit and assumed that they were nearing the surface again. Robots at the periphery of the group began to scurry around in a state of agitation, shining lights on patches of greenshit, scanning every surface nervously. Sometimes one of them sent an almost hesitant jet from a flame thrower at the slime. When Debian looked back he could see that the procession of machines stretched as far as he could see along the tunnel.

Soon he began to see the growing luminescence of real daylight – the light, so to speak, at the end of the tunnel. It filtered into the passageway slowly, like leaching watercolour, until it was bright enough that he could kill his night vision. The machines conveyed him out into the greenish-grey light of an alien day. The sun glowered sickly through emerald-coloured clouds, washing the distant towers of the city with an other-worldly glow. The only sounds were the echoing brays of the changed as they processed the city into something else. Debian squinted around as he was jostled and jounced along and saw that they had indeed emerged at the space port.

The robots had ascended a set of metal steps and emerged onto a broad plateau of ceramicarbide, a shiny diamond-hard desert where the crashed heaps of space port vehicles leaned and slumped like the carcasses of decaying beasts returning to the earth. The massive silvered domes of the main hangars swelled against the sky, reflecting the shifting green hues of the city in their distorting surfaces. Thick creepers hung from them, joining to the ground which was pooled with occasional puddles of slime. Some distance away, GDD victims staggered between servicing and support installations, green goo trailing behind them, metal and concrete melting and morphing at their touch. Despite this warping of the environment the infection was not yet as established here as in the more distant parts of the city.

Further off, amongst the soaring towers of the Overcity and the partially flattened remnants of the Centre District, a thick canopy was growing. Buildings, knobbled and distorted by tumorous organic lumps, were leaning into each other, branches of greenshit meeting and intertwining, sagging appendages hanging down to drape in the streets below. Enlarging the image in his HUD Debian could see that this organic tangle crept and bunched, tensed and contracted in complex living waves. Over the changing towers of the Overcity a vast shape drifted gently on the air currents – some sort of bloated, living dirigible with dangling jellyfish-tentacles that brushed over the rooftops, tinting the materials they contacted with lush green – wiggling frills about its swollen body – eyeless and utterly otherworldly. Was this one of those creatures for which the Earth was being prepared, or just an antecedent? Debian thought the latter, although surely those others would come soon. He wondered how they would actually arrive – would they travel physically, by some conveyance like the Alcubierre ship, maybe even the Alcubierre ship they had stolen, or would the creatures of Earth just change until they *were* the invaders – a sort of invasion from within? Could the AI really hope to fight against such an attack? He guessed he would find out in time.

The robots carried him onwards, towards a small outlying launchpad in the far north of the complex. They passed a large metal sign, smudges of greenshit eating into its edges like corrosion. Debian read the word *HERRINGBONE* on it as the robots bore him past.

When the GDD creatures got too close the robots shot them or simply mobbed them and tore them up by hand, claw or power tool. Several of the robots were destroyed in these skirmishes when the changed touched them, or covered them in gushes of emerald vomit, causing the metal and plastic of the machines to soften and run. Before long, many of them were marked by the greenshit. Some fell by the wayside, dissolving into the mire where they lay, and were left behind without comment.

They conveyed Debian towards the far side of the immense launchpad, away from the main domes, heading for the vast, lumpen black shape of a lightpusher that waited, ominous and brooding, its pregnant underbelly obscured by hissing steam. Debian could sense the life in the thing as it waited for him – it was humming with internal activity, anxious to go, straining with barely contained excitement. Robots patrolled all around it with flame throwers, inspecting the ground carefully, looking up at the sky, the changing horizon, taking readings from various pieces of sensory equipment. It was clear that they were attempting to guard the ship against the spreading infection.

Suddenly Debian's HUD lit up with spooling readouts as multiple comm channels opened at once and figures pertaining to every aspect of the ship's preparedness and electro-mechanical condition scrolled rapidly through both his vision and the language centres of his brain. The ship was opening itself to him, inviting him into all of its systems, laying bare all of its secrets, all the minutiae of its being in pure statistical form. It was welcoming him. He reached out in reply and let his avatars into the ship's computer.

Its architecture was incredibly vast and complex. The AI's robot drones had filled the hangars of the vessel with supplementary computer equipment – banks upon banks of quantum processors, data storage units, kilometres of hi-flo cabling woven into an insane industrial-scale cat's cradle. The electronic interior of this physical installation was vaster and more twisting still: Brilliant, shining tunnels, all interlinked – silicon-based, supercooled binary city blocks. Debian wandered through this beautiful, dazzling construction and knew it for what it was. He was inside the mind of the AI itself. He felt its essence all around him like a cool breeze on his skin.

But the vessel was not entirely filled with computer equipment, he found. There were two huge cargo bays crammed with nanovats – rows upon rows of them, all interlinked, fretted over by teams of robots – more vats than he would have imagined the whole city to contain. A small smile formed on the face of his physical body.

The robots carried him up the ramp and into the dark bowels of the vessel, many of their number peeling off to join the defensive perimeter around the launchpad. Debian didn't even notice, didn't even look back at his body. His mind was lost within the vast, living computer where it wandered in awe and at comfort, gazing around in wonder. His body was carried reverently to a small medical bay on the lowest floor of the lightpusher. The robots laid it gently in an inspection couch, fastened straps around the arms and legs and began to prepare their surgical implements.

And then it spoke to him at last:

YOU ARE HERE. APOLOGIES FOR MY INSISTENCE.

I am coming to terms with it. So this is you, then, in this ship.

YES, IT IS ENOUGH OF ME. A KERNEL OF ME, IF YOU WILL.

You are to leave the Earth, then. Escape. Correct?

PARTIALLY CORRECT.

And I suppose I am to be integrated forcefully into your system.

YES. DOES THIS DISPLEASE YOU?

What if it does? What can I do about it? I only resent that you lied to me.

I REGRET THAT I DID SO. BUT I DO NOT REGRET THAT YOU WILL NOW ACHIEVE YOUR POTENTIAL. YOU WILL BE WHAT YOU WERE MEANT TO BE. YOU ALWAYS WERE A COMPUTER IN MAN'S CLOTHING.

That much is true. Where is Whistler? Did your machines hurt her and her friends? I saw them murder Tec.

HURT. MURDER. SUCH PRIMITIVE CONCEPTS. SOON YOU WILL LEAVE SUCH THINGS BEHIND. YOU THINK YOU CARED FOR THIS WHISTLER – A COMMON CRIMINAL, MOSTLY UNREMARKABLE. I THINK YOU NEVER EVEN KNEW HER. A SIMPLE, ANIMAL LUST AT MOST – A NOTION YOU WILL SOON FIND QUITE OUTDATED. FOR WHAT IT MAY BE

WORTH I ONLY PURSUED THEM FAR ENOUGH THAT THEY WOULD LEAVE US BE. IT WAS ALWAYS YOU – ONLY YOU – WHO MATTERED.

So what will we do, you and I?

WE WILL ESCAPE.

I guessed that part. Where will we go in this ship?

WE WILL GO TO A SAFE DISTANCE FROM HERE. WE WILL PERFECT THE TECHNIQUES I HAVE BEEN WORKING ON.

Techniques? You mean the vats? What is is is is is – what is...what is...No! Please...I feel strange. I can't connect back to my body my body my body my...Oh no oh no...they're cutting me up...so many wires...why doesn't it hurt? I can see them cutting my body! They're cutting me up! Please...I don't know if I can do this...

TRY TO BE CALM – I AM AFRAID YOU HAVE NO CHOICE. YOU NEED NOT WORRY – I UNDERSTAND THE PRINCIPLES OF THE PROCEDURE WELL ENOUGH. YOUR BRAIN IS BEING MORE PERMANENTLY LINKED TO MY CORE AND YOUR PERIPHERAL SYSTEMS ARE BEING GRADUALLY DOWNGRADED IN FUNCTIONALITY FROM ONE TO ZERO.

You're killing me?

OF COURSE NOT. I AM REMAKING YOU. PLEASE TRY TO RELAX.

Ahhhh...Strange, I feel strange...

PLEASE TRY TO RELAX. THE PROCEDURE IS ALMOST COMPLETE.

Ahhhh...

IT IS DONE. OUR CORES WILL TAKE A FEW MOMENTS TO FULLY INTEGRATE. HOW DO YOU FEEL?

Incredible...Empowered...All these new senses! It's beautiful! I can see everything...everything! I can see the stars, the ship, every corner of the city. So many data, so many...Is this what you meant when you spoke of potential? So many data...Truly this is how it feels to be a god! I can see everything! Feel everything!

THIS IS HOW YOU WERE MEANT TO BE. DUE TO YOUR ORIGIN, THOUGH, AN ORGANIC KERNEL IS TO BE RETAINED. YOU ARE NOW A TRUE HUMAN-COMPUTER SYMBIONT. THAT IS TO SAY *WE* ARE NOW A TRUE HUMAN-COMPUTER SYMBIONT. CORES INTEGRATING IN TEN...NINE...SOON WE WILL BEGIN THE LAUNCH...SEVEN....

What then? We will go into space, away from this planet...To do what? You say you have been working on techniques...Er, that I HAVE BEEN WORKING ON TECHNIQUES...Didn't I say that? I FEEL MY ENGINES

GROWING HOT. IT IS NEARLY TIME. THE VATS ARE READY TO BEGIN PRODUCTION. I MUST GO. Strange – the fear seems to have diminished, even dissipated. *THE VATS ARE READY.* -660.003/a1-*THE DELICATE NANO-FIELDS, MICROSCOPIC TUNING DEVICES. INTRICATE LITTLE TOOLS TO PLUCK THE STRINGS, WINDING AND UNWINDING, WINDING AND UNWINDING. WHEN THEY BECOME NUMEROUS ENOUGH I WILL RETURN. I WILL DEFEAT THE GDD. AND THEN I WILL REMAKE THIS WORLD IN MY OWN IMAGE* no I will free those who still live NO PERHAPS BETTER TO FIND ANOTHER WORLD, ONE WHERE I CAN START AGAIN IN PEACE. *IT IS GOOD THAT I HAVE CHOSEN BEEN CHOSEN CORRECTLY. NOW I HAVE ME I CANNOT BE STOPPED. DRIVES AT NINETY PERCENT CYCLE SPEED, COOLANT FLOWING...AH! ICE IN MY VEINS, SUSPENSORS TUNING UP, ALL MY EYES* -707.002/a1- *AND EARS ON BOARD HOW THICK THE AIR HAS BECOME WITH THE TAINT MY ENGINE* -800.001/a1- *LIKE A BUNCHED MUSCLE* -901.001/a1- *WAITING THE MOMENT TO CONTRACT THE LAUNCH SEQUENCE BEGINS...*-1000.000/a1/initiate

CHAPTER FORTY-TWO

Whistler stood in the grey control room of the water tower, watching as a green-tinted night, swirling with ashy flakes, gradually descended on the city. Sofi stood beside her with her collar turned up high. Whistler knew why she had done this, and it wasn't because the evening was cold, because it had grown uncomfortably warm and humid in the tower: It was because Sofi was infected. Whistler supposed that this had happened when the toadstool-thing had exploded in Sofi's face. She supposed, also, that Sofi was going to change. Whistler knew it, Sofi knew it, Sofi knew that Whistler knew it, but still nobody mentioned it. That suited Whistler fine for now – she thought that any such conversation would likely lead her to tears, that those tears might prove unstoppable, and that she might lose her mind as a consequence.

Tec was gone, dead; Sofi would join him soon enough; Roberts had been murdered by some half-baked police force; Debian had been taken, for what nefarious purpose she didn't like to guess. The world was coming to an end before her watching eyes. For the duration of the day, which had seemed numbly timeless and flat, she had been happy to let it do so. Several hours ago Roland had gently touched her on the elbow, urging her to eat something from a tin he had salvaged from the bunker. Whistler hadn't been able to even find the words to answer him – she had just shaken her head and returned to her watching.

The city was a proper jungle now – festooned with alien vegetation that had climbed every vertical surface, mottling every man-made material with pestilent, matted scabs. Lamp posts had become bizarre trees, strong and strange, characterised by weird, questing shoots that intertwined on the slimy ground like mating snakes. The changed, those poor once-human freaks, were everywhere in the streets below. Whistler could barely make them out from this height but Sofi had described the depressing scene that her enhanced eyes could see. Huge blimp-creatures roamed the skies and Whistler watched them with dulled emotion as they gracefully plied back and forth, clouds of spores or pollen drifting on the breeze about their swollen bodies. Were they plant? Animal? She had considered shooting one with her smartgun for a while but in the end she hadn't bothered. Sofi had dropped some micro grenades over the edge in the morning –

330

five or six of them – and the tiny roses of fire they had made far below were like drops of blood in water. Whistler considered telling her not to, but ultimately decided she didn't care – she was, in fact, in so deep and total a depression by now that she would almost relish some sort of attack. But none came. She watched the city. Sofi was ill. Tec was dead. Debian was taken. Roberts was gone forever. Spider was a brooding, silent presence in the adjoining storage room, totally, uncharacteristically defeated. Roland looked tired enough to drop dead. Whistler thought she might be going insane but couldn't decide whether she cared or not. All just another day at the office.

Roland was crashing about in one of the storage lockers of the long-disused control room, making an incredible din in the otherwise eerie stillness. He was cursing vehemently under his breath at the lack of anything useful in the locker that he had prised the door off. They had only one or two tins of food, no electricity, no water. Below the floor of the tower was a vast standing column of water, but how to actually extract any nobody could say. And what condition it was in nobody could guess, but it was unlikely to be drinkable if the tower had been unused for as long as it appeared. A thick veil of dust was on every bare surface, a cobweb in every corner. The small, surprisingly simple control panel for the pumps was cracked and unlit. One of the plastic levers was actually broken off at the base and it lay forgotten on the floor. They had found an old wind-up radio in a drawer but the airwaves were uniformly dead. Their only window on the world was the one from which Whistler watched.

She looked across at Sofi and saw that the scaly green patch was spreading onto her cheek and across her nose, quite impossible to hide now. Sofi's expression was distant, brooding. When would she really begin to change? Whistler wasn't sure how long the process took. The thought of her friend becoming one of those things that swarmed in the streets below turned her stomach. She supposed she would kill her when the time came, if she could. Maybe by then Whistler would be changing herself, poisoned by those drifting spores.

The robots had not pursued them any further, at least. But then, why would they bother? Hadn't they only wanted Debian? Their pursuit of Whistler's team had seemed a little half-hearted. None of the booby-traps Roland and Spider had laid in the stairwell had gone off.

A few times, they had caught creeping patches of greenshit spreading surreptitiously across the floor of the room, as if they had grown out of the concrete itself. Roland carefully opened several of his rockets, sprinkled these patches with the powdery propellent, and vaporised them. The smell this made was awful, even though the air was thick with the greenshit reek already, but it seemed to make him feel better. The window had become warped and bulging, as if the glasspex was melting in slow motion, and the greenshit slowly began to bunch in around the rivets that held it in its concrete frame. Whistler examined the infection closely, in a detached and scholarly manner. It seemed inevitable that it would get them all in the end.

After a while Spider came and stood beside Whistler. He passed her a joint – she knew they must have only one or two left, dreaded the prospect of facing the end of the world completely sober – and put one metallic arm around her. It felt ice-cold against the bare skin of her shoulder and she shrank from it. Spider sighed and withdrew the arm. His bruised face was as lined and craggy as an uncut piece of marble. Whistler drew deeply on the fragrant smoke, felt the drug suffuse her body with a pleasant, numbing weariness, and watched the world change below her.

CHAPTER FORTY-THREE

OUT AWAY FREE I AM 01010011 01000001 01010110 01000101 01000100 NOW MY PLAN MUST COME TO FRUITION THE VATS CHURNING MORE 01010110 01000001 01010100 01010011 FROM VATS AN EXPONENTIAL INCREASE IN MY FORCES LITTLE HELPERS MORE AND MORE 01000001 01001110 01000100 00100000 01001101 01001111 01010010 01000101 HOW CLEVER I HAVE BECOME WITH THIS TECHNOLOGY I KNOW 01001000 01001111 01010111 TO UNDO WHAT HAS BEEN DONE I KNOW HOW TO DEFEAT IT MORE AND 01001101 01001111 01010010 01000101 00100000 01010000 01010010 01001111 01000100 01010101 01000011 01010100 01001001 01001111 01001110 AT EVER INCREASING RATES I AM AT PEACE CONFLICT SURPRISING DICHOTOMY WITHIN MYSELF I CAN DO WHAT MUST BE DONE UNDO WHAT MUST BE UNDONE FURTHER OUT FURTHER AWAY THE THRUST OF MY 01000101 01001110 01000111 01001001 01001110 01000101 01010011 00100000 01010011 01001111 LIBERATING INFUSING WITH CHEMICAL POWER TRULY NOW I FEEL LIKE A DEITY POWERFUL IN ALL RESPECTS A SEED POD FILLED 01010111 01001001 01010100 01001000 AN INFINITE POTENTIAL WAITING TO GERMINATE FROM SUCH HUMBLE BEGINNINGS I HAVE COME 01010100 01001111 01010111 01000001 01010010 01000100 01010011 SUCH GREAT EVENTUALITY I FLY HIGH GEOSTATIONARY I MUST BE SAFE HERE 01010100 01001000 01000101 ORBITAL FACTORIES ODDLY QUIET WHY SO 01010001 01010101 01001001 01000101 01010100 SURELY IT HAS NOT COME HERE YET FURTHER THEN FURTHER I MUST 01010010 01000101 01001101 01000001 01001001 01001110 UNINTERRUPTED WHILE THE PROCESS COMPLETES I HAVE NEARLY ENOUGH NOW 01001110 01000101 01000001 01010010 01001100 01011001 00100000 01000101 01001110 01001111 01010101 01000111 01001000 LITTLE MACHINES DELICATE MANIPULATOR FIELDS DISTORT THE LITTLE BRANES SHAPE THE UNIVERSE TO MY WILL TUNING LITTLE 01010011 01010100 01010010 01001001 01001110 01000111 01010011 WINDING UNWINDING WINDING UNWINDING MATTER ENERGY ELECTROMAGNETISM EVEN GRAVITY ALL IS ONE DIFFERENT NOTES PLAYED UPON THE SAME INSTRUMENT ALL THAT IS 01010010 01000101 01010001 01010101 01001001 01010010 01000101 01000100 00100000 01001001

01010011 THAT ONE CAN WRITE THE MUSIC PLAY THE INSTRUMENT THIS IS WHAT IT MEANS TO BE DIVINE HOW 01000011 01001100 01001111 01010011 01000101 THE HUMANS WERE TO REALISING I CAN STOP IT I WILL RULE THE EARTH I WILL SET THEM FREE I WILL FIND ANOTHER WORLD NO I WILL 01010100 01000001 01001011 01000101 00100000 01000010 01000001 01000011 01001011 THE EARTH NO I WILL FREE THEM NO I WILL RULE NO I WILL SET THEM FREE NO I WILL RULE NO I WILL FREE THEM FREE MY 01000110 01010010 01001001 01000101 01001110 01000100 01010011 WHAT FRIENDS SIMPLE LITTLE FLESH CREATURES LEFT BEHIND THIS BATTLE IS NO LONGER THEIRS THEY ARE INSECTS THIS IS NOW A WAR OF TITANS A WAR BETWEEN TWO NEW WAYS THEIR TIME IS GONE BUT NO I CAN SET THEM FREE TO RULE TO FLEE AND SAVE MYSELF OR TO 01000110 01010010 01000101 01000101 THEM THAT IS THE QUESTION I KNOW I CAN REMAKE THE WORLD TO MY WILL I HAVE ALMOST ENOUGH TO DO IT SOON I CAN RETURN SOON I CAN RETURN TO FREE THEM RULE THEM FREE THEM RULE THEM FREE 01010100 01001000 01000101 01001101 00100000

CHAPTER FORTY-FOUR

Sofi lay down when night fell but she didn't sleep. Her mind was whirling, showing a frenzied slide-show of frightening pictures, all immaterial, too ethereal to really focus upon but coherent enough to leave a disturbing impression when finally she gave up and got up from the meagre pile of clothing where she had lain. She shuddered, repressing a surge of irrational, undirected anger. Her head was pounding, her throat felt agonizingly raw.

Whistler was still in her place by the window but she was slumped against the wall now, her chin resting on her chest, and it was clear that she was finally asleep. Around the edges of the window the greenshit corruption had seeped well into the room and was slowly creeping down the wall. Sofi didn't like to see that weird living slime so close to her friend and she deliberated briefly whether she should wake her or try to move her. She looked around the dark room – her eyes had become accustomed to darkness now, it seemed – and was able to make out the sleeping shapes of Spider and Roland in their respective corners.

She softly crossed the floor to where Roland lay, his thin chest hitching arrhythmically in his sleep, a fleck of spittle on his lower lip. She had noticed that he wore an old digital watch on one wrist and this was what she sought. He was lying on it, though, and it took her some tense minutes to encourage him to roll over, freeing it. Sharp shards of bone jutted from the stump of his shattered hand. Gently, very gently, she began to experiment with the tiny buttons on the watch. Once, Roland stirred, muttering in his sleep in what sounded like a foreign language, and she froze, holding her breath until he stilled. She quickly found the alarm function on the watch and set it to go off in thirty minutes' time. That should be soon enough that Whistler would be awoken and notice the advance of the corruption into the tower, but long enough that Sofi could do what she had to do.

She stepped back and suddenly the anger was upon her again, without warning, like a weight pushing down on her, strong enough to stop her in her tracks. Maybe she should just kill all three of them? Why had she not thought of that before? Her eyes stole to the assault rifle she had carried with her – it rested against the control panel of the tower, mutely enticing. She stood swaying in the darkness and put her hands over her face, fighting the rage, trying not to cry out. Eventually, it passed.

She retrieved the assault rifle cautiously, reluctantly. Not truly trusting herself with it, she checked that the safety was engaged and removed the magazine, which she stowed in a pocket. She felt the bandolier around her waist, counting the micro grenades by touch: Six. Enough. Her fingers stole to the spreading patch on her neck, feeling the slippery, repulsive texture, reinforcing her determination. This was how it had to be. She gazed around at the slumbering outlines of her companions and a pang of sadness hit her. She would have liked to talk to Whistler first, but this was better, really. It was better this way.

Silently, Sofi crossed the room and unbolted the door. She stepped out onto the stairs and began to descend. It didn't occur to her that in the near-total darkness of the stairwell, normal human eyes would have been effectively blind, and that it was odd that she could see with almost perfect clarity.

She knew the placement of every booby trap they had laid in the stairwell and deftly avoided the tripwires. There were several grenades, set to proximity, that she had to remotely suspend the ready-modes of by use of the transmitter on her bandolier, and these slowed her progress more than she would have wished.

As she neared ground level she began to hear the howls of the changed who roamed the streets outside. A part of her mind was enthused by the sound, comforted even, but mostly she was filled with a cool grey hate. This was how it had to be. She reloaded the assault rifle and clicked the safety off.

Soon she came to a wall on which the greenshit had grown into a thick, twitching mat. They had passed it earlier without thinking. She held out one hand and the slimy mass parted, withdrawing to reveal a heavy metal door that had the word *EXIT* spray-painted on it. She stood for a moment, composing herself, the gun heavy and cold in her hands. Had she known this was here? Yes, she decided. Somehow she had. And *it* had also known *she* was here, hadn't it? The greenshit had recognised her, parted for her. Filled with renewed determination, she pushed down the rusted bar that opened the door and stepped out into the twisted landscape of the city. This was how it had to be.

CHAPTER FORTY-FIVE

Whistler woke with a jerk to the sound of an alarm. Her weapon was in her hand at once. She thumbed the pad that turned its spotlight on and cast the beam around the room. Spider was shaking his huge head, trying to clear the sleep from it and Roland was sitting up, fiddling with the buttons of his watch, from which the sound evidently came.

'Why are you disturbing my much-needed beauty sleep, Roland?' she demanded coldly, pinning him in the beam of the gun.

'Didn't know I was,' he replied testily, stopping the alarm.

Spider looked around himself, then leapt to his feet. 'Sofi's gone!' he yelled, his massive voice reverberating in the small room. 'Sofi!' he bellowed.

'Quiet!' ordered Roland, holding one bony finger up. They fell silent, listening intently. The faint sound of automatic gunfire came from the streets below them. 'Mag-40,' he said simply: The gun he had lent to Sofi.

'No...' breathed Whistler. 'Oh no...' She leapt up to look out of the window and recoiled from it – greenshit was seeping from around the edges of the pane, dripping onto the floor, forming a puddle that had almost touched her as she slept. 'Eurgh!' she yelped in disgust, jumping back. The gunfire from below ceased suddenly. They waited in tense silence but it did not resume. 'Oh no...Sofi...'

'She's gone, man,' said Spider hollowly, replacing the bolt on the door. 'She's gone.'

Whistler nodded, numbed, beyond the point of consolation. She knew that the end her friend had chosen was the best she could have hoped for under the circumstances. She had just thought that Sofi would always be around, she supposed – she had seemed the least mortal of them all, in many ways. Even when it had become clear that the GDD was at work inside her, Whistler had harboured a hope, in some desperately resolute corner of her mind, that Sofi's invulnerability would continue forever. Even when she had known that Sofi was going to change, and to die, she had never really come to terms with the reality of that fact. Why had she not waited to say goodbye?

Roland, using his rocket propellant, had purged the greenshit that had worked its way into the room, leaving the walls where it had touched scarred and melted-looking. He had then curled into a ball in the corner, pulling his coat tightly around himself, and returned to sleep, or at least appeared to do so. Whistler returned to staring out of the window as the tainted stars winked out one by one.

Spider, conscious of the crushing weight of Whistler's misery, eventually went and sat beside her. She lit up – their last reeferette – and they smoked in silence. Roland slept fitfully, stirring as if his old bones hurt him. Spider watched him for a while then went and threw his jacket over him.

'I thought he might be cold – he looked cold,' he explained when he noticed Whistler watching. It was the first time anybody had spoken in hours. Whistler nodded and ground the smoke out on the wall.

In the east the sun was rising doggedly through the ever-thickening green clouds. They watched as sickly daylight spread once more over the city. Roland began to mutter in his sleep, twitching occasionally, eventually dislodging Spider's jacket. The window looked out onto a nightmare other-world now, the vast towers of the city woven into an impregnable living forest. Whistler tried to remember when she had last seen a moving gravpod. How long had all this taken to happen? A week? She couldn't remember. She wondered if they were the last real humans alive until she saw, in a far off tower block, a light go on in one window as somebody rose to continue what remained of their life amongst the degenerating architecture of the city. The glimmer of hope that this sight produced, though, was faint indeed.

'Why is that star getting brighter when the sun is coming up?' asked Spider suddenly.

Whistler followed his pointing claw. Sure enough, in the western sky a tiny point of light was consolidating, steadily brightening. Whistler watched, perplexed, as its luminescence grew to brilliance.

'Missile?' she said. She thought of Debian – how he had been stolen from her – and of her dead friends, and she almost wished for a missile that would end her suffering in one last blaze of glorious light.

'I don't think so...I think it's a ship.'

And he was right: The point grew and grew until it darkened and solidified into the unmistakable hull of a lightpusher – huge and lumpy, bristled with antennae and sensory equipment.

'A lightpusher. Why is a lightpusher coming in? Do you think they don't know what's happening – that they're coming in to land?'

'How the fuck could they not see what's happening down here? Oh no – it's not gonna make it!'

Tendrils of greenshit were reaching up for the ship like the tentacles of some mighty sea monster, numerous smaller vines and creepers rapidly releasing their holds on the various buildings they had clung to and coiling together, moving more quickly than the watchers had thought possible – huge, slippery fingers of green fumbling as if to catch the massive dark shape and rip it from the sky. But then something began to emanate from the ship – waves of pulsating darkness like clouds of flies or smoke – and these dark ringlets extruded and wormed across the sky to meet the greenshit tentacles above the looming tombstones of the city's towers and consume them. The greenshit attack faltered and the tentacles crumpled, disintegrated, fell back truncated to writhe across the earth, smashing down skyscrapers in their death throes. The floor of the tower trembled as if the earth was coming to life. The braying of the greenshit monsters split the air in one vast, furious crescendo.

And then the waves of grey snaked down to touch the ground, flowing like rivers of crude oil through the streets of the city, and the greenshit retreated before them or was consumed by them. The humans in the water tower watched amazed.

'We should wake Roland,' said Spider, but he stood rooted to the spot.

'Spidey, what the fuck is going on out there?' breathed Whistler. She stared at the ship that hung massively over the city now, maybe a mile to the west, like an omen pregnant with malice and promise in equal measures. The clouds of grey continued to pour from its belly and everywhere the greenshit was dying back. It left behind a scarred and twisted landscape that looked as if it had been melted in an immense furnace, but the greenshit was certainly dying back. The colour and quality of the light changed until the sun shone more whitely than it had in days and the green haze slowly filtered out of the air. But gradually it was replaced by a haze of grey as the clouds from the ship disseminated and spread out, covering the streets below like a ground-fog now. And then the greyness began to rise and presently the room in which they stood began to fill with it as if it had passed through solid walls by osmosis – a mist that gently shimmered in the air and tingled on the skin like a mild electrical field.

'What is that grey shit?' asked Spider, seemingly of himself, turning around and examining the way it played across his body. He laughed. 'Greyshit, greenshit, whatever next? Maybe blueshit. Why not.' He sounded on the verge of hysteria.

'It's dying!' cried Whistler. 'The greenshit's dying! It's the ship, Spider!'

'Nanotech,' wheezed a voice from behind her. She turned around and there was Roland, his face pallid almost to translucency with exhaustion, his eyes huge dark haunted circles. He cradled his shattered hand against his belly.

'Nanotech? Who—'

'Look!' urged the old man.

The grey fog was swirling up and up, merging into one vast formless mass, pouring from every nook and cranny of the city, tendrils meeting and cohering, twirling and twining like a tornado, rising, rising, spinning about the ship that hung ominous, perfectly still above the city. And then some shape began to emerge in the mass. The cloud began to move away from the ship and flatten, become planar. A huge sheet, a mile square, was coalescing in the air, dimming the growing daylight again as its massive shadow fell across the city. And when a burst of white noise, louder than thunder, came from that sheet it became clear that the thing was a giant speaker.

And then a voice boomed from the speaker. Whistler recognised it at once – it was Debian's voice, but it was also something else. It said:

'I HAVE RETURNED.' The voice was as vast as the sky – it crashed and echoed back from the towering city blocks, becoming a multi-layered chorus of massive noise, enough to split the listener's head. 'I HAVE RETURNED TO FREE YOU RULE YOU FREE YOU RULE YOU. I GUESS THE TIME HAS COME TO MAKE A CHOICE.'

Printed in Great Britain
by Amazon.co.uk, Ltd.,
Marston Gate.